"We don't have to be enemies . . . "

Nick said as Tasha told herself to pay attention. She couldn't afford *not* to.

"Until I get a chance to talk to either Mimi Castle or Jonas Baker," he said, taking one step closer to her, "we'll be seeing a lot of each other."

She met his gaze, and Tasha knew what he was saying. She wasn't going to get rid of him until he was satisfied.

A man with money, charm, and a stubborn streak wide enough to match her own could be nothing but trouble. And if that man had dark brown eyes and a lean jaw and shoulders broad enough to land a plane on . . . well, that was an entirely different kind of trouble that Tasha *so* didn't need at the moment . . .

OUTSTANDING PRAISE FOR
MAUREEN CHILD AND HER NOVELS

"Maureen Child infuses her writing with the perfect blend of laughter, tears and romance. Her well-crafted characters, humor, and understanding of what it means to be part of a family make each of her novels a treat to be savored."

—Jill Marie Landis, author of *Magnolia Creek*

"Maureen Child always writes a guaranteed winner, and this is no exception. Heartwarming, sexy and impossible to put down."

—Susan Mallery, author of *Married for a Month*

ST. MARTIN'S PAPERBACKS TITLES
BY MAUREEN CHILD

Finding You

Knowing You

Loving You

LOVING YOU

MAUREEN CHILD

St. Martin's Paperbacks

LOVING YOU

ISBN: 0-312-97844-8

Printed in the United States of America

St. Martin's Paperbacks edition / June 2003

St. Martin's Paperbacks are published by St. Martin's Press, 175 Fifth Avenue, New York, NY 10010.

10 9 8 7 6 5 4 3 2 1

To the real Tasha and all of the other lost children like her. May you find your way home.

Chapter 1

For the first time in his life, the cameras *weren't* focused on Nick Candellano.

He didn't like it.

Nick had spent years in the limelight. As an NFL all-pro running back, he'd had more cameras flashed in his face than a member of the Kennedy family. Hell, he'd even been featured in one of *People* magazine's Sexiest Bachelor articles. He'd done radio, TV, and print interviews and was glib enough to charm his way through any situation. Kids had been known to stand in line outside the stadium for hours just to get his autograph.

And now?

"You're still in my shot," Bill, the cameraman, muttered.

"Right." Biting down hard on the quick flash of temper that jittered along his spine, Nick took a single long step to the right. Wouldn't want to mess up the camera angle. No telling when they might get another chance to film an earthshaking athletic contest like this one.

Pushing one hand through his hair, he squinted into the afternoon sunlight and let his gaze slide across the playing field. The players were in position. The ball was in play. The crowd roared, half of them cheering, the other half heckling the officials.

It should have been familiar. Comforting, almost, to a man who'd spent most of his life suiting up for a game. The only problem here was, the players were high school girls and they were playing *soccer,* for God's sake.

And it was Nick's job to cover it for the local TV station.

The taste of bitterness filled his mouth, but he choked it back down. A new leaf, he reminded himself. That's what he was doing here. Starting fresh. A new career. Something he could do even *with* a bum knee.

Christ though.

Girls' soccer?

A man had to start somewhere, right? Nick shifted position, taking the weight off the bad right knee that had ended his career. While the pain shimmered along his nerve endings, he couldn't help thinking, as he often did, about that one play that had sidelined his career. If not for that one stinkin' tackle that had sent his body east and his knee west, he'd still be playing. Still be signing autographs. Still be doing what he loved doing.

Instead, he was standing on the sidelines, in a bone-chilling early November wind, getting dust on his Gucci loafers, trying to look interested in a play-off game that meant nothing to anyone not attending either Santiago or St. Anne's High.

Local TV my ass, he thought. He should be working at ESPN. Probably would have been except for the one guy who'd voted no to Nick's application. Seems the man still held a grudge about some comments Nick had once made about their coverage of a game. So instead of the big time, here he was, working at a station that included farm reports in the local news. But he had plans. He'd work his way up. Be at ESPN where he belonged. Doing commentary for football games—interviewing players—*something* that would allow him to stay a part of the game he loved. But until then, he got the shit jobs.

And they didn't come much shittier than this.

Out on the neatly trimmed grass, one of the girls from St. Anne's kicked a well-aimed ball at the net, and when the goalie missed it, the game was suddenly over. Screaming teenage girls swarmed across the field, shrieking and laughing as they jumped at one another in celebration.

A momentary twinge jabbed at Nick's heart and he almost felt a kinship with the high-schoolers. He'd done a lot of those victory dances himself. He'd been in the center of the locker-room festivities after a big win. He'd popped a few champagne corks and showered in the foamy stuff, blinking back tears as the alcohol nearly blinded him.

Damn, he missed it.

He missed everything about it.

"Okay, that's it," Bill announced as he straightened up from behind the camera. Glancing at Nick, he said, "You wanna get an interview with the coach first, or with the girls?"

It was like being asked if he'd rather be shot to death or stabbed.

But this was his life, now. And bitching about it wasn't going to move him up the ladder or get him to ESPN. So he'd choose the lesser of two evils. He just didn't think he was up to trying to interview some high school soccer player and listening to her "um" and "oh" and "uh" her way through a conversation.

"The coach," Nick said, and scooped one hand through his hair again. He checked his tie, smoothed one hand down the front of his camel brown sport jacket, then fell into step behind Bill.

The stands emptied of people and they all seemed intent on getting in his way. Bill was a few yards ahead of him, and Nick was in no hurry to catch up.

"Hey, aren't you Nick Candellano?"

Nick stopped, caught by the awed tone in the voice coming from right behind him. Turning, he looked down at a short balding man with a wide grin.

"You are," the guy said, nearly breathless with excitement, "Nick Candellano."

Fond memories reared up and Nick basked in the glow of them for a second or two.

The guy shook his head and blew out a breath. "Man. Imagine that. Seeing you here. I remember the time you took the ball and ran it back eighty-five yards for a TD." He sighed. "Never saw a run like it—before or since. Man, you cut through those other guys like they weren't even there."

Nick remembered, too. "Yeah," he said, enjoying this quick trip down memory lane. "That was the Atlanta game. Ninety-eight. Good game."

"*Great* game," the shorter man corrected. "You were awesome, man."

Pride swelled along with the memories and puffed out Nick's chest. Hell, maybe this wouldn't be such a bad gig after all. He still had lots of fans out there. Running into one or two of them now and then would cheer him up and give the fans something to talk about when they went home to dinner.

"Thanks," he said, automatically offering his right hand. Giving the man the smile he used to reserve for close-up postgame interviews, he said, "Appreciate it. Always good to meet a fan."

The little guy's grin went even wider as he slapped a manila envelope into Nick's waiting hand. "Good to meet you, too, man. Oh. And you've been served."

"Served?"

"It was great meeting you, though." The short man was already turning to leave.

What the hell was going on? Served? As in served with a lawsuit? Who would be suing him? Nick stared down at the envelope as if waiting for it to open up and announce itself. When it didn't, he lifted his gaze to the retreating back of the little guy who'd sounded like a fan.

"Hey, Nick," Bill called from the sidelines, "you coming?"

The cameraman's voice suddenly sounded muffled—but that was probably because of the sudden roaring in Nick's ears. A cold trickle slipped through his bloodstream. He gave his head a shake, but the roaring was still there. This couldn't be good. His hand fisted around the envelope as if he could squeeze the truth out of it. "What the hell's going on?" he demanded.

The bald guy chuckled as he kept walking. "Read all about it, Nick. Oh, by the way, congratulations. It's a boy."

Tasha Flynn finished the comb-out on Edna Garret's hair, then stood back and aimed a torrent of hair spray at the woman's head. Naturally, the stream of toxins didn't shut Edna up. But then, at this point, why bother?

At eighty, the old woman had probably inhaled enough hair spray over her lifetime to put a nice, glossy shine on her lungs already. What was another coat?

"So anyway," Edna was saying, "when I found out that Francine Chase was gambling away the rent money, I just knew her husband was going to leave her. What man in his right mind would put up with that?"

"Richard Chase should have," a woman under the dryer piped up. Tilting the old-fashioned space helmet dryer back so she could get in a little gossip herself, Alice Tucker stuck her head farther out, stared at Edna, and said, "Francine was the only woman who would have put up with Dick's meandering eye."

"It wasn't just his eye that meandered," Lorraine Tuttle said with a chuckle.

Tasha rolled her eyes at the gossip. The same women kicked around the same topics of conversation every Tuesday. You'd think they'd run out of things to talk about. But no. Every week, they showed up to be washed, curled, and dried. And every week, they had more dirt to dish.

The FBI should know about these women.

But there was a comforting sameness to the routine. A familiarity that told Tasha everything in her world was as it should be. She glanced around the interior of the small shop and smiled to herself. Three hair dryers, only one of them occupied, sat against one wall. Opposite them were three comfortable chairs clustered around a low table littered with hairstyle magazines. Wooden shelves marched along one wall, stuffed to bursting with hair products and supplies. The pink-and-white linoleum was peeling up in one corner, but it was clean, scrubbed nightly by Tasha herself. The wide window overlooking the front yard was sparkling, and a thick slice of sunlight jutted through the glass beneath the half-opened blinds.

She supposed that to most people, the place wouldn't look like much. But to Tasha, it was everything. It was home. Stability. A future.

This was her place.

Where she belonged.

"What do you think, Tasha?" Edna asked.

"Hmm? What do I think?" She glanced into the mirror, ignoring the handful of postcards tucked into the edges of the glass, and met the older woman's direct stare. "I think you're finished, Edna."

The older woman sniffed and waved an impatient hand. "I don't mean my hair, girl. I mean what do you think about roving Dick?"

Tasha's lips twitched as she met Edna's still sharp blue eyes. "I try not to think about roving dicks of any kind."

Heck, it'd been so long since she'd been on a date or come anywhere near a man who wasn't at the shop to pick up his wife, Tasha was pretty sure she could qualify for sainthood. Which, she thought wryly, in her case, was really saying something.

"Smart girl," Edna said as Tasha yanked the Velcro closure at her neck free and snapped the hair-littered plastic cape up and off of her. "You'll find men are usually more trouble than they're worth."

From under the dryer, Alice snorted. "This from a woman with four dead husbands."

One of Edna's steel gray eyebrows swept up. "And all four of them were—"

Whatever she'd been about to say was cut off when the door swung open so quickly, it slammed into the wall with a crash. Tasha whipped around in time to watch her framed print of Tahiti hit the floor. The boy standing in the open doorway hunched his shoulders as it fell, winced, and said, "Sorry."

"Like a bull in a china shop," Edna muttered, but her smile took the sting out of her words.

Jonas Baker, eleven years old and already he was taller than Tasha. Which, she kept reminding him, wasn't that difficult. Since she stood only five-foot-two, most good-sized kids could pass her height at a walk. His dark brown hair fell across his forehead in a sweep that dusted his eyelashes and had the boy continually squinting or swinging his head to one side to clear his vision.

Attempts at a haircut had so far failed.

Thin and gangly, his body seemed to be a collection of sharp angles. And if, like a puppy, he grew into the size of his feet, he'd end up at least seven feet tall. But at the moment, he was just a kid. And the center of Tasha's heart.

"How was school?" she asked as she took Edna's money without bothering to count it. Heck, Edna knew the prices at Castle's Salon better than Tasha did. But then, why wouldn't she? The old woman had been a customer here for forty years. Tasha'd only been here seven.

And before that, there'd been only—

Nope. No point in going down that road. The past didn't matter. Anything beyond her arrival on Mimi Castle's doorstep was ancient history and better forgotten than revisited.

Especially now.

"It was okay," Jonas said with a shrug that could

mean anything from "school was boring" to "I won the Nobel Prize."

Though the Nobel Prize was a long shot, there were other things to be considered. Like homework, for instance. Or that math test she'd helped him prepare for.

"How about your test?" Tasha asked, stuffing Edna's money into her jeans pocket and giving it a satisfying pat. "How'd you do?"

"Okay," he said again, and Tasha wondered if they gave lessons in evasive maneuvers in junior high these days. Or maybe it was just genetic. Become a preteen, forget how to talk. A couple of years ago—heck, even *one* year ago—Jonas would have come into the shop bursting to tell Tasha or Mimi what he'd done in school. He would have told all the ladies some dumb knock-knock jokes and then complained of starvation.

But times change, Tasha told herself.

People die.

Kids grow up.

And secrets were born.

She buried the ache in her heart that always leaped into life when she thought of Mimi Castle, and forced a smile that didn't quite reach her eyes. God, she missed Mimi.

Jonas grunted to the women clustered in the shop portion of the Victorian, then ducked through the connecting doorway that would take him into the main house.

Tasha was right behind him.

Just because he was closing up, trying to shut her out of his life, didn't mean Tasha was going to stand by and let it happen.

She hurried through the service porch, with barely a glance at the mound of laundry waiting to be washed.

She didn't spare a glance at the dishes in the sink as she moved through the kitchen. As she quickened her steps, her sandals clicked noisily against the scarred wood floor of the dining room.

Tasha caught him at the base of the stairs. He might be younger, but she was quicker.

"Hey," she asked, reaching out for him to slow him down, "what's the big rush?"

"No rush," Jonas said, and slipped out from under the hand she'd laid on his shoulder.

Tasha ignored the tiny pang around her heart as she let her hand fall to her side. There was something going on here. Something that kept him from meeting her eyes.

And a tiny tendril of fear rippled through her. Heck, she knew better than anyone what kinds of things were out there in the world, just waiting for a chance to snatch at a kid. Just the thought that he might have already stumbled into trouble tore at her.

"Jonas," she said, reaching for him again before he could scoot out of range, "what's going on?"

He flipped his hair back, then looked at her through those wide brown eyes of his. "Nothing, Tasha," he said with an "I'm so innocent, how could you not believe me?" expression on his face. "Everything's cool."

"Cool, huh?"

"Totally."

Tasha smoothed his hair back from his face and he didn't pull away, so she counted that as a plus. "You're not in trouble or anything, are you?"

"No way." He actually looked insulted.

"Would you tell me if you were?"

He grinned. "No way."

That smile of his jolted her heart. She hadn't seen

it very often lately and she'd missed it. God, she loved this kid. She smiled back at him. "Okay then. Go on up and do your homework."

His whole body moped. "Aw, man. Come on, Tasha. How about a half hour of TV and *then* homework?"

"Let me guess," she said. "The Sports Channel."

He nodded.

"Fine," she said to his back as he raced up the stairs, making enough noise for six kids his size. As his bedroom door slammed shut, she shouted, "A half hour. I'll be checking!"

Jonas tossed his backpack onto the floor, dropped onto his mattress, and propped a pillow under his chest as he lay on his stomach, grabbed the remote, and pushed the ON button. The TV flickered briefly, and for one short second Jonas was afraid the old set wasn't going to come on this time. Heck, it was older than him; it was bound to go out sooner or later. "Just not today, okay?" he said softly.

As if it had heard him, the picture rolled wildly, jittered like someone was shaking the set, and then suddenly straightened itself out.

He whistled out a relieved breath and punched in the right channel. The camera moved in for a close-up on the reporter's familiar face and Jonas studied the man carefully.

When the reporter smiled into the camera, Jonas smiled back. His stomach jumped like millions of butterflies were bumping into each other down there. He slapped one hand against his belly, trying to tame them, but it didn't work. There was just too much going on.

Too much about to happen.

He'd waited for this for so long, Jonas didn't know whether to be excited or scared. He knew Tasha would be mad when she found out. But sometimes a guy just had to do stuff that girls didn't understand.

Another guy would get it, though.

Jonas looked at the reporter again. "You'll understand, won't you?"

CHAPTER 2

"A paternity suit, can you believe it?" Jesus, even saying the words out loud gave Nick a cold chill that rattled his spine before settling in his gut. Beads of sweat popped out on his forehead. He knew because his head was pounding as though they'd had to batter their way through his skull.

Paternity?

Him?

Jackson Wyatt, Nick's brother-in-law and, more important at the moment, his attorney, looked up and said, "How about you shut up for a minute and let me read the paperwork?"

"Fine, fine, read." Nick waved a hand at the other man and stalked around the confines of Jackson's office.

Set in an old brick building at the end of Main Street in Chandler, the only law office in town was huge. Bookshelves lined with leather-bound books crowded most of one wall, floor to ceiling. Jackson's desk sat in front of them, an acre of carved wood, littered with neat stacks of papers and manila envelopes. In the middle of the room, overstuffed oxblood leather couches sat opposite each other atop a floral area rug. The faded colors in the carpet looked rich against the gleaming wood plank floor.

Nick stopped pacing to stare blankly at a spear of sunlight streaming in through the wide window. Thank God Jackson had been here, working, when Nick called. Otherwise, Nick would have had to go to the house to see Jackson and get his advice. The problem with that was, he'd have had to listen to Carla's advice, too.

Shit.

If his baby sister found out about this, the first thing she'd do—well, after hitting Nick in the head with whatever was handy—would be tell Mama. And once Mama Candellano discovered there was a possible extra grandchild running around . . . the planet wouldn't be big enough to hide Nick.

Not that he wanted to hide. Hell, like any other upstanding, self-respecting Candellano, when faced with a problem, his first instinct was to plant his feet and fight it out. But when there was no one to punch, he had to go about things a different way. Hence, the lawyer.

Nick started pacing again, unable to stand still while his insides fisted, relaxed, and fisted again. Damn it, how could someone just sue him like this? No warning? No angry letters or demanding phone calls? Nick scraped one hand across his face. Christ. A lawsuit. Naming *him*, for God's sake, as the father of an eleven-year-old boy.

Eleven.

While Nick paced, his brain picked its way through a jumble of thoughts to come up with the ability to subtract. He was thirty-three now. Eleven years ago, he'd been twenty-two. He groaned tightly. Crap. His rookie year in the NFL. Fresh out of college and feeling . . . well, to be honest, he'd been feeling any woman who came into range.

And there were plenty of them in that category. Football groupies, hangers-on, party girls—they'd all been way too handy back then. But in his defense, there weren't many men who could have walked through a mine field of willing women without getting caught up in one or two explosions.

It had been part and parcel of the dream. Nick had worked his ass off all through high school and then college. He'd been a number two draft pick, and when he signed his first contract his wildest fantasies came true. More money than he knew what to do with and hot and cold running women.

Jesus. It was a wonder he'd even survived his playing days. Between the late-night parties, the weekend orgies, and the actual playing of football, he'd gone through his twenties in an exhausted stupor. A tired but well-contented man. Still, his indulgences had cost him his girlfriend, Stevie Ryan—well, Stevie Candellano now, since she'd married Nick's twin brother, Paul, just a month ago.

Christ, he was living a soap opera.

And the head writer, Fate, had just thrown him a helluva curve.

This whole thing was a nightmare.

"For God's sake, I can't be somebody's father," he muttered.

"Jonas Baker disagrees," Jackson said quietly.

"Who the hell is this kid?" Nick demanded, stopping alongside the front window that looked over Chandler's Main Street.

"Your son?" Jackson offered.

Nick shuddered. "Don't say it."

"I'm reading it."

"Well, read to yourself."

"Ignoring it won't change anything, Nick."

"I know that. That's why I'm here, talking to you."

Jackson leaned back in his chair, ruffling the edges of the subpoena with a thumb as he watched his brother-in-law. Maybe it hadn't been such a good idea for Nick to move back closer to Chandler. A few weeks ago, the Candellano family had thought it a brilliant plan. Nick had wanted to get back closer to the people who mattered in his life. To get out of San Jose and the anonymity of living in a city where no one gave a damn about him.

But if he'd stayed in the city, he'd have found a lawyer who didn't have to try to keep this secret from his wife. Lawyer-client confidentiality meant nothing when it came to Carla's family. Somehow, she *would* find out what was going on with her brother. And then she'd kill Jackson for not telling her himself.

Oh, yeah. This was going to be lots of fun.

Straightening up in his chair, he leaned forward, planting both elbows on his desktop as he stared at his brother-in-law. Nick looked like hell. His dark brown hair had been stabbed through by nervous fingers until it stood out from his head. Brown eyes looked worried, and the muscle twitching in Nick's jaw let Jackson know that he was a man on the edge.

"The suit says that the boy's mother, Margie Baker, claimed you fathered her son." Jackson tapped his fingertips against the paperwork.

Nick frowned, shook his head, and shrugged helplessly. "I don't remember the name."

"Not surprising," Jackson allowed. "It was a long time ago."

A long time ago. But if he'd made a child, shouldn't he at least remember what that child's mother looked like? Had he really been so self-indulgent that names and faces of the women he'd had sex with were nothing more than a blurred stream in his memory? Something a lot like shame stirred inside him, and Nick didn't like it. Hell, he'd been young and stupid and rich. A lethal combination.

Nick turned to stare out the window. Beyond the glass, Chandler was settling in for the evening. No late-night clubbing in Chandler. This was no party town. Just a quiet little suburb, hardly more than a speck on the road to bigger and better places. Tourists loved the place, though, and brought in a fortune in souvenir dollars. The summer crowds faded into the fall foliage people, who gave way to the winter carnival group, who eventually stepped aside for the spring festivals, and then it was summer again and the whole cycle started over. No, there was no excitement in Chandler. He'd learned that as a kid. But there was something else here Nick had never found anywhere else. The comfort of the familiar. And right now, he could use a little of that comfort. The sense of peace that being here, where he belonged, usually brought him.

Squinting into the sunshine, he asked, his voice low and suddenly weary, "Why isn't the boy's mother suing me? Why'd she leave it to the kid?"

"You didn't read everything?"

"No."

"Margie Baker died two years ago."

Nick's chin hit his chest. "Damn." Bracing both hands against the edges of the window, he leaned forward, shaking his head as that little piece of news drilled through his brain. A woman he couldn't remember had given birth to a child he hadn't known about, and now, eleven years later, the shit had finally rolled downhill.

Lifting his head again, he stared out at Main Street and squinted into the late-afternoon light. What was left of the sun slammed against his eyes, and Nick told himself that was the reason his head was suddenly pounding. It couldn't be sympathy for a kid he hadn't even known existed yesterday.

Still, a twinge of pity stirred inside him and he wondered, whether he wanted to or not, what kind of kid would have the balls to sue his own father.

And at that sobering thought, he stiffened, resisting accepting the cloak of parenthood, even in his own brain.

Pity aside, he wasn't going to stand still and let this kid ruin his life. It was all a mistake. It had to be. Hell, anybody could claim to have been with him—and Nick wouldn't have been able to confirm or deny it. Suddenly disgusted with himself, he realized it was no wonder he'd lost Stevie. He'd been with so many women back then, no one face stood out from the crowd. And what did that say about him?

But no way was he a father. He'd been careful. Even back then. Hell, he'd bought condoms by the gross in those days. Taking a deep breath, he let it out again slowly, reassuring himself that he was no doubt in the clear. The fact that condoms weren't a hundred percent effective didn't even blink on his internal radar screen. He'd done the right thing. He'd protected himself, and the women he'd been with, from disease and from pregnancy, damn it.

The poor kid, whoever he was, was grabbing at straws. Looking for a famous father to rescue him. Well, Nick couldn't blame the kid for trying to look out for himself. Nick had been doing the same thing for years. But he wasn't going to be the fall guy here. He was nobody's meal ticket. He wasn't going to accept responsibility for a child that wasn't his.

So what he had to do here was meet the kid, face-to-face, get him to admit it was all some sort of sick joke, and then end it—hopefully before the newspapers got wind of this story. There were just too many so-called journalists who'd *love* the idea of toppling yet another former—God, he hated the word *former*—sports hero.

"What're you thinking?" Jackson asked.

Nick nodded to himself as his thoughts jelled and he settled on his plan. "I'm thinking," he said softly, "that maybe this is something I should take care of myself."

"That's probably not a good idea."

"Jackson," Nick said, and pushed away from the window to turn and face the man behind the desk. "You take care of the legal side of this and let me handle the kid myself."

Shaking his head, Jackson stood up, came around the desk, and crossed the room to stop in front of Nick. "You can't just confront this boy—he's a minor. You'll have to go through his foster mother."

Foster mother.

Shit.

Those two words painted a mental image Nick really didn't want. Visions of a kid with no one and nothing to call his own roared through Nick's brain and he had to fight down another stab of pity. Jonas Baker had lost his home, his mother, his world. Nick had grown up surrounded by more love than he'd been able to handle at times. With two parents, two brothers, and a kid sister to make his life a living hell. And he wouldn't have had it any other way.

The idea of a kid being on his own was so alien to Nick that he had a hard time picturing it. But just because Nick could feel for the kid didn't mean he was going to take the rap for this. It wasn't his fault. This wasn't his son, and Nick had to prove it.

One thing he didn't plan on doing was having the threat of paternity hanging around his neck like a noose for the rest of his life. Nope. There were enough Candellano grandchildren already. And if there were going to be more, they wouldn't be coming from him. He liked his role of favored uncle just fine. He could see his brothers' and sister's kids, play with them, spoil them a little, then run like hell for the peace and quiet of his own place.

Being a father just wasn't in his game plan.

Now all he had to do was convince this boy that he had the wrong guy. "Fine," he said, feeling more in control than he had since the moment that process server had slapped the papers into his hand. "I'll talk to the foster mother, then the kid."

"I still don't think this is a good idea."

"I'm not going to just sit around and wait, Jackson."

His brother-in-law stared at him for a long minute or two, then finally nodded. "All right, fine. Go see the woman." He turned and walked back to his desk. Grabbing up a pen and paper, he scribbled the name and address down, then handed the paper to Nick as he came up beside him.

"She lives just outside Santa Cruz."

Nick glanced at the paper. "Mimi Castle." He chuckled as visions of a chubby blonde with poodles in tow leaped into his mind. "Now *there's* a name."

"If she refuses to let you see the boy," Jackson warned, "drop it, Nick, and leave it to me."

A woman? Nick thought. Refusing him something? That'd be the day. He gave Jackson the million-dollar smile that had once graced toothpaste commercials. The same smile that had been known to melt female hearts at a hundred yards. "Trust me on this, Jackson," he said. "Mimi's gonna love me."

By six-thirty, all Tasha wanted was a long soak in a hot bath and about ten hours of sleep. But she still had too much to do.

She shifted wet clothes from the washing machine to the dryer, then yanked the knob on the old washer to start up another load. Water streamed into the chipped tub, and while she waited for it to fill, Tasha stared out the window at the darkness.

Beyond the yard, lamplight spilled out of her closest neighbors' windows, almost a half-mile away, looking like bright patches of yellow fabric in an all-black quilt. The ocean wind danced in and out of the trees, and a leafless tree limb scraped eerily against the windowpane, sounding like fingernails on a chalkboard.

She shivered, reached for the detergent, and tossed a scoopful into the already agitating water. Then she threw the clothes in, slammed the lid down, and moved into the kitchen. No time to stand around and idly watch the night pass. There was just too much to do.

Once the last of her customers left, Tasha had to deal with the rest of her life. Laundry, cooking, cleaning, making sure Jonas did his homework and hit the showers. There never seemed to be enough time for everything, and not for the first time, she wondered how Mimi had made it all look so easy.

She stopped short and smiled to herself. "She was Mimi, that's how," she muttered. And that said it all, didn't it? Mimi Castle had been one of a kind. Unique. From the long rope of silver hair she'd worn in a braid that dangled to her waist, right down to the hot pink polish on her toes. Age hadn't meant a thing to Mimi. If she liked something, she wore it and would cheerfully tell anyone who didn't like it to "shove off."

At seventy, Mimi had still been a force of nature. She started every morning by draping herself in her beloved turquoise jewelry—from earrings and dozens of necklaces and armbands to the concho belt she habitually wore around her waist. Her long skirts usually dusted the tops of her worn leather moccasins, and the wildly flowered peasant blouses she favored combined to create the perfect picture of an elderly hippie.

Her lined face was perpetually wreathed in a smile that welcomed the world and warmed the heart. She cried over telephone commercials and laughed loud enough to rattle the dishes.

And Tasha missed her desperately.

Only seventeen when she'd first encountered Mimi, Tasha had been on the streets, homeless, for two years. She'd run away from a home where her parents had chosen Jack Daniel's over their only child. And despite the fear and loneliness that accompanied a life on the streets, it had been better than what she'd run from.

And then there was Mimi. Mimi had taken her in, offered her love and a home. The older woman hadn't been Tasha's foster mother—officially—but for ten years she'd been more of a *real* mother than Tasha had ever known before.

And the ache of missing Mimi never went away.

Tasha reached into the hot soapy water, found the sponge, and on autopilot wiped the first of what looked like a hundred dishes. The hot water seemed to soak into her bones, her blood, and warmed her through. Bubbles frothed against her skin and she watched them slide away under the stream of hot water gushing from the tap. There was something peaceful, nearly comforting, about the act of washing dishes. Maybe it was remembering those plates on the table and the conversations you'd had over the meal. And maybe it was just a mindless task that left you free enough to wander whatever mental freeways you felt like traveling.

"God, Mimi, what am I supposed to do?" she asked, then held her breath, almost waiting to hear an answer. When none came, she sighed and kept talking. Even if Mimi couldn't reply, Tasha knew she was listening. "Something's up with Jonas." There. She'd said it. She hadn't wanted to even think the words, but bringing them out in the open, if only to the ghost of a woman she wished were still here, actually felt pretty good. As if once the words were said, things couldn't get worse.

"Now *there's* a direct challenge to the gods," she said softly. Though how things could get worse, she just didn't know. "And maybe you don't *want* to know, Tasha," she told herself, and got back to the matter at hand. "Mimi, he's hiding something. I don't know what it is, but he won't talk to me about it. If you were still here, you'd find a way to make him spill his guts inside fifteen minutes."

Mimi'd always had a gift for getting people to open up to her. There was always such understanding, such acceptance, shining from her eyes, a person just knew he could trust her.

Trust.

It all came down to trust, didn't it? Tasha had believed in Mimi, trusted her, despite the fact that she'd learned the hard way to trust *no one.* Then Jonas had come along and the three of them became a family. A unit—indivisible. Or so they'd thought, until a sudden heart attack six months ago had split up the Three Musketeers forever. Mimi had been the heart of them. She'd been their center. The glue that held them all together.

And without her, Tasha was just as lost as poor Jonas.

"Hey!" Jonas shouted from the living room. "There's somebody at the door!"

"Well, see who it is," she called back, and shook her head in disgust. What was it about almost-teenagers? He'd used up more energy calling for help than it would have cost him to get off his butt and answer the door himself.

"My show's on," he wailed.

"Fine." His show. Heck, he shouldn't be watching TV anyway. He should be doing homework. Turning off the water, Tasha grabbed up a dish towel and dried her hands as she walked through the house. As she walked past Jonas, she flicked the end of the towel at his head.

"Hey, no fair."

"Go do your homework," she said.

"Right after the show, Tasha," he said, tipping his head back to look up at her. A slow, crooked grin curved his mouth and it had the effect he'd hoped for.

"Okay, ten more minutes. *Then* homework."

Someone on the porch knocked again, three solid thumps that sounded more like a battering ram than a set of knuckles, and Tasha hurried on. Grabbing the cold brass knob, she gave it a turn and yanked the door open.

Tall, dark, and gorgeous looked back at her. In the yellow glow of the porch light the man's brown eyes gleamed almost like amber. His dark brown hair was wind-ruffled and just the slightest hint of a five o'clock shadow bristled on his lean cheeks. His nose looked like it had been broken at some point in his life, but somehow it added character to his face without making him look menacing.

Of course, how menacing could any man look while wearing loafers with little tassels on them? A *GQ* hit man, maybe? The stray thought had her half-smiling as she asked, "Can I help you?"

Okay, Nick thought, *not* what he'd been expecting. If this was Mimi Castle, then foster mothers had been getting a bad rap for way too many years.

She wasn't very tall. Probably would hit him in the middle of his chest. Thick, wavy hair the color of dark fire framed her face, and sharp green eyes watched him. A truly incredible mouth curved in a secretive smile that almost distracted him from the rest of her. She might be short, but not an inch of her was wasted. Her long-sleeved T-shirt clung to her breasts, then scraped down along her rib cage and tucked in at a narrow waist. Her jeans were worn and faded and dipped low enough at her waist to display her belly button and about an inch of pale skin. Bare feet and silver toe rings completed the picture of easy sensuality.

She was almost enough to make him forget why he was there. Almost. But if she was Mimi, then Jonas couldn't be far away. Better to get this done and over, misunderstandings cleared up. Then maybe he and Mimi could have dinner or something.

"Hello?" she said, waving one hand back and forth in front of his face. "Earth to intruder."

"Huh?" He inhaled sharply. "Oh." Chuckling, he shook his head and gave her his most endearing smile. That slightly crooked grin that had always smoothed rough paths before him.

But instead of turning into the puddle of goo he'd expected, she sighed, said, "We don't want any," and closed the door.

Stunned, Nick just stood there.

He was still standing there when she turned off the porch light and darkness reached for him.

CHAPTER 3

Nick blinked, opened his mouth, then snapped it shut again.

He stared at the closed door, waiting for it to open again. Hell, he couldn't believe it had closed in the first place. Hadn't she seen his smile?

Shifting position uneasily, he glanced around at the quiet darkness around him, reassuring himself no one else had witnessed that. But just as he'd been when he first parked his Corvette in the gravel driveway, he was alone. The Victorian stood smack in the middle of what had to be at least a couple of acres of land. The nearest neighbor was no more than a lamplight gleam in the dark.

Maybe that was it, he told himself. The house was a little isolated—and a woman who looked like *that* was bound to be a little nervous opening the door to a stranger at night. It wasn't *him* in particular she'd shut the door on. She would have done the same to anyone.

So all he had to do was convince her he was harmless.

Determined, he knocked on the door one more time.

The porch light winked on and Nick blinked again

at the sudden spill of light. Then the door opened and there she was, the redhead with the great mouth, framed in the narrow opening, backlit by lamplight, glaring at him. From inside the house he heard the unmistakable sound of *The Simpsons.*

Had to be the kid. The boy at the root of his current problem.

But he wasn't dealing with Jonas Baker yet. First he had to get past the small, curvy sentinel. Nick tried his patented "all the women love me" smile again, focusing every bit of his attention on her.

No reaction.

Man.

"Look," she said, "I don't want to be rude, but I don't need a vacuum, I don't buy Avon, and I'm too busy to accept Jesus just at the moment, so go away, okay?"

He couldn't believe it. He was getting the brush-off, *again*? No way. As the door swung closed again, he took a step forward. "Hey, hold on. I'm not a salesman and I'm not delivering pamphlets."

She paused, sighed heavily, and said, "Fine. Are you lost? The freeway's just up the road another couple of miles. You can't miss it."

"I'm not lost, either." Jesus. He'd never had such a hard time trying to get a woman to listen to him. Of course, most of the time, he was wining and dining them and whisking them outside to stand under the moonlight. Apparently, it was a whole different story by porch light. "Are you always this friendly?"

"Only to uninvited guests." Tasha leaned against the edge of the door, tilted her head to one side, and stared at him. He looked a little more frustrated than he had a minute ago, but that *so* wasn't her problem. In the yellow glow of the overhead light his dark brown hair shone as if streaked with gold dust. His dark eyes fixed on hers and she could have sworn she actually *felt* a little jolt of electricity.

Great.

Now her hormones wake up?

Fighting a reaction she didn't want, Tasha snapped, "So? What's this about then?"

"Are you Mimi Castle?"

"No," she said, and her stomach flipped wildly. Straightening up, she felt her mouth go dry and her palms go damp. A stranger? Asking about Mimi? This couldn't be a good thing.

He blew out a breath and frowned. "I need to speak to her."

Tasha stiffened and her eyes narrowed as she looked at him more closely. Even while her insides fluttered and swirled, she told herself he couldn't be with Social Services. Not with those expensive shoes—not to mention his car, she thought, shifting her gaze to the driveway and the Corvette parked behind her battered VW van. So if he wasn't a state snooper, who the hell was he and why did he want Mimi?

And what did it matter? she reminded herself. She didn't care who he was or who he worked for. He wasn't welcome here. The point was to get rid of him. Fast.

"She's not home."

"Are you the baby-sitter?"

"Is that really your business?" Good. Keep talking. Don't let your throat close up. Sound confident.

"Defensive, aren't you?"

"Nosy," she countered, "aren't you?"

"Lady, why are you making this so hard?"

"Why in the hell should I make anything easy? I don't know you from a spot in the road."

His jaw worked and she could almost hear him grind his back teeth together in mounting frustration. It took him a couple of minutes, but he got himself together again enough to ask, "Fine. Okay. When'll Ms. Castle be back?"

Never, Tasha thought, and wished for the thousandth time that things were different. That Mimi was just off on one of her weekend "adventures." But her latest adventure was forever, and wishing wouldn't change a damn thing, as Tasha knew better than anyone else.

She inhaled sharply, lifted her chin, looked him dead in the eye, and lied. She was getting pretty good at it. And for someone who hated a lie more than anything else, that was saying something. "Who knows? She'll come back when she feels like it and not before."

Mr. Tassel Loafer didn't like that one bit. His sharply defined features twisted into a scowl and he reached up to shove one hand impatiently through his hair. "Look," he said, taking another step closer. "This is important. I have to see her. Talk to her."

As casually as she could manage, Tasha lifted one hand, grabbed the screen door handle, snicked it completely closed, and flipped the lock. A flimsy barrier, she knew, but it was better than nothing. Just in case Gucci Guy decided to press the issue.

"Well, she's not here, so you can't."

"It's about her foster son," he said tightly, "Jonas Baker."

Everything inside Tasha went cold and still. There it was. Plainly said. Jonas. He was here about Jonas. Fear rippled along her spine, but she managed to keep from shivering. It was never a good thing to let your opponent know that you were rattled. And she'd learned long ago to *never* show fear. Even when you were choking on it.

She took another long, hard look at him. Those dark brown eyes of his were fixed on her face and she tried to read what might be written there. But all she could see was his frustration.

She didn't want to ask. Didn't want to invite him even an inch further into their lives. She wanted to make this guy go away and leave them alone. But she couldn't afford to send him off without at least getting an idea as to what was going on. Why he was so interested in Mimi. After all, she told herself grimly, know your enemy.

"What about Jonas?" she demanded, keeping her voice low. There wasn't really a need for quiet, though. Jonas kept the TV high enough to block the sound of machine-gun fire.

"Is he here?"

"Of course he's here, he lives here."

Gucci smiled again and nodded stiffly. "Sure. Stupid question. Okay, since Mimi's not here, can I talk to him?"

"No," Tasha said sharply. "Mister, I've already told you. I don't know you from a hole in the wall. Why in the hell would I let you inside my house to talk to Jonas?"

He blew out a breath that ruffled his hair. Brown eyes narrowed as he considered her a full minute before he said tightly, "That's between me and Ms. Castle. And Jonas."

"Swell," she countered, and congratulated herself silently when her voice didn't shake. So much for getting a little information. "Then you can wait for Mimi to get back to take care of it."

"This can't wait—"

She shut the door and gave the dead bolt a fast spin. Then slipping the chain into place, she turned around and leaned against the door, as if bracing her back against the solid oak panel to keep the intruder out.

"Who was it?" Jonas called out.

Trouble, she thought, her brain wheeling with the possibilities. But she shouted back, "No one. Just some salesman!"

Another lie.

She reached up and rubbed the center of her forehead with her fingertips. The volume of the TV seemed to reach inside her head to play on the last few nerves that weren't already shrieking. Dropping her hand to her side, she shouted, "Turn off the TV and do your homework!"

"Ta—sha . . ." Jonas drew her name out until it sounded like a six-syllable word.

"Now, Jonas," she said, and waited a heartbeat or two before he complied. Silence dropped on the old house like a warm blanket and Tasha breathed a sigh of pure relief.

Jonas, on the other hand, slouched through the living room, down the hall, and to the stairs. He shot her one angry glance over his shoulder, then stomped up the stairs, each pounding step an exclamation point to his disgust. When he reached the top of the stairs, he went to his room and slammed the door with enough force to rattle the windows downstairs.

Tasha winced at the demonstration, then pushed away from the door and headed into the kitchen to finish the dishes. She stared into the window above the sink but didn't see the blackness outside. Instead, she focused on her own reflection. "He's mad," she told her mirrored self, "but he's safe." He was here. In his own home. With her.

Where he belonged.

Where he would stay.

When he woke up the next morning, Nick was still feeling the frustration that had had him kicking his way down a graveled drive, then peeling out of Mimi Castle's driveway. And not even pushing the Vette to ninety on the way home or feeling the oncoming wind slap at his face had done a damn thing to make him feel better.

If he'd only been able to get past the redhead, he might've been able to straighten out the situation then and there. But wouldn't you know that when he most needed his legendary charm, it had deserted him?

He didn't have a clue who the redhead was—and under different circumstances, he'd have been anxious to find out. Instantly an image of her leaped into his brain and those green eyes of hers hit him just as hard in memory as they had in person.

Damn it.

But she wasn't the real problem. She was just blocking his way to it.

Jonas Baker was beginning to feel like an ax hanging over his head. Hell, he'd only known about the kid for twenty-four hours and already Nick had been pushed to the edge of his patience.

Yeah, parenthood was a real treat.

Whoa. His brain stopped, backed up, and erased that word, *parenthood.* He wasn't this kid's father. No way, nohow. All he had to do was convince the kid. If he could get a few minutes alone with the boy, Nick was sure he'd find a way to settle this mess without courtrooms. Or the media.

He knew he wasn't the father. Couldn't be. The kid was probably a fan. A fan with fantasies. A bit of hero worship gone bad, that's all. Nick could straighten him out. Give him a pep talk. Kids liked that kind of shit. Build up the boy's self-esteem a little. Tell him that this was no way to meet your football heroes. Then he'd sign a few photographs. . . . hell, maybe he'd give the kid one of his old jerseys. Nick grinned. Yeah. That was it. No fuss, no muss.

Jackson would want him to take a DNA paternity test. But hell, he didn't need it. Didn't want it. Why put the kid through that, anyway?

And a small voice in the back of his mind whispered, *Besides, if the press got hold of a DNA test . . . they'd have a field day.*

His head was pounding with a rhythmic slam that felt as though his brain were sliding from side to side to bang against his temples. He hadn't had a headache like that since his last hangover. And since he hadn't been drinking, there was no reason for the—shit. He finally located the source of the noise battering at his head and muttered every vicious curse he could think of.

Throwing the blankets back, he swung his legs off the bed and sat up. Bare feet hit the cold hardwood floor and he shivered as he reached for the gray sweats strewn across a nearby chair. Standing up, he tugged the pants up over his naked ass and headed for the window on the far side of the room.

That pounding accompanied every step he took as

if he were a dancer in a well-choreographed show. Wincing as the hammering sound smashed against his caffeine-starved system, he threw the window up, stuck his head outside, and almost groaned as the sun slammed into his eyes. Jesus Christ. Did people actually get up this early on purpose?

Pulling in a gulp of air, he yelled, "What the hell's going on?"

"Good morning, Nick!"

Nothing good about it as far as he could see. Nick glared at the cheerful little man standing on a ladder not two feet away. Hank Marconi, of Marconi's Construction, grinned at him. Barrel-chested, Hank had thick gray hair, twinkling eyes, and a nose that took up half of his face. Actually, he looked like a short Italian Santa. Normally, Hank was so short Nick had to practically bend over to look the man in the eye. However, this morning the little guy was perched on a ten-foot aluminum ladder and staring at Nick eyeball-to-eyeball.

"Hank," Nick asked, his voice rough with the lack of sleep scratching at his throat, "why are you torturing me?"

The man's wide blue eyes fairly sparkled. Humor creased his features and he shook dangerously as a laugh rumbled through his compact body. "Torture? Ah, Nick, your papa and me, we used to be up with the birds every morning."

"Papa's dead," Nick reminded his father's oldest friend.

"God rest his soul," Hank muttered, and crossed himself quickly. Since he was holding the hammer in his right hand, it was a miracle he didn't knock himself out.

"Lack of sleep probably did him in early, Hank," Nick said, despite hearing the plea in his voice. "Are you trying to kill me?"

Hank laughed and shook his head, sending that wild gray hair into a tangle of waves that a lot of women would have cheerfully done him in for. "Hey, Nick, I'm just fixing the eaves." He used his hammer as a pointer to indicate the missing boards along the roofline. "You remember? We talked about it a couple days ago?"

Remember? Okay, yeah. Nick had a vague recollection of some conversation about eaves. But then, who could be sure? There'd been so many conversations about so many things that needed fixing, how could he possibly keep them all straight?

And who the hell would have expected work to start at the crack of dawn?

Shaking his head and blinking into the morning sun, Nick shivered slightly as the cool November air brushed against his bare chest. Winter was coming fast, and if he wanted to be able to keep the wind, not to mention the rain, out of this wreck of a house, he supposed he'd have to put up with the construction guys.

"Okay," he said, and spoke up again quickly as Hank lifted his hammer to slam yet another nail into the bare wood. "But can you just give me five minutes to get dressed and downstairs before you start hammering again?"

"Late night?" Hank asked with a wink and a smile.

"Something like that," Nick assured him, then ducked back into the bedroom and closed the window. While he grabbed up jeans, underwear, and a sweater and headed for the bathroom, he told himself that not so long ago, Hank's assessment would have been right.

Up until a month or so ago, Nick had been trying to drink his way through every bottle of liquor in Northern California. He'd had more hangovers than a frat house in Homecoming Week and had even had the dubious honor of being arrested by his own brother for drunk driving.

Just remembering that little incident made him cringe. Hell, he was lucky he hadn't killed somebody. As it was, the only damage had been to the reverend's lawn goose. Which the reverend's wife had no intention of letting Nick forget, anytime soon.

A man could really screw up his life without hardly trying, he thought. All it took was a little depression and a lot of booze. But things were different now, he reminded himself. He'd turned over a new leaf. Started fresh.

Just like with this house. Not too long ago, he'd been living in a cold, lifeless condo in San Jose. Far from the town where he'd grown up, from the family he loved despite their combined craziness. He'd lived alone and insulated from everything save his own popularity. And what had it gotten him?

Truckloads of trouble.

So he'd moved back to Chandler. Back to his past, in the hopes that it would jump-start his future. And since he was making a fresh start, he'd decided to go all the way. Why buy some new, characterless place that would end up being nothing more than a carbon copy of that god-awful condo? Nope. Not Nick. He'd bought a run-down place at the opposite end of town from his mother's house.

Hey, he wanted to come back home, but he wasn't completely nuts.

The house sat at the edge of the woods, not far from

the small lake that ran along the border of Chandler. Back here, among the trees, the nearby ocean sounded like nothing more than a hushed heartbeat, drifting through the forest and sighing on the wind. Here he was close enough to his roots to get support—and far enough away to retain his sanity.

At least, whatever sanity was left him after the remodel was finished.

He'd hired the Marconi family to make the renovations, and they'd assured him that in no time at all he'd have the house of his dreams.

They just hadn't specified that those dreams would be nightmares.

Shaking his head, Nick stepped into the shower, flipped on the water, and sucked in a gulp of air as the frigid water drilled a gaping hole through his chest.

"Jesus!"

His shout drew a peal of laughter that drifted in through the tiny window above the tub.

"Sorry, Nick!" one of Hank's daughters shouted. "Had to turn off the water heater this morning. Working on the gas line."

"Great," he said, through clenched teeth. If this house remodel didn't kill him, Nick thought, nothing would.

After the world's fastest shower, Nick got dressed and jammed his feet into a pair of sneakers. Heading downstairs, he stepped over cables and wires and tried to ignore the tarpaulin-covered area that used to be a semihabitable living room.

Muttering under his breath, he turned toward the kitchen, hoping the Marconis had left the electricity on. He needed coffee. Gallons of it.

"Nick . . . *hi.*"

"Hi, Mike," he said, nodding to Hank's third daughter as she pulled her blond head out from under the sink and stood up. She gave him a soft smile and a pout she'd perfected years ago in high school. He ignored it. Safer that way. "You guys leave me any coffee this time?"

Josefina, "Jo," Marconi, the oldest daughter, walked into the kitchen just in time to answer that. She flipped a dark brown ponytail over one shoulder and cocked a hip. "You said you wouldn't be here today. We shut everything off to get at the wiring. And the gas." She shot a look at her younger sister and smirked. "Cool your jets, Mikey."

Mike, Michaela, huffed out an impatient breath, but relaxed the femme fatale look, which helped Nick relax a little. He didn't need Hank Marconi coming after him with a shotgun, demanding he do the right thing by one of his precious girls.

Well, the morning just kept getting better and better. "This is great. And what do I do for coffee?"

"What we do," Sam said as she stepped into the room and stopped between her sisters. She pulled a white painter's cap off her head and sent a mass of long reddish brown hair tumbling down to her shoulders. Grinning, she held up a tall paper cup with the Leaf and Bean logo. "Go to Stevie's place."

Nick studied first one sister, then the next. The Marconis were so different, you'd never know they were related by looking at them. A blonde, a brunette, and a redhead, the Marconi girls were full partners in their father's construction business. Thankfully for their sakes, they'd taken after their mother—tall, slim, and gorgeous—rather than their father in the looks department.

The Candellano kids and the Marconis had gone to school together. Hell, he'd even dated Sam once or twice, before hooking up with Stevie—and right this minute, Nick could cheerfully murder all three Marconi women.

"You're killing me, you know that, right?"

"Suck it up, football star," Samantha said, grinning.

Nick grimaced.

"Hey, the place is gonna be great," Jo told him.

"When?" Nick asked.

Mike, answered, and Nick said the words right along with her. "Three or four weeks."

She grinned at him and sent him a slow wink.

Samantha jabbed her with an elbow to the stomach.

Nick paid no attention. Three or four weeks. No surprise there. It was the same response he'd been getting from the whole family ever since this remodel had started two weeks ago.

"C'mon, you guys," he argued. "It's not that big a house."

"Hell," Sam countered with a derisive snort and a glare at her youngest sister, "it's almost not a house. I'd call it more like one step up from a shack."

"Now," Nick argued pointedly.

"Hey," Mike said, abandoning the flirtatious pose long enough to defend her family's work, "it's over fifty years old. The pipes and the wiring alone belong in a museum."

Nick shot a look at her. "But everything was working until you guys ripped the guts out of it."

"Working for how long, though?" Jo asked. "Until you woke up floating downstairs one night 'cause the pipes burst? Or until an electrical fire turned the whole place to ash?"

"Fine," Nick muttered, surrendering to the inevitable. "I give up. I'm going to Stevie's for coffee."

"Excellent idea," Sam said. "Bring us back a few more, huh?"

He stopped dead, hunched his shoulders, then kept on walking. Perfect. He was three for three. Career. Life. House. All screwed. He opened the car door and glanced up, half-expecting to see a plague of frogs descending on him.

Somebody crashed into Jonas from behind, then ran past him, down the crowded hall. He hardly noticed. Heck, the school hallways were always packed. A guy could get run over and then trampled to death and probably nobody'd notice until the bell rang and you could see the body.

"You hear anything?"

"Huh?"

Jonas spun around and grinned at his best friend. Alex Medina, clutching one strap of his overloaded backpack, grinned back. "I said, did you hear anything yet?"

"No." Jonas slammed his locker door shut, the loud clang rising up and then disappearing in the roar of sound created by several hundred kids. "Nothing. But the lawyer said that it might take a while."

Alex shook his head and fell into step beside Jonas as the boy started walking toward his first-period class. "Man. It's all gonna happen, isn't it? I mean, you've got the lawyer and everything. You're really doing it."

"Told you I was gonna," Jonas said, and swallowed back the tight ball of nerves that seemed permanently lodged in the middle of his throat.

For two days now, he'd been waiting. He didn't know if he could last much longer. For so long, he'd thought about doing this. About setting everything into motion. And now that he finally had, there was only one thing that worried him.

What if his father didn't want to be found?

Chapter 4

"So, *talk.* What was he like?" Molly Watson, friend and co-operator of Castle's, tapped her foot. She tipped her head to one side and her perfectly cut midnight black hair stayed in place. Tiny points and wedges of hair flattered her small face and made her look like a mischievous pixie. Impatience had her drumming her blood-red nails against the arm of the chair as she waited for more information on Tasha's mystery man.

At eight-thirty, there was still a half hour before the first customer arrived and things started hopping in the shop. Tasha glanced around. Not much had changed in here since Mimi's death. And there was familiarity and comfort in that. It was still a three-chair shop, which meant they were busy enough to keep ahead of the bills and small enough to stay cozy.

Shifting her gaze back to Molly, Tasha sighed. They never scheduled customers before nine in the morning, giving themselves that extra half hour to catch up on the bills or to chat or even to do each other's hair. This morning, though, the conversation was strained and Tasha couldn't shake the weird sensation of impending doom that kept tugging at her insides.

Ridiculous.

Everything was fine.

Even if Tassel Loafer came back, which she was pretty sure he would, she would handle it. She'd get through it—just as she'd gotten through every other rotten situation in her life. Atta way, Tash, she told herself silently. All she had to do was remember all of the other crap she'd managed to survive.

And now she had more motivation than ever—because it wasn't only her own life at stake here . . . it was Jonas's.

Sitting at her workstation, directly opposite Molly, Tasha wondered if she should have said anything at all about Tassel Loafer. Maybe she should have kept the weird visit from a stranger to herself.

In the old days, she would have. But her life was different, now. *She* was different, now. She didn't have to carry all of her burdens alone anymore. She had friends. Like Molly.

"Are you gonna tell me what he was like or not?" Molly prompted.

"How do I know?" Tasha finally said. "I got rid of him as fast as I could." Though God knew, he hadn't been easy to get rid of. But then, guys like him—gorgeous and charm personified, rich, too, judging by the clothes—probably weren't used to hearing the word *no* very often.

Molly was not appeased. Dangling one foot off the chair, she gave herself a push against one of the pink cabinets and sent the chair into a slow spin. When she came back full circle, she stopped the spin with a slap against the counter and said, "At least you could give me a clue about what he *looks* like."

Tasha didn't even have to dredge up her memory to describe him. Hadn't his image been dancing across her brain all night? She shifted uncomfortably in the chair as she pictured his eyes, dark and filled with frustration. "He looked," she said, "like temptation."

"Mmmm . . . sounds promising." Molly waved a hand at her. "More."

"Tall," she said. "And gorgeous, in an I-know-I'm-great-try-not-to-faint-at-my-feet sort of way."

"Intriguing," Molly murmured, then tipped her head to one side to study Tasha. "Tall?"

Tasha snorted. "Look who you're talking to. From my vantage point, *everybody's* tall." But as she remembered it, he was *really* tall. And lean. And muscled. And dangerous, damn it.

"Good point." Molly nodded. "Okay, how was he dressed?"

"Expensively." Tasha leaned back in her chair and folded both arms across the T-shirt across which bold letters spelled out: **Castle's Salon**. "I already told you about the loafers."

Her friend nodded. "That's right. The tassels. And he wanted to talk to Mimi."

Both women turned to glance at the postcards stuck into the frame of the mirror. A second or two ticked past.

"Okay, bad," Molly said.

"*And* Jonas," Tasha pointed out.

"Okay, *really* bad," Molly agreed, and idly ruffled one hand through her hair. Every hair fell perfectly back into place and Tasha felt a quick rush of pleasure. Damn, she did a good haircut.

"But," Molly added, "he *did* leave after you told him to."

"Not the first time," Tasha argued. "The second time, I didn't give him much choice. Slammed the door in his face and didn't open it again."

"Well, if he'd been a cop," Molly offered eagerly, "he wouldn't have left at all."

She'd already considered that option and rejected it. During a certain time in her life, Tasha had had more reason than most to become intimately acquainted with the police. And though her instincts had faded with time, she was pretty sure she could still spot an undercover man, and Tassel Loafer didn't set off those warning bells inside her. No, he set off a completely *different* early alert system. Which she really didn't want to think about at the moment. Or ever. Tasha shook her head. "Trust me on this. *No* cop dresses that well."

"Private detective?" Molly ventured.

"Hired by who?" Tasha countered, sitting up and shoving both hands through her hair in frustration. "And for what reason? No. You've been reading too many mystery novels again."

"Then who do *you* think he was?"

"I don't know," she said softly. "And that's what worries me."

"Maybe he won't be back."

Tasha shook her head. He'd be back. The guy had *determined* written all over his face. A look that said, "I've never been denied anything in my life, and I don't plan to start now. Step aside, or get run over, lady." Tasha shivered. "He'll be back, Moll. There's not a doubt in my mind. He'll be back."

She just wished she knew what to do about him when he did show up.

• • •

Nick drove straight to the Leaf and Bean from what was left of his house.

The place was busy.

Polished wood and soft lights made the coffeehouse look warm, welcoming on a cold morning. Sunlight streamed through the front window and danced off the wood walls and tables. From the overhead beams oversize baskets hung on silver chains, trailing enough flowers and ferns to start up a good-sized rain forest. And over it all, the rich, tantalizing aroma of coffee and fresh-baked pastries filled the air.

The Leaf and Bean was a gathering place in town, once the summer tourists were gone. The locals came out of the woodwork, reclaiming their town for the winter months. Well, at least in the early mornings. In cold weather, the tourists really didn't get moving until afternoon. Then the tiny town of Chandler would get wrapped up in the spirit of the winter carnival and catering to the day-trippers who flocked to town to take part in the festivities.

In the mornings, though, the locals huddled around the small round tables scattered across the gleaming wooden floor at the Leaf and Bean. Conversations rose and fell like waves battering against the shore.

Only a half hour or so away from Monterey, Chandler was a world unto itself. A throwback to a gentler era, the wide Main Street looked like something out of a Norman Rockwell painting. With forests and a lake on one side of town and the ocean on the other, Chandler had the best of everything—an easy commute to a big city but the comfort and irritations of a small town. The local gossips spread news faster than the

New York Times, and there wasn't a kid in town who could get away with anything. But there was a sense of community here you just didn't find most places.

The Candellanos had been in Chandler for years. Like most of the Italian families in the area, they'd been drawn to Northern California generations ago, by the fishing industry, the canneries, and the vineyards. They'd stayed, raised their families, and become a part of the tapestry that was California.

Familiar faces dotted the crowd in the coffee shop and a few of them turned to smile at Nick as he walked across the room. He nodded in greeting but kept walking, hoping no one would start a conversation until he'd had some coffee.

Following his nose, he stepped up close, rested his forearms on the gleaming wooden counter, and glanced at his twin brother, Paul. Fraternal twins, the two of them were absolutely *nothing* alike. Either in looks or in personalities. But they shared a closeness that only another set of twins would understand. "Aren't you supposed to be at work?"

Paul shrugged and winked at his new wife. "I'm going in late today."

Nick shook his head and watched as Stevie and Paul shared one of those secret, incredibly intimate looks that only couples understood. Electricity arcing between the newlyweds nearly singed Nick's eyebrows. Amazing.

Before Stevie had entered his life completely, Paul would never have considered missing work. The man's brain was as fast and complicated as the computer programs he designed. But apparently, he'd found something with Stevie that was bigger—more important to him than the work that had always been his driving ambition.

A small twinge of envy spiked through Nick, then disappeared again almost before he could be surprised at it. After all, he'd never wanted a steady relationship—a marriage. Hell, if he'd been interested in that, he wouldn't have blown it with Stevie years ago. Even as he thought it, he realized that his time with Stevie felt like another lifetime ago. Now, when he looked at her, he saw . . . a sister. Paul's wife.

Weird.

"So what's up with you?" Paul asked, splintering Nick's thoughts.

"I'm hiding out from the Marconis."

"A little loud over there?" Stevie asked, reaching behind her for a pot of coffee sitting on a warmer. From beneath the counter, she pulled out a bright yellow mug, filled it to the brim, and slid it across the counter to Nick.

He bent his head and inhaled, sucking in the rich aroma that cleared his head and opened his eyes. "God bless you, my child."

Stevie laughed and leaned into Paul's side before asking, "So what happened to you last night?"

He picked up his mug, took a long sip, and let the hot dark brew slide down his throat, like a blessing from above. "Last night?"

"You were supposed to come over for dinner?" Paul reminded him, nodding his head toward his wife. "Stevie was cooking?"

"Oh, yeah." Nick scraped one hand across his face. Hell, he'd forgotten all about the dinner in the face of his sudden could-be parenthood. Hardly surprising. Looking up at his twin, Nick thought for a minute about telling Paul what was going on. Asking him what he thought about it.

But then he realized that Paul would probably tell Stevie, who would tell Carla, and then Mama was bound to find out and—good God. No. Best to keep the food chain of the Candellano family in mind.

"Forgot," he said abruptly. "Got busy down at the station. You know, doing some editing and dubbing on the tape we did yesterday." They didn't need to know that only one cameraman had been at the game, which probably meant that the whole segment would boil down to about ten seconds of airtime.

"That's right. The play-off," Paul said. "Who won?"

"St. Anne's little darlings wiped the field with Santiago." And that's all he could remember about the game he'd had to sit through for more than two hours. Not only had he been bored out of his skull, but the odds were that when the ten-second segment aired, Nick would be sliced neatly out of it.

Perfect.

Oh, yeah. His future was looking brighter all the damn time.

"Didn't love it, huh?" Paul asked as Stevie smiled and walked past him, carrying two pots of coffee out to the crowd.

Nick laughed shortly and took another sip of coffee. "Not so much." He stared down at the coffee, studying the dark surface, trying to let his mind go blank. But it wasn't working. One thought chased another through his brain, and all of them were centered on an eleven-year-old kid out to screw up Nick's life.

He needed to talk to Mimi Castle. Needed to talk to *somebody*. Paul? he thought again. Sure, he was married now, but the twin thing was a strong bond. Paul could keep a secret. And Paul was so damn logical and clear-thinking, he'd be able to look at the problem coolly, dispassionately, and maybe he'd be able to think of something Nick hadn't considered yet.

Nodding to himself, Nick looked up at his brother, ready to take the risk and dump everything on him. But Paul wasn't looking at him. His gaze was fixed on Stevie. Following her as she moved through the crowd, laughing and talking with her customers as she refilled cups. The expression on Paul's face told Nick that his brother was nowhere near cool and logical. Hell, he looked like he was ready to grab Stevie up and carry her into the office for a little extension on their honeymoon.

Nope. No help from this quarter. And really, maybe it was just as well. Nick needed to get a grip on this himself.

His problem.

His solution.

"Hey, Paul!"

His twin brother tore his gaze from Stevie, looked over at Nick, and grinned sheepishly.

"Sorry. Zoned out on you, didn't I?"

"I'm getting used to it," Nick said dryly. "Ever since you and Stevie got back from Ireland, you've been like you're on another planet."

Paul leaned against the bar top and waggled both eyebrows. "Honeymoons, Nick. You ought to try one sometime."

"Just what I need," he muttered. First a kid, then a wife. Oh, yeah. That'd be great. Swallowing the last of his coffee, he straightened up. "As long as you're back there, give me five coffees to go."

"Five?" One of Paul's eyebrows lifted.

"One for me—"

"The Marconis get the rest?"

"If it'll get 'em to hurry, I'll bring 'em their coffee every damn day."

Once he had the coffees ready to go, he picked up the cardboard tray and looked at Paul and Stevie again. He'd never seen his brother happier. Never seen Stevie so completely in love. Marriage could work, he thought. For some, the whole family thing was just right. For him . . . not a chance.

Bills.

The great equalizer.

With a break between customers, Tasha snatched at the extra half hour in her day. Settling in the small office tucked into the back of the shop, she pulled out her checkbook and got down to the business of throwing money down a rat hole. Or, to be precise, several rat holes. Well, okay, not throwing it away. But paying bills was enough to give anybody a headache. There just never seemed to be enough money to go around. More often than not, she ended up juggling with all the panache of a circus act. But there was no applause when she finished her performance.

Pay this one, wait on that one—eventually everyone got their turn. But things were tight, no mistake.

She hadn't even realized how much Mimi's Social Security checks had helped out. How could she have, though? While Mimi was alive, the older woman insisted they stick to a strict code of "don't worry, be happy." That old reggae song had been one of Mimi's favorites, since it perfectly encapsulated her outlook on life. "Don't sweat the small stuff," she was always saying.

"But this isn't small stuff, Mimi," Tasha whispered.

"This is life stuff, and it's getting so tight, any minute now, I'm gonna start squeaking." Heck, just trying to keep the old house from falling down around their feet was eating up a lot of hair money.

Tasha filed the paid phone bill, then reached for the Edison envelope. Bracing herself, she closed her eyes as she pulled the statement out. Slowly, cautiously, she opened her right eye and took a peek at the amount due. Instantly her left eye flew open. "Eighty-five bucks?"

Flipping the folded bill open, she scanned it quickly, all the time remembering Jonas's habit of entering a room and hitting a light switch. Of course, he never bothered to turn the lights *off*. Even in broad daylight, the kid left a trail of brilliant illumination behind him.

"He must have lived in a cave in a former life," she muttered, and picked up a pen to write the check. "I swear, I'm going to buy him a miner's hat. Or a flashlight."

But she wouldn't do either and she knew it. She'd just keep doing what she'd been doing . . . turning the lights off behind him—only more often. Eleven-year-old boys just weren't any good at all about remembering anything but the location of the fridge.

"Which brings us to the grocery bill." She glanced at the amount of this week's check and shook her head. "Amazing how much that boy can eat."

Mimi used to say that children went into feeding frenzies just before they started growing in leaps and bounds. "Well," Tasha said, smiling, "judging by the food intake, if Mimi was right, Jonas should be a foot taller inside a month."

But then, a lot could happen in a month, couldn't it? Dropping the pen, Tasha leaned back in her chair and let her gaze slide around the room. Just six months ago, she'd thought things were pretty good.

And then, overnight, Mimi was gone.

Scrubbing one hand over her eyes to keep the threat of tears at bay, Tasha forced her mind onto a different track. Like this little room, for instance.

When she'd taken over doing the shop's books a year ago, Tasha'd convinced Mimi to let her paint the office. There was only so much pink a person could take. Well, a person other than Mimi. The older woman should have been a Mary Kay rep. She'd loved pink. In all its shades. Thankfully, she'd kept most of the pink in the beauty shop portion of the house, which Tasha would never think of changing. Mimi's stamp was all over the shop, and there it would stay.

But here, in the office, the walls were now a soft blue, with white paint sponged on top of the base coat until the walls looked like a blue sky studded with soft white clouds. It was soothing and cool and . . . hers. Tasha's spot. The one spot in the house where she felt as though she really had earned her place here.

Everything else had been a gift.

She closed her eyes and let her mind drift back across the years to the moment she had first found her way out of the darkness. It was ten long years ago. Mimi Castle had looked into Tasha's eyes and seen something no one else, including Tasha, had ever seen.

Someone worth saving.

Rain in LA wasn't pretty.

Water choked in the gutters blocked by trash, and broken neon signs flashed in darkly ominous colors off the puddles stretched across the streets.

Fancy cars with fancier drivers splashed through the rivers in the street, splattering anyone who hap-

pened to be close to curbside. But since leaving her home behind her to live on the streets, Tasha'd found ways to keep dry. Huddling in doorways with thick arches overhead, and crouching beneath boxes piled up in an alley, and stretching out under the freeway overpasses.

She kept her mouth shut and her gaze down. She steered clear of the boozers—she'd had enough of that life, thanks, before she ran away from a home she rarely thought about anymore. She begged for quarters and cashed in cans at the recycling center—and sometimes, when it got too cold for her pride to keep her warm, she stopped in at one of the missions downtown. There she could get a hot meal and clean sheets, and all for the price of listening to some do-gooder telling her she'd be better off at home.

But what did they know? Even sitting here shivering in the cold rain was better than what she'd left behind.

The old woman stopped her car under a streetlight and pulled a map from her glove compartment. Tasha spotted her right away. A pink Cadillac, especially an old one, was going to attract attention. From her vantage point in the doorway, Tasha saw a cluster of guys across the street, eyeing the old woman and no doubt making some quick plans.

Her gaze shifting back to the woman in the car, Tasha felt a small twinge of worry. Why, she wasn't sure. She'd learned long ago to look out for number one. So why was this one woman's safety suddenly an issue? But Tasha had also learned to listen to her instincts. Sometimes they were all that kept you alive.

Grumbling, she stepped out from beneath the archway and was instantly pelted by tiny, icy knives of rain. She pushed her sodden, dirty hair out of her eyes and squinted into the driving rain. Still furious at both the woman and herself for caring, Tasha stomped to the driver's side window.

The woman rolled it down, telling Tasha right away that she didn't have a single ounce of self-preservation. She had to be at least sixty, but she wore her long gray hair in a thick braid that lay across her left shoulder. Her face was lined, but she didn't look . . . used up, like so many people Tasha knew did.

"Lady," Tasha said, bending low enough to look into the woman's soft blue eyes, "you'd better get out of here. Quick."

"I will as soon as I figure out where I am," the woman said, smiling. Then her features softened into concern. "You look half-frozen, honey."

The warmth of the car nearly singed her skin, the shock of it went so deep. She'd been cold for so long, *frozen* didn't even come close to describing her anymore. But that wasn't the point. Tasha glanced back over her shoulder and noticed that the guys were starting to move. Turning around again, she said quietly, quickly, "You see those guys behind me?"

The woman looked, then shifted her gaze back to Tasha. "Yes. . . ."

"They're looking to take your car and they won't much care what happens to you in the taking."

Those soft blue eyes went hard, and just for an instant Tasha thought maybe the old lady wasn't such a dummy after all. But that thought was shot to hell the minute the woman said, "Okay then, you'd better get in so we can go."

"Huh?"

Reaching across the front seat, the woman unlocked

the passenger side door, then sat back and repeated, "Get in. We'd better hurry."

"Lady," Tasha said, "I'm not going anywhere."

"The name's Mimi," the old woman said and gave Tasha a direct stare that seemed to look deep enough to see her soul—if she had one. With their gazes locked the woman said, "I'm not going anywhere without you."

Crazy. That's what she was. Crazy. Too nuts to be out on her own. Tasha looked over her shoulder again. The three men stepped off the curb, moving as a single entity. Danger pulsed off them as clearly as the shattered glow of neon dusting them with a weird red light.

"Lady . . ." she tried again.

"Get in or help me fight them off," Mimi said flatly.

Frustrated, torn between wanting to run and wanting to get into the warm, dry car, Tasha blew out a disgusted breath, then sprinted to the other side of the car. The minute she was inside and the door slammed behind her, Mimi stepped on the gas. The old Caddy peeled away from the curb and sent a fantail of dirty water spraying over the three men like a tiny tidal wave.

Their curses rang out loud and clear and only got louder when Mimi stuck her left arm out the window and gave them a prom wave.

"Tasha!"

Her eyes flew open and she jumped, startled, as she turned to look at Molly, standing in the open doorway, one hand on the brass knob.

Tasha slapped one hand to her chest and said, "Christ, you scared me to death."

"Join the club," her friend said. "Thought you were

in a coma or something. I called you three times." She frowned. "You okay?"

"Fine," she said, and released the last wisps of memory before rejoining the present. "What's up, anyway?"

"What's up is . . . Tassel Loafer was here."

Tasha's insides went cold and still. Weird. She was pretty sure her heart had stopped beating, too. She swallowed hard. "When?"

"Pretty much now." The deep voice came from right behind Molly, and as he stepped into view, Tasha knew her heart had started again. Because it was practically skipping in her chest. That couldn't be a good thing.

Heck, she'd seen handsome men before. Rich ones, too. Just never here. In the shop. In her world.

And the faster she could get rid of him, the better.

Chapter 5

Nick took a long look at the redhead and damned if she didn't look better in daylight than she did by porch light.

Her skin was pale, creamy, but for the sprinkle of freckles across her nose and cheeks. That full mouth of hers was thinned into a dangerous grim line, but it didn't detract from the whole picture. Her thick shoulder-length hair was pulled up into a ponytail high at the back of her head. The dark red mass, streaked through with blond and pale red strands, fell down against her slender neck, and Nick felt the urge to reach out and touch it. Just to see if it was as soft as it looked.

Then her meadow green eyes narrowed on him as she stood up to her full, less-than-impressive height, and Nick figured touching of any kind might get his hand bitten off.

"Hey," the dark-haired woman said as she turned to gape at him. "I told you to wait outside."

He shrugged. "I didn't."

"Yeah, I can see that." Blowing out a breath, she turned back to the redhead and said, "I'm sorry, Tash. I didn't know he was following me. Those tassels are pretty damn quiet."

"I cheated," Nick said. "Wore Reeboks."

He damn sure didn't like being called Tassel Loafer. Might be time to pitch those puppies, he thought, Gucci or not.

"It's okay, Molly," the redhead said, and gave him a look she probably saved for spiders, just before she squashed them.

Nick never took his gaze off her, even when her friend said, "You want me to stay?"

"No thanks, Molly. I'll be fine."

When the dark-haired woman turned to leave, Nick spared her a quick look and caught the gleam of warning shining in her eyes. Jesus. Did he have *serial killer* tattooed on his forehead?

He forced himself to smile at the dark-haired woman with the hard eyes. "I don't need you to stay, either."

"Cute," she said, but her tone told him she didn't mean it. "I'll be right outside if you need me," she told the redhead. Then she was gone, into the hideously pink and strictly female lair of the beauty parlor.

Seemed as though he'd caught them all flat-footed. Which was, he admitted silently, just what he'd been aiming for. He could have called first, he supposed. Mimi Castle was in the phone book. He'd checked. But if he'd called, the redhead would have just told him to stay away. And if she was going to do that anyway, he'd just as soon make her say it in person.

Hell, just looking at her had been worth the trip. Her T-shirt defined curves that were incredibly generous considering how tiny she was everywhere else. And her worn, faded jeans clung to her short but shapely legs like a second skin. She wore sandals on her feet and a silver ankle bracelet that matched the toe rings peeped at him from beneath the hem of her jeans.

After indulging in a good long look, he lifted his gaze to the slogan on her shirt, then up to her eyes. His lips quirked. "Nice to see you again."

"What do you want?" she demanded.

"Now what kind of hello is that?"

"The kind you get when you walk into my house without an invitation."

Nick stepped into the tiny office and watched her back up. He frowned to himself. He wasn't trying to scare her, for God's sake. Hell, he *liked* women. And they generally liked him back. Until her.

And he'd never frightened a woman in his life.

"Wasn't exactly uninvited." He jerked his head in the direction of the shop. "Your friend . . ."

"Molly."

He nodded and gave her his most charming smile. "Molly. Well, she told me to wait and—"

She backed up another step until she'd placed the small, incredibly organized desk in between them. "—and you took that to mean 'Come on in, stranger.' Sure. I could see how that would happen."

"Okay, look." Nick gave up on the charming smile and tried for harmless. "I can see we got off on the wrong foot, but there's no reason why we can't behave like adults."

"Does that usually work?" she asked, throwing him off-balance a little.

"Huh? Does what work?"

"That little smile," she snapped. Narrowing her eyes on him, she continued, "Flash a dimple and I'm supposed to curl up and whimper?"

He blinked at her.

"Because I'm just too busy to do any adoring today." Deliberately she picked up a sheaf of papers from the center of the desk, effectively dismissing him. "So if you'll excuse me . . ."

Nick closed the door of the office and leaned one shoulder against it. She wasn't making this easy and damned if he didn't resent it a little. This was his life here, hanging by a thread over a media chasm filled with popping camera flashes and frenzied reporters. And to do a damn thing about saving his own ass, he was forced to deal with a tiny tyrant who, he thought, watching her, wasn't nearly as calm and cool as she was trying to appear.

Her hands shook as she straightened an already perfectly neat desk. She aligned papers and envelopes into tidy rows and flipped the pens and pencils around until they were arranged on the spotless blotter according to length.

And through it all, she studiously, determinedly, avoided noticing he was in the room.

Nick really didn't have a clue how to handle this. He'd never had to work so hard to get a woman to simply *talk* to him. Hell, he'd never even *had* to do the talking himself.

A twinge of shame had him admitting that she'd been right. All he'd ever had to do was flash a smile and suddenly doors were opened and women were willing. So okay. Made sense that something this important was going to require a little work on his part, right? But she didn't have to be such a hard-ass about this. He waited for her to stop fiddling with the damn desk before asking, "Does that usually work?"

"What?" She glanced up at him.

"The ice maiden routine." Nick shook his head while keeping his gaze locked with hers. "I mean, if you're waiting for me to tuck my tail in and run, you've got a long wait coming."

She stood up straight, planted both hands on her hips, and cocked her head, swinging that ponytail in a dark red wave. He'd struck a nerve. Satisfaction rumbled through Nick, and it surprised him just how good it had been to throw her own words back at her.

"What is it you want?" she asked, and before he could answer, she added quickly, "I've already told you Mimi's not here."

"But you didn't tell me when she'd be back."

She swallowed hard and shifted her gaze away from his. "I don't know exactly."

"You're not a very good liar."

Her head snapped up and she glared at him. If he'd needed proof that she was lying, that was it. She was too damn defensive.

"You don't know anything about me," she said flatly.

"I know I make you nervous."

She snorted a laugh and folded her arms beneath her breasts. "No ego problems with you, are there?"

Nick grinned. She looked so pissed, it was hard not to. "Don't hear you denying it."

"I'm not nervous," she countered, "just annoyed."

"Then my work here is done," Nick said.

"So you'll be leaving."

"Just as soon as you tell me when Mimi will be back."

"I *still* don't know."

"Take a guess."

"Look." Clearly flustered, the redhead blew out a breath and huffed it back in again. "Mimi comes and goes as she pleases, okay?"

Oh, she was nervous. And it wasn't just him causing those nerves. There was something else going on here, Nick thought. Something she didn't want to think about, much less talk about. And though his curiosity was piqued, he told himself to let it go. What did it matter to him what secrets the redhead wanted to keep? All he was concerned about here was the noose around his own neck and the kid who was waiting to knock the trapdoor out from under his feet.

"Why don't you just leave your number and I'll have Mimi call you when she—"

"This can't wait."

She reached up to smooth back a stray lock of hair that had slipped free of the band holding the ponytail in place. "I can't help you."

"Can't or won't?"

She threw her hands wide and let them slap against her thighs. "Look, you come into my house, *uninvited*, try to order things around to suit you, and I don't even know who the hell you are."

"Damn. You're right."

He laughed shortly and came away from the door, straightening up and holding his right hand out. Well, this could explain a lot. He was so used to being recognized, it hadn't even occurred to him that she wouldn't know who he was. "In all the arguing, I forgot to introduce myself."

She stared at his outstretched hand as if it were a snake, poised to strike. Deliberately she folded her arms across her chest again. After a long uncomfortable minute or two, Nick folded his fingers into a fist and lowered his hand to his side.

"I'm Nick Candellano."

He waited for recognition to kick in. After all, he'd

only just left the San Jose Saints. A month ago, there was a huge article in the local paper about his retirement, complete with pictures. He'd done an interview two weeks ago that aired on CBS. And yet . . . Nick shifted position uncomfortably as she simply stared at him.

"Am I supposed to be impressed?" she asked finally.

Nick jerked his head back, surprised. She didn't even know his *name*? Had she been living in a cave or something? "Well, yeah," he said, and to hell with any pretense of humility. "Most people get a charge out of meeting me."

One corner of her mouth quirked, and even that hint of a smile, wry though it was, did something spectacular to her eyes.

"Sorry to disappoint you," she said, "but I've never heard of you."

"I play football. For the San Jose Saints. Well, I did. I'm a—*was* a running back."

She shook her head. "And that means exactly what?"

"You don't know football, either?"

"Nope."

"Great. This day just keeps getting better and better."

"Just what I was thinking," she muttered so softly he almost missed it.

Nick studied her and swallowed back the bitter pill of being a nobody. Something he was going to have to get used to. And it wouldn't be easy. He liked being recognized. Liked having kids lined up outside the stadium waiting for an autograph. Liked being ushered to the best table at a top restaurant. When it came down to it, there wasn't a single damn thing he *didn't* like about it.

Except the fact that it was over.

Okay, fine. Let it go. Concentrate on the current problem. "So. You don't know me." He shoved both hands into his jeans pockets. "That makes us even then, because I still don't know you."

"Tasha Flynn," she said, biting off each word to make sure he understood that she gave the information grudgingly.

"Flynn. Irish."

"Wow," she said tightly. "A football player *and* a genealogist."

"Irish explains the red hair," he mused, ignoring her jibe. "*And* the temper."

"Yeah? Well, *your* name's not Irish, so how do we explain you?"

"Hey, I'm not the hostile one here," Nick reminded her.

"No, you're just the idiot who can't tell when he's not wanted." Tasha's insides were vibrating. Anger, frustration, and pure unadulterated fear rippled through her in alternating waves until she wasn't sure which was which anymore. But did it really matter? For whatever reason, Mr. Football had invaded her home and didn't show any sign of leaving.

She could always call the police.

Oh, yeah, Tash. Great plan. Let's get the authorities involved. Then they'll want to talk to Mimi and things'll only get worse.

Nope. There was no cavalry riding to the rescue. This one was up to her.

She stared up at the man who for whatever reason had decided to make himself a part of her world. *Way* too tall for her liking. As short as she was, people tended to look at her and see not a woman but a child. Thank heaven for the red hair. If she were *blond* and short, she'd never get respect.

Today he was wearing a navy blue sweater over a white T-shirt—she could just barely see the edge of it beneath the neck of the sweater. His blue jeans were as worn as hers and she told herself not to notice how long and lean his legs were. The running shoes he wore were a real departure from the tassel loafers of the day before. But she wasn't fooled. She'd been shoe shopping with Jonas and had to dial him back from the super-expensive shoes he always drooled over. That particular brand of tennis shoe sold for around a hundred and fifty dollars.

Tasha had to cut four heads of hair to earn that much money—and that was only if tips were good.

Whether he was wearing intimidating designer wear or the "just plain folks" outfit, Nick Candellano had money behind him. So whatever it was he wanted, he could afford to stay as long as it would take him to succeed.

"I really think we've done all we can do today," Tasha said as she inched around him in the confined space and tried for the door. "I've got things to do and I'm sure you must have a ball to throw around or something—"

"I didn't throw the ball," he said, stepping to one side to block her progress. "I caught the ball."

"Uh-huh." He was standing too close to her. Not hard to do, really, considering how small the office was. Still, she backed up.

"But I don't do that anymore," he said. "I quit."

"That's a shame." She wasn't even listening now;

her thoughts were centered on ending this little conversation, even though she knew she should be finding out exactly why he was here.

"We don't have to be enemies," he said, and Tasha told herself to pay attention. She couldn't afford *not* to. Until she could get rid of him, she had to listen.

"We don't have to be *anything,*" she said.

"Until I get a chance to talk to either Mimi Castle or Jonas Baker," he said, taking one step closer to her, "we'll be seeing a lot of each other."

She met his gaze and Tasha knew he meant what he was saying. She wasn't going to get rid of him until he was satisfied.

A man with money, charm, and a stubborn streak wide enough to match her own could be nothing but trouble. And if that man had dark brown eyes and a lean jaw and shoulders broad enough to land a plane on . . . well, that was an entirely different kind of trouble that Tasha *so* didn't need at the moment.

Nick Candellano.

Professional football player.

Of course, she only had his word for that, she thought. She wouldn't know a pro football player from . . . well, from anything. But why would he lie about it? No. He was who he said he was.

So why would he want to talk to Mimi about *anything*? The only "sport" Mimi had known anything about was video poker. And what could Jonas have to do with the world this man traveled in? Like most boys his age, Jonas followed football and baseball and hockey and, well, whatever sport happened to be in season. But she'd never heard him talk about Nick Candellano in particular—so how did Candellano know about Jonas?

A brisk knock at the door startled both of them.

Molly pushed it open, stuck her head inside, and looked from Nick to Tasha. Worry shaded her eyes as she said, "Sorry, Tash. But Mrs. Sorenson's here and getting crankier by the minute."

"Right. I'll be there in a sec."

Molly shot Nick a quick, almost admiring glance, then backed out, closing the door behind her.

"I've got to get back to work."

"About Jonas Baker . . ."

Jonas. Though her stomach jittered with a fresh assault of nerves, Tasha stood her ground. As anxious as she was to get this man out of her shop, her house, she had to get to the bottom of his visits. Had to know exactly what she was fighting. Or she'd never be able to fight back.

Steeling herself, she straightened her spine, lifted her chin, and looked him dead in the eye. "I don't have any more time to play games with you, Mr. Candellano," she said tightly, trying to keep her voice from shaking. "Since Mimi's not here, you'll just have to deal with me. So let's have it. Why are you here? What do you want with Jonas?"

He responded to the banked fury in her voice. "You think I *want* to be here? I didn't start this, red. The kid did."

"What are you talking about? Jonas started what?"

He pushed one hand through his hair, then scraped his palm across his face as if even he couldn't believe what he was about to say.

Tasha braced herself, but even then she wasn't prepared.

"The kid's *suing* me."

"What?" She felt her eyes bug out and wouldn't have been surprised to see them pop out of her head and roll across the desk.

"He's suing *me.*" This time, the emphasis was on him and Tasha knew that's where his real interest lay. Not in Jonas or Mimi or even her. Nick Candellano was out for himself.

Big surprise.

"He can't be suing you," she said. "He's only eleven years old."

"Yeah, well, his lawyer's not a kid."

"Lawyer?"

He nodded stiffly. "Oh, it's official. I got served with papers yesterday."

"I can't believe this." What had Jonas been thinking? He knew that she was trying to stay below the state's radar. He knew that with Mimi gone, their little family was on tenuous ground.

"*You* can't believe it?" He choked out a laugh that sounded as if it hurt his throat.

Tasha, on the other hand, couldn't find a thing to laugh about. Hundreds of thoughts raced through her mind, chasing one another, faster and faster, until her brain was a blur. "What, uh . . ." She sucked in a deep breath, blew it out again, and forced herself to ask, "What's he suing you *for,* exactly?"

Nick shoved his hands into his jeans pockets and rocked back and forth on his heels. His jaw worked as if he was trying to force the words out. Finally, when she felt as though she couldn't stand the suspense a moment longer, he blurted it out.

"Paternity."

Tasha plopped onto the edge of the desk, like a puppet whose strings had been cut.

"The kid says *I'm* his father."

Oh God.

Jonas, what have you done?

Chapter 6

Something was wrong.

Carla Candellano Wyatt knew it the minute she walked into her husband's office. Jackson shot her a look that practically *screamed* "guilt." And her brother Nick actually winced when he looked at her.

Jackson's secretary had been out to lunch when Carla arrived, so naturally she'd just knocked on the door and opened it. After all, when you were showing up to surprise your brand-new husband with a lunch-time seduction, the whole point was surprise, right?

Only problem was, she was the surprised one. Her brother and husband had shut up the moment she opened the door, but the "kid caught with his hand in the cookie jar" expression they were both wearing was a pretty good indication that something important was going on. Something neither one of them was telling *her*. "Okay," she said, shutting the door behind her, "what's up?"

"Huh? What do you mean?" Nick said, and, too late, tried to adopt a nonchalant air. He shoved his hands into the back pockets of his jeans and unconsciously shifted his feet into a wide-apart stance, as if expecting a fight. His big brown eyes went soft and innocent, but Carla wasn't fooled. She'd seen that same expression too many times while watching Nick try to finesse his way out of trouble. Their parents had never bought his act and she wasn't buying it now, either.

"Don't give me that, Nick," she said, and crossed the room toward him. Her boots clicked loudly into the sudden silence as she walked across the wood floor. "You suck at lying. Always have. Something's up and I want to know what it is."

Nick didn't answer, just shot a helpless look across the room to Jackson.

Carla followed his gaze and stared at her husband for a long second.

He shook his head. "Leave it alone, honey."

She smirked at him. Poor man. He hadn't known the Candellanos long enough to realize that was a useless plea. "Not likely." Turning her head, she gave her brother her undivided attention again.

"Go away, Carla," Nick said tightly.

"Not a chance," Carla told him. Hey, this was family. Nick wouldn't have stopped by to see Jackson for no reason in the middle of a workday. So that meant this was an official visit. Man-to-lawyer. Up until about a month ago, Nick had been acting like the biggest ass in Northern California. He'd spent most of his time diving for the bottom of a bottle of scotch—and finding it. He'd alienated his family, fought with his twin, and, in general, managed to piss off everyone who loved him.

Suddenly she remembered the night their older brother, Tony, had tossed Nick's drunk butt into a jail cell, and instantly Carla's insides twisted. That night, all he'd done was smash Reverend Michaels's lawn goose. Had Nick gotten into some real trouble this time? Something serious? Her stomach churned into a tight knot of dread. If he needed a lawyer, then Carla needed to know why. How in the hell could she help her family if she didn't know what was going on?

"Talk to me, Nick," she said flatly.

"Jesus, Carla," Nick said, jerking his hands free of his pockets to throw them high in disgust. "This is none of your business."

She snorted a laugh that had nothing to do with humor and shook her head. "Oh, please. Like that's ever stopped a Candellano."

Nick scooped one hand through his hair, pushing it back from his face, and in that one split second, Carla saw worry in his eyes. That sent a cold chill sweeping through her. Nick *never* worried. He went through life sailing by on his charm, his easygoing nature, and the fact that he could kick at a rock and have it turn out to be a diamond. In fact, blowing out his knee playing football was the first really bad thing that had ever happened to him. Which probably explained why he hadn't handled it very well.

Ordinarily, the world pretty much treated Nick like a king. And worry was something new for him.

"Fine," he said, meeting her gaze. "Just for today, stop being a Candellano and remember you're a Wyatt now, okay? Fight the inner need to jump in and tell me what to do."

Carla paid no attention to that—and she was pretty sure Nick had known even when he said it that she wouldn't. He'd been her brother way too long to think she could be put off that easy.

"Not gonna happen."

"I'm not talking to you about this, Carla."

"And no way I'm backing off. I want to know what's going on," she said, ignoring Nick's refusal to speak. Heck, she'd find a way to make him talk, and they both knew it. For now, though, she shifted her gaze from her brother to her husband. Staring at Jackson, she narrowed her eyes and pinned him with a steely look.

But her husband didn't fold, which was only slightly irritating. After all, what woman wanted a weenie for a husband? Much better to have a stubborn man you could fight with than to have a man you could walk all over. Still, she felt a flash of annoyance when Jackson lifted both hands and said, "Sorry, Carla. Attorney-client confidentiality—"

"Your *client*?" she interrupted him, zeroing in on that one important word. So it *was* an official visit. Uneasiness danced through her veins. Great. That meant that for some reason, Nick *needed* a lawyer. That couldn't be good news. "Why is Nick your client?"

"Because he wanted the best?" Jackson tried.

"Good effort," she told him, and promised herself to make his life miserable later. At the moment, though, she spun around to stare up into her brother's eyes. "Do you talk to me or do I tell Mama that you're Jackson's 'client' and let her get it out of you?"

A disgusted whoosh of air shot from Nick's lungs as he scowled at his sister. "Pulling out the big guns is really sinking low this early in the fight."

"I go with what works," she said with a shrug.

That scowl deepened. But in spite of his best efforts, a chill swept along Nick's spine. *Nobody* wanted to be on Mama's bad side. Mama had raised four children with a firm hand and—as far as her kids were concerned—an all-seeing eye. Her hugs were legendary, as were her steely stares that could convince a kid to confess to anything in less than ten seconds. Now, though her children were grown, Mama Candellano was still a force to be reckoned with. And the ultimate threat. "Aren't we a little old for you to be tattling to Mama?"

"I repeat . . ."

"Christ, Carla, you're like a dog with a bone, aren't you?"

"What do you think?"

He loomed over her, trying for intimidation. It didn't work. Never had. Disgusted, he viciously rubbed the back of his neck. Finally he said, "I think life would be easier if I were an only child."

"Yeah, well, that wish and five bucks'll buy you a latte at Stevie's." Carla plopped both hands at her hips and dared him to look away. "Now tell me what's up."

Nick stared down at his younger sister. Her curly dark brown hair surrounded her face and fell to her shoulders in wild abandon. She wore a sweatshirt, jeans, and her ratty old cowboy boots and looked just as fierce as a grizzly. He recognized the glint in her brown eyes, too. She might be married now and stepmother to a little girl, but at her heart and soul she was still and would always *be* a Candellano.

Ordinarily, he might have been pleased by that knowledge. His family was tight. Always had been. They stood up for one another and weren't afraid to kick a little butt when it was needed—as evidenced by the crap he'd been getting from the family for the last couple of months. He loved them all, but damn it, he wished to hell Carla was more intent on her own new family right now than on him. Because Carla just wouldn't give up and walk away.

Until she found out what she wanted, she was going to hound him until he was nothing but raw meat.

Man, the day he'd had, dealing with tough women. First Tasha Flynn practically pushes him out of her house, green eyes flashing; then his own sister turns on him. Nick's head was pounding. Hell, his ears were still ringing from Tasha's temper. She'd shouted at him the whole time she was shoving him through the pink hell of a beauty parlor and out the door.

She hadn't bothered to keep quiet in front of their audience of very interested ladies in various stages of hairdos. And once his feet hit the porch, she'd told him in no uncertain terms to stay the hell away. When she'd slammed the door in his face, the resulting breeze had ruffled his hair and dented his ego.

Well, he'd love to be able to do just what she wanted. But until he had a chance to talk to the kid and smooth this mess over before it got even more out of hand, that wouldn't be happening.

"Carla," Jackson said, standing up behind his desk, "back off. . . ."

She never took her gaze off Nick. "Butt out, Jackson." Then, to soften her words a little, she added, "I love you, but this is between me and my brother."

Nick looked over Carla's head to Jackson and nodded. Then shifting his gaze back to his sister, Nick surrendered to the inevitable. He'd had it fighting with temper-driven, determined women today.

"Okay," he said, holding both hands up as if she were holding a gun on him. "You win."

"Was there ever any doubt?" Carla folded her arms across her chest, tipped her head to one side, and prompted, "Now, what's going on?" Her voice was filled with a concern that warmed him, despite the situation. Family. It all came down to family.

The question was, would his *family* now include his *son*?

"Is he really your dad?"

Jonas nodded and looked down at the eight-by-ten glossy color photo of Nick Candellano. It was an action shot, of Nick, wearing his San Jose Saints uniform, except for the helmet. They didn't wear helmets in pictures, so people could see the players' faces. The photographer had caught Nick mid-leap, catching a pass, and his wide smile seemed to be aimed directly at Jonas. Scrawled across the bottom of the photo were the words: *Running Backs Rule! Best Wishes, Nick Candellano.*

It was the same thing written on all of the pictures he'd received from Nick. Sometimes the color ink was different and sometimes the way he signed his name changed, but other than that, they were just the same. Jonas had written four letters to his dad, telling him where he lived and how Nick could get in touch with him. Then he'd spent days watching the mailbox, waiting for a letter from his father.

But all he ever got was those pictures.

"He is." Jonas looked at Tommy Malone. "He sends me pictures special, whenever I ask him to."

Tommy took the picture and held it carefully by the edges, so his fingers wouldn't get it all dirty. "That's pretty cool, but how come you wanna sell 'em?"

Jonas rubbed the back of hand under his nose. " 'Cause I don't need all of 'em." And Tasha's birthday was coming up and he might need money and he could always get more pictures of his father.

"I don't have five bucks," Tommy said. "I've only got three."

Jonas thought about it for a long minute. Three dollars was better than nothing. "Okay, three."

Tommy grinned at him, dug into his jeans pocket, and pulled out three crumpled one-dollar bills. He handed them to Jonas, then wandered off, across the playground, still admiring the photo of his favorite football player.

The first bell rang and the crowds of kids started wandering closer to the brick school buildings. Lunch recess was almost over. Noise rose up on the cold November wind and drifted across the overgrown lawn toward the asphalt. Tetherball ropes and chains clanged against poles, and basketballs thumped against backboards. The lunch ladies wandered through the crowds of shouting kids, blowing silver whistles that shrieked for attention, yet still went unnoticed.

"Are you selling all of 'em?" Alex asked as he sat down next to Jonas.

"Yep." Leaning back against the old tree in the middle of the field, Jonas scooted over, making room for his pal. Tree bark bit into his back, right through his sweatshirt. He tipped his head back and stared up through the leafless limbs at the gray clouds overhead. The wind blew hard and sent the tree branches into a wild dance that made them kind of look like skeleton arms clapping together.

"My dad'll get me more as soon as I meet him."

"When's that gonna be?"

"Don't know for sure," Jonas said, and tore his gaze away from the storm clouds crashing across the sky. "But it'll be soon."

It had to be soon. 'Cause with Mimi dead and Tasha

worried all the time, it was getting a little scary at home. He kept expecting to see Ms. Walker from Social Services pull into the driveway to take him away. Every time one of Tasha's customers drove up to the house, Jonas's stomach did a weird rolling thing that made him think he might barf. He always had to run to the window and look out to make sure it wasn't Ms. Walker's green Volkswagen parked outside.

Ms. Walker was always saying how important Jonas was to her, but he didn't like the way she kind of crinkled up her nose when she came inside. Like the house was dirty or something, and it totally wasn't, 'cause Tasha was always cleaning and making him pick up his dirty socks and stuff out of the living room.

But Ms. Walker didn't like the house and she hadn't liked Mimi, either. But 'cause Mimi was old, Ms. Walker treated her better. Nicer, kind of. But she treated Tasha like she was stupid, and pretty soon she'd probably take him away. Even though Tasha said it wouldn't happen, Jonas couldn't take the chance. He had to be sure. He didn't want to go away again. He liked his house. And Tasha. And he wanted to stay. So he needed his real dad to help.

And he would. Nick wouldn't let him down.

"Think he'll take us to some games before the season's over?" Alex asked. "I bet he can get us down on the field by the team and everything."

"Sure he can," Jonas said, nodding as if trying to convince himself as much as Alex. "Maybe we could even go to the Super Bowl."

"Wow. . . ." His best friend's voice, filled with awe, drew that one word out like a song.

Jonas smiled to himself. He wasn't lying to his friend. He knew Nick would do all the things Jonas said he would, as soon he knew about him. That's what dads did.

The second bell rang and the boys reluctantly got up and headed toward history class—visions of the Super Bowl game dancing in their heads.

By the time Jonas got home from school, Tasha had worn a rut through the living room carpet with her pacing.

She still wasn't sure how she'd managed to get the football player out of the shop. All she remembered was a lot of vague sputtering and arguing. Well, that and a few women whistling at him as Tasha pushed and shoved him through the shop and out the door. Once she had him on the porch, she'd closed the door in his face and hadn't taken another easy breath until she heard his Corvette roar into life and rush off down the road.

And even then, breathing was tough.

Air strangled in her throat.

Her lungs heaved, she felt light-headed, and her stomach was doing a whirligig thing that had her seriously worried about tossing her cookies.

Somehow, she'd pulled herself together enough to do Mrs. Sorenson's hair, then the other two appointments she'd had scheduled for today. It hadn't been nearly as easy to keep from talking to Molly about what was happening. She'd just had time to give her friend the headlines, then it had been back to work.

As if thinking about the woman had conjured her up, Molly spoke up from the doorway between the dining room and the living room.

"He's not here yet?"

"No." Tasha shot her a quick look, then kept pacing, never breaking stride. Heck, she was in a rhythm, now. Twenty-one steps, turn, twenty-one steps back.

"What do you think's going on?"

"I don't know."

"Is Jonas really this guy's son?"

"I don't *know.*" Too many questions. Not enough answers. Oh God. Her head pounded in time with her footsteps. Her heartbeat seemed to hammer out the count as she continued. Nineteen, twenty, twenty-one, *turn.*

"What'll you do if he is?"

Tasha's steps staggered. She lost count, then stopped dead. She shoved one hand through her hair and yanked at it, as if the sharp pain stinging her scalp could take her mind off everything else. It didn't work.

"I don't know," she said again, and her voice was just a sigh of exasperation and worry. Her hand dropped to her side and her shoulders slumped. She felt as though she'd been beaten up. Her body was limp. Her knees were like water and her stomach was spinning. Surprised she was still standing, she admitted quietly, "I don't know anything."

She stared at a square of sunlight outlined on the scarred wooden floor, but she wasn't seeing it. Instead, her mind filled with the image of Nick Candellano's face—and then Jonas's. There *were* similarities, she thought. The dark hair, the eyes. And that smile. *Oh God.*

If it was true, she'd lose Jonas. If it wasn't true, then why was Candellano here? And even if Jonas wasn't this guy's son, then the stink made and the investigation would surely turn up the fact that Mimi was dead. And then Social Services would take Jonas away from her and whether Candellano got the boy or not, Jonas would be gone, just the same.

And Tasha would be alone.

Again.

At twenty-seven, she'd be as alone as she had been at seventeen, when Mimi had first found her. Only alone would be so much worse now—because now she knew what *family* could be like. Bitterness filled her mouth, snaked down her throat, and stained her soul. She should have known. Should have guessed that the good life she'd made for herself couldn't last. Wouldn't last. Things like that just didn't happen to people like her.

She scrubbed both hands across her face, wiping away the single tear sliding down her cheek. Her throat closed around a knot she knew wouldn't be disappearing anytime soon.

"Tasha?"

She looked at Molly.

"He's here."

"What?"

"Jonas," Molly said, nodding toward the front window.

Tasha shifted her gaze to the view of the wide lawn that needed mowing. Cold wind pushed at the tree limbs and ruffled the hair of the boy with his head down. Jonas was dragging his new backpack across the grass and kicking at a rock as he walked slowly toward the house. A brief smile tugged at her mouth. No one could dawdle like a kid. And Jonas did it better than most.

Knowing he had chores and homework to face once he set foot inside the house, he could make that walk from the bus stop to the front door last a lifetime. It was a routine. One they were both used to. The welcome home. The arguing about vacuuming. The plea bargaining for a little TV time before homework.

It was business as usual.

Their little world.

The same one that, right at the moment, was teetering on the brink of destruction.

Tasha never took her gaze off Jonas as she said, "Go away, Molly."

"Right." But before she left, the other woman added, "Take it easy on him, Tash. He's just a kid."

"Yeah, I know." He was a kid. *Her* kid. Her family. And she was going to see to it that it stayed that way.

Striding across the room, she pulled the front door open and stepped into the cold bite of the November afternoon. The wind pushed at her, almost as if some invisible hand were trying to keep her in the house. Keep her from asking questions she really didn't want to put voice to. But there was no avoiding it. No ducking the issue. Jonas had started something that they were just going to have to face. Together.

She shook her head, tossing her hair out of her eyes, then walked to the edge of the porch. Jonas stopped at the bottom of the steps, looked up, and grinned.

That smile shot straight to her heart. He was such a *little* guy. And though she was barely old enough to be his mother, Jonas was more *her* son than Nick Candellano's. She loved him with a fierceness that only ten years ago she wouldn't have thought possible.

Back then, she'd figured love was just a word people used to hurt each other: *I love you, so you have to do what I say. I love you, so when I hit you, it means I care. I love you, so shut the hell up and get me a beer.*

Love hadn't meant a damn thing to her until Mimi.

And then, just two years ago, Jonas had joined their little family. With him and Mimi, Tasha had discovered what life should really be about. And she wouldn't lose it now. *Couldn't* lose it.

"Hi, Tash," he said, flipping his too-long hair back out of his eyes.

"Hi yourself." Dropping to the top step, she sat down and patted the place beside her. "Sit down, Jonas."

He frowned, lines forming between his eyebrows as his eyes narrowed on her. "Something wrong?"

"I just want to talk to you."

He took the first step, then stopped. Worried, he asked, "Did my teacher call you?"

One red eyebrow arched as she looked at him. "No. Is there some reason she's going to?"

He shrugged and gave her that smile again. The same half-smile she'd seen on Nick Candellano's handsome face earlier. And her heart clutched. "She maybe might not be happy about maybe my history test."

A smile struggled to be born inside her and failed miserably. Ordinarily she almost enjoyed hearing Jonas's last-ditch attempts to soften a blow one of his teachers would be delivering. But today she'd already had a blow that had taken the heart out of her.

Nodding, she said, "We'll talk about history later."

Grabbing the reprieve while he could, Jonas grinned again and clomped up the stairs. How was it, she wondered, that one small boy could sound like a battalion of elephants when he walked? When he reached the top step, he swung his backpack at the doorway, and when it slid through the opening, he threw both hands high and said, "Touchdown!"

Football.

Football *players.*

Tasha's stomach swirled again and she had to swallow hard to keep from losing her lunch. Jonas plopped down beside her and nudged her arm with his shoulder. "So what are we talking about?" he asked.

She looked down at him and just for a minute let herself enjoy the sweet innocence shining in his eyes. Eyes that now reminded her too much of the man who'd ripped the floor from beneath her feet just a few hours ago.

At eleven years old, Jonas was still more of a kid than a preteen. And despite losing his mother and going into the system at eight and a half, he'd managed to retain a sweet optimism that never ceased to amaze Tasha. Even when Mimi had died, Jonas had been the one to remind Tasha that they still had each other.

They'd clung together through the pain of loss, and now, just a few months later, Tasha thought they were stronger than ever. So why then had he gone searching for his real father? Why had he taken the risk? Why was he willing to gamble everything they had for the chance at something he'd never known?

The only way to find the answers to the questions haunting her was to ask. So, keeping her gaze locked with his, she cleared her throat and said, "A man came to see me today."

"Yeah?" He smiled, eyes wide. "A date?"

"No," Tasha said, and reached out to smooth his hair back from his face. Her fingertips lingered a moment, then she dropped her hand to his forearm. Holding on to him, she said, "He was really here to see Mimi . . ."

"Uh-oh."

". . . or *you.*"

"Me?" His gaze shifted from hers. "Um . . . who was it?"

Did he inch slightly away from her, or was it just her imagination?

"Nick Candellano."

"He was *here*?" Jonas looked quickly around him as if he were expecting the man to be hiding behind a plant, waiting to jump out and yell, "Surprise!"

Excitement fairly rippled out around him in a thick wave that danced across Tasha before it disappeared into the bone-numbing wind.

"Where is he now?" he demanded.

"He's gone."

"Why didn't he wait?"

"Because I wouldn't let him."

Jonas's gaze snapped back to hers, and Tasha's heart hurt at the accusation aimed at her. "You sent him *away*?"

"I wanted to talk to you first and—"

"But I've been *waiting*. . . ."

He tried to pull away, but Tasha's hand on his arm held him still. "Jonas, he says you're suing him for paternity."

"I had to 'cause he wouldn't answer my letters and—"

"But why, Jonas? Why?"

" 'Cause he's my dad," the boy said, and his voice broke on the word. Tears welled up in his eyes and spilled over, racing one another down his reddened cheeks.

"How do you know that?" Tasha asked, her voice quiet, filled with the pain of watching him hurt.

"My mom told me," he said. "She always said it. That he was my dad."

"You should have told me what you were doing," she said, trying to choose her words carefully.

"You woulda said no."

"Probably." It cost her some to admit it, but it was the truth and she'd never lied to the boy before. Lies only caused more grief. But yes, she would have prevented him from opening up this can of worms that just might rise up and devour them all. Because to protect him, to protect what they had, she was willing to do just about anything. "Jonas, you know we can't let anyone find out about Mimi."

"He won't tell," the boy said quickly, eagerly.

"We don't know that," she said, and silently she thought that Nick Candellano had struck her as the kind of man who would do whatever it took to cover his own ass. Maybe she was wrong about that, but she wasn't willing to bet their lives on it.

"I'm sorry, Tasha," Jonas said, and his bottom lip quivered until he bit down on it. "I didn't want to make you mad or anything, but I had to do it. I just had to."

"Jonas . . ."

And then the boy who was always insisting he was "almost a teenager" did something he hadn't done in too long to remember. He threw himself into Tasha's embrace, laid his head on her shoulder, and let the tears flow. "He'll help," he said, the words choking on his body-shaking sobs. "He will."

Oh God. She soothed him with long, steady strokes of her hand along his spine, but the force of his crying shook her to the bone. He was so small, she thought. So young. So trusting. And so damn fragile. Her heart broke for him even as her mind raced, trying to figure out every possible complication. Oh, she wished he hadn't done it. Would do anything to undo it.

Through the tears, though, he gulped loudly and said, "He's my *dad.*"

Those three little words seemed to sum it all up for the boy. And in a way, Tasha couldn't blame him. He was holding out for the American dream. Heck, he saw it every night on television. Even the damn commercials showcased Mom and Dad and the kids. She supposed the advertisers were trying to appeal to Middle America. But God, didn't anyone guess what those *family* things did to kids who didn't *have* families in the traditional sense?

When she was a kid, she'd sneered at them. Known them for the joke they were. No one she had known lived that kind of life, had that kind of love and warmth. So she hadn't been tortured with the "what ifs" that were driving Jonas today.

But he was different.

He was younger than she'd been at his age.

He was hurt.

He'd pinned his dreams on an egotistical football player who couldn't give a shit about the boy who might be his son.

Jonas didn't see that, though.

He just *wanted.*

And when he didn't get it, he was going to be crushed.

Chapter 7

"You have a *son*?"

Nick winced when his sister's voice hit a note only dogs should have been able to hear. Jesus. Hadn't he had enough crap already in the last couple of days? Did he really need a big spoonful of Candellano on top of it?

"I didn't say I had a son," he snapped, biting off each word. "I said *the kid* says I have a son."

"Oh, big difference."

"There is a difference, thanks," Nick said, and stalked across Jackson's office. Being a wise man, Carla's husband had already left brother and sister alone. Claiming to have been worried about paperwork that his secretary "might have" misplaced, Jackson had found an escape. The lucky bastard.

"This is why I told you to stay out of it."

"How can I?" she demanded, leaping to her feet and marching to his side. "I'm supposed to pretend I don't know I've got a nephew out there somewhere?"

"Not somewhere," Nick muttered. "Christ, he's not lost at sea. He lives outside Santa Cruz."

"And I'm just now finding out about him?"

"Hell, *I* just found out about him yesterday."

"And whose fault is that?" She crossed her arms over her chest. The toe of her right boot tapped loudly against the floor and sounded, for some reason, like the clock of fate numbering out the seconds of Nick's life. Well, at least his life as he'd known it. Because if this kid really was his son, everything was going to change.

Thoughts Ping-Ponged in his head and he didn't like a damn one of them. Carla couldn't say anything to him that he hadn't already said to himself. But naturally, that knowledge wouldn't have stopped her, even if he'd told her so.

Still, he wasn't going to just stand there and make like a target for Carla. If no one else was going to defend him, then it was up to Nick himself. "Damn it, how was I supposed to look out for a kid I didn't know existed?"

"No." Carla took a step closer to him and jabbed him in the chest with her index finger. "I think the better question is, *How could you have been so stupid as to make a child and not know it?*"

"Thanks," Nick said, sneering at her. This was great. Spending this time with his sister made him remember exactly *why* when they were kids he used to kidnap her Barbies and hide them. "Man, Carla, you're really the one to have around when you're feeling like shit already."

"Well, God, Nick. What do you expect me to say?" She threw her hands high. "There's a little boy out there who's part of our family and none of us, including his father, *know* him."

He scrubbed one hand across his face.

"Where is he living? Who takes care of him?"

"His foster mother is—"

"*Foster* mother?" Carla's voice hit that weird note again and he could have sworn he heard the muted sounds of every dog in town barking in response. "Foster mother. A Candellano kid has a foster mother."

Yeah, he'd known going in that that piece of news would hit the family like an 18-wheeler. To the Candellanos, family was everything. And knowing that one of their own—just a kid—was out in the world undefended by them would be enough to have them all ready to kill Nick.

"Jesus, Nick."

Her barbs hit hard and he felt every one of them like the tip of a knife blade, whittling at his skin. But damn it, he was being hanged here with no proof of his guilt. "I don't have a son," he repeated, and wasn't sure if he was trying to convince Carla or himself. At this point, he'd take either one. "I have a *fan.*"

"What?" She looked at him like he was nuts.

Hell. Maybe he was.

"That's all this is," he said, warming to the one thought he'd been clinging to since being served with the lawsuit yesterday. "The kid's obviously had a hard time of it. His mother's dead, he's in a foster home—of *course* he dreams up this fantasy. He picks somebody famous. Somebody who even looks like him a little. And he dreams it all up."

"He *looks* like you?"

Figured she'd pick up on that. Blowing out a disgusted, frustrated rush of air, Nick snapped, "Damn it, Carla, I look a little like Tom Cruise, but *we're* not related."

She snorted. "Oh, yeah. In your dreams, big brother. Besides, this is different. Most eleven-year-olds don't hire lawyers to make their dreams come true."

"Okay," Nick said, walking away from Carla's too-knowing gaze to pace the confines of Jackson's office again. His fingertips scraped along the backs of the overstuffed sofas as he moved past. "So he's a little more determined than your average kid. But that doesn't make his fantasy a reality. It doesn't make *me* his father."

"Then take a DNA test," she suggested. "Settle this."

"I will. If it comes to that."

"Why not now?"

"Think about it. If the media were to get hold of this . . ."

"So," she said knowingly, "we're worried about you now, are we?"

Well, that sounded shitty. Even to him. "I just want a chance to talk to the kid. To sit him down—without that tiny storm trooper around—and talk to him, man-to-man."

"Or boy-to-boy . . ." she mused.

"Cute. Don't you have a husband to torture?"

"There's plenty to go around."

"Good to know."

"Storm over?" Jackson spoke up from the door he'd cracked open just wide enough to risk his life.

Carla's golden retriever, Abbey, who'd been left in the outer office, woofed in a low, throaty half-roar and pushed at the door until it swung open and she could enter the room. Tail up, the golden pranced across the floor, her nails clicking madly as she walked up to Carla and plopped down on her butt.

"Yeah, it's done," Nick said, without giving Carla a chance to answer.

"For now," his sister piped up. She smoothed one

hand across the top of the dog's head and watched her husband approach warily. When he was close enough, Jackson took a chance, dropping one arm around her shoulders, and Carla instinctively leaned back into his chest.

"What time is it?" Nick asked suddenly, realizing that he and his sister had been going around and around for what felt like hours.

Jackson glanced at his watch. "Three-fifteen. Why?"

Jesus, he and Carla had been going around for a long time. "School's out by now, right?"

"Yeah. . . ."

"Good." Nick headed for the door.

"Are you going to see him?" Carla called out.

"Yes. And *this* time, I'm actually going to see him." If that meant he'd have to steamroll the little redhead, then he'd try to enjoy the ride. Nick stopped at the door and looked back over his shoulder at his sister. "Don't spill your guts to Mama about this, Carla."

"I won't say anything."

He turned to leave, then stopped cold when she added, "Yet."

Damn it.

Jonas could hardly sit still. He should have been doing his homework upstairs. But he was just too excited. So instead, Tasha had let him stay in the living room to watch TV. But he wasn't watching it. He flipped the channels on the TV, hardly seeing the flashes of color zipping past his eyes. Snatches of dialogue snapped in the air, quickly changing from news channels to cartoons and old reruns of *The X-Files*. But he wasn't paying attention, anyway.

His mind was way too busy to concentrate on some dumb show. All he could think of was that Nick had been there. In *his* house. His dad had really come to see him. And that kind of made it okay that he never answered Jonas's letters. 'Cause when it mattered most . . . he'd shown up himself.

Jonas had sorta worried about going to Legal Aid. But he could still remember how excited the lawyer had been when Jonas told him his dad's name. And it must've been the right thing to do, 'cause Nick had actually come to the house to see him.

If Tasha hadn't sent him away, Jonas and his dad could be out front right now, playing catch or something. He smiled to himself at the thought. Having a dad was gonna be great. For the first time ever, he'd have a dad standing on the sidelines at his Pop Warner football games. Nick would yell Jonas's name and maybe call him *pal* or *sport* or something cool like that. He grinned as he imagined walking off the field and Nick meeting him, being all proud. Then he'd pat Jonas on the back and put his arm around Jonas's shoulders and they'd talk about the game and laugh and stuff.

And the best part, Jonas thought as he flipped past local news, then quickly turned back to it, just to have the TV on Nick's channel, was, Jonas would be like the other guys. He'd have his dad with him. And they'd go out with the team for pizza and Nick'd talk to the other dads about how great his kid was. He smiled, enjoying the movie playing in his head, and scowled when a knock on the door interrupted it.

"I'll get it, Tasha," he called out. Tossing the remote onto the magazine-littered table in front of him, Jonas stood up and headed for the door. Grabbing the cool brass knob, he gave it a turn, yanked the door open, and swallowed his bubble gum.

"Hi. You must be Jonas."

He nodded and opened and closed his mouth a few times. Nick Candellano. His father. Right here. In front of him. Standing on his porch. Jonas blinked and almost rubbed his eyes, but he was too afraid that if he did that, Nick would disappear and this would turn out to be some really great dream.

He looked different close up, Jonas thought. Taller. Bigger. But his smile was the same as in the pictures. And his voice sounded just like he did on TV. This was so cool.

"I'm Nick Candellano," the man said, unnecessarily.

"Uh-huh." Now *his* voice sounded weird. He cleared his throat. "I know."

"I thought you and I could have a little talk."

"A talk?" Jonas stared up at him and hardly noticed how fast his stomach was spinning. His dad. *Here.*

Finally.

"Yeah," he said eagerly, "sure. You wanna come in?"

"Thanks."

Jonas stepped back to let his father inside and just managed to keep from reaching out to touch him. Wow.

"Who was at the—" Tasha's words arrived just a second before she did. Her tennis shoes squeaked against the wood floor when she skidded to a stop. Jonas watched her face freeze up like it did the last time he got an F in math. Oh, man.

"Hello again," Nick said, and Jonas's gaze flicked between his father and Tasha.

"What are you doing back here?" she demanded.

"Told you I'd be back."

"And I told you not to bother."

"Why don't you—" Nick stopped short and shot a look at Jonas. He wasn't going to shout at the kid's "family." At least not in front of him. But damn. Looking into those wide brown eyes, Nick felt a pang of genuine concern rattle through him. Dark brown hair, brown eyes, and a stubborn chin. The kid could be his. And if he was? Jesus. God help them both.

Before that thought had a chance to take hold, he pushed it aside. No way. He'd been careful. Brown hair, brown eyes. What did that really mean, anyway? Probably half the people in the world were brown and brown. It was average.

"I don't think this is a good idea," the redhead said, and Nick shifted his gaze to watch her approach.

Hell, she looked like she wanted to drop-kick him. His gaze shifted, giving her a slow look from head to toe. She was wearing those faded, soft-looking jeans again and a dark red sweatshirt that hid the curvy figure he knew lay beneath it. Her grass green eyes shot cold knives at him, and even at a distance he felt the chill she was giving off.

What did it say about him, he wondered, that the flash of desire she sparked in him didn't disappear despite the fury in her eyes?

And she might be mad, but she didn't worry him. Hell, she was no bigger than a kicker—if he had to, he could take her. Not that he'd even try to take her—well, he wouldn't mind *taking* her—but he figured if she had a temper like his sister, at the very least he could outrun her. But first things first.

"Yeah, well," Nick said, shoving his hands into his

back pockets, "good idea or not, I'm here and I'm not leaving until I have a talk with Jonas."

Just saying the boy's name out loud made this whole situation seem more real than it had in the last two days. Before, he'd been more or less a faceless threat. A threat to Nick's freedom. His future. His lifestyle. But now . . . here Jonas stood, staring up at Nick like he was a hero.

Something inside him turned over, even while he fought it. Hell, he'd had kids look at him like that before. Every game day, there were dozens of 'em waiting outside the stadium. Clamoring for autographs or a handshake, they were delighted with a couple minutes of your time and walked away telling their friends how cool you were.

But this was different, his brain argued. This was personal. This kid didn't want a few minutes. He wanted a lifetime. He wanted commitment. From *Nick* of all people. Man, if this wasn't some weird-ass kind of cosmic joke, he didn't know what would qualify.

Scraping one hand across his face, Nick tore his gaze from the kid's. If this was gonna work, he had to retain some distance. And staring into those eyes full of hopes and dreams wasn't the way to maintain it.

"Jonas . . ." The redhead spoke up and her voice was flat, even.

"Tasha, come on. He's my *dad,*" the boy pleaded.

Jesus. There was that word again. Nick could see she didn't like it any more than he did. All she wanted was for him to disappear. Well, hey, honey, he thought. That makes two of us.

"Just let me talk to the boy," he said tightly. "What could it hurt?"

She sucked in a gulp of air and folded both arms across her chest. He could almost see thoughts racing through her mind, and none of them were making her happy. That fabulous mouth of hers flattened into a grim slash and her eyes narrowed as she considered him. Then her gaze shifted to the boy and Nick watched her features soften until her beauty was ripe enough to steal his breath. Whatever she thought of *him,* Nick told himself, she loved that kid.

Another long minute passed in anxious silence and Nick damn near *felt* the boy's excitement rippling off of him in thick waves. Tasha must have sensed it, too, and obviously didn't have the heart to squash it.

"Okay," she said, and Jonas practically danced in place. "Fifteen minutes," she added quickly, which earned her a whine from Jonas and a grateful sigh from Nick.

Hell, he wanted to talk to the kid, but fifteen minutes was more than enough time. What he had to say could be summed up pretty quickly. All he had to do was explain how being a fan was one thing, but making up stories was something else. Once that was done, he'd give the kid the stuff he'd left out in the car; then he'd be gone. And he could get back to rebuilding his life. To getting onto a track that would lead him somewhere beyond the dead end he'd found himself in when his career ended.

"C'mon . . ." The kid paused as if not quite sure what to call him, then settled for, "Nick. I'll show you my room."

The boy sprinted ahead of Nick and shot up the stairs, making enough noise, as he went, for ten kids. Nick's gaze shifted from the kid to the redhead, and when he met those green eyes of hers, he damn near took a step backward. He caught himself just in time.

"If you hurt him," she threatened, "I swear I'll—"

He shot a quick look at the stairs to make sure the kid was out of earshot. Then he took a step toward her and snapped, "Christ, what do you think I am?"

"Don't you get it, football hero?" she asked quietly, her voice filled with ice. "This isn't about *you.*"

God damn it. Was she blind or something? His life was riding on this. Sure, he didn't want to see the kid crushed, but none of this had been *his* idea. A spurt of something dark and dangerous shot through him, and Nick's head snapped back as he stared at her. "You know, lady, you and I need to—"

"*We* don't need to do anything." She cut him off cleanly. Her eyes flashed green fire and Nick could have sworn she singed him from across the room. "Jonas is waiting for you. Take your fifteen minutes, then I want you out of here."

She turned her back and walked away. Nick watched her go as ribbons of fury snaked through him. Hell, he'd never been thrown out of *anywhere* as often as this redhead was pitching him out of her house. And damn it, that kind of shit just didn't happen to Nick Candellano.

Couldn't she see he was trying to do the right thing here? Okay, so what if his main concern wasn't the kid? He hadn't started this and he almost shouted that after her. But he figured she wouldn't care, wouldn't stop to fight it out with him, and that was something he wasn't used to. In his family, people chose sides and jumped into the battle. They didn't fire a shot and walk away. They stuck around until everyone was battered and bloody—figuratively speaking, of course—and the argument was finished.

"Hey, Nick . . ." Jonas's voice hurtled at him from the top of the stairs. Nick had to remind himself that he wasn't here to convince the redhead that he was a great guy. Though it went against the grain to have *any* woman give him the brush-off, he was here to get the kid off his ass. Gently, of course, but definitely *off*.

"Yeah," he called back, his gaze still locked on the doorway through which Tasha had disappeared. "Coming."

Then he pushed her out of his thoughts and turned for the stairs. Ready to tackle the biggest game of his career.

Tasha grabbed the kitchen timer and carried it into the dining room. Her knees felt weak, so she pulled a chair out, its legs scraping against the wood floor with a screech. Plopping down into it, she set the timer for fifteen minutes, then put it down on the table in front of her. Fifteen and not one minute more.

The whir of the timer sounded like a drunken bee, buzzing through her brain. Her head pounded, her heart raced. In memory, she saw his eyes again. Nick's eyes. Dark and deep. And she shivered. He threatened everything she held dear just by being here. Yet at the same time, he touched something inside her that had been cold and empty for way too long.

Her gaze locked on the open doorway between the dining room and the living room. From where she sat, she could just see the bottom step of the staircase, but in her mind's eye she saw Jonas's bedroom—and Nick Candellano invading her world.

• • •

"Come on," Jonas said from the last doorway on the left.

Nick walked slowly, checking the place out as he went. The old house had seen better days. Fifty years ago, the house was probably a beauty. But now, like an old woman, the Victorian's beauty was more memory than reality. The stair runner was threadbare; some of the wallpaper at the head of the stairs was peeling away at the baseboard. The wood floors were old and scarred but clean, and his footsteps seemed to echo down the long hallway.

"This is my room," Jonas was saying as Nick got closer.

He tried not to notice the excited gleam in the kid's eyes. Tried not to feel anything as he stepped past the boy who might be his son, into the bedroom.

Nick took a deep breath and instantly regretted it.

Like every kid, Jonas was a slob.

The room was big. As big as the room Nick had once shared with his twin brother, Paul. A dresser stood on one side of the room, crowded on either side by stuffed bookcases. Two walls had windows that overlooked the side and backyards and let in enough sunlight to display the mess in all its glory. A single bed was dead center of the room and surrounded by discarded books and piles of—judging by the smell of sweat—*dirty* clothes. The walls were decorated with sports posters. Baseball players hung alongside basketball stars and hockey players. There were *two* of Nick in his playing days, and it felt a little weird to stare up into his own eyes.

Hell, he even remembered the days those pictures had been taken. Flying high on his own success, Nick had been on top of the world. Everything rolling his way, a part of him had been sure that the ride would last forever. At the top of his game, he had money, fans, women, and everything else he'd ever wanted.

Now all he was, was another guy on a fading poster. And the hard truth of that rattled around inside him like a handful of BBs. Cold, hard little pellets of truth, hammering at his guts, tearing away what he'd once been and leaving him damn uncertain about a future that wasn't looking any too bright.

Finally, though, he shifted his gaze from his past and looked at the kid wandering around the room. Jonas stopped beside a small collection of football trophies. Hell, Nick had dozens just like them, stuffed in a closet at his mother's house.

The boy's fingers danced across the cold metal surface of one as he said, "I got these. I play football, too. Just like you."

"Yeah?" Okay, safe territory. Talk football. Good a segue as anything, right? "What position do you play?"

"Tight end," Jonas said, one corner of his mouth lifting into a proud smile.

"Yeah?" Hey. The kid was a running back. *Just like the old man?* Nope, he thought. Don't go there. "You any good?"

"I'm fast," Jonas said with a hard nod. "Just like you."

"Great." *Ah, Christ.* "I'll have to come see you play sometime."

"Yeah?" The boy stepped closer, eagerness etched into his features and a brilliant light shining in his dark brown eyes. "You will? When? We have a game on Saturday and—"

The kid kept talking. Words flying out of his mouth like bullets from a machine gun. And every word hit

Nick like a fist. Jesus. Why hadn't he kept his mouth shut? He makes an idle comment and the kid takes it like a solemn vow. *I'm an idiot.* Nick scraped one hand across his face and tried to ignore the shaft of guilt that stabbed at him. It wasn't a comfortable feeling and Christ knew he didn't experience it often. Purposely. Nick lived his life looking out for Nick Candellano. It was easy. It was safe. Start worrying about the rest of the world and you ended up getting sucked into all kinds of shit.

"We'll see . . ." Nick hedged, and winced just a bit. Hell, his parents used to say that to them all the time when they didn't want to say no and hear the whining, but weren't prepared to say yes, either.

Jonas probably recognized the stalling tactic for what it was, because some of the shine left his eyes. But to give the kid credit, he smiled again quickly and walked to a paper-littered desk in the far corner.

Nick sat down on the edge of the bed and braced his forearms on his thighs. Watching the kid, he tried to come up with just the right words to burst the boy's balloon. While he thought about it, Jonas picked up a silver-edged framed photo and walked toward him.

The boy smiled at the picture, then turned it around to Nick. Holding it proudly, he said, "See? This is my mom. That's how I knew you were my dad. 'Cause she told me about you."

Nick swallowed hard and accepted the picture. The frame felt cold and stiff in his hands, and as he stared down into the smiling face of an attractive smiling brunette, he searched his memory desperately. But Jonas was eleven now. And that was a hell of a long time to try to remember a single face out of what had been, at the time, *dozens* of women.

Nick felt the kid's expectations as if they were a living thing in the room with him and the boy. Jonas was practically vibrating with excitement and Nick found himself almost . . . *almost* wanting to be able to say, *Yes. I remember her. I loved her a lot and I'm your long-lost dad. Everything's going to be great.*

Hell, it would be better than the truth. Because the truth was going to kill the kid.

Nick didn't know the woman's face. He didn't remember her. She was pretty, but a lot of women were pretty. They'd *all* been pretty back then. For all he knew, he *had* slept with her, but he was damned if he'd made her pregnant.

He'd been too careful.

Hadn't he?

"You remember my mom, right?" Jonas asked after a long, painful moment of silence had crawled past.

Damn it. What the hell could he possibly say to this kid? That he'd boinked so many women he couldn't possibly pick one from the crowd at this late date? Could he really tell Jonas that his mother hadn't been memorable enough to etch herself into Nick's brain? That she'd been nothing more than a quick diversion?

And what if he hadn't been as careful as he'd been saying? What if after hours of drinking and partying, the condom had been forgotten? What if it just plain hadn't worked? What then? Then, he thought, he might actually be staring at his son, and could he really tell his own flesh and blood what a shit he was?

Shame slapped at him and it was such a new experience, it nearly took his breath away.

"You remember, right?"

"Jonas . . ."

The boy must have read something in Nick's features because he started talking fast again. Words tumbled out of his mouth in a wild rush, as if chasing each other in a desperate bid to keep Nick from speaking and ruining everything.

"Her name was Margie," Jonas said. "Margie Baker. And she was really pretty. She had a nice laugh and she told me . . . she *told* me that you were my dad, and my mom never lied to me." He shook his head fiercely, sending that brown hair of his into a dance across and into his eyes. "Never once. Ever."

Nick sighed and avoided what felt like a punishing stare from the woman in the photograph. "Look, Jonas, I—"

"No. You *do* remember her. I know you do. Margie. Margie Baker."

Jesus.

"You *have* to remember her, 'cause I'm the only one who does and you're my dad so you have to, too."

Nick took a deep breath to steady the well of pity he hadn't expected to feel so deeply. Every self-defense mechanism inside him was screaming at him to tell the kid the truth and make his getaway. Sure, the boy would be hurt, but was that Nick's fault? No. Jonas's mother had started all this when she'd pulled Nick's name out of a hat and labeled him Daddy Dearest.

Yet her memory was cherished and Jonas was now looking at Nick like he'd just crawled out from under a rock. He wasn't used to that, damn it. People *liked* Nick Candellano. Admired him. Looked up to him.

Damn it all to hell, he *missed* that. He missed being sought after. Being hounded for autographs. Being the target of paparazzi whenever he went to some five-star party. He'd lost so much in the last couple of months. Football, the one thing he'd ever been good at. His career. The future he'd mapped out for himself. Everything. Gone.

Regret pooled in his mouth and he had to choke it down. *Do yourself a favor, Nick. Tell the kid the hard truth and get the hell outta Dodge.* But he couldn't do it. He couldn't look into the eyes of one of his last remaining fans and let that go, too.

"I don't know," he said softly. "Maybe I did know her."

Jonas smiled.

And Nick felt like a hero again.

CHAPTER 8

"I knew it." Nodding, Jonas snatched the photo from Nick and hugged it to his narrow chest, folding his arms over it protectively. His smile widened. "I knew it. My mom never lied to me. Never."

Oh, man. Almost from the moment the words had left his mouth, Nick had regretted the impulse to keep the kid's hopes alive. He hadn't done the boy any favors. And he'd only made things worse for himself. Well, hell. A full day's work in less than thirty seconds.

"Jonas . . ."

"I knew you'd remember." The boy looked so earnest, so determined to force memory into life, Nick almost ached for him. But Jonas wasn't finished. "You had to—'cause my mom was really pretty. And nice. And she loved you." Despite a trembling smile, tears sprang up to fill his eyes and Jonas freed one hand long enough to swipe them away.

He didn't know what to do, damn it. Nick was no good with kids. Not one-on-one. Talking to a group of them he was fine—he could joke and talk about football—but dealing with one little boy's misery was just beyond him.

Maybe he should have done it Jackson's way after all. Maybe he never should have come here. Wasn't he just making this a bigger mess than it had been to begin with? Making it harder for the kid to ultimately let go of his fantasy?

But he knew damn well that a DNA test would never have convinced Jonas anyway. An adult would take the results of a test and accept them at face value. But Jonas was just a kid. He wouldn't care what a test had to say one way or the other. He'd put his faith in his mother's word—because that was all of her he had left.

And who the hell was Nick to take that from him?

"She was pretty, huh?"

Hope and pride and fear mingled together in the boy's big brown eyes and stirred something inside Nick he'd never felt before. He wasn't entirely sure what it was, but it was damned uncomfortable.

Nick stood up, feeling the need to move, even if it was only to walk around the cluttered room. His gaze drifted across the dirty laundry, ripped-up sneakers, and crumpled papers dotting the floor surrounding a trash can. Cleats coated with dried mud lay at the foot of the bed, and Jonas's football pads had been tossed onto the floor of the closet. His clean football uniform was folded on a chair and his helmet lay on the floor nearby. It all reminded Nick so much of his own room when he was a boy. Between his own sports stuff and Paul's boy-genius chemistry sets, they'd hardly had room to walk.

But there was a difference between the Candellano boys' room and Jonas's. In the Candellano house, Nick's parents had always been close by. He'd grown up surrounded by security and love, and he'd never had to doubt who he belonged to.

Jonas . . . all he had was the currently missing foster mother and the ferocious gorgeous redhead downstairs. The poor kid was clinging to the memory of his mother and to the dream of the father he wanted.

What a joke. If Jonas only knew him better, he'd see that Nick was nobody's idea of a dad. The kind of man Jonas wanted, needed, for a father was the kind who would have told him the truth instead of dodging it to make himself feel better. Nick scraped one hand across the back of his neck. He had to say something. He just wasn't sure what. Turning to look at the boy, he said, "Jonas—"

"Your time's up."

Nick and Jonas both turned to look at Tasha, standing in the open doorway. Arms folded across her chest, she stood there like a guardian angel—all she needed was a sword and a shield. Her hair looked wild, as if she'd been running nervous fingers through it. Her eyes were wide and worried, and Nick was pretty sure if he listened hard enough, he'd be able to hear her heart pounding like a bass drum in a parade. "What?"

"Your fifteen minutes are up," she said, meeting his gaze and silently daring him to argue. "It's time for you to go."

"Tasha . . ." Jonas scooted away from the bed and took a step or two toward Nick. "He just got here."

She stared at the boy for a long minute and Nick knew the instant she noticed Jonas's teary eyes. Her face went cold and hard, and when she shifted her gaze to look at him again, Nick had a strange urge to cross himself. Jesus. Mother bears had *nothing* on this woman.

"Leave," she said tightly.

"I'm going." He'd had his fifteen minutes, and absolutely nothing had been solved. Everything was still up in the air, the kid was still convinced he was his father, and Nick had deliberately dropped his opportunity to say, "No, I'm not."

Tasha stood aside in the doorway to make room for Nick to pass her into the hall. She flattened herself on the doorjamb and *still* he managed to brush against her. Instinctively she sucked in a breath and unthinkingly drew in the scent of his aftershave. Something cool, expensive, and all male. Oh boy. She closed her eyes briefly, then opened them again. When Jonas started after Nick, she stopped him. "No. You stay up here. Do your homework."

"I want to walk with him."

"And I want to talk to him." Actually, Tasha wanted to strangle him, but she didn't think she should tell Jonas that. By the look on his face, the little boy had already had enough emotional wrenching for one afternoon.

"It's okay, sport," Nick said from behind her. "I'll come by again in a few days."

Jonas's whole face lit up when Nick Candellano called him *sport*. And Tasha wanted to scream. Already he was having an influence on Jonas. Already he was making inroads into *her* family. Her fingers curled tightly around the doorknob and squeezed until her knuckles went white.

"Don't forget," Jonas called out, even as Tasha pulled his door closed, "my game is Saturday. At the park!" The door shut firmly, but Jonas's voice carried through the wood. "Three o'clock!"

Blowing out a short frustrated breath that ruffled the wisp of bangs on her forehead, Tasha started down the long hall toward the stairs. She didn't breathe again until she was well in front of Nick. She couldn't risk getting another whiff of that aftershave. Nick fell into step behind her. She felt his steady gaze on her back as surely as she would have his touch, and her blood heated, thickening in her veins even as fear tugged at the pit of her stomach.

She fought the feelings—*all* of them.

Tasha didn't want to be attracted to him. There was no good there. And worse, she didn't want to be afraid. Oh, she wasn't scared of *him*. Just what his presence might mean. This house, this life she'd built for herself—fear wasn't a part of it. It wasn't a part of her world anymore. And she couldn't go back.

His heavy footsteps echoed into the stillness and she even resented that. It was as if somehow he was imprinting himself on her house as well as the boy she loved like her own.

At the foot of the stairs, she took a left and kept walking. Headed for the door, she concentrated on it as if her life depended on it. Once past that oak barrier, she'd have him outside, and if she had anything at all to do with it, Nick would *remain* outside this house. Every step she took, though, she felt his gaze on her.

Tiny needles of awareness trickled along her spine and Tasha tried to shake them off. This was no time to let her long-comatose hormones out for a test drive. No matter what her physical reaction to him was, this man was her enemy. He represented a huge threat to everything she loved. If he really was Jonas's father, then he could take the boy from her in an instant. And even if he wasn't a blood relation at all, his very presence, his involvement with them, could bring down the authorities on their heads, and Jonas would be taken away by Social Services.

Either way, Jonas would be gone.

She opened the door and stepped onto the porch. Instantly the cold air slapped at her and she took a deep breath, hoping the chill of it would be enough to quiet the burning inside her. It didn't help, so she kept moving.

Tasha paused only long enough to make sure he was still following her, then she headed down the short set of steps to the flower-lined walkway.

In the gray cloud-washed afternoon sunlight, the flowers Mimi had loved so much looked bedraggled, hopeless. As if they'd picked up on Tasha's turmoil and were drooping in solidarity. The truth, though, was far less comforting. She'd let the flower beds go. She'd been too busy doing hair and saving money and raising Jonas and trying to avoid the terrifying Ms. Walker of Social Services.

The lawn that needed mowing and the flowers at half-mast were just the tip of the iceberg, too. The old house needed painting, storm shutters needed to be put up before winter got too much older, and her car needed a tune-up.

Head suddenly throbbing, Tasha rubbed her eyes with her fingertips and told herself that at least she'd managed to bury her hormones beneath other worries. She kept walking, down the curving sidewalk toward the gravel drive where Mr. Wonderful's Corvette waited, looking like a perfect rose in a bouquet of weeds.

"So, are you going to stop walking anytime soon?" Nick's voice prodded at her, pushing her dangerously close to the tattered edge of her control.

Her tennis shoes hit the drive and she turned around quickly, gravel scraping beneath her feet. Looking up into his dark brown eyes, Tasha demanded, "What did you say to him?"

Nick planted his feet wide apart, crossed his arms over his chest, and cocked his head to one side. "That's none of your business."

"Wrong, hotshot." She stepped in closer. "Anything that has to do with Jonas *is* my business."

"Yeah?" he countered. "If he's so damn important to you, and you hate having me around so much, why didn't you stop him from suing me?"

A rush of air escaped her. "I didn't know about it."

He smiled, and in the gloomy sunlight, that smile sparked something in his eyes that Tasha tried to ignore. Unfortunately, her body noticed and her blood hummed.

"So he surprised you, too," he said, his voice softer now, friendlier. As if they were on the same side in this. And a part of her almost wished they were. She was so tired of standing alone. But she knew darn well that being alone was the only sure way to be safe.

A cold breeze ruffled his dark brown hair as he leaned up against the Corvette, one hand at the top of the windshield frame. He looked like a magazine ad. Then he inclined his head toward her and gave her that half-smile again. It didn't seem to matter that it was a practiced move. Her body responded as though he'd meant it for her alone.

This was *not* a man to be dealing with when her resistance levels were low.

"Yeah," she admitted, pushing her hair out of her eyes as the wind shifted direction. It swirled around them briefly, then disappeared, leaving only a chill that stealthily crept through her. "You could say he surprised me, too."

Nick nodded, breathed deeply, blew air out in a rush, then looked deep into her eyes. "He says his mother told him I was his father."

One simple sentence and she felt the gravel drive shift beneath her feet, almost as if it were quicksand. A knot lodged in her throat, but Tasha swallowed it down and forced herself to ask, "Are you?"

He pushed away from the car and shoved one hand through his hair in either frustration or irritation. She couldn't decide which.

"No. I don't know. Maybe. Probably not."

Hope that this would all be over quickly died inside her. "Well, as long as you're sure . . ." She choked out a harsh laugh that scraped her throat and shook her soul.

"Hey, it was more than eleven years ago."

She shook her head in disbelief and stared up at him. "God, you actually think that's an excuse, don't you?"

He scrubbed one hand across his jaw. "That's a lot of years."

"As hard as this may be for you to believe, *most* people remember who they've slept with."

"Fine." He shoved both hands in his pockets, then jerked them back out again, as if he wasn't sure exactly what to do. "I'm a pig."

"You said that, I didn't."

Shaking his head, he let his arms drop to his sides. "You want to tell me why you hate my guts when you don't even know me?"

"I don't have to know you. I know your type." Tasha told herself that this was a good thing. Better she keep in mind now that Nick Candellano was a player. He looked at women and never saw their faces. Just blonde, brunette, or redhead. No one was special.

No one held a place in his mind or heart. And if she was dumb enough to give into her hormonal urges, she'd be nothing more than a passing blip on his radar screen.

He snorted a laugh, but he didn't sound amused. "My type? This I've got to hear."

"No problem." She took a step closer to him, and the gravel beneath her feet screamed into the midday quiet. Tipping her head way back to stare up into his eyes, she wished for just a second or two that she was taller, just so the glaring would be easier. "You think women are here just to throw rose petals in front of you when you walk by."

"What?"

"You're rich and good-looking, so you think the world is yours. Women aren't *people* to you, they're conquests. You don't care about any of them," she continued. "It's quantity you're interested in, not quality."

"Really?" His voice went tight and a muscle in his jaw twitched. Otherwise, he didn't move. "And you get all of this from knowing me for two whole days?"

Tasha smirked at him. "I got that in the first five minutes."

He shifted position then, as if uncomfortable. Gravel crunched, the wind blew, and steam seemed to be coming from his ears. Apparently, she'd struck a nerve.

"I don't owe you or anybody an explanation for how I lived my life. Then *or* now."

"Is that right?"

He crossed his arms over his chest and Tasha told herself to ignore just how big he was. To pay no attention to the broadness of his chest. After all, legions of women had been there before her and none of them remained.

"Yeah, that's right."

"I think there's a little boy who might argue with you."

His shoulders slumped and a defeated glint shone briefly in his eyes. "Look, whatever you think of me, it doesn't really matter. All that matters now is settling this."

"*That* I'll agree with."

He laughed shortly again. "A peace treaty?"

"A truce."

"I'll take it," he said, and held out his right hand.

Tasha stared at it for a long moment. Calling a truce with him might not be the best way to go, but at the moment it was all she could think of. Maybe if she worked *with* him, she could get rid of him that much faster. Steeling herself, she slipped her hand into his. His fingers curled around hers and a heat she'd never felt before blossomed and spread through her like a wildfire decimating the foothills.

His eyebrows lifted, and she knew he felt it, too. She tried to pull her hand free, but he tightened his grip on her. A buzz of something dark and dangerous and *way* too tempting raced through her bloodstream. Her heartbeat quickened; her mouth went dry and still; he held on to her. Flames licked at her center, and when his thumb stroked over the back of her hand, Tasha knew she couldn't take any more. She yanked hard, freeing herself from his grasp. Her skin tingled and she rubbed her palm against her jeans as if she could wipe away even the memory of his touch. God knew it would be safer if she could.

"Okay then," she said, and cursed silently when she heard the tremor in her own voice. She cleared her throat and tried again. "A truce."

He rubbed his fingertips together as if he could still feel her hand in his. "Now that we're on the same side, sort of, what exactly do we do next?"

"That depends," she said, grateful for something else to think about. "What did you tell Jonas?"

He scowled, looked past her at the bare-limbed trees lining the front yard, then reluctantly shifted his gaze back to hers. "Not much."

"But what?"

"I told him that maybe I remembered his mother."

"Oh God."

Clearly disgusted, Nick frowned, rubbed his mouth with one hand, and muttered, "He looked at me all teary-eyed and I couldn't—"

"What?" she prodded. "Tell him the truth?"

"Yeah."

"So you lied."

"Sometimes a lie is kinder."

"Only liars think so."

"Man," he said, huffing out a breath. "You're a hard woman, Tasha Flynn."

Unexpectedly a sheen of tears clouded her vision and she was horrified. She blinked them back quickly and prayed he hadn't noticed. She wasn't hard. Sometimes she thought life would be easier if only she were. Then at least, the chances of having her heart steamrollered would have been tiny.

"I just don't like lies," she said with a sniff. "Lies only create more problems. The truth is simple. It's easy to remember and you don't stumble trying to keep the details straight."

His eyes narrowed on her. "Are you okay?"

"I'm fine." Not really, but she would be. As soon as he left. So that wasn't really a lie, was it?

"Look, I'm sorry. I handled things with Jonas badly. I admit that. But what do you want me to say?"

She looked up at him and didn't see his charming smile this time. This time she saw a man who held the power to shatter her family, to break Jonas's heart. "I want you to say you're going away."

"Wish I could," he admitted with a wry smile, "but I can't."

"You could have if you'd just told him you weren't his father."

"I couldn't do that, either."

"What exactly *can* you do, Mr. Candellano?"

"Nick."

"What?" She blinked up at him.

"Call me Nick."

"Why should I?"

He shrugged. "Why not? We're locked into this situation together. We've called a truce. Might as well be friends."

Friends? No way. Just standing this close to him, she felt as though she needed a chastity belt. Nick Candellano was a walking orgasm. Everything about him sent warning bells clanging in her head. Anytime she got within three feet of him, she could feel the electricity arcing between them, practically burning the air. Shaking his hand had nearly set her body on fire. No. There wasn't a chance in hell the two of them could *ever* be friends. And she wouldn't allow anything else.

Tasha shook her head. "We're not going to be friends, *Nick*." She sucked in a gulp of air and said a silent *thank you* heavenward when she didn't get another taste of his aftershave. "To you, Jonas is a problem to be solved. To me, he's a little boy to be protected. That puts us on opposite sides. Even with a truce."

"I don't want to hurt him," he argued, and the flash of heat in his eyes convinced her as his words couldn't.

Tasha nodded slowly. "Okay, maybe you don't. But you will."

"Thanks for the vote of confidence."

"You want confidence?" she asked quietly. "Then do the right thing."

"Happy to," he said. "Just what would that be?"

Go away! she screamed silently. But that wouldn't solve anything and she knew it. Until Jonas was convinced that this man wasn't his father, she'd never be rid of Nick Candellano.

"I don't know," she finally said. "I just don't know."

Three days later, Nick was still twisting at the end of a long rope, hoping it didn't form a noose.

He walked across the small park, toward the playing field. Along both sidelines, groups of people were standing or sprawled in sand chairs, shouting encouragement and yelling at the ref. Coolers and thermoses dotted the grass, and the shouts, like a magnet, drew Nick closer.

He'd already spotted Tasha. Sitting all by herself at the far end of the field, she was perched on the edge of a folding chair, hands braced on her knees, gaze fixed on the game. Her fiery hair was pulled into a ponytail that whipped around in the ever-present wind and looked like flames dancing in a hearth.

He tore his gaze away from her to glance at the playing field where two squads of little boys pretended to be men. Standing in the grip of a cold, fierce wind that rushed across the open spaces to push past him like a stranger, Nick took a quick trip down memory lane. Listening to the sounds of the crowd took him back to his own childhood. To a time when everything was simple. Easy. When running down a field and scoring a touchdown meant an ice-cream sundae after the game. When he could look to the sidelines and see his family, cheering him on.

When the future was far away and still looked bright.

Dismissing the past, he headed toward Tasha.

She glanced up as he came near and he saw surprise register in her eyes. "I didn't expect to see you," she said.

"Didn't expect to come," he admitted, and dropped to the grass beside her chair. Drawing his knees up, he draped his forearms across them, then shifted a sideways glance at her. Christ, she was gorgeous. The wind made her cheeks pink and the handful of freckles across her nose stand out in gold relief. Her eyes were as deep and dark a green as the bulky sweater she wore over her jeans and sparkled like polished emeralds. She looked fresh and young and impossibly beautiful.

Something inside Nick tightened into knots, squeezed hard, then eased off, yet the sudden tension within remained. For the first time since he'd met her, she wasn't looking at him like he was a disease waiting to be cured. And Jesus, when her eyes were smiling, she was lethal.

Man, he hadn't counted on her.

She turned her gaze on him and Nick felt the solid punch of those eyes. "So why are you here?" she asked.

He shrugged. "I was invited." And he was hoping she'd leave it at that, since he couldn't give her any other reason. Hell, he wasn't sure himself why he was there. He'd spent the last three days trying to get lost in work, to attempt to put Jonas Baker—and Tasha Flynn—out of his mind. But that had been less than successful. As the low man on the totem pole, he had fewer things to do at work than a water boy at a swim meet.

Frustration was riding him hard. He wasn't used to doing nothing, even if he *was* getting paid a ridiculous amount for it. He wanted to do . . . hell, *something*. Working for television wasn't turning out to be the dream job he'd expected.

Since he was fifteen years old, he'd been working out or practicing or playing football. Now he could hardly hit the treadmill without his knee screaming and reminding him exactly how much he'd lost. He was no longer part of a team. He had no goal to shoot for, no driving desire to push himself to be the best. He was too often alone, and quickly discovering that Nick Candellano wasn't someone he wanted to spend that much time with.

Plus, there was no peace to be found in his house. Not with the Marconis crawling all over the place pounding hammers and clanging on pipes.

So, he was here. And just what did it say about his life, he wondered silently, when an afternoon at a Pop Warner game—with a kid who was suing him—was the best thing he had going?

"Where is he?" Nick asked, shoving his thoughts to the back of his brain. God knew there'd be plenty of time later to think. His gaze locked on the small herd of tiny tacklers, one squad in filthy white, the other in faded red.

"Number twenty-two. In white," Tasha answered, her gaze, too, fixed on the game.

Nick watched Jonas. God, he looked small out there. Skinny white legs poking out of the knee-length football pants. His cleats were muddy and his white socks drooped down around his ankles. The kid's uniform was covered in grass stains, giving witness to how many times he'd been knocked on his ass. But when the ball was snapped, Jonas took off like a shot. Zigging and zagging his way through the other team, he raced downfield, outran his blockers, then leaped up to snag a pass aimed right at him.

Nick's heart jumped to his throat and his hands closed around his knees as if he could somehow help the kid hold on to the ball. When Jonas turned and hit the ground running for the goal line, fifty yards away, Nick's heart pounded.

The screams and shouts of the crowd faded into the distance as he focused solely on the one small boy headed for glory. Memories skirted through Nick's mind again in a wild rush of color and sensation. He knew just how Jonas felt when the triumphant boy spiked the ball on the ground, then turned to jump up and down with his friends.

And for a split second, Nick envied Jonas that feeling that was now lost to him forever.

Beside Nick, Tasha was on her feet, two fingers in her mouth and whistling like she was hailing a cab in New York City. Then she glanced down at Nick, eyes bright, a proud grin on her face that lit up all the dark places inside him.

"Did you see that?" she demanded.

"Yeah," he said, standing up to get a better look at that gorgeous smile. "He's pretty good."

"Good?" Tasha repeated, then shook her head. "He's terrific."

Nick nodded and shifted his gaze to the field, where the refs were calling the game over. Jonas's victorious team started the screaming again and bolted for the sidelines and their own private cheerleaders.

Jonas, too, yanked his helmet off and came running straight to Tasha. Nick knew the instant the boy spotted him. Jonas's dirty, sweat-streaked features brightened as if a hundred candles were burning inside him, and he ran forward as if looking for another touchdown.

"You came!" he shouted as he slid to a stop right in front of them.

"Had to see you play," Nick said.

"Did ya see my touchdown?"

Tasha stepped forward and smoothed the boy's sweaty hair back from his forehead.

"I saw it." Nick grinned. "That was a great run."

"See? I'm just like you."

Just like you. The words echoed in Nick's mind and repeated over and over again like a chant. For the kid's sake, Nick hoped not. Nick had spent most of his life devoting so much time to football . . . that now that he was required to find a *real* life, he wasn't sure what to look for. He wouldn't wish that on anybody.

"Are you comin' for pizza?"

"What?"

Tasha looked from Jonas to Nick and paused before saying, "After a game, the kids and the parents go for pizza."

"You wanna come?" Jonas asked, and hope blossomed on his face.

Nick's gaze shifted from the boy to Tasha. He could see she was hoping he'd say, "No thanks." And he probably should have. But instead, he heard himself say, "Why not?"

Chapter 9

The noise level at the Pizza Palace was enough to make grown men weep.

But Nick, Tasha thought as she watched him from across the room, seemed to be enjoying himself. Surrounded by Jonas and his friends—and a few of the boys' fathers—he was practically holding court. He'd been the star of the show since he'd arrived and Tasha couldn't even resent him for it. How could she, when all it took was one look at Jonas to convince her the boy had never been happier?

Jonas was soaking it all in, like a flower left out in the sun too long and then blessed with rain. He darn near glowed in the reflected admiration bouncing off Nick.

Watching Jonas with the man he thought of as a father was enough to break Tasha's heart. The little boy was so excited and so . . . *proud.* For the first time ever, Jonas had been one of the guys after the game. He, too, had had a 'father' there for him. And though Tasha was pleased for him, she was worried, too. This was all going to end, badly, one way or another. Either Nick would prove to be his father and take Jonas from Tasha

. . . or Nick *wasn't* his father and Jonas would lose him. Or worse yet, Social Services would catch on to the truth about Mimi and throw the boy back into the system, and he would lose Tasha *and* Nick.

How would Jonas stand it? How would he hold up after having his heart broken? And how could Tasha possibly stand by and watch it happen?

There was so much hanging in the balance, she thought, her stomach twisting into knots of anxiety and good old-fashioned fear. Too much for her to relax her guard.

"He's much more handsome in person, isn't he?"

"Hmm?" Tasha tore her gaze away from Jonas to look at Betty Wilkes, one of the team mothers. Betty always looked harried, from her mismatched socks to the gray roots of her blond hair. "Who?"

"Pssh!" The woman playfully slapped at Tasha's shoulder. "Nick, that's who."

"Oh." Of course. Who else would they be talking about? The kids' moms were just as fascinated by Nick as their husbands.

"I mean, I used to watch him play," Betty said, "not like I had any choice, my husband never misses a Saints game, but . . ." She took a deep breath and let it slide out in a slow rush of approval. "In person, he's so . . ." She waved her hands, shook her head, and tried to find a word to describe him. When she couldn't, she gave it up and just sighed.

"That about covers it," Tasha agreed, letting her gaze slide back to the tall, broad-shouldered man with the wide smile. Even from a distance, she felt the heat of his gaze when he turned his head to look right at her. She sucked in a gulp of air.

"Well . . ." Betty said, leaning in close, "have something you'd like to share with the class?"

Well, at least she knew she wasn't crazy. There really was something going on here between her and Nick. Now why didn't that knowledge make her feel any better?

"*No,*" Tasha said tightly. She didn't have anything she wanted to talk to Betty about. However, she could see herself spilling her guts to Molly in the morning. Chewing at her bottom lip, Tasha slid off the bench seat, leaving Betty hanging in the gossip wind, so to speak.

But she'd recover. At the moment, all Tasha wanted was a little space. Not easy to find in the madness that was the Pizza Palace. Between the screaming kids, the beeps and shrieks of the video games, and the piped-in music bouncing off the neon orange walls, the place was every kid's dream—and every adult's nightmare.

Almost every adult, she amended silently as she watched Nick playing to the crowd. Kids and their parents and even a few of the teenage waiters circled Nick like planets orbiting the sun. As she watched, he turned slowly in place, giving each of them a little brief eye contact, and she wondered if he actually practiced the move. Without even trying, he had every one of those people thinking *they* were the center of Nick's attention.

He was smooth. And good-looking enough to be declared bad for a woman's health. And charming. And . . . Nick dropped one hand onto Jonas's shoulder and the boy leaned into him. Tasha sighed and her heart ached. Even in a crowd, the man had remembered *why* he was there. By drawing Jonas into his circle, he'd made the boy a part of it all. And Jonas was clearly loving it.

How could she fight to protect Jonas from something he wanted so badly?

She shifted her gaze to Nick and caught him watching her. One corner of his mouth lifted into a small private smile that reached across the room and curled up into a warm knot at the pit of her stomach. She found herself smiling back until she realized he'd done it again. He'd made *her* feel like the center of his attention, too.

No doubt about it. A man with that much personal power was a man to keep a wary eye on.

"That was so cool," Jonas said as he rushed into the house and tossed his shoulder pads onto the staircase. Turning back around, he looked at Nick, his face beaming. "The guys really liked you. I could tell."

Tasha scooped up the mail from the floor, where it had fallen through the slot in the front door, then moved past the two of them. Nick watched her as she carried the envelopes and circulars into the dining room. She'd been damn quiet since leaving the pizza joint. Made him wonder why. And that made him wonder why the hell he cared. His gaze still on her, he said, "I had a good time, too, Jonas."

"I knew you would," the boy crowed. "And you'll go to the next game, too, huh?"

Nick smiled. His gaze shifted to the little boy and basked in the warmth radiating from the kid's grin. Hell, it had been a pretty good night. He'd been worried about the whole spending time with Jonas thing, but it had really been fun. Talking to the boy's teammates and their parents about football. Reliving a few of his more memorable moments. Nick rocked back on his heels and shoved both hands into his back pockets. He'd been worried for nothing. It was easy doing the father thing.

Not that he *was* a father or anything.

Tasha dropped her purse onto the dining room table and Nick looked over at her as she flipped through the mail. He saw her pause over a postcard, her fingertips tracing whatever glossy picture was there; then she dropped it onto the stack and turned around to meet his gaze. Her green eyes carried a solid punch even from across the room, and he wondered what she was thinking. Usually her expression left him no doubt at all about where her brain was.

Tasha wasn't like most other women he knew. She didn't play mind games. Didn't pretend to be fascinated by him or football. Didn't discreetly laugh or muffle a yawn. She yelled when she wanted to, challenged him whenever she thought he was stepping over a line she'd drawn in the sand, and she flashed that amazing smile of hers when she was happy.

With her, what you saw was what you got. Until tonight. Now there were shadows haunting her brilliant green eyes. Secrets hidden behind that nervous chewing of her lip. And damned if he didn't want to know what they were.

"Jonas," she said, ripping her gaze from Nick's in order to confront the still chattering boy. He looked at her as she said, "It's time for you to take a shower."

"But we were still talkin'," Jonas said.

"Jonas," Tasha said firmly, though her voice was tinged with fatigue, "it's been a long day. You're tired and sweaty. Say good night and go upstairs."

He wanted to argue, Nick could see it in the kid's face. And he flashed back to his own childhood when he and Paul would put up a last-ditch effort at gaining a few extra minutes. But they'd never won those battles and apparently Jonas didn't, either. Being a bright kid, he saved his breath and caved early.

"Okay, but—" He looked up at Nick. "Are you gonna be here when I get out?"

Tempting thought. A little extra one-on-one time with Tasha and maybe he'd be able to coax that truce into something a little friendlier. But even as he thought about it, he glanced at her expression. No welcome there. Just those intriguing shadows.

"No," he said, shifting a look at Jonas. "I'd better go."

"But you'll come back, right?"

Jesus, how did anybody stand a chance against those big brown eyes? The kid packed so much hope and expectation into a single glance that his feelings were stripped bare. And Nick felt a flicker of unease. How could *anyone* live up to what this boy wanted, dreamed of having? Him, least of all. Had he really just thought this thing was *easy*? "I—"

"Jonas," Tasha cut into the conversation before Nick could either agree to return or dodge the question. He was so busy being grateful for the rescue that he didn't know what he might have said. Maybe it was best for everyone that way.

"Go take a shower."

"Aw. . . ." Shoulders slumped in exaggerated defeat, the boy turned and headed for the stairs. He paused to pick up his pads and sling them over his shoulder. Then, drooping with every step, he slouched up the stairs like a man headed to the gallows. When he hit the top of the staircase, though, he stopped and looked down at Nick.

"I almost forgot. Can you get me some more of those pictures?" he asked.

"Pictures?"

"Yeah." Jonas grinned. "Like the other ones you sent me, with you catching a pass, and you signed 'em, too, so you have to sign the new ones, too, 'kay?"

Signed pictures? "When did I send you pictures?"

Jonas leaned over the banister, dangling his shoulder pads by one dirty strap hooked around his index finger. "I wrote letters to you and you sent 'em."

Fan letters. Signed pictures. It took a second or two, but things clicked in. "Did you send your letters to the stadium?"

"Uh-huh."

That explained it. Any letters sent to the players via the football stadium were automatically forwarded to the players' PR people. Since his second season with the Saints, Nick had used a secretary his business manager had hired. The secretary and whoever *she* hired answered the letters, signed the photos, and kept the fans happy. Nick never saw the letters himself. Like most of the other players, he'd been too busy practicing and playing the game to have time to deal with letters.

And to tell the truth, it had never bothered him before. He hadn't given a single thought to the people writing to him. Celebrities got fan mail. That was just part of the job. And celebrities hired people to answer the mail. Also part of the job. So why, all of a sudden, was Nick feeling like a shit for not knowing that this kid, who might be his *son,* had written to him and gotten a generic reply along with a forged signature on a photograph?

He pulled his hands from his pockets and folded his

arms across his chest. Looking up at Jonas, he said, "I'll get you some more."

The kid lit up like a Christmas tree and Nick told himself he shouldn't feel bad if the boy didn't mind. But it didn't seem to help.

When Jonas was out of sight, Nick pushed thoughts of fan mail and photos out of his mind and turned toward Tasha. He felt her withdraw even before she took a cautious step backward. Her gaze lifted to his and he wished again he knew what she was thinking. Strange, though, he couldn't remember *ever* worrying before about a woman's thoughts. He'd been too busy admiring their hair, their eyes, their mouths. But Tasha . . . for some damn reason, he could admire the package while still wanting to know what was inside.

How new and intriguing was that?

"Thanks for coming," she said, though he saw how much it cost her.

"Wasn't easy, was it?"

"What?"

"Thanking me for being here when you really want me gone?"

She blew out a breath, reached up, and yanked the rubber band off her ponytail. Instantly her hair tumbled down to her shoulders in a thick, rich mass that made his hands itch to touch it. "Look, it's nothing personal. . . ."

"You know," he said softly, "I'd rather it was." He didn't understand it himself. But damned if he wanted to be lumped in with every other male she'd chase from the door. Hell, if she was going to hate him, he at least wanted that hatred to be specific to *him.* And if *that* wasn't twisted, he didn't know what was.

"What are you talking about?"

"Damned if I know," he muttered, and kept his arms folded tight across his chest, to keep from reaching out for her. Hell, knowing her, she'd probably take his hand off at the elbow if he tried it.

Truce or no truce.

"I appreciate what you did for Jonas tonight, but—"

"Who was the postcard from?"

She stopped. "What?"

"The postcard you were looking at. Who sent it?"

Her gaze shifted from his, then back again. "Mimi."

"Yeah? Where is she?"

Tasha sucked in a breath and released it in a rush. "Paris."

Nick nodded, even though he wasn't buying it. There was something else, he thought. Something she wasn't saying. "Paris is beautiful. You ever been there?"

She laughed, short and sharp. "No."

"You should go," he said, and in his mind he was already seeing her there at the little café he knew on the Champ de Mars. His imagination painted a clear vision of the two of them, tucked behind a small glass-topped brass table. They would sit and sip wine and watch the incredibly fast-paced French traffic roar past. They would chuckle at the tourists and sniff at strangers as the locals did. And much later, when the summer sun was setting, late into the night, they would stroll along the champ to the Eiffel Tower. There they'd stand in the encroaching darkness and watch as the tiny white lights on the tower blinked into life.

"Sure," she said, shaking her head and dispelling the images in his mind. "I'll put that right onto my 'to do' list."

Nick glanced around the interior of the house, noting again the age of the place. Shabby but clean, old but cared for. Okay, there wasn't much money here. But Mimi had managed it, hadn't she? He looked at Tasha again. Maybe she didn't see trips to Paris in her future, but she should, he thought. Everyone should see those things. Whether they did them or not, it was important to at least dream about them.

But he had the distinct feeling that Tasha Flynn was too rooted to the hardscrabble reality of life to let her dreams run wild.

"So Mimi does Paris while you stay here and take care of Jonas and everything else?"

She stiffened and he was struck by her loyalty. Not only to Jonas, but also to a woman who apparently dumped all the work of running a house, a shop, and a kid on *her*.

"Mimi likes to travel," she said tightly.

"And you don't."

"I've seen enough, thanks." The words came clipped and pointed, and hinted at yet *more* secrets. Secrets Nick wanted in on.

"What have you seen, Tasha Flynn," he murmured, "that makes you so unwilling to see anything else?"

She surprised them both when tears suddenly swam in her eyes. "You should go." She sniffed, blinked her eyes frantically, and somehow, thankfully, managed to keep those tears from falling.

But she hadn't been able to hide them, and they tore at Nick. Just knowing they were so close to the surface made him want to discover their source. Made him want to stand in front of her to make sure no other fast-talking clod brought them into life again.

"Tasha, I—"

"Just go, okay?" She stepped up, grabbed the edge of the door, and clenched it so tightly, her knuckles went white.

"I'm going." Turning around, he stepped through the doorway and onto the porch. There he stopped and looked back over his shoulder at her. Backlit by the house lights shimmering behind her, she looked small and *way* too alone. "But I'll be back."

She tried a laugh, but it nearly strangled her. Still, she said, "Who're you? The Terminator?"

Okay, he could play light-hearted with the best of 'em. In a deliberately hideous imitation of Schwarzenegger's already horrible accent, Nick said those words again. "I'll be back."

And when the smile on her face stayed put, he felt almost as good as he had the last time he'd scored a touchdown.

Sunday dinner at Mama's.

In any other family, that probably would have meant a pleasant evening, good food, and a visit with the brothers and sisters.

To Nick it was something else.

It was the Colosseum in Rome, filled with lions just off a hunger strike, and he was the fattest Christian in town.

He sat in his car and stared at the house where he'd grown up. It hadn't changed much. Well, except for the paint. Every few years, Mama got some bug up her . . . and decided to stir things up a little. This year, the answer to Mama's decorating binge had been, God help them all, bright, bilious blue with pale green trim on the shutters and dark green trim on the porch railings and floor.

If Papa could see it . . . hell. If Papa could see it, he wouldn't have cared. If it made Mama happy, then it had been all right with her husband. It didn't really bother Nick, either, until he was drafted into the painting team and forced to look at the god-awful colors close up.

Nick's fingers drummed on the leather-wrapped steering wheel. He was stalling. He knew it. Wouldn't have even tried to deny it. Any member of his family, except for his mother, of course, would have understood.

At one time or another, they'd all dawdled outside like condemned prisoners getting one last stroll around the prison yard.

He glanced into the rearview mirror and took a long thoughtful look at the road behind him. The road that could take him back to Tasha's place. He'd been thinking about going back ever since leaving, the night before.

He could just fire up the engine, slide the car into reverse, and get the hell outta Dodge. But just the thought of having to pay the penance for that sent a shiver down his spine. Missing a Sunday dinner was only excused if you were at death's door.

And God help you if you weren't really dying.

No way was he getting out of this, so he might as well get it over with. Grumbling to himself, he climbed out of the car, slammed the door, and hesitated again, on the driveway. From inside the house, lamplight shone through the glistening windowpanes to dot the lawn below. The kitchen door was open, and on the wind, Nick caught a whiff of something incredible, and it was that scent more than anything else that got him moving again.

Nobody cooked like Mama Candellano.

Gravel crunched beneath his feet; the wind coming in off the ocean pushed at him as if trying to get him to the house in a hurry. And the roar of the sea pulsed in the air around him.

He passed his brother Tony's Ford Bronco and Paul's 4Runner parked in the driveway ahead of him. His sister, Carla, wouldn't have had to drive, since she, Jackson, and Reese, Jackson's little girl, lived just down the road.

Carla.

The weak link.

If she'd already spilled her guts to Mama, then Nick was walking into what would turn out to be his wake. If she hadn't, then Nick was in for a long evening trying to dodge his sister's questions.

Shaking his head, he took the back steps, grabbed hold of the doorknob, and paused, listening.

Voices greeted him.

Not single, distinct voices.

Not in this house.

Here it was a riot of sound and conversation. Here the Candellanos outshouted each other. Here everybody talked at once. If you waited for your turn, you might never be heard from.

Steeling himself, he wrenched the door open and stepped into a wall of heat and noise and incredible aromas.

Before anyone could notice him and spoil the moment, Nick concentrated on the scents swirling around him. He inhaled sharply, deeply, savoring the mouth-watering aroma of Mama's sauce. Basil and onion and the spicy tang of Italian sweet sausages flavored the air thickly enough that he should have been able to bite it instead of breathe it. On the stove a pan lid rattled with the steam building up beneath it, and as his sister, Carla, pulled open the oven door, a new, richer blast of scent reached out for him and grabbed his throat.

Calzones.

Even better. *Sausage* calzones. With a side of spaghettini. Oh, man. Nick braced himself, because he knew whatever else the night might bring, he'd at least have a hearty last meal.

"Wipe your feet!" Mama's voice rang out over the crowd. But that wasn't surprising. She'd had to be louder than anyone else over the years, just to make sure they all knew who was in charge.

Dutifully Nick scraped the bottoms of his loafers against the mat on the top step, then walked into the kitchen.

"Tony, if they take away the parking spot in front of the Leaf and Bean," Stevie was arguing, "I'll lose all kinds of business."

"Not my call," Tony answered, grabbing a bread stick out of the tall blue glass jar in the middle of the table. "Take it up with the City Council."

"Yeah, like that'll help." Stevie snatched the bread stick from him. "I might as well talk it over with the Terrible Three for all the good the council will do me."

"Also not my problem," Tony said, dismissing the council and the town gossips while taking another bread stick while glancing at Paul. "Curb your wife."

"What was that?" Stevie nearly shrieked, narrowing blue eyes on Tony until Nick's reflexes kicked in, warning him to duck and stay out of range.

"Whoa. . . ." Paul wisely backed up and away from

the brewing war. "You're on your own, big brother."

"Mama," Beth said, pushing her auburn hair behind her ears, "Tony's been bugging me about making cannoli for weeks. You said you'd talk me through it."

"I will, I will," Mama promised as she wiped her hands on a sparkling white apron. She hurried across the room, swatting at Paul to get him out of her way, then reached up to cup Nick's face in her palms. "Hello, Nicky. You're late."

Warm brown eyes stared up at him. Mama's long graying hair was kept up in a tight bun on top of her head and she wore a dress Nick could swear was twenty years old. But she looked as she always did . . . starched, neat, and utterly Mama.

"Good to see you, too, Mama." He smiled and accepted her welcome kiss gratefully. She wasn't swinging a broom at his head, which meant Carla had—so far—kept her big mouth shut.

He slid a glance at his sister and saw her clamp her lips together. Good. It looked like it was physically painful for her to keep a secret. Small consolation. That's what she got for sticking her nose into his business in the first place.

"Hey, Nick," Jackson said as he stepped up, holding out a cold bottle of beer.

"Hi." Nick took it, unscrewed the top, and lifted the bottle for a long drink. Mama hustled back over to the stove, where Beth started in on her again about cannoli recipes.

On the other side of the table, Tony and Stevie were still arguing, and if anyone had asked, Nick would have put five bucks on Stevie coming out the winner. Carla's dog, Abbey, lay beneath the kitchen table, keeping a hopeful eye out for any dropped tidbits. Tina, Tony's toddler, sat right beside the big dog, pounding its head in affectionate "pats."

"Anything . . . *new*?" Jackson asked in a low-pitched mutter that was missed in the general din.

"No," Nick admitted, curling his fingers tightly around the icy bottle. He'd gotten to know Jonas a little better, had breached some of Tasha's defenses, but hadn't come any closer to solving his problems. "Nothing's been settled."

Jackson blew out a frustrated breath. "We could take care of this in a snap with the test," he whispered.

"Not yet." Now that he'd come to know the kid, Nick wanted to take care of this himself. Find a way to get the boy to understand that Nick wasn't his father. Without having to rub the kid's nose in a test that would name his mother a liar and his dreams a fraud.

"Damn it, Nick—"

"What're you two whispering about, as if I didn't know?" Carla asked, sidling up to stand next to her husband.

Nick glared at her. "Butt out, Carla."

"Not likely."

"Carla honey," Jackson said, bending in as if to kiss her cheek, "go away."

"You, too?"

"Jesus," Nick muttered, taking another long sip of beer. "Why couldn't you have been that little brother we wanted? Or better yet, a puppy?"

"Love you, too."

"Mommy!" Reese came racing up to Carla and grabbed her hand.

Despite her frustration with Nick, Carla instantly smiled at Reese and gave the child her full attention. "What is it, sweetie?"

"Come see the table," the tiny blonde said, tugging at Carla's hand. "I set it and Tina helped me."

"I bet," Nick said softly, thinking about Tony's toddler trying to set a table.

"Well," Reese admitted with a shrug, "she tried."

"Okay, I'm coming," Carla said, but shot Nick a look as she left the room.

He didn't have to be a mind reader to know what that look meant. This wasn't over. Not by a long shot.

"Nicky!" Mama called out his name, giving him the distraction he so desperately wanted. "You carry the calzones into the dining room. Paul, you get the salad, and, Tony, bring the wine."

Calzones, Nick thought as he inhaled the scent of Mama's homemade sausage-and-cheese sandwiches. Triangles of pastry dough were filled with sauce and sausage and mozzarella cheese, then baked until they were a golden brown. Freshly grated Parmesan had been sprinkled over the tops of the calzones and was already melting into the hot sandwiches. More sauce bubbled on the stove behind him, and as Mama filled her huge dark blue pasta bowl with al dente spaghettini, Nick told himself that if the lions smelled half as good, the Christians had probably *danced* into the arena.

Chapter 10

Tasha hadn't had the chance to talk to Molly all day. With a couple of walk-in clients needing attention, along with their scheduled appointments, they'd both been pretty much racing from customer to customer all day.

Now, though, there was time to breathe. And eat. And talk.

The old brass chandelier hung low over the dining table, sending a warm glow of light spilling into the room. The yellow flowered wallpaper looked soft and comforting rather than faded, and the wood floorboards gleamed with reflected light. Sitting on opposite sides of the wide dining room table, Molly and Tasha dug into the dozen or so white cartons in front of them.

"Try the Moo Shu Pork," Molly said around a mouthful. "It's terrific."

"I think Jonas took the last of it upstairs," Tasha told her, and reached for the carton of beef and broccoli. Maneuvering her chopsticks with practiced ease, she helped herself to some broccoli before passing the carton to Molly.

"How's he doing?" Molly asked, shooting a quick look toward the stairs as if half-expecting the boy to pop up. "You know, with Tassel Loafer hanging around?"

Tasha shrugged. She really wasn't sure how Jonas was doing. He hadn't been talking to her as much lately. It was as if the closer he felt to Nick, the further he felt from Tasha. Almost as if he were choosing sides. And she was losing.

Her heart twisted and, no longer hungry, she set her chopsticks down.

"He's not talking to me, Mol," she said, tracing the tip of her finger across one of the gold-colored roses decorating the vinyl tablecloth.

"That's not so unusual," Molly said softly. "Kids are weird."

"Not Jonas," Tasha argued. "At least, not until lately."

"He's got a lot on his mind, poor kid."

"I know. But he's got stars in his eyes, too." Tasha looked at her friend, and in the soft glow of the overhead light, Molly's eyes shone with sympathy and ready understanding. "Nick comes around and Jonas feels like a king. You should have seen him after the game yesterday. All of the other kids were hanging on him, trying to be his best buddy—and he was loving it. He felt so . . . *important*."

Molly set down the carton she was holding and asked, "Is that such a bad thing? I mean, the kid's had a rough life. Maybe he should enjoy the attention."

"I know, and no, it's not a bad thing, but what happens when it's over?" Tasha asked, swiveling in her seat to prop her tired feet up on the chair next to her. "What then? How does Jonas deal with losing something he always wanted? Does he get his heart broken and then spend the rest of his life pretending different? Does he run away and keep running?"

"Hey," Molly said quietly, reaching across the table to lay her hand atop Tasha's. "Who're we talking about here? Jonas . . . or *you*?"

Tasha inhaled sharply, deeply, and then let the air slide out of her lungs in a long, slow exhale. And still she felt no more in control than she had a moment ago. She grabbed Molly's fingers, gave them a squeeze, then let go, to scrape her hair back from her face. "I don't know," she admitted. "Both, maybe?"

"You know, Tash, this doesn't *have* to become a disaster."

"Oh, yeah?"

"Yeah." Molly grinned slyly and grabbed up the carton closest to her. Sniffing and wrinkling her nose, she quickly put the squid down and reached for something else. "Jesus, why does Jonas ask for that stuff and then not eat it?" Spotting the orange chicken, she smiled and took a bite. "I mean, clearly, there's something going on between you and this guy. Maybe you could just talk to him. Be honest. Tell him the truth and that you need his help."

"Ah." Tasha nodded even as her heart turned to stone in her chest. "Great plan." She held up one hand and ticked off items on her fingers as she talked. "Let's see, you want me to tell him that Mimi's dead and we're pretending she isn't so we can hide from Social Services."

"Well . . ."

"Oh. And then I can tell him that the county's already rejected me as a foster mother because of my 'colorful' past."

"Tash . . ." Molly grimaced tightly.

Warming to her theme, Tasha kept going. "Then to finish up, I can tell him that I've been saving money like a crazy person so I can pack up Jonas and run away from the law."

"Okay, shoot me now." Molly lifted both hands in surrender. "Bad idea."

"Ha! Understatement. It's right up there with Noah saying, 'I think it's gonna rain.' "

"Funny."

"I try."

Sighing, Molly set both elbows on the table and leaned in toward Tasha. "How's the savings account looking, anyway?"

"Funny you should ask," she said, and lifted one hip off the chair to pull something from her back pocket. The savings passbook looked just as worn as Tasha felt at the moment. But then, she pulled it out of her dresser to look at it often enough to have the damn thing falling apart. She flipped it open and checked the balance, even though she knew the total, down to the last penny, by heart. "So far, we have a grand total of eight thousand, four hundred seventy-three dollars, and sixty-seven cents."

Molly whistled. "That's not bad."

Tasha ran her fingers over the numbers as if reassuring herself that they were really there. "Not bad, but not great, either. A guy who buys top-of-the-line tennis shoes and those ridiculous loafers is going to have a lot more money behind him than I do."

Molly smiled. "I've got money, too, and you know you can have it."

Tasha looked at the woman across from her and felt a huge swell of emotion rise up and nearly choke her. Molly Watson, friend extraordinaire. The thought of leaving Molly and this house, this place, where she'd made a home for herself nearly broke her heart.

Through the lonely years on her own, living on the street, and even before that, living in a house that fed on the anger writhing inside it, she'd dreamed of this. Having one place to call hers. Having friends and a job and enough food to eat and people to love.

Knowing that she was on the verge of losing it all tore at her. Still . . . stiffening her spine, she straightened her shoulders and lifted her chin. To protect Jonas, she'd walk away—run, if she had to. And start again somewhere else.

But no matter where she ended up, this place would always be home.

"You know I can't let you do that," Tasha said, tucking the passbook back into her pocket. "You're saving for your wedding, Mol. But I love you for offering."

"Hmph." Molly sat back and shook her head. "By the time Jim gets around to asking me, I'll be fifty."

"Think how much you'll have saved by then."

Molly smiled. "Fine. You won't take the money."

"Nope." Tasha shook her head and reached for the orange chicken. "I will, however, take this."

While they ate, Tasha's gaze slid to one side and landed on the latest postcard she'd received from "Mimi"—in reality Helen Simmons, another of Mimi's loyal customers. The glossy photo of the Champs-Elysées only served to remind Tasha of the narrow ledge she was clinging to.

They couldn't pull this subterfuge off forever. Ms. Walker wouldn't believe the traveling excuse much longer. Thankfully, the day-to-day insanity of trying to battle bureaucratic red tape, not to mention the hundred or so cases assigned to her, Ms. Walker didn't have a lot of time to devote to one hard-to-reach foster mother.

The minute that changed, though, the game would be over.

Huddled in that Cadillac, safe from the cold and rain and basking in the heat blasting from the vents on the dashboard, Tasha took stock of her savior. An old hippie with a do-gooder personality. Well, she wouldn't be staying with the old woman long. The rain pounded at the car, slamming tiny wet fists against the roof and the hood, bouncing off the street in front of them, illuminated by the headlights until they looked like fistfuls of diamonds tossed to earth in a rage.

"You look hungry," Mimi said. "We'll stop for a good hot supper and that'll make you feel better."

Tasha just stared at her. Where Tasha came from, people didn't do something for nothing. There was always a catch attached to favors. "What do you want from me, lady?" she asked.

Mimi smiled and shook her head. "All I want is a little conversation," she said. "It's a little lonely, driving by yourself."

"Most people just turn on the radio," Tasha said.

Mimi laughed and the sound rolled out around Tasha, carrying as much warmth as the heated air pouring from the vents. "Ah, but I'm not like most people, now am I?"

"Right. You can let me off anywhere," Tasha said, glancing at the older woman in the driver's seat.

"In the rain?" Mimi said with a shake of her head. "I don't think so."

Tasha sighed. God, that car heater felt good. Every bone in her body almost felt liquid with the delicious sensation of warm air defrosting the ice inside her. But even if she dried out completely, she'd only have to go back out into the cold, wet night. Best to get it over with. "Look, lady, it was nice of you to get me away from those guys, but . . ."

"What?" Mimi asked with a grin. "You have a train to catch? Some appointment?"

"What's it to you, anyway?" Tasha asked.

"I don't know," Mimi said thoughtfully. "Let's just say I've taken a liking to you."

"Swell." Just what she needed. A crazy old hippie as her new best friend.

"Do you believe in fate?"

There wasn't much Tasha believed in. Especially fate. If she did, then she'd have to believe that she somehow deserved being beaten to shit for no good reason. Bad luck she could accept. Getting screwed was something she was used to. But fate? "No."

"Well, I do believe. You know, in fate, the gods, karma, whatever you want to call it." Mimi signaled a left turn and steered the boat of a car down yet another dark street, glittering in patches where unbroken street lamps tried to dispel the gloom. "And I believe there's a reason I was on that street tonight."

"Yeah. You were lost."

"I never get lost. I have an excellent sense of direction."

"You were lost tonight."

"Exactly my point. There was a reason for me to be there," Mimi said, then glanced at Tasha in the soft glow of the dashboard lights. "And a reason you were there, too."

"I should probably tell you," Tasha said, "if you're taking me off to enlist me in your Church of Take the

Suckers to the Cleaner's, I don't have anything for you to take."

Mimi chuckled and shook her head. "Don't worry about that, honey. I told you, there was a reason for us to meet."

Heat seeped more firmly into Tasha's bones and she felt her eyelids drooping. She was so comfortable. So warm. So dry. And the quiet music drifting from the car radio sort of lulled her into a half-sleep. "So what's the reason?" she mumbled.

"I don't know yet," Mimi said quietly, and took another glance at the old-before-her-time girl beside her. The poor child was already asleep. "Rest, honey," Mimi said. "We'll discover the reason for finding each other sooner or later."

Tasha woke up with a start, sitting straight up in bed and staring into the darkness of her room. Heart pounding, eyes filled with tears, she swore she could almost smell Mimi's perfume, that wonderful mix of flowers and oranges.

That long-ago night, Tasha had slept all the way to Santa Barbara. When she awakened, Mimi had stopped at a diner, and over the first hot meal Tasha'd had since her last bowl of soup at the mission, Mimi had offered her the world.

Outside, rain hammered at the old house, plinking against the windowpane and tapping on the roof. Probably the reason for her dream. The rain. It always made her remember that one lucky night when her life had finally taken a good turn.

Tossing the quilt back, she swung her legs off the bed and climbed out. She walked across the room toward the window where a weird half-light came spilling through into the shadows. Lightning flashed and thunder rumbled. Rain pelted at her, trying to get in. Trying to force its way back into her life. To make her that cold, lonely, frightened girl again.

But she wouldn't go back.

No matter what happened, she'd had Mimi in her life. And now she had Jonas. She wasn't alone. She wasn't a kid.

And these days when she got scared, she fought back.

Nick hit the stairs first thing in the morning. Wearing jeans and a sweat shirt, he took a left at the base of the staircase and headed through the kitchen. Ignoring the clanging coming from beneath the sink, he stepped over Michaela's outstretched legs and headed for the back door.

After the storm, the air was clear and crisp and cold. He paused long enough to take a moment to enjoy the view from his new back porch. A semicircle of trees surrounded the small lake that lay at the bottom of a shallow slope just behind his house. Birds skittered across the surface of the still water, no doubt fishing for breakfast. A family of ducks paddled through the reeds waving delicately in the wind, and from a distance, despite the slam of hammers against wood, he heard the muted roar of the ocean.

He should go fishing. He hadn't been fishing in . . . hell. Years. He wondered if Jonas had ever been fishing, and the instant that thought wandered through his brain, Nick realized just how involved he was getting with the kid. Christ. Scowling out at the lake, he asked himself when the hell he'd lost direction. He was supposed to have had this straightened out by now. Instead, he was getting in deeper and deeper.

With a flutter of wings, a big male duck dropped from the sky to settle gracefully on the water's surface, not far from the little family grouping.

Father duck? Nick wondered. If so, he was showing up sort of late in the ducklings' lives. They were already half-grown. Hmm. A metaphor? No, he decided. It was way too early to be thinking about duck metaphors for his own screwed-up life.

He forgot about the stupid ducks and took another big gulp of air, drawing the damp and cold deep within him. A beautiful morning. And one he'd probably enjoy a lot more if he hadn't been up all night chasing leaks in the roof. Of course, he wouldn't have gotten much sleep anyway—not with thoughts of Tasha sliding through his mind all night. She was there. In his brain. In his blood. And he didn't know how to get her out—or even if he wanted to.

"Jo!" he shouted, taking the back steps down to the wet, muddy grass.

"Yeah?" She leaned over the edge of the roof, her long dark brown ponytail hanging over one shoulder to swing in the wind.

"I thought you were supposed to be putting the new roof on yesterday." Nick backed up, his tennis shoes slid in the mud, and he fought to maintain balance.

"Got half of it done, then the storm blew in, and . . ." She shrugged.

"I *know* about the damn storm." Nick didn't even bother to try to charm her. The Marconis had known him long enough to be immune. "I was the one up all night emptying pots that were catching the leaks."

"Hey," she said, clearly offended. "Nick, this place is a wreck and I'm working as fast as I can. You think you can do better, you're welcome to crawl on up here and give me a hand."

"Fine," he muttered. Never argue with a woman, he reminded himself. Especially one holding a hammer. He reached up to shove both hands through his hair and just managed to keep from yanking it out of his head. "You gonna finish it today?"

She sniffed and pulled back from the edge. "If people leave me alone and it doesn't rain . . . *maybe.*"

Nick stared at the spot where she used to be and told himself, "Brilliant. Just fucking brilliant. Piss off the woman who's fixing your roof."

"Jesus, you're a lot of fun in the morning, aren't you?"

Nick turned to look at Samantha as she walked up carrying a can of paint. She had a splotch of white across her nose, testifying to the fresh paint on the porch railing. Nick's gaze dropped to his palms. Sure enough. Twin streaks of white paint. Which meant, he thought with a tired sigh, white paint in his hair, too.

"Rough night," he said as Sam checked out his hair and stifled a laugh.

"Poor baby." There wasn't an ounce of sympathy in her tone. "You could probably use some coffee, huh?"

"God, yes."

"Good. Bring us some when you go to Stevie's, okay?"

She walked past him like he wasn't there, and Nick was left alone in the muddy grass, wondering just when it was he'd lost complete control of his life.

"Any more news from Ms. Walker?" Edna Garret squinted into the mirror as she tried to meet Tasha's gaze and failed.

Tasha smiled anyway. Edna couldn't see two feet in front of her without her Coke-bottle-thick glasses. At eighty, the woman had outlived four husbands and was currently on the lookout for number five. She was also one of the loyal "sending postcards from Mimi" crowd, so Tasha would always love her.

"Nothing lately," she said, and lightly dragged a fine-tooth comb over the back of Edna's thin hair. It was a lovely shade of pinkish gray and had been permed within an inch of its life. Each tight curl clung to Edna's scalp as if terrified it would fall off and join the rest of her missing hair. Grabbing up a can of hair spray, Tasha shot a fine aerosol stream at the woman's head. "But I don't know how long we can keep up the pretense."

Edna reached back and patted Tasha's hand. "As long as we have to, honey."

"Damn straight." Molly grinned as she looked up from the washbowl in the back of the room. "Don't worry. It's working, Tash."

"What's working?"

Every woman in the place swiveled her head toward the open doorway. Tasha's breath staggered from her lungs. Nick Candellano stood there, framed in the open doorway, his wide shoulders nearly brushing the jambs on either side of him. He wore a long-sleeved blood-red dress shirt, open at the throat, and a pair of black slacks with a crease so sharp it looked lethal. Her gaze dropped to his feet. No tassel loafers. Lifting her gaze again, she stared into his eyes and felt something inside her quake a bit.

"What're you doing here?"

He shrugged and stepped into the beauty salon. He looked way too big to be taking up room in the small pink shop. Holding a to-go cup in one hand and a large dark green box in the other, he said, "On my way to work. Wanted to talk to you for a minute."

"I'm busy," she said, and wished to heaven she was just starting Edna's hairdo rather than finishing it.

"Five minutes." He held the box up. "I brought a bribe."

"What kind of bribe?" Edna's nose twitched. "Smells almost as good as he looks."

Tasha just stared at the older woman. Then her gaze shifted to encompass the other women in the place and she noted with an inward sigh that every last one of them was eyeing Nick like he was the last candy bar in town.

"It *is* good," he said with a smile meant to disarm the most wary of women. Walking toward Tasha, he held her gaze with his as he handed the box to the old woman. "Stopped by my sister-in-law's store for coffee, so I picked up some of her goodies, too."

"I like a handsome man who brings presents." Edna opened the box and cooed. "Girls, would you take a whiff of these?"

The two older women in the waiting area sprang out of their chairs and clustered around Edna. Even Molly left Sarah Hastings dripping wet in the sink and came over for a look.

Nick stared into Tasha's eyes as he said, "Stevie's known for her biscotti, and her muffins are legendary." He shrugged. "I brought both."

"Oh God," Molly said around a crunching mouthful. She waved a chocolate-dipped biscotti in the air like a tiny baton. "She *makes* these? From *scratch*?"

"Uh-huh."

"Tash, you gotta try one of these," Molly urged,

dipping her hand back into the box to come up with another one.

"Later," Tasha said tightly. Inhaling sharply, she nodded at Nick and said, "Five minutes."

Leaving the women to fight over the baked goods like starving hounds on a banquet, Tasha led the way into her office. Once inside, she waited for Nick to follow her, then closed the door behind him. Leaning back against it, she looked up at him.

"What is it?"

"Well, that's friendly."

"You want friendly?" she asked, folding her arms across her chest. "Step back out into the shop. Those baked goods just bought you a whole bunch of friends."

Some guard dogs they were, she thought. Waltz a good-looking man past them and they drooled. Dangle a little chocolate in front of them and they all caved in. Even Molly.

Nick pushed one hand through his hair, turned away from her, then just as quickly spun back around to face her. "I was thinking. If it's okay with you, I thought I'd pick Jonas up from school today."

She stiffened. "Why?"

"Because we need to talk, him and me." Shaking his head, Nick threw his hands high, then let them slap against his sides.

"Father-to-son?" she asked.

He winced. "Something like that."

"No," she said flatly, staring at the man who had the power to end her family. Since waking up from that dream the night before, she'd been doing a lot of thinking. And the only thing she knew for sure was that she had to protect Jonas. She was all he had. She would protect him from the state's foster care system, where children were lost under layers of red tape and piles of papers—and she would protect him from this man. The man who might be the father Jonas wanted so badly. "It's not 'something like that,' Nick. It either is or isn't. You are his father or you're not. You remember his mother or you don't."

"I don't, okay?" The words were torn from him and she could see he didn't like the sound of them any more than she did. He wasn't saying he didn't know her. Only that he didn't remember her. There was a difference. She wanted him to say that there was no chance he was the boy's father. But it looked as though neither of them was going to get what they wanted—at least not today.

He looked like he wanted—needed—to pace. But there was nowhere to go. No place to move to. Between the small desk and the one chair, the room was pretty much used up. So rather than move, he took a long, deep breath, then blew it out in one frustrated rush. "Look. This isn't easy for me. I don't know anything about being a father. Never wanted to learn. The *idea* of becoming a father never occurred to me."

"That's what this is about, isn't it?" she asked, coming away from the door to face him. Fury licked at her soul, chewed at her heart. Leaning toward him, she tilted her head back to make sure she was glaring right into his dark brown eyes. "It's not easy. That's what's bugging you. The great Nick Candellano is used to easy. Well, welcome to the real world, pal."

"Easy?" He laughed shortly. "Listen, red. I've been working my ass off my whole life. Running, lifting weights, training. Working through heat that'd suck the air out of your lungs and through cold so deep the water in the sidelines jug had ice skimmed across the top of it."

He leaned in at her until they were nose-to-nose. Neither one of them was willing to give an inch.

Tasha opened her mouth, but he cut her off before she could laugh in his arrogant face.

"I've worked through broken bones and muscles so sore they were screaming." He loomed over her, matching her, glare for glare. "And then in *one* miserable second, it was all over. One fucking tackle that went the wrong way and my knee was blown. I'm done. Finished. At thirty-fucking-three, I'm through. Everything I worked for my whole damn life is gone forever. So don't talk to me about easy, lady."

"You delusional . . ." Tasha surrendered to the temper inside and let it boil to the surface. Planting both hands on his chest, she shoved him as hard as she could and had the satisfaction of pushing him until the backs of his thighs pressed against her desk.

"That's your idea of a rough life?" she countered hotly. "Playing a game? Hearing the applause? Cashing a single paycheck that's probably more than most people will earn in a lifetime?" She snorted a choked-off laugh that scraped her throat and brought tears to her eyes. "Well, poor you. Poor Nick Candellano. Getting your picture taken all the time must have been hell on you. What a nightmare." Sarcasm dripped from her voice and he actually winced, but she kept going, on a roll now and unable, and unwilling, to stop. "Your knee got wrecked. Poor you. You can't play in a game anymore. My heart bleeds."

"I don't need this crap from you," he said through clenched teeth.

"Why not?" she asked. "Hitting a nerve, am I? A

little too close to home? So you were injured. Your knee got hurt. How about having the local thug beat the crap out of you because he wants the few bucks you made cleaning out some old lady's garage? How about not being able to afford to go to the hospital? How about *that,* Mr. Ballplayer?"

A dark flush painted his cheekbones. But he wouldn't back down. "You don't know me."

"I know enough," she said. "All your weight lifting and your workouts? Did you have a place to sleep? Food? Family?"

He frowned at her, his jaw working as if he wanted to speak, but forced himself to be quiet. To let her have her say and get it over with.

"Do you know what it's like to sleep in an alley?" Tasha asked, even though a small corner of her mind was shrieking at her to shut up. She didn't want his pity. Didn't need him to know that the misery of life with her parents had driven her, at fifteen, to the streets. She didn't discuss that with anyone. She didn't even like to remember a time when she was more used to being slapped than spoken to. She never thought about the pain of not being loved by her own parents. The nightmares had stopped long ago and the life she'd built was the only one that interested her.

She'd run away at fifteen, lived on the streets until she was seventeen—and then, thank God, Mimi had entered her life. And now, at twenty-seven, Tasha *knew* what love was. *Knew* that people like Nick Candellano had lived a wildly different childhood than she had.

She didn't want to talk about any of this. But her emotions were in charge now and she couldn't choke the words off. "Have you ever cashed in aluminum cans to buy a hamburger?" She shook her head, sending her hair into a wild tangle around her face. Scooping it back and out of her eyes, she locked gazes with him and kept right on, as if a cork had popped, releasing a torrent of words she'd never thought to say to anyone. "Of course you haven't. When you were sixteen, what did you worry about, football star? Making the team? Who to ask to the prom?" She jabbed her index finger against his chest as if she could drill right through bone to reach his heart. "Well, I worried about the guy sleeping in the box next to me. I learned how to sleep with one eye open. I learned to eat when I could, 'cause there might not be anything tomorrow. I learned that you don't trust anyone and that *nothing* comes easy." She took a long, deep breath. "So don't tell me your sad tales, rich man. They don't mean jack to me."

Nick just looked at her.

What the hell could he say?

Her cheeks were flushed with fury, her eyes sparkling like ice chips in the sun. Her breath was ragged and she looked like she wanted to kick him.

Hell, maybe he should let her.

If the purpose of that tirade was to make him feel like a prick, then she was batting a thousand. "Tasha . . ."

"Swear to God," she said, backing up until the closed door was at her back again. "If you say you're sorry . . ."

The room was practically vibrating with an energy that pulsed around him like a live thing. He wasn't sure what to do. What to say. For the first time in his life, Nick Candellano was speechless. He'd been whining about his bad breaks to a woman who'd had more than her share and still managed to come out whole. Together.

He shook his head warily, sadly. "Are you kidding? Sorry for you? No. Hard to feel sorry for a woman who's been turning my dreams into X-rated films lately."

She sucked in a quick breath.

"Can I be sorry for the kid you were?" he asked. "Damn right I can."

"I'm not that kid anymore," she whispered, and even her voice sounded hollow, as if she'd emptied herself and now there was nothing left. "I left her behind a long time ago."

"Maybe," he said, and took a step closer to her. He moved slowly, carefully, as he would if trying to approach a feral kitten. Prepared for her to run, hoping she wouldn't. His heart ached for what she'd been through, even while another, larger part of him admired the hell out of her. Not many people could come through what she had and remain in one piece. "But I think," he said, his voice soft, gentle, "a part of that girl is still here. In you."

"You're wrong," she said, shaking her head until a single stray tear snaked along her cheek.

"I don't think so."

She reached up and impatiently brushed that tear away with the back of her hand. Then she straightened up, lifted her chin, and met his gaze squarely. "Look, I'm sorry I dumped on you. But I'd appreciate it if you'd just forget it."

He shook his head. "Can't do that," he said, lifting one hand to cup her cheek. "I'm too damned impressed." His thumb stroked across the damp spot on her soft skin.

She laughed shortly, shakily. "Yeah, I'm impressive."

"Red," he said, and bent his head until he was no more than a breath away from her face . . . her mouth, "you have no idea what you do to me."

"I'm not *trying* to do *anything* to you," she whispered.

"And that's the hell of it," he said, staring into those green eyes as if hoping to find something he hadn't known he'd lost. "You don't even have to try."

Then, because he couldn't help himself, because he never would have forgiven himself if he hadn't . . . he kissed her. A soft, tender brush of his lips across hers. And the sizzling heat of that one brief touch of her flesh shot through him. In a moment, it was over and he pulled his head back to stare at her as if he'd never seen her before. Jesus. What was happening to him?

He straightened, shoving his hands deep into his pockets so that he wouldn't grab her and drag her down to the floor with him. She was one tough woman. Forged of steel, but with a soft inner core that called to something deep inside him. He'd never met a woman like Tasha Flynn before.

She tugged at his heart even while she heated his blood and he wanted her so badly he ached with it.

Ah, Jesus. He was in serious trouble. "I'm gonna go now," he said quickly, before he said or did something really stupid.

She moved to one side and Nick pulled his hands from his pockets, grabbing the doorknob. He paused, looked at her again, and slowly, cautiously, lifted his left hand to her cheek.

Her eyes closed briefly at the contact.

"You really are something else, Tasha Flynn."

Her eyes opened. "And you're damn annoying, Nick Candellano."

One corner of his mouth quirked. "So I've been told." He let his hand fall to his side but rubbed his fingers together as if he could still feel her skin. "Oh, yeah. About Jonas . . ."

She swallowed hard and nodded. "You can pick him up. Three o'clock. Edison Elementary."

"I'll be there."

She nodded. "Don't be late. And have him home by six for dinner."

"I know this is gonna sound strange . . . but you can trust me," he said, and stepped through the door, closing it after him.

Tasha leaned forward, resting her forehead against the door. Her heart was pounding and the sting of tears burned at the backs of her eyes. Jesus.

She ran her tongue across her lower lip. She could still taste him. How could a brush of two mouths be so . . . soul-shaking . . . so unnerving?

Things had just gotten a lot more complicated.

CHAPTER 11

Tasha slumped onto the chair, and now that it was *way* too late, she slapped one hand across her big mouth. Horses? Barn door? *Good God.*

Oh, this was so bad in so many ways.

She jumped up from the chair and paced frantically. Of course, in the tiny office, that consisted of three quick steps, a turn, and three quick steps. Oh, Mimi, she thought, the shit just doesn't get any deeper than this.

The office door swung open and Molly stuck her head inside. "Hey, Mr. Cute Butt just left. He wasn't looking too happy and—"

Tasha looked at her friend and grimaced.

"Uh-oh," Molly said, stepping inside and closing the door behind her. "Okay, compared to you, he looked like he was headed to a party. What's going on?"

Tasha inhaled sharply, deeply, and hoped the extra air would calm the swarms of butterflies in her stomach. It didn't. "Oh God. I told him."

"Told him what?"

"Too much."

"About Mimi?" Molly's voice squeaked.

"No, about *me.*" Tasha scraped her hair back from her face with both hands and then let it all fall again to form a dark red curtain on either side of her face. She only wished she could hide behind it. But that wouldn't help. It wouldn't take back everything she'd said to Nick. It wouldn't wipe away the expression on his face when he looked at her. It wouldn't turn back time to help her dig herself out of this mess. So instead of hiding, she blurted, "I actually told him about me living on the streets."

"Ohhhh. . . ." Molly's eyes went wide.

"Yeah. Then I told him he was a wimp, whining about his injury and his football career ending when *I* slept in alleys." Tasha nodded violently. She really had said all of it. Oh God. She still could hardly believe it. Stuff she'd buried. Stuff she tried to never *think* about anymore.

"How'd he take it?"

"*Stunned* would be a good word." Shaking her head, Tasha swallowed hard, to keep the sudden roll of nausea where it belonged.

"Maybe it'll be okay." Molly shrugged helplessly. "I mean, why would he care, right?"

"Sure. Why would he care? The fact that he's rich and settled and famous and could take Jonas away from me in a heartbeat if he wanted to, that should be enough." She eased down to sit on the corner of the desk. "Why should he be interested in the new ammunition I just handed him?"

Molly hissed in a breath. "Right."

"But there's more."

"More?" Molly slumped back against the door. "Jesus. What else is left?"

"I kissed him."

"You—" Molly came away from the door like she was on a spring.

"Well, technically, *he* kissed *me*," Tasha corrected before Molly could get her question out. "But there was definitely kissing."

"*Lips* kissing?"

"No," Tasha said, sarcasm dripping from her voice, "*hand* kissing. Yes, lips. And maybe, just a hint of tongue."

"Whoa." Molly's eyebrows shot up. "Was he as good as I think he is, just by looking at him?"

"Better."

"Whoa."

"Yeah." Tasha rubbed one hand across her mouth, but all she succeeded in doing was reminding herself of that kiss. The soft, gentle brush of his mouth on hers. The snaking ribbons of electricity that sizzled through her.

"Well, this might work out okay then."

"What?" Tasha's gaze snapped to Molly and she could have sworn she actually saw the wheels in her friend's mind whirling.

"Hey, if you can't beat 'em, join 'em."

"Join 'em how?"

"This could be worse, you know. At least he's really cute and a good kisser, judging by the glassy shine in your eyes."

"Which has to do with what?"

"Everything." Molly leaned back against the door again, folded her arms over her chest, and gave Tasha a sly smile. "He likes you, you like him, you get married, and you *both* get Jonas."

Tasha shook her head, then stared at her friend for a long minute. She couldn't even argue with a statement as dumb as that one. Tasha Flynn was so *not* Nick Candellano's type. She didn't have a family. Didn't come from a good home. Hell, she'd lived on the streets as a kid. That's not exactly the kind of woman Nick was going to take home to Mother. Nope. Molly, bless her heart, was just a romantic—with a blind eye. "You know, Molly, sometimes I worry about you."

Evelyn Walker sat at her computer and stared blankly at the screen. The clutter of noise surrounding her—raised voices, the clatter of fingers on keyboards, and the weeping of a solitary child—never touched her.

She was used to it.

Thirty years working in child welfare had made her immune to the sound of tears as well as to the various and sundry excuses people came up with to sidestep her inquiries.

People like Tasha Flynn.

Sitting poker-straight, Evelyn reached for the wafer-thin bone china cup at her elbow. Lifting the rose-bedecked cup to her lips, she took a dainty sip of her still warm Earl Grey tea. Tasha Flynn was hiding something.

Evelyn knew it.

She felt it.

She could smell a lie from a hundred yards off.

Setting her cup gently back down on its matching saucer, she stared at the file, lying open across her desk. Jonas Baker. One of dozens of children she was responsible for, the boy stared back at her, unsmiling in the official photo. Evelyn tapped her fingertips against the paper-littered blotter as she considered his case.

Eleven years old and in the care of a woman so

flighty she'd been on "vacation" for six months. Evelyn's mouth puckered as if she'd bitten into something especially sour. Mimi Castle was undignified, unconventional, and annoying in the extreme. However, the woman had been a foster mother for so many years, she was thought of as a saint in the Santa Cruz area.

Which left Evelyn in the minority when she filed complaints about the woman's frequent displays of unorthodox behavior. For heaven's sake, what woman of seventy actually held a car wash in her front yard to benefit a stranded sea lion? And as for her "hippie" tendencies . . . Evelyn unconsciously straightened in her chair and tugged at her pale blue suit jacket. A woman as old as Mimi had no business wearing braids and moccasins.

But as flighty as the older woman was, Evelyn was forced to admit that Mimi Castle had *never* been incommunicado this long before. Something was wrong. Unfortunately, since Jonas was being well cared for and fed, that put him light-years ahead of the other children she was sworn to protect. So Mimi Castle would stay on Evelyn's back burner a while longer.

But sooner or later—when she could find a little extra time in one of her too-short days—Evelyn would discover whatever it was Tasha Flynn was so determined to hide.

The drive to the small television station outside San Jose was long, familiar, and didn't require a hell of a lot of attention. The truth was, Nick could have driven it in his sleep. So that left his brain plenty of time to wander.

Usually, if left to its own devices, his mind shot

directly to his playing days. Recalling the glory moments, play-by-play. He could remember all of the truly great ones with amazing clarity, as if those small pieces in time had been carved deep into his brain.

Without even trying, he could recapture the heady sensation of a victory run. The thrill of crossing the goal line just a breath ahead of some three-hundred-pounder intent on destroying him. In his thoughts, Nick heard the roar of the crowd and the shrill shriek of the ref's whistle. He remembered exactly how it felt to be standing on the sidelines with his teammates. How their breath puffed into clouds of fog in front of their face masks during the winter games. How spring and summer practice sessions could sweat the life out of a man.

And how good it had been to be a part of something . . . special.

But today he couldn't get Tasha's words out of his mind. He saw her as she must have been. Young, alone. Scared. What had she been running from? What had been so bad that she'd chosen outright danger rather than staying put? Did she have a family somewhere? Someone who might be looking for her? Worrying about her? Or had they been happy to see her go?

Jesus, what kind of family was that? He couldn't even get his mind around that one. To a Candellano, there was nothing more important than family. His mother would have walked into fire for any one of her kids. They'd all known it. His brothers, his sister, and he had all grown up secure in the knowledge that no matter what, they were safe. Loved.

Had Tasha *ever* had that?

Sunlight speared through the bank of dark clouds overhead and sliced right through the windshield and into his eyes. Nick reached for his sunglasses, tugged them on, and squinted anyway. Hell, he felt like his head was going to explode, and at the moment that sounded like a vacation.

He couldn't forget the look in her eyes when she'd faced him down. Couldn't forget the taste of her when she'd—so briefly—kissed him back. Couldn't forget too damn much about her. She was slipping into his life. Into his . . . heart?

Her face filled his mind and it seemed as though he could even taste her scent. No exclusive, expensive perfume for Tasha. She smelled of flowery shampoos and soap and . . . he chuckled and shook his head. Hair spray. Yet somehow those scents combined to become something alluring. Something that was pure Tasha. Something that drove him to distraction the moment he came close enough to catch a hint of her scent.

That woman touched places in him he hadn't been sure existed. Scowling, he reached up to adjust his sunglasses, then scrubbed his hand across his mouth. Damn it, he could still taste her. That one sweet, soft, too-damn-brief kiss had ignited the embers that had been smoking inside him for days. Heat pooled in his belly and reached out with hungry talons to drag across his nerve endings. He wanted her. Wanted her so badly, his whole body ached with it.

And the wanting was something he wasn't used to. Oh, he'd wanted women before. But that had been simple desire. A quick flash of need that was just as quickly eased. But this wanting went deeper.

Ever since he'd first laid eyes on her, he hadn't so much as *thought* about another woman, and that was just not like him. He blew out an exasperated breath, changed lanes, and honked the horn at the idiot merging onto the freeway in front of him, traveling at little more than a crawl. Maybe that was it, he thought, just a little desperately. He'd been so involved with Tasha and Jonas, he'd forgotten about having a life. Getting out. Seeing people. *Women.* Maybe he just needed to get laid.

As much as he'd like to believe that, he couldn't.

It wasn't just sex he wanted.

It was sex with Tasha.

"Okay, enough already," he snapped through gritted teeth. Reaching out, he flipped on the radio, and, instantly a clash of guitars and a slam of drums blasted from the speakers. Good. Just what he needed to get rid of the soft, sexual thoughts invading his brain.

Deliberately he turned his brain from the problem of Tasha to the problem of Jonas. He propped his elbow on the top of the car door, adjusted the lie of his sunglasses again, and squinted into the distance. Jonas. A great kid, but Jesus. This whole thing was spinning way out of control. Every time he saw the boy, Nick was digging his own grave just a little deeper. He was getting sucked into a whirlpool of emotions that he wasn't sure he'd be able to deal with.

If he handled things Jackson's way, there'd be some fallout from the media, maybe. But at least everything would be cut-and-dried. He'd know. Jonas would know. One way or the other.

But maybe . . . Nick wasn't ready to know.

Maybe he just wasn't ready yet to give up on whatever the hell it was he'd found.

Shit.

When his cell phone rang, Nick gratefully lunged at it. Anything was better than his own company at the moment. He turned off the radio and impatiently shoved the earpiece into place, stabbed the SEND button, and growled, "Yeah?"

"Nice talkin' to you, too."

"Travis. Good." Nick hit his left turn signal and squeezed past a slow-moving pickup truck. Keeping his gaze fixed to the road, he asked, "Do you have that address for me?"

"No problem," his agent said, "but why exactly are you going to see the fan mail machine in action?"

Nick frowned. "Because maybe it's time I found out just who was writing to me and what *I'm* saying in response. So, will you call my house and leave the information on the answering machine?"

"Sure. Now, on to business."

"Shoot." His hands fisted on the steering wheel and he punched the accelerator just for the hell of it. Wind screamed past him, shoving through his hair and reducing the sound of Travis's voice to an annoying buzz.

"The Make-A-Wish Foundation is asking for one of your jerseys for their auction again this year."

Nick smiled. He'd always enjoyed going to that auction. Gave him a chance to visit with some sick kids and to feel like he was making a difference. "No problem. Hell, we can offer my helmet, too. Not like I'll be using it."

"Right. So. Anything else you need?"

"A less confusing life?" Nick suggested.

"Hey, if I could offer that, I'd charge twenty percent."

"You would, wouldn't you?" Another driver came up fast behind Nick. The black SUV tore past the Vette doing at least ninety, and when the driver took a swerving left to pass, he just missed clipping the front bumper of the Corvette. "You dumb son of a bitch!" Nick shouted, just to push his heart back down from his throat.

"Problem?" Travis asked.

"Just a moron escaped from the asylum for the day."

"Must be on the freeway."

"Good guess."

"Anyway, there's nothing else?"

"No, thanks."

What he needed his agent couldn't find for him. Hell, he had a job. It wasn't ESPN, but that'd come. Eventually, he guessed. Everybody knew rookies didn't go in and play first string right off. He'd have to work his way up to the big leagues, just as he'd had to prove himself on the playing field. Besides, it wasn't as though he *needed* the work. He'd made more money playing ball than three men could spend in one lifetime.

It was just . . . he *wanted* to work. To be a part of the game he loved. In some way, he wanted to stay connected to football. It was all he knew. All he'd ever wanted. All he'd ever planned on doing.

"Okay." His agent started talking again. "I'll call your place and leave the address you wanted and—"

"Travis," Nick said suddenly, "did you ever think maybe you were in the wrong line of work?"

"What? Is that a complaint?"

"No. I mean," Nick said, trying to explain to Travis what he didn't really understand himself, "do you ever think about what road you might have gone down if you hadn't ended up on the one you're on at the moment?"

"Have you been drinking again?"

Nick snorted a laugh. Well, so much for philosophy. "Forget it. Hell, I don't even know what I'm talking about." Frowning, he tipped his sunglasses down and stared off at a smudge of black rising on the horizon. "Travis, I'll call you later." He ended the call and kept driving, more slowly now as the traffic began to back up.

Scowling into the distance, he watched as twists of smoke drifted and danced on the ever-present wind. Horns blared and tempers shortened as the freeway choked down to not much more than a parking lot. Cars inched along the highway, crawling across the asphalt, getting ever nearer to what had to be a hell of an accident.

Ominous black smoke had thickened into a column. It lifted into the air, twisting, writhing, as it reached for the sky. Nick shuddered. It looked like the hand of death, stretching out greedy fingers as it tossed its latest soul toward heaven.

Instinct and twelve years of Catholic school had him crossing himself for the sake of whoever was lying in the wreckage beneath that smoke.

Sirens screamed as police cars, tire trucks, and ambulances raced along the shoulder. Traffic inched closer, closer, until at last Nick was driving past the scene of a one-car accident.

The black SUV that had passed him in a blur of speed only minutes ago was now lying on its top like an upended turtle. Smoke billowed and poured from beneath the hood and the chassis. Already, bright orange flames were licking at the black paint, blistering, searing.

He didn't want to look but couldn't help himself. Instinct had him wanting to stop, get out, and see if he could help. But dozens of firefighters and cops were already bustling around the scene and wouldn't thank civilians for butting in—no matter how well intentioned. So Nick sat in his car, hands fisted around the steering wheel, squeezing the leather-bound wheel to combat his own sense of helplessness.

Traffic moved again. Haltingly cars chugged forward. Cops blew whistles, shouted, and waved their arms to clear a path for the ambulances and paramedics while their comrades tried to pull the poor bastard out of what was left of his car.

Not ten minutes ago, the driver of that SUV had been in such a damn hurry to get where he was going, he'd taken risks that hadn't paid off. He'd been alive and impatient and Nick had cursed him for it. Now, he wouldn't be arriving anywhere.

A cold chill slipped along Nick's spine and he stepped carefully on the accelerator as traffic moved past the scene of the accident. Choices. It all came down to choices. Football player or doctor. Hairdresser or scientist. Alive . . . or dead. In his rearview mirror Nick watched the smoke until it was nothing more than an indistinct smear in the distance.

And all he could think was just how quickly life . . . everything . . . could be over.

Chapter 12

Jonas was at the front of the mob and had to move fast or get run down by the scattering horde of kids spilling out of the school. When the final bell rang, things got crazy as every kid in the building tried to be the first one out. Even the air smelled better once school was out for the day, and everybody was in a hurry to have fun.

Somebody crashed into him from behind, yelled, "Sorry," and kept running. Jonas didn't even look up. Instead, he kept counting his money. For the third time, he flipped through the dollar bills and smiled to himself when he got up to, "Nine. Nine whole dollars."

"You already counted it like a hundred times," Alex said, and elbowed him in the ribs. "Whatcha gonna do with it?"

"I told you. Tasha's birthday."

Alex grinned and rubbed his palms together. "Yeah, or the game center at Bullwinkle's."

Jonas thought about it for a minute and almost caved in as visions of Space Blasters dazzled his brain. But then he remembered Tasha and shook his head. "Uh-uh. I'm gonna get Tasha something nice."

"Not with nine bucks."

"Dave Hackett's gonna buy a picture, too, so that'll be five more."

Alex shrugged, tossed his dark brown hair out of his eyes, and trudged along beside Jonas as he headed for the front of campus. A cold wind pushed at them and the boys ducked their heads and charged through it like they were tackling a linebacker. Black clouds stacked up in the sky, bouncing into each other, and the distant roll of thunder whispered a warning.

"You have the picture?" Dave yelled as he raced up to join them. With his blond hair shaved short, Dave Hackett looked like a bald fifth grader. But nobody told him that, 'cause Dave was kinda big and he might not like it and a black eye was hard to explain to people.

"Yeah, I've got it." Jonas dropped his backpack to the ground, then knelt beside it and tugged at the zipper. Pulling out a blue San Jose Saints folder, he opened it and took out his last signed picture of Nick. Holding it carefully at the edges, Jonas stared down at his father's smiling face and felt bad about selling his last picture. But he needed the money and Nick said he'd get him more, so that'd be okay, and besides, he had Nick for real now. The pictures weren't *all* he had of him anymore. Now he didn't have to pretend to know Nick and stuff. Now he could see him all the time.

"Okay, here." Jonas stood up and handed the picture over before he could feel bad about it.

"Cool." Dave took the picture and looked at it for a second. Then he frowned. "Hey, how come he signed his name different?"

"Huh?"

Dave scowled at him. "I saw the picture Tommy

Malone bought off you and the handwriting looked different than this one does."

"So?" Jonas had noticed that, too. But it didn't really matter. "Can't a guy change the way he signs his name? Don't you sometimes?"

"Yeah, but—"

"So no big deal."

After a minute or two, Dave shrugged and pulled a crumpled five-dollar bill from his jeans pocket. He handed it over, then looked at Jonas and asked, "So can I meet him, too?"

Already mentally adding the five dollars to his nine, Jonas was hardly paying attention. "What?"

"Nick Candellano. You said he's your dad. So can I meet him?"

Jonas stood up and hefted his too-heavy backpack over his left shoulder. It would be kinda neat if he could get Nick to come to the school, so everybody could see Jonas with him. He smiled thinking about how all the guys would really be surprised and how Nick would call him *sport* again, only this time in front of everybody.

Enjoying the visions swimming through his mind, Jonas indulged himself. Heck, even the principal would want to meet Nick. And then Mr. Viggo would tell Nick what a great son he had and how smart Jonas was and everything—as long as Mr. Viggo didn't tell Nick about the water balloon war behind the science building, then everything would be really great.

Smiling at Dave, he said, "Sure, I'll ask my dad to come sometime and—"

"He's here now."

"Huh?" Nick? Here? Jonas swiveled his head quickly, his gaze sweeping across the grassy yard behind him and the asphalt playground. That quick look encompassed the basketball courts, the handball squares, and the tetherball circles. But all he saw was kids. Everywhere. With a couple of teachers wandering through, still blowing their dumb whistles and shouting. He turned slowly, letting his gaze sweep across everything that was familiar. "Where is he?"

"There."

Jonas shifted a look at a spot just in front of the school, and there he was. Funny, he'd never noticed him. Probably 'cause the red Corvette was so low to the ground, it was blocked by the crowds of kids streaming along the sidewalk in front of it. And if he hadn't known to be looking for him, Jonas never would have noticed Nick, leaning against the car, arms folded across his chest—because there were a few grown-ups surrounding him and he was hard to see. They were all talking and looking at him like he was a movie star or something.

Pride flickered inside Jonas, then was quickly snuffed when he noticed Ms. Carmichael, his English teacher. Worry darted through him, but then Jonas figured since she was smiling, she maybe wasn't telling Nick about that whole report he was supposed to do and how he hadn't finished it yet and it was late.

Besides, he thought, his insides getting all excited again, this was too cool to be worried about. Nick was *here*. At the school. And everybody could see him.

"Sure," Jonas said, already headed toward the Vette. "You can meet him now. You, too, Alex."

The boys moved through the crowd like little eels, slithering in and out of the moving mob of kids, their gazes locked on Nick.

Nick saw them coming. He'd been watching them

for a few minutes—long enough to wonder just what kind of transaction Jonas had made under the big tree. It was too far away for Nick to see much more than money and something else exchanging hands. Dread reared up inside him and he wondered frantically what a little kid Jonas's age could possibly be selling . . . or buying. Dozens of ideas, each more scary than the last, raced through his brain and he wondered how parents did it. How did they manage to keep from worrying themselves into heart attacks on a daily basis? How did they send their kids off to school and not be terrified by what they might encounter there?

Jesus.

Being tackled by a three-hundred-pounder out for blood suddenly seemed like small potatoes. This whole parenthood thing could kill you.

And to top off the worry, Nick hadn't been able to show it, since he was caught, having to smile and nod in all the right places while a few fans asked for autographs and talked about old times. Ordinarily, there was nothing he liked better than listening to people talk about the fan's-eye view of one of his games. He enjoyed reliving great runs and game-winning touchdowns. And he'd always gotten a charge out of giving the fans a little lift. He knew they'd go home and tell their wives, brothers, sisters, whatever, about meeting him, and it was fun knowing he'd be the star of stories that would probably be told for years.

And also, any other time, he might be more than a little interested in Jean Carmichael. She'd introduced herself as an English teacher and Nick could hardly believe it. All of his teachers had been old crones who liked nothing better than making kids' lives miserable.

But Ms. Carmichael was gorgeous, curvy, and more than obviously interested.

Which didn't explain why *he* wasn't.

But Nick pushed that worry aside for later as he watched Jonas approach. The boy squirted through the edges of the crowd like toothpaste from a tube and grinned up at Nick as he rushed toward the Vette.

"Hi!"

"Hi yourself, sport," Nick said, and ruffled the kid's sweaty hair. God, he hoped everything was all right. What had Jonas been selling . . . buying? Nick nodded absently at the adults and one by one they drifted off into the crowd. Well, all but the teacher with the great legs. She hovered just a foot or two away as if waiting for him to turn his attention back to her. Nick couldn't bring himself to care.

Moving in a little closer to him, Jonas mimicked Nick's position and leaned against the Vette himself, as if proving to his friends it was okay. "This is Dave and this is my best friend, Alex. You guys, this is Nick." He took a breath, held it, and added, "My dad."

Nick winced inwardly but didn't say anything to contradict the kid. He remembered too clearly what it was like trying to look good in front of your friends. All an adult had to do was say the wrong thing and a guy could be branded for life. So he grinned at the boys, then shook hands solemnly. "Good to meet you guys."

"Wow," the stocky blond kid muttered, jaw hanging open and eyes bugged until it looked like they were about to roll down his cheeks.

"Hi." Alex swung his too-long hair out of his eyes in an action so like Jonas's habitual movement, Nick almost wondered if they'd choreographed it. It wasn't easy after all, being cool.

"Are you picking me up today?" Jonas asked.

"Yeah." Nick looked down at him, trying to read the boy's eyes. But all he saw was excitement, pleasure at seeing Nick, and he felt a responsibility for this boy's dreams that was heavier than anything he'd ever experienced before. "Tasha said it was all right."

The boy grinned and his dark brown eyes shone like 100-watt bulbs were inside them. "That's great."

Yeah, great, Nick thought. If he hadn't been here, he wouldn't have seen Jonas and his friends doing some kind of deal and he wouldn't now be forced to confront a kid who thought of him as a hero. Well, hell. Even heroes had bad days, right?

"Hey, Nick," Dave said as he held out an eight-by-ten photo. "Would you sign this again? And this time put my name on it?"

"You bet." Nick took the picture, glanced at it, then turned a thoughtful gaze on Jonas. Was this what they'd been doing? Was Jonas selling Nick's pictures? That *would* explain why the boy had asked for more of them. But why? he wondered, and knew the question would have to wait. "You have a pen?"

"Yeah." Jonas bent over, dug through his backpack, came up with a chewed-on white pen, and handed it to him.

Nick pushed away from the car, took a few steps toward the long, low hood, and laid the photo down on the engine-warmed surface. Before he signed it, he looked at the signature already there. *Running Backs Rule, Nick Candellano.* Now he did wince. How corny was that? And who'd come up with it? And why hadn't he known about it before?

Because, he admitted silently, he hadn't cared enough to find out. Which said a lot for the man he was, right?

Not only was it a stupid signature, but the words were written in a scrawl that was nothing like his own. He frowned slightly as he realized that there were pictures of him, just like this one, all over the country. Generically signed by people who'd never even *seen* him, these pictures were tacked up to bedroom walls, taped onto lockers, and stuck into scrapbooks. And every one of those people who had a picture of him was convinced that he had a small, personal piece of Nick Candellano. That somehow he'd cared enough to take the time to sign his own name.

He couldn't help wondering how those fans would feel if they knew the pictures were churned out of an office in Santa Cruz that Nick had never even visited.

But he couldn't change the past. Only the future. And right here, right now, he'd do his best to salvage this one small situation. Gritting his teeth, he shook his head and wrote in a close facsimile to the scrawl across the top of the photo: *To Dave—any friend of Jonas is a friend of mine—Nick Candellano.* He straightened up, handed the picture to the kid, and watched a grin spread across the boy's face as he read it.

"Wow, thanks, Nick."

"No problem," he said, though there were several that he could think of at the moment.

"There's the bus." Alex hitched his backpack higher onto his shoulder and raised one hand in a half-assed salute to Jonas. "I'll call you later. Bye, Nick."

Dave and Alex raced off toward the school bus, disappearing into the crowd of kids jostling for position at the head of the line.

Overhead, the clouds thickened and thunder growled, a little closer now. Nick shot a look at the sky and was silently thankful he'd stopped on the way here to put the top up on the Vette. He shifted his gaze to Jonas. "Hop in."

The kid's face went neon bright. "Cool!"

Jonas clambered into the car and had already buckled up by the time Nick got in. He snapped his seatbelt into place, fired up the engine, and listened to the throaty roar for a second or two before sliding the car into gear and steering carefully through the stream of kids.

"This is a great car," Jonas said, and ran one hand across the cream-colored leather seats.

"I like it, too." Nick felt like he needed a dozen pairs of eyes to make it out of the lot without flattening a herd of running, laughing children. There were hundreds of them, each one of them determined to get a quick start on freedom. Jesus, he remembered the joy of being set free for the day. The world was a wide-open treasure, just waiting to be explored, and there were hours to go before having to report in for school again.

"It's way better than Tasha's van. I mean, her car kinda smells like flowers, ya know? Real girl stuff," Jonas was saying, and Nick listened with half an ear, too intent on escaping the parking lot to pay close attention. "It's kinda old, too, and sort of coughs when she starts it, like this. . . ." He instantly went into a gagging choking sound that was way too realistic.

Out on the street, Nick glanced at the boy beside him, then stepped on the gas. He wasn't really sure how to gently introduce the question that was tugging at the edges of his mind, so rather than beat around the proverbial bush, he just said what he was thinking. "What were you and your friends doing out under that tree?"

Jonas shot him a quick look, then let his gaze slide away, to the passenger window, where he stared at the passing houses as if watching a fascinating movie. "What d'ya mean?"

"Stalling tactic," Nick said, nodding. "Pretty good. I used it myself a lot."

"Huh?" The boy turned to look at Nick and widened his eyes until they were practically shouting *innocent.* And that was almost enough by itself to convince Nick he just might be the kid's father after all. That ability to look sweet as pie *had* to be genetic.

"Save it for Tasha," Nick advised, giving the kid a slight smile. "I *invented* that 'who, me?' look."

A second or two ticked past before the boy gave it up with a sigh that fluttered the hair hanging over his eyes. Then he shrugged and fiddled with the strap of his backpack, sitting on the floor between his knees. "I was just selling Dave that picture."

Okay, relief really could feel almost like a good stiff drink. It poured through Nick's veins and pooled in the pit of his stomach. Not that he'd actually thought the kid might be buying or selling drugs, but these days you just never knew.

Nodding, Nick hit his right turn blinker, steered the car around the corner, and flashed the boy a quick look. "You mean you were selling your friend the pictures you got for free."

"Well . . . *yeah. . . .*"

"Why?"

That shrug again. A really annoying gesture, Nick

thought, and wondered why he'd never noticed that before.

"I needed the money."

"For what?" And before the kid could do it again, Nick ordered, "Don't shrug. Talk."

Jonas caught himself in the act, then swiveled his head to look up at Nick. Squinting past the hair in his eyes, he said, "Tasha's birthday's comin' and I wanted to get her something and I figured you could get me more pictures if you wanted and then I could make more money and get her something nice, you know?"

Jesus.

The kid hadn't even taken a breath.

He knew he should stop the boy from selling those publicity pictures. It wasn't fair to sell what any fan could get just by writing a letter. But at the same time, he remembered what it had been like when he was a kid trying to get money to buy Mama a present. He'd worked for the neighbors, washed cars, done whatever he could, trying to get something nice. Could he really blame Jonas for doing the same things?

Nick sighed. "When's Tasha's birthday?"

Jonas smiled. "Next week. It's the eighteenth. And I wanna get her something really nice this year 'cause she's been so worried about—" He broke off and shifted his gaze away from Nick's.

"What's she worried about?" Nick asked, surprising himself with just how much he cared about the answer to the question. "Me?"

"Kinda. But there's other stuff, too."

What could possibly scare that woman? Nick wondered. With all she'd accomplished and overcome, what would have the power to worry her? And why did it bother him so much to know that she was frightened?

The light turned green and Nick moved with the traffic and changed lanes to take the freeway entrance.

"Where we goin'?" Jonas asked.

"My house," Nick told him, making up his mind just as the rain began to fall. In the rain, the Marconis wouldn't be working. No one would see Jonas at his house and ask questions he wasn't prepared to answer yet.

He didn't know if he could be everything the boy wanted him to be, but he could at least help him buy a present for a woman who was fast becoming as important to Nick as she was to Jonas. "If you want to earn money to buy Tasha a present, you can do some chores for me."

The pot of stew at the back of the stove bubbled gently, sending clouds of richly scented steam into the air. The windows overlooking the backyard were fogged over and rain pelted at the other side of the glass. Alone, Tasha wandered from the kitchen, through the empty dining room, and into the quiet living room. Her footsteps echoed and sounded overly loud in the cavernous house. The Victorian was like a mother whose children had all grown up and left her.

Abandoned, silent, filled with memories.

Tasha let her gaze sweep across the familiar rooms and she realized with a shudder that she could still lose Jonas. That she might be here, alone in this house, trying to remember the sound of his too-big feet clambering up the stairs.

When her heart ached at the thought, she pushed it

away, not wanting to torture herself. Instead, she walked to the front door, pulled it open, and stepped out onto the porch.

Wrapping her arms around her middle, she shivered slightly and turned her face into the wind. Rain hammered the yard and puddled at the foot of the steps. The leafless trees along the front of the house swayed like naked dancers and rattled their limbs to keep time. Tasha stepped to the edge of the wide porch and squinted into the windblown wet as she watched for a set of headlights that didn't come.

She never should have let Nick pick Jonas up from school. "Of course, you never should have told him about you living on the streets, either," she muttered, more to hear the sound of her own voice in the quiet than anything else. Tasha grimaced tightly and let her head fall back. Staring up at the porch roof, she whispered, "Then you let him kiss you. Real smart. Tell the enemy that you used to be a homeless person, then play tonsil hockey. Really smooth."

Okay, not quite tonsil hockey. The kiss had been too . . . gentle for that. But there'd been hints of what could happen. Promises of more to come in that tender brushing of lips. And it didn't make Tasha feel any better to silently admit that she *wanted* more. She shouldn't. But what a person *should* want and what she *actually* wanted were usually two very different things.

She hadn't even been able to lose herself in work, either. Once the rain had started, her clients had called one by one to cancel their appointments. So Tasha'd had most of the day to wander through the big empty house and analyze everything she'd said to Nick. And every second of that so-brief kiss. She knew it was nothing. Just a kiss. Nothing special. Nothing life-altering.

To a man like Nick Candellano, kisses were just appetizers. And she wasn't about to be anyone's main course, so that left them exactly . . . where?

Straightening up, she walked over to the rail and leaned on it, tempted to stick her head under the steady runoff from the roof. Nature's cold shower. But she had a feeling it wouldn't help.

The phone rang. Swiveling her head, she glanced at the open front door and the slice of lamplight spilling through it. The phone rang again, shrill in the silence. Somehow, she knew it would be him. Heading into the house, she picked up the portable phone on the third ring. "Hello?"

"It's not six yet," Nick said, "so I'm not officially late."

His voice was low and soft and silky and sent shivers along her spine that had nothing to do with the cold wind slipping through the open front door. She glanced at the clock on the VCR. He was late bringing Jonas back and she didn't want to be amused. "It's a quarter to," she told him, and shut the door before walking into the living room to curl up in one corner of the overstuffed sofa. "So, unless you're driving down our street, you're late."

"Technically, yes."

"Just technically?"

"Okay, literally, too."

She smiled, damn it. The sound of his voice was warm and liquid and she didn't want to be affected by it, but she was.

"You're smiling, aren't you?" he asked.

"No."

"Liar."

"Nick," she said on a sigh, "why aren't you here?"

"Jonas isn't finished earning money yet."

"What?"

"It's guy stuff," he assured her, and Tasha felt a twinge at the edges of her heart. Guy stuff. Which left Tasha out in the cold. How could she compete with a man who might be Jonas's father? How could she hope to provide everything Jonas needed when she so clearly couldn't even give him "guy stuff"?

It hurt to admit she'd already lost a part of the boy to the man whose attentions Jonas had so needed. Every little boy needed a man to look up to. To emulate. The question was, was Nick Candellano the right kind of role model?

"Tasha? You there?"

"Yeah," she said, drawing her knees up under her. "I'm here and his dinner's ready."

"Dinner. Sounds good. What're we having?" Nick asked.

"We?"

"Ahh . . . Tasha. On a cold and rainy night, you wouldn't let a man leave your house . . . hungry, would you?"

Had his voice dropped an octave or two? Her stomach skittered nervously and she swallowed hard, reminding herself that one kiss didn't mean anything. That Nick Candellano was a man used to women falling at his feet. That *she* didn't fall at *anyone's* feet.

"Look, Nick, I—"

"I've been thinking about you today," he interrupted her smoothly.

Her grip on the phone tightened until she thought she might just crumble the thing into dust. "Why?"

"You're the kind of woman who tends to haunt a man's mind."

She tried to laugh, but the chuckle dried up in her throat and almost strangled her. "Great. Like a horror movie?"

He sighed and she could have sworn she felt the brush of his warm breath right through the phone. "No. . . ." One word, and so much lay within it.

"Nick . . ." She had to get him to stop. She didn't want to be attracted to him and wouldn't allow anything to happen between them.

"Don't say it," he said, his voice scraping along her spine again in a deep rumble that seemed to echo throughout her body. "Don't say something you might have to take back later."

Tasha shoved one hand through her hair and tried not to notice the tremor in her fingers. He wasn't even in the room with her and still he'd managed to set her blood on fire and stir her nerves until she felt nearly dizzy.

After a long moment or two, Nick inhaled deeply and blew the air out in a rush. "Okay. So. Jonas is about finished sweeping out the garage. We'll be at your place by six-thirty."

"All right."

"You gonna feed me?" he asked, and she heard the smile in his voice.

"I'll give you dinner," Tasha said. "But that's the only appetite that's going to be satisfied."

"It's a start, Tasha," he said quietly. "It's a start."

CHAPTER 13

Just mom and dad and son, sitting around the dinner table. It was weird. A little surreal.

And *way* too comfortable.

A small voice in Tasha's mind fought against that comfort even as a larger part of her hungered for it. Secretly, in a corner of her heart she rarely acknowledged, she'd been longing for just such a traditional, cozy setting all her life. It didn't make sense. It wasn't as if she'd ever known that kind of simple comfort. And maybe that's why the hunger had remained so strong. If she'd once had it and lost it, at least she could tell herself that once upon a time it had all been hers. She could have clung to the memory. Taken it out and dusted it occasionally. But since she'd never known that little pleasure, a piece of her heart was still convinced that she was owed it. That one day . . . It was stupid and she knew it, but that didn't seem to stop the feelings that crept through her.

Outside, rain pelted the windows and hammered at the roof. Thunder rumbled and lightning flashed in brief, brilliant stabs of light that winked in and out of existence, illuminating the dining room like a spotlight flickering on and off a stage.

Inside, there was warmth and laughter and a sense of—she didn't want to use the word *family*. But that's what leaped to the front of her mind. Somehow, someway, Nick Candellano had insinuated himself so deep into their lives that it wouldn't be only Jonas to miss him when he eventually left—and he *would* leave, she knew. He wasn't here because he wanted to be. He'd be here only long enough to straighten out this situation with Jonas. Then he'd be gone. Back to his own life. Back to his own world—where little boys and former-runaway beauticians weren't wanted and didn't belong.

At the thought of him leaving, though, she felt a twinge of something she was pretty sure was pain—and she resented it. She hadn't asked Nick to step into her life and screw with it. She hadn't *wanted* a man to wake up feelings she'd thought long buried. And now she didn't *want* him to go, damn it. But she wasn't the important one here.

"Then what happened?" Jonas asked breathlessly, his gaze locked on Nick.

Nick moved the salt and pepper shakers around on the table, representing opposing football players, then slid the Parmesan cheese—*him*—around both of them toward an invisible goal line. "I faked 'em both out, did a half-turn and swept around one side—then made a dash for the end zone. *Touchdown!*"

Jonas cheered as if the play had just happened.

Nick grinned, first at the boy, then at Tasha. The full power of that grin hit her hard, and her breath staggered in her lungs. Thankfully, he shifted his gaze back to Jonas a heartbeat later and Tasha could breathe again.

"I wish you were still playing so I could go and watch you," Jonas said wistfully.

Nick sighed. "I wish I was still playing, too." Then

he shrugged. "I could take you to the stadium, show you around."

Jonas practically vibrated in his chair.

Tasha tensed. *Take him to the stadium.* There it was. A blatant symbol of how much ground she was losing. Nick strolled in and lit up Jonas's world like Vegas at midnight and Tasha was the drag. The homework tyrant. Nick was vacation. Tasha was drudgery.

Nick would take him.

Resentment pooled in the pit of her stomach as her gaze slid toward Nick. Focused on Jonas, the man was unaware of her fury, and even while she admitted that, she told herself she was overreacting. He wasn't saying he was going to throw the boy in an RV and hit the road. It was just a visit to the stadium.

God, she was losing it completely.

"Can I see the locker room?" Jonas asked.

"You bet." Nick took a drink of his iced tea. "I'll take you out onto the field, too."

"Wow, cool." Jonas's eyes shone with anticipation and an excitement that worried Tasha. The boy was flying so high, the inevitable fall was bound to crush him.

Sympathy welled up inside her as she watched the sparkle in Jonas's eyes and the delighted grin that split his features as he responded to Nick. She glanced across the table to Nick and watched his expressions shift and change as he launched into yet another story about his football-playing days. Looking back at Jonas, she saw how the boy ate it all up. Every word soaked into him as though he were a sponge and Nick a puddle.

How long before that sparkle was gone—replaced by tears? And how would she be able to help Jonas through the misery when she, too, would be wrapped up in pain?

Tasha reached for her coffee and took a long sip. How had Nick done it? For years, she'd protected her heart, guarded it against everyone—until Mimi. And then Jonas. For them, she'd opened herself up to the risk of pain, but she'd found love. And a family—and they'd filled all but one of the empty corners of her heart. She'd been happy, damn it. Happier than she'd ever thought to be. Then Mimi was gone, but even through the pain of loss and the fear of losing Jonas, there'd still been the comfort of the world she'd created and her place in it. Now Nick was here and everything was unsettled again.

He'd sneaked past her defenses. She hadn't seen him coming. Hadn't thought she would respond as, no doubt, countless women before her had responded to him. And now that she had, she didn't have a clue what to do about it.

"What do you think, Tasha?"

"Hmm?" She blinked, disoriented as if waking up from a nap, and shifted a glance at first Jonas, then Nick. "Think about what?"

"Jonas asked me to take him to the father-son camp-out next month."

Oh, Jonas. Her heart ached for the little boy who so wanted to be just like the other guys. He'd never had a father-son weekend. The closest he ever came was tagging along with Alex and his father. And though Mr. Medina was a sweetheart and worked hard to treat Jonas just as he did his own son, she knew Jonas felt the difference. He'd been on the outside looking in for too long. Like a kid with his nose pressed against a toy store window, he watched while everyone else played.

She knew he wanted it, but damn it, she wished he'd said something to her first. Maybe she could have talked him out of it. But as she looked into the boy's big brown eyes, she knew that was a forlorn hope.

"Jonas . . ."

"It'd be great, Tasha," the boy said, words racing out of his mouth in a wild attempt to keep her from popping his balloon. "Alex and his dad are going again and we could camp next to them and—"

"Jonas, I'm sure Mr. Medina would let you go with him and Alex again."

His features twisted into a mask of stubbornness she recognized. When his heart and mind were set on something, Jonas had a head like a rock. "I don't want to go with them. I want to go with my own dad." He looked at Nick. "You'll go, won't you?"

Tasha looked at him, too. She waited for him to say *something*. To remind the boy that none of them knew for sure that Nick was his father. That they shouldn't take the relationship for granted. But he didn't say any of that. He looked as though he wanted to sprint for the door, but to give him his due, he met Jonas's hopeful, nearly desperate gaze calmly.

"I, uh—"

"We don't have to stay the whole weekend," Jonas said, trying to make it easy.

"Jonas," Tasha put in, wanting to help and not sure what to do about it.

"It's not that," Nick said, and flicked a quick look at Tasha before turning back to face Jonas. "But a father-son thing is pretty important and—"

"I know," Jonas interrupted him, and there was just the slightest shine of panic in his eyes now. Tasha's heart ached for him. It was as if he knew and feared he was losing ground, so he scrambled even harder. "That's why I want to go. 'Cause you're my dad and I want everybody to know and—"

"I know, but—" Nick started.

"Jonas," Tasha interrupted them both. She wasn't sure why. Maybe if she'd let Nick ramble a few more minutes, he might have gotten around to a little truth telling. To try to ease the boy down from the cloud of dreams he'd been drifting on for days. But she'd never know that now. "Jonas, why don't you let Nick think about it for a day or two? I'm sure he's got to check to see if he's free or not."

Disappointment turned Jonas's spine into a noodle. He slumped bonelessly in his chair, and for a minute Tasha was afraid he'd just ooze right down onto the floor. Then he found an outlet. He kicked one sneakered foot against the table leg and rattled the dishes.

"Jonas . . ."

"I'll go."

"All right!" Instantly Jonas shot straight up in his chair and punched one fist high in victory. "That's *so* cool. It's gonna be great. You'll see. You'll like it and we can cook over a fire and . . ."

While Jonas rambled excitedly, Nick shifted a look at Tasha and shrugged helplessly.

Tasha bit down hard on her bottom lip to keep from saying something she didn't want Jonas to hear. Didn't Nick see that the more time he gave the boy, the more it would tear Jonas apart when Nick's visits ended? Didn't he know that by facing the truth of the situation, no matter what it was, he would be doing Jonas a favor? Didn't he care?

Facing the truth wouldn't be easy for *her*, either. If Nick was Jonas's father, then she would lose him to a man she wasn't sure deserved him. If Nick *wasn't* his father, then she still stood a good chance of losing this child of her heart to the state. But even she couldn't let the situation drift endlessly.

When she thought she could talk without shrieking, she interrupted the boy's excited monologue, "You're finished eating, Jonas, so go up and do your homework."

"Aw, Tasha. . . ." He flipped his hair back out of his eyes and that one little action sparked something inside her.

"And tomorrow, I'm cutting your hair."

He looked horrified. "No way."

"You're going blind."

"I can see okay."

"Not for long."

Jonas blew out an impatient breath. "Tasha, I gotta talk to Nick about the camp-out and—"

But Nick was standing up, shaking his head. "A smart man knows when not to argue with a woman," he said. "We'll talk later. Right now, you go on and do your homework."

"Aw . . . all right." Disgusted but moving, Jonas slid out of his chair and started for the stairs. Feet shuffling, head down and shaking in disgust, he muttered, "Sometimes being a kid just sucks."

"You ain't seen nothin' yet," Nick said softly.

But Tasha hardly noticed—she was just too stunned. Hurt warred with disbelief and ballooned in her chest until it was painful just to breathe. Tears burned at the backs of her eyes, but she refused to let them fall, keeping them at bay by sheer force of will.

She listened to Jonas's footsteps as he slogged up the stairs like a beaten man. Every step hammered against her heart. Every stomp echoed in her mind. She was losing him. Little by little, she was losing the boy who meant everything to her.

And she didn't know how to stop this runaway train headed for disaster. Upstairs, Jonas's bedroom door slammed, and she winced at the crash.

"What's wrong?"

Tasha stared at Nick and shook her head. He didn't get it. He didn't even know what had just happened. What he'd done. Damn it. She was hurt and he was clueless. *So* not a good sign.

"Tasha?"

She swallowed past the knot lodged in her throat and forced air into her lungs. God, she wanted to tell him. But admitting anything now would just give him more power over her. Once he knew he could hurt her, he'd do it again. People always did. It was human nature. So she lied. Something she'd been doing too much of since meeting him. "Nothing."

"You're a lousy liar. Have I mentioned that before?"

She fixed him with a glare that should have curled his hair. "And as an expert, you would know, right?" Tasha stood up, too, and walked toward the living room. Toward the front door, which she would open and wait for Nick to walk through.

"Where'd that come from?" He caught up with her in a few long steps. He grabbed her upper arm and dragged her to a stop before she could get across the room. His brown eyes narrowed on her and he had the nerve, she thought, to look confused. And insulted.

Tasha yanked free of his grip and pushed one hand through her hair, dragging her nails along her scalp. Just to distract herself from the lingering pain inside. Keeping her voice low to make sure Jonas didn't overhear anything, she said, "I don't want to talk about it. Just never mind."

"Oh, no." He laughed shortly, but there was no humor in the quiet, harsh sound. "None of that female mind game shit." He flicked a glance past her toward the staircase, then looked back into her eyes again. "Say what you mean and don't give me that old 'if you don't know then I'm not going to tell you' crap."

Tasha swung her hair back and glared up at him. She wanted to scream at him and couldn't. Her voice came in a low hush that scraped her throat and fed her pain. "I don't *have* to say anything to you. Except good-bye."

She took another step, but he grabbed her arm again. Tasha blew out a frustrated breath and stared down at his hand on her arm until he let her go again.

"I just want to know what the hell I did wrong. How'd we go from *Leave It to Beaver* to *The Twilight Zone* in less than ten seconds?"

"You watched too much TV as a kid."

"Too much now, too. Not the point."

"What *is* the point, then?"

"I want to know what the hell set you off. What bug, exactly, crawled up your ass and died?"

"That was charming," she said with a tight smile. "Thanks."

"Fine. I'm a pig with no manners. Just curiosity. So talk."

"You don't get it at all, do you?"

He snorted a laugh and glanced around the empty room as if looking for witnesses to speak up on his behalf. "I think I've made that pretty clear, yeah."

"You told Jonas what to do."

"What?"

"You told him to go do his homework."

He stared at her for a long minute. "You're kidding, right?"

"*And* he did it."

"This is nuts." He shook his head and watched her through wide, confused eyes. "You're still talking in circles. Cut the female mind warp and just say what's buggin' you."

"*You* are bugging me." She poked at his chest with her index finger. "You and your 'I'm so great and every kid's dream of a dad' attitude."

"I'm nobody's idea of a great dad. Never said I was."

"You didn't have to. You roll in here with your Corvette and your 'Hi, sport.' " She swaggered a little as she said that, in a ludicrous imitation of him, just for effect. "Who can compete with that? Not me," she said, walking a slow circle around him. Crossing her arms over her chest, she kept talking, and as she did, she felt that knot in her throat tighten until she was pretty sure she was about to choke. Yet she couldn't stop. Couldn't let it go. "You're going to a father-son thing with him. I can't give him that. I'm just Tasha. Old news. You're the football hero come to save the day." She circled in front of him and unfolded her arms long enough to poke his chest again, then kept walking. "And then you tell him to do homework and he does it. He took an order from you and fought it from me. He *did* what you told him to do." Behind him now, she gave him a shove that didn't budge him an inch.

She wanted to push him out of the house. Out of their lives. Out of Jonas's heart and out of her mind. But Nick Candellano was damn near immovable. He was staking a claim on her world and he didn't even really want it. He was doing it because it was easy. God, the hardest thing she'd ever done was keep her world together. And without even trying, he was destroying it.

"Just to be clear," Nick asked, his voice low and dangerous, "I told him to do his homework and I'm the devil?" He turned around to look at her again.

"Yes," she blurted. "No. Hell."

"Well, as long as you're sure . . ."

Tasha's gaze snapped up to his and she saw the smile in his dark brown eyes.

But she wasn't appeased. It didn't help. His charm was just a balm on an open wound. And the pain squeezed her chest until she heard herself whisper, "You're taking him from me." Oh God, just saying the words tore at her heart and made her eyes burn with tears that shimmered up from her soul. "A piece at a time, you're taking him," she continued brokenly, "and I can't fight it. I don't know how. Or even if I should."

A single tear trickled from the corner of her eye and arrowed straight into Nick's heart. Jesus Christ. Watching a strong woman cry was enough to kill a man. Knowing he'd caused it just hammered the nails into his coffin.

"Christ, Tasha," he said, keeping his voice low, soft, in a sad attempt at soothing her. "I'm not trying to take him from you. I'm just trying to do the right thing."

She angrily swiped the tear away with the back of her hand. "That doesn't make me feel any better."

"I've never been in this position before," Nick said, and knew it for a gigantic understatement. "And I'm not even sure what the right thing is anymore." She opened her mouth to say something, but he hurried on and cut her off before she could get started. "All I know for sure is, I've let down a lot of people over the years. And I don't want Jonas added to the list."

She swallowed hard. "I'm glad of that, anyway. But don't you see? You're only here because you *might* be his dad. What if you're not? What then?"

"I don't know." He reached for her, dropping both hands onto her shoulders. So narrow, he thought. So fragile to be carrying so many burdens. "And you're right. Jonas was the first reason I came here. But now, he's not the only reason."

"Don't," she said softly, but her heart wasn't in it. Her eyes darkened despite the haunting shadow of pain and he read a quickening there that set off sparks inside him.

"Tasha . . ." He slid his hands up and down her arms, rubbing, caressing, soothing. What the hell was he supposed to say? He wasn't interested in her? He didn't want her so much he could hardly breathe? He was sorry for fucking up her life? He had a feeling she wouldn't want to hear any of it anyway.

Damn it, there was no win here. If he was Jonas's father, then he and Tasha—not to mention the long-missing Mimi—were going to have to decide where to go from here, together. If he wasn't Jonas's father, then this was all for nothing. He wouldn't have any reason to come back here. To spend time with the boy.

With Tasha.

He looked down into those grass green eyes and suddenly couldn't stand the idea of never seeing her again.

When had that happened?

When had Tasha become important enough to *really* matter?

"What?" she whispered as he continued to stare at her.

"I'm just . . ." He shook his head, then shifted his hands, sliding up the length of her arms, along her shoulders, and up to cup her face in his palms. "You keep surprising me, Tasha," he said.

She reached up and covered his hands with her own. She tried to pull his hands away, but he wouldn't budge. The warmth of her skin beneath his palms was something he didn't want to surrender just yet.

"Nick . . ."

"You know when I kissed you before?"

"It was a mistake." She swallowed hard, her gaze locked with his. Her eyes shone in the lamplight and dazzled him with a beauty that was soul deep.

"It was too short," he said, lowering his head slowly, inch by inch, toward hers. "Too quick, too soft, too good to not repeat."

Her breath came fast and furious and as he dipped lower, closer, her breath fanned his cheeks and fueled the flames within. His thumbs stroked her damp cheekbones, sliding across her smooth, pale skin with a touch so light, it was almost the *promise* of a touch.

"I think we need to try it again," he murmured when his mouth was just a kiss away from hers.

"I can't think when you're this close," she admitted.

Nick smiled. "Good."

Then he claimed her mouth with his, lips moving over hers at first gently, tenderly. But as she leaned into him, he gave himself up to the want within and took her mouth in a plundering kiss that ravaged him and left her gasping.

He parted her lips with his tongue, sweeping into her warmth, exploring, discovering her secrets. Her hands came up slowly to wrap around his neck and she held on, her hands fisting in his hair.

He shifted slightly, changing his grip on her, wrapping his arms around her middle and clutching her close. Close enough that the thundering of her heart echoed within him. He felt each clamoring breath rushing in and out of her lungs. Each small sigh that whispered from the back of her throat.

She leaned into him closely, and the hard tips of her nipples pressed into his body and set him on fire.

He lavished attention on her mouth. The mouth that had driven him to distraction from the moment they'd met. And it wasn't enough. He needed more.

He needed *all.*

But a moment later, when she pulled her head back, breaking the kiss and gulping in air like a woman about to drown, he knew he wouldn't be getting it. Not tonight, anyway.

"Jonas," she whispered the warning brokenly, leaning her forehead against his chest.

He rested his chin on top of her head and fought to steady his own heartbeat. When he thought he could talk without whimpering, Nick tried for humor, saying, "Let him get his own girl."

"You have to go." She let go of him, her hands sliding down his arms and then drifting away from him completely, severing a touch that he hadn't known would be so . . . compelling.

He felt empty, damn it. Without her hands on him, he felt empty.

And that scared the shit out of him.

"Yeah," he said, and took one long step backward. Better to keep a safe distance between them. A light-year or two should do the trick. "I'd better go. Now."

He headed for the front door before he could change his mind, throw logic *and* Tasha to the floor, and say to hell with doing the right thing. He damn sure hoped she wouldn't notice that he was walking a little bow-legged. Hell, he hadn't hurt this bad since high school.

He didn't look back. Didn't trust himself to look into those eyes of hers and still be able to leave. Didn't want to know if she was as torn up and on edge as he was. Didn't think he could leave if he knew she wanted him as bad as he wanted her.

Jesus.

He walked out the front door and down the steps, tipping his face up into the cold rain. He scraped his hair back and let the drops hammer against his skin like icy slaps from heaven.

But it was going to have to rain a hell of a lot harder to put out the fire Tasha had started.

From the top of the stairs Jonas watched Tasha close the front door and fall back against it like she was too weak to stand up or something. He moved out of the light and stepped farther into the shadows, so she wouldn't know he'd seen her kissing Nick.

Weird stuff was spinning in his head. Jonas had come out of his room to remind Nick about his next football game, 'cause he'd said he would go, but just in case he forgot . . . But then he saw Nick and Tasha arguing real quiet, so he couldn't hear what they were saying.

But they looked really mad, so he figured he'd stay there to keep watch, 'cause he really liked Nick, but he had to take care of Tasha, right? But then Nick kissed her and Tasha kissed him back and then Jonas couldn't leave 'cause it was just too . . . weird.

He swung his hair back from his face—thought maybe Tasha was right about the haircut thing—and looked at Tasha again. She didn't look mad anymore. She was smiling, sort of. And she looked kind of like Molly looked whenever her boyfriend came to pick her up from work. All shiny-eyed and kind of excited.

And he wasn't real sure how he felt about that.

Chapter 14

"I fired them."

"Who?" Paul asked.

"Two nanas." Nick yanked at his hair with enough strength to snatch himself bald. But the accompanying pain didn't quite diminish the guilt chewing at his insides. He'd needed to tell somebody about it. Hell, Nick admitted silently, he'd needed to talk about everything. Which was why he was standing here on his brother's backyard deck confessing to something he still didn't believe himself. "I fired two little old nanas."

Paul laughed shortly, then forced his grin into submission when he caught Nick's dirty look. "That probably didn't do much for your karma."

"Funny. Thanks. I really needed that." Paul could make jokes. He wasn't the one who'd had to look two little old ladies in the eye and tell them they were out of a job.

Nick'd gone to the address Travis had left on his answering machine, determined to view the "fan mail machine" in action. But he hadn't been prepared for the truth. He wasn't quite sure what he'd been expecting, but it sure as hell hadn't been two grandmotherly types, sitting at a long folding table, signing pictures of *him.* They'd offered him tea and cookies, showed him pictures of their grandchildren, then given him a tour of the square, joyless office where they toiled, pretending to be a professional football player.

Ridiculous, he thought now, with a shake of his head. The sight of those two old women writing "Running Backs Rule" was something that would stay with him for a while. The whole damn thing was just so idiotic. Frank Sinatra crooning from a small boom box, tea steeping in a flowered pot beneath a crocheted cozy, and homemade cookies in a Tupperware container. Nanas. That's who had been signing his pictures. Little old ladies making some extra cash by practicing their penmanship, which, he thought, as he recalled the careless scrawls he'd seen, could use some work.

"Christ, Nick." Paul laughed and reached for his beer. "Relax. It's not like you foreclosed on an orphanage or something."

"It was like firing Mama."

Paul shuddered. "That's not even funny."

"You're tellin' me," Nick said, disgusted. "Those women were *mad.*"

"You were *scared* of 'em?"

"Damn straight." Scowling, he added, "Though they cheered up fast when I gave them a hefty 'retirement' bonus."

Paul hooted with laughter. "You paid 'em off?"

"You bet. Otherwise I'd have been looking over my shoulder for the rest of my life." He eyed his brother solemnly. "Don't ever piss off a grandma."

"I'll remember that."

Nick took a seat in the pine Adirondack chair opposite his twin brother. Setting his bottle of beer down on the round pine table between them, he propped his elbows on the varnished surface and cupped his head in his hands. His brain felt as if it were expanding, getting too big for his skull. Which would go a long way toward explaining the pounding headache that pulsed in time with his heartbeat.

He'd been batting a thousand since dinner at Tasha's place the night before. Agreeing to a father-son campout. Kissing Tasha and discovering a brand-new world that he'd had to turn his back on—and then capping it all off by waking up bright and early this morning to piss off two old women who had looked like they could have cheerfully murdered him.

Yeah, things couldn't get much better. Oh, wait.

There *was* more.

The letters he'd retrieved from the dueling nanas' office. Before he'd fired them, the two women had shown him three file cabinets where every fan letter received had been neatly tucked away alphabetically. Under "B," he'd found all four of the letters Jonas had written him. The childish, painfully careful handwriting had tugged at his heart even while it nudged his conscience. If he'd been paying attention to business instead of feeling sorry for himself, he'd have known about Jonas months ago.

He'd already read those letters twice—and now they were burning a hole in his back pocket.

"What's going on, Nick?"

He looked at his brother. Paul was the calm one. The logical one. The one Mama insisted was the most like their father. Paul had always been able to look at any situation and see both sides. It had been a real irritating quality when they were kids. Now it was just what Nick needed. Besides, Paul was the one person Nick knew he could count on to be completely honest with him. They were more than brothers, they were twins. And that bond went deeper than most people would ever understand.

Reaching for his back pocket, Nick pulled out the four letters Jonas had written to him. He ran his fingertips across the wrinkled papers, then tossed them onto the table, letting them slide across the varnished wood toward Paul. Grabbing up his beer, Nick took a long drink and said, "Read these. Then we'll talk."

"Tasha, you *can't* run away."

"Why not?" Tasha looked over her shoulder at Molly, standing in the doorway of Mimi's bedroom. Going up onto her toes, Tasha reached for the top shelf, where Mimi's old suitcase was stored.

"For one thing, Jonas will never go."

"Of course he'll go, if I say we go."

"He won't leave Mr. Wonderful."

Nick. It always came back to Nick. Gritting her teeth, Tasha stretched, her fingertips scraping at the old blue Samsonite, but she didn't budge it. "Damn it." She swatted the blasted thing, and still it didn't even topple. When Mimi stacked things, they stayed stacked. Nerves jangled inside Tasha and her brain skittered uneasily from thought to thought and couldn't seem to find a happy one to land on.

She rubbed her eyes with the tips of her fingers, but it didn't help. She'd hardly slept all night, thanks to the fantasies her imagination had continued to pump through her mind.

Served her right, she thought. She never should have

let him get that close. And she damn sure shouldn't let him do it again.

So why did she want him to so badly?

"Hello? Earth to Tasha."

"I'm here," she muttered, pushing thoughts of Nick and wild fantasies to a small dark corner of her mind where they would stay . . . until the next time she tried to sleep. "And I heard you. Jonas won't want to leave Nick."

"Exactly."

"Fine." Tasha turned around, whipped her hair back from her face, and stared at Molly. "You're right. He probably won't want to go. But I'm still in charge. He'll do what I tell him to do."

Molly pushed away from the doorjamb, walked slowly across the room, and then plopped onto Mimi's old four-poster. "And you want to tell him to pack up his little backpack and start hiding?"

Tasha winced at the image. "No."

"Then don't."

"Easy for you to say." Tasha stepped away from the closet and walked across the glossy hardwood floor toward the wide window overlooking the backyard. Beyond the glass, the day was cloudy and gray. Cold wind shuffled through the leafless trees and rolled Jonas's football aimlessly across the brown lawn. Mimi's chrysanthemums were bedraggled now, past their prime, but still lending splotches of color to the otherwise drab day. Tasha's gaze locked onto the bright yellow and purple flowers as if they were a shining light of hope in a sea of misery.

The mattress creaked as Molly leaned back and propped her head on one elbow. "It's not too late to try *my* idea."

"Which one is that?"

"You know, marry Nick and both of you have Jonas?"

"Marry him." Tasha huffed out a breath. "Sure. I'll just make a note and take care of that this afternoon. I can already see the society column in the paper. 'Millionaire Football Player Marries Runaway Beautician.' " She gave a pretend sniff and touched an invisible hankie to her eye. "It's so beautiful."

"Sarcasm isn't pretty."

"Yeah," Tasha said wryly, "but it gets the job done."

Molly just looked at her. "Tash, you can't run."

"Why not? I have before."

"That's why not."

Tasha shifted her gaze from Molly back to the windblown world beyond the glass and waited for her to continue. That she would was never in doubt.

"You're not that kid anymore, Tash. You've got a life here," Molly pointed out. "A job. A house. People who depend on you. And you have *me*."

At that, Tasha glanced at her friend again. Molly's grin tipped up one corner of her mouth. Her pixielike haircut framed her face in spiked tufts that gave her an impish look. That effect faded along with her smile as she said, "Seriously, Tash. You can't just take off and start over every time you're threatened."

Tasha wrapped her arms around her middle and let Molly's words sink in. She knew her friend was right. But logic didn't have a damn thing to do with what she was feeling. Her emotions were swirling through her body, churning in the pit of her stomach, and short-circuiting what was left of her brain.

The one clear thought that kept pounding itself home was, Run. Take Jonas and run.

Turning her back on the window, she slumped down, perched on the edge of the windowsill, and braced her hands on her knees. Blowing out a breath, she looked at Molly. "How can I stay and lose Jonas?"

"Jeez, pessimist much?"

"Hello?" Tasha sat up straight, reached up, and scooped her hair back from her face. "Have you been paying attention? 'Cause if you've missed an episode or two, let me just bring you up-to-date."

Pushing up from the windowsill, Tasha stalked toward the bed and didn't stop until her knees bumped into the mattress. Staring down at her best friend, she said, "You should have seen Jonas this morning. He almost *floated* out the door to go to his game. All he can talk about is this father-son camp-out."

"So?" Molly said, rolling over and sitting up. "Why shouldn't he be excited? Tasha, he's never had this. Never been one of the guys. Never had a dad."

"Don't you think I know that?" Tasha sat down and flopped back, letting Mimi's pillows catch her when she fell. She inhaled sharply and drew Mimi's scent deep within her. The soft floral perfume Mimi had preferred seemed to cling to this room, strong enough to haunt, faint enough to remind Tasha that the woman who once wore it was gone. What she wouldn't give to hear Mimi's laughter-shadowed voice telling her to get a grip. Tasha smiled to herself in spite of everything. Mimi's advice had always been short and to the point: *Do what you can and do it the best you can. Everything else will take care of itself.*

And right now, Tasha wished more than ever that Mimi was still here. That Jonas was safe. That Nick had never appeared in their lives.

And hell, as long as she was at it . . . wished for a million bucks. That had just as much chance of happening as any of the rest of it.

Her heart ached for Jonas, but he was too young to protect himself. That was her job. And not having a dad at all was *way* better than having a father who did nothing but break your heart. That much she knew all too well from experience. "He's counting on Nick. Counting on him too much."

"You can't protect him from everything."

"I can try."

Molly reached out and laid her hand atop Tasha's. "You're not Wonder Woman, Tash. Life happens. People get hurt. Then they get better and they go on." She paused a minute, then added, "*You* did."

Tasha stared up at the water-stained ceiling. Too many years of a leaky roof had left permanent marks on the old wood. Just as too many years of neglect and abuse had left marks on Tasha's heart and soul that were still there, despite the time that had passed. A part of her wondered if old hurts ever really disappeared. Or were they just buried under new ones?

"He'll have you, Tash. One way or the other, he'll still have you."

"Maybe." Tasha turned her head on the ancient tapestry pillow to look at Molly. "Maybe he'll have me. But if Nick is his father, then I'll lose him. And if Nick *isn't* his father, I might still lose him. The only sure way I have of keeping Jonas safe is to run."

Molly sat back, leaned against one of the thick pine posts at the foot of the bed, and stared at Tasha through narrowed, thoughtful eyes. "To keep him safe, or just to keep him?"

"What?"

Molly shrugged and picked at a loose thread in the old lace bedspread. "It's just that I keep hearing what *you* want for Jonas. I don't hear you wondering about what *Jonas* wants for Jonas."

"He's a kid."

"Who's had to grow up fast. Nobody should know that better than you."

"My point exactly."

"Tasha, think about it for a minute, okay?" Molly leaned forward, her gaze locked with Tasha's. "Remember what it was like when you ran away."

"I remember," she said, not needing the moment or two to dredge up the past. It was always with her, just one breath away. It haunted her when she least expected it. A scent, a sound, would awaken the memories, and in an instant she could find herself back in an alley, hiding in shadows.

The fears and hurts she kept under lock and key suddenly slipped from their cages to snake through her chest and wrap cold fingers around her heart. It had been terrifying. To be all alone. No one to turn to. No one to talk to. No one to trust. And still, it had been better than the home where she hadn't felt loved or safe.

"Now ask yourself," Molly whispered. "Do you want Jonas to have those same memories? Do you really want him to be a runaway, too?"

"It wouldn't be the same. He wouldn't be alone."

"He'd be running."

"With me," Tasha said tightly.

"And when do you stop running, Tash?"

She'd thought she had. She'd thought she'd found a

home. She'd thought this was her place. Here in the Victorian where she'd learned to trust again. To love again. But if keeping Jonas safe meant leaving it all behind, she would do it.

Did she want to take Jonas from the place he loved, from his friends, his home? Did she want to live under assumed names and keep skipping ahead of Social Services and nosy neighbors? Did she want to sentence him to the same kind of uncertainties she'd known until Mimi had turned her life around?

And was it really only Jonas she was worried about? If she couldn't be honest with Molly, the least she could do was admit the truth to herself. Nick scared her. Not just for Jonas's sake, but for her own. He made her nervous. He shook the foundations of her little world with the strength of a 6.0 earthquake. He made her want things she knew she couldn't have. And yet she couldn't stop the wanting.

But would running change that? she wondered. Wouldn't Nick's eyes, his smile, his touch, remain in her mind and haunt her no matter where she went?

She shifted a look at her friend. "How do I stop running, Molly?"

Molly smiled and shook her head. "I don't know. Maybe it's as simple as just taking a stand and refusing to move."

Tasha flung one arm across her eyes. "I take a stand and I could lose everything."

Molly flopped down onto her stomach and stretched out beside Tasha and lifted her friend's arm off her eyes. When their gazes met, she said, "Tash, the only way you could possibly lose that kid is if you deliberately try to keep him away from the man he thinks is his dad. Do that, and Jonas might never forgive you."

. . .

"He's your *son*?" Paul set the letters down onto the table and stared at Nick through wide astonished eyes. "You have a *kid*?"

Nick huffed out a breath. Jesus, it was a relief that Paul knew what was going on. Sure, he could have talked to Carla, but he was pretty sure how she felt about this whole thing already. It was Paul's cool head he needed now.

"I don't know," Nick finally said. "Maybe. Possibly. Probably. Damn it, I'm not sure."

"The boy sounds sure."

Nick slumped back in his chair and tented his fingers atop his chest. "Of course he's sure. He believes his mother."

"What do you believe?"

"That's why I'm here, Paul. I don't know what to think. Or believe." He scraped one hand across his face. "I saw a picture of his mom. I don't remember her."

"Jesus."

"Exactly. And I can't tell the kid that, can I?"

Paul winced. "Guess not. Have you had a DNA test done?"

"No."

"Why the hell not?" Paul's eyes flashed behind his glasses, and as if he suddenly felt as though they were blocking his view, he snatched them off and set them aside. "Christ, Nick. That should have been the first thing to do."

"That's what Jackson said."

"*He* knows?"

"He's a lawyer."

"Yeah, but if Jackson knows, then Carla—"

"She knows, too."

"Man." Paul whistled low and long. "And she hasn't told Mama yet?"

"It's a miracle, I know."

"One that can't last," Paul warned him.

"Yeah, I know."

"What're you doing about this?"

"I'm spending time with him." Nick sighed. "Going to his football games."

"He plays football?"

"Receiver," Nick said, smiling, and he felt that ripple of pride that he'd become so accustomed to since meeting Jonas.

"Like father, like son?" Paul asked.

"Maybe."

"So why not do the DNA test and have your answer?"

"What if it's the wrong answer?"

"Which one is the right one?"

"I don't know anymore," Nick admitted, and could hardly believe it himself. When this had all started, he'd wanted it settled and to be on his way again. He'd thought only of placating Jonas long enough for the kid to back off. He hadn't wanted to even consider the possibility of being Jonas's father. Now, though, he didn't like the idea of *not* being his father, either. Yeah, he was great parent material. "At first all I could think about was my own ass. Getting it clear without the media getting wind of all this."

"Yeah? What about now?" Paul's steady gaze locked on him.

"Now . . . damn it, you should see him, Paul." Nick chuckled softly. "He even looks like me. And Christ, what an operator. He plays Tasha like we used to work Mama."

"Tasha?" Paul's eyebrows lifted.

"Yeah. His foster mother—or not really his foster mother. She's off traveling somewhere, but Tasha takes care of him and she's . . ." He blew out a breath and reached for his beer again. "Driving me nuts."

"This is getting interesting."

Nick snorted a laugh. "Then I'm telling it wrong."

"You?" Paul laughed shortly. "Woman troubles?"

"Jesus. She's got me all tied up in knots. I don't know whether to kiss her or tie her to a chair and gag her so she can't argue with me."

"This is getting better and better." Paul's grin flashed.

"Thanks for your support," Nick said wryly.

"Hey, it's about time it happened to you."

"What?"

"You finally found something more important to you than *you*."

"Now what do I do about it?"

"Enjoy it?" Paul suggested. "Hell, I plan on enjoying the show. In fact, I want a front row seat."

"You're my brother. You're supposed to be on my side."

"I am on your side, Nick. Hell, seeing you thinking about something else besides football is enough to make me want to go buy this Tasha a drink."

Nick pushed himself out of the chair and stalked to the edge of the redwood deck Paul had just finished adding to the back of the house. Staring out into the woods lining the edge of the property, he looked through the gray naked branches of the trees, straight toward the highway that led to Tasha. And Jonas. He rubbed the back of his neck with a vicious grip. "I don't know what to do here, Paul. I don't want to fuck this up. Like I've fucked up so much of my life."

"Then don't."

"Yeah, that's easy." He shook his head and stuffed both hands into his jeans pockets.

"Didn't say it was easy," Paul said, and, standing, crossed the deck to stop beside his twin. "We all make choices, Nick. Big ones, little ones. They're all important one way or the other, and sometimes you don't find out for years if it was the right choice or not."

"Comforting."

Paul slapped his shoulder. "All you can do is make the best call possible at the time. Then hope to hell it all works out."

"Hope? That's it? That's all you can give me?"

Paul shrugged. "Sometimes, that's all you need. Make a choice, Nick. Chances are, it'll be the right one."

Choices.

It was all about choices. Hadn't he been telling himself that just the other day? In his mind's eye he saw that accident on the freeway again, and felt a cold chill sweep through him. One wrong move and everything he'd come to care for could be lost.

The question was, did he trust himself to make the right choices?

CHAPTER 15

"Isn't he something?" Alex Medina's mom sidled up close to Tasha and pointed.

She needn't have bothered.

Tasha knew just who Rose Medina was talking about. Nick Candellano, boy wonder. He was here again. At Jonas's football game. She hadn't expected to see him. And frankly, after the little chat she'd had with Molly just a couple of hours ago, she wasn't really ready to see him again. But then, if she was going to be honest with herself, she'd probably *never* be ready to see him. There was no bracing herself as far as Nick was concerned. Every time she saw him, her pulse kicked into high gear and her knees turned into water. So just how was she supposed to prepare for that?

"I swear," Rose said on a sigh, "if I wasn't a happily married woman, I'd chase him until he dropped."

Tasha smiled at her. The other woman was short and round, and her dark brown eyes flashed with mischief while dimples creased her cheeks. Rose talked a good game, but she was completely nuts about her husband, Eduardo. "He probably wouldn't run if it was you chasing him, Rose."

"Ha! You're a sweetie, Tasha." The other woman grinned and reached out to squeeze her forearm. "But you're a lousy liar."

"So I've heard," Tasha said, her gaze shifting to Nick, as it did whenever he was near. Just watching him from a distance was enough to make her blood hum. Which was *so* not a good thing. It could have been, Tasha thought, if things were different. Molly's suggestion echoed in her mind: *marry Nick and both of you have Jonas.* But that wasn't an option. She didn't belong in his world and she couldn't allow him into hers.

Rose wandered off, back to where her husband stood on the sidelines, shouting encouragement to his son and the rest of the kids. Tasha hardly noticed. Her gaze still focused on Nick, she tried to ignore the flash of heat that shot through her. But it was pointless. She couldn't ignore what he did to her any more than she could avoid worrying about what would happen next.

She felt as if she were on a tightrope stretched across a pool loaded with sharks. One wrong move and down she went, to be a midnight snack for a hungry great white. And once that great white was finished with her, she'd be nothing more than a memory, if that. She huffed out a frustrated breath, shoved her hands into the pockets of her navy blue sweatshirt, and fingered her car keys.

Tiny cheerleaders bounced and jumped, waving crepe paper pom-poms. Parents shouted, coaches blew whistles, and the solid thump of small padded bodies being tackled underscored it all. The wind tugged at Tasha's hair, whipping it across her eyes, and when she shook her head to clear her vision, she saw Nick, watching her.

She couldn't see his eyes. He was too far away. But she *felt* the heat of his gaze. As surely as she would have felt a touch, and Tasha shivered as anticipation inched along her spine and settled somewhere deep inside her.

Stupid. What had happened to her sense of self-preservation, for God's sake? Had she been too comfortable the last few years? Had she completely forgotten just how dangerous it was to let someone get too close? What in the hell was she doing?

Nick walked toward her, his long jean-clad legs carrying him quickly across the grassy field. The dark red sweater he wore accentuated his broad chest and muscular arms. As he came closer, she studied his eyes, the slightly crooked smile tilting one corner of his mouth, his wind-ruffled dark brown hair. Her mouth went dry and a spiral of sensations slipped through her body like ribbon dropping free of a spool.

He stopped just an arm's reach away. "Hi."

The wind carried his scent to her, subtly expensive with just a hint of spice and a whole lot of man. She drew it deeper inside, damn it.

Tasha forced a smile. "Didn't expect to see you here today."

He shrugged. "Promised Jonas."

A promise. And he'd kept it. That should make her feel better. But it didn't. Promises were too readily given and too easily broken. Jonas believed in him. For the boy's sake, Tasha simply couldn't. "There's a lot of that going on lately."

"Yeah, I know." He shoved his hands into the back pockets of his worn, faded jeans. "Tasha—"

Behind him, on the field, Jonas's team scored another touchdown and the kids went nuts. The herd of tiny cheerleaders raced toward the goalposts, where they struck a pose and waited in hope of an extra point.

"They're doing well," Nick said.

"I'm sure you've been a big help." There. That wasn't hard. Be nice. Be cooperative. Be careful.

Nick's eyebrows lifted, but he gave her a smile. "It's fun, helping out. Never thought about coaching, but . . . I'm enjoying it more than I expected to." She nodded. He nodded. Silence stretched out between them like a cord pulled to just this side of snapping.

She should say something. Anything. It would be better than simply standing there, looking at him and letting her thoughts run wild.

Nick cleared his throat and pulled his hands from his pockets. "Anyway. I wanted to ask you. Jonas needs to go shopping and I told him I'd take him tomorrow. If that's okay with you."

Caught off-guard, Tasha glanced past him at the field, as if expecting Jonas to pop up and explain this. When he didn't, she said, "Shopping? For what?"

Nick leaned in. "For you."

"Me?"

"Your birthday?" he prompted.

Surprise slapped at her. With everything going on in her life at the moment, she hadn't given a single thought to her birthday. Without Mimi to hound her about it and start the ritual teasing a month in advance of the event, it had slipped past her entirely. "Huh. I'd forgotten all about it."

"Jonas hasn't."

That touched her so deeply, she felt the sudden sting of tears in her eyes. After losing Mimi, she and Jonas had clung together, tightening the bonds between them. And Tasha had been so worried that those bonds were loosening now, unraveling like an old tapestry. Things had changed too much lately. Everything was shifting, morphing into something she didn't know quite how to handle. Her fears had nearly choked her, but Jonas . . . She swallowed hard past the knot in her throat. Even with finding the "father" he'd longed for, Jonas had remembered her. A sweet ache settled in her heart. "He doesn't have to buy me anything," she said softly.

"He's not doing it because he *has* to," Nick told her gently. "He *loves* you."

She blew out a breath and tried to steady her emotions. But that was near impossible lately. She felt as though she was on a roller coaster—never sure if she was on the uphill climb or the sweeping, roaring downward plunge. Everything she was feeling lately was so charged, so changeable, it was as if she didn't know whether she was coming or going anymore. Heck, she'd teared up and cried more in the last couple of weeks than she had in years.

"Yeah," she said, looking past Nick to the squad of dirty little boys in oversize uniforms. One of those little monsters was all hers, and that knowledge warmed her even as she worried about it. "I know he does."

"So why do you look like you're about to cry?" Nick stared at her, his dark brown eyes shining with emotions that shifted and changed so quickly, she couldn't identify them. And maybe that was just as well.

"I'm not gonna cry," she lied, and not for the first time realized that she did that a lot around Nick. Why did he get to her so? Why couldn't she just give in to the nearly overwhelming urge to lean into him and feel his arms wrap around her? She mentally squashed that thought almost as quickly as it appeared. "Just sinus trouble."

"Right." Nick's mouth quirked as he stepped closer and reached out one hand to cup her cheek.

Tasha sniffed, sucked in a gulp of cold air, and told herself not to react. But his thumb stroked her skin and kindled a new slow-burning fire within her. She closed her eyes and resisted the urge to turn her face into his touch, to feel more of the heat he created. Why did this have to be so hard? Why couldn't she ignore him and what he did to her? She'd never really wanted a man in her life. Never *allowed* a man in her life. Why did she have to start now? With *him* of all people?

"Nick . . ." She took a half step back, moving away from his touch while she could still manage it. He let his hand drop to his side, but his gaze caught hers and held. "We shouldn't, uh . . ." Tasha waved one hand as if searching the air for just the right words to tell him to back off. Unfortunately, she came up empty.

"Probably not," he admitted. "But I want you anyway."

"Oh God."

Nick smiled again and licked his lips before saying, "He's got nothing to do with what's between us, Tasha."

"There can't *be* anything between us, Nick." The fact that her voice broke and shook just a little probably took the conviction from that argument.

"Too late." His eyes darkened and Tasha wouldn't have thought that possible. Dark brown eyes went black and seemed to draw her in, deeper and deeper, until she thought she might never be able to get free.

She tore her gaze from his. "It's never too late."

"It was too late that first day."

She looked back at him. Couldn't help herself. No other man in her life had gotten this close to her. And a part of Tasha was terrified. After all, just exactly how was a twenty-seven-year-old virgin *supposed* to act? What if she did something wrong? What if she let him in and he broke her heart? What if he laughed at her because she was inexperienced? What if . . .

"The minute you slammed the door on me," Nick argued with a half-smile, "I was toast."

She forced a laugh that didn't come anywhere close to sounding amused. "Thrive on rejection, do you?"

"It gets my attention," he admitted, then added, "*You've* got my attention."

A cold wind raced across the field, tugged at the V neck of her sweater, then slipped down beneath it, teasing her skin with icy fingers. Her nipples went taut, but she had the distinct feeling that fact had more to do with *him* than the chill of the wind.

God, how could she be this *hot* when the wind was racing and thunderclouds were chasing one another across the sky? The scent of rain was in the air and a distant roar of thunder sounded like angry whispers.

Nick's gaze moved over her slowly, from head to toe and back again. Flames licked at her insides and reflected back at her from the depths of his eyes. A heat she didn't know what to do with swamped her.

As probably the oldest virgin in California, Tasha had no clue about how she should handle the desire she saw in his eyes. All she'd ever learned was how to say no. She'd never even thought about saying yes before.

Her virginity had been the one thing she'd been able to hold on to. The one piece of herself that had remained hers—even during those scary two years on the streets. Back then, she'd seen other girls her age trade their bodies for warmth. For comfort. Even for food.

But once that trade had been made, those same girls had found it all too easy to sell what they'd already given away.

Tasha had seen it time after time and had vowed to stay far from that slippery slope into emptiness. And until meeting Nick Candellano, she'd never even been tempted to break that vow.

Now, though, she saw desire in his eyes, the set of his jaw, and the way his hands fisted and relaxed at his sides, as if he was just managing to keep from grabbing her. And that thought welcomed memories from the night before, when he'd held her close, when he'd kissed her and awakened sensations she'd never experienced before.

Tasha's throat closed up tight and she was pretty sure she was about to hyperventilate. Wouldn't that be attractive?

Want shimmered between them like a living, breathing thing. Electricity hummed in the air and she wouldn't have been surprised to see lightning arc across the cloud-tossed sky in response.

"Nick . . . we can't—"

Who knew what might have happened if they hadn't suddenly been surrounded by fifty eleven-year-olds screaming for pizza? The game obviously over, both teams were racing toward the parking lot and their parents' cars and didn't much care who they had to trample along the way. Nick grabbed Tasha's forearm and pulled her up close to him. Holding her back to his front, he wrapped his arms around her and held on tight as the sea of children rushed past them.

She felt his breath on her cheek. Felt his hard, muscled arms resting just beneath her breasts. Felt the thundering beat of his heart against her back. And Tasha's blood turned to fire. Right there, on a muddy field, with storm clouds overhead and a noisy crowd surrounding them, she felt a quickening inside her that she'd never known before. She felt his erection press against her and she squirmed in his arms, instinctively trying to ease the pulsing ache that had settled low in her body.

"Christ, Tasha," Nick growled, bending low enough that his throaty whisper rumbled gently in her ear. "If you keep moving like that, we're in deep shit."

She froze.

He chuckled, his breath fanning against her cheek, dusting her hair. He dipped his head closer and kissed the tip of her ear. She shivered.

"It's no good, y'know," he said, and his voice was a low hum of sound, carrying just beneath the screams and shouts of hungry children. "Standing still or moving, you do things to me."

"I'm not—"

"And stop saying you're not trying to." He cut her off neatly. Shifting one hand, he casually brushed his palm across her breast, scraping gently across her nipple.

She sucked in a gulp of air like a drowning woman.

"It doesn't seem to matter that you're not trying," he continued, and caressed her one last quick time before turning her loose and taking a step back. "I'm gonna have to have you."

Everything in her tightened.

Her breath caught in her lungs.

She had to lock her knees to keep upright.

Yet she managed to look him in the eye and meet the hunger there. "I don't think—"

He laughed shortly and shook his head. "Don't say something you're gonna have to take back."

"Pretty sure of yourself, aren't you?" Tasha asked, and wondered wildly where the hell Jonas was and why wasn't he racing up to them so they could stop talking about this and she could take a breath without going up in flames? And oh God, there goes the whole hyperventilating thing again.

"Usually, yeah," Nick admitted, and watched her meadow green eyes turn the color of pine trees in winter. There was passion there. Deep, rich passion, and he knew that if he didn't have her soon, he was going to lose what was left of his mind. "But when it comes to you," he said, amazed that he was willing to own up to this, "I don't know jack. You mess me up, Tasha."

"Yeah, well . . ."

"And I think I'm getting to you, too." He grinned when she looked away from him. "And real soon we're going to have to do something about that."

"Hey, Tasha!" Jonas shouted, and her head whipped around to find the boy in the crowd. When she did, a wide, genuine smile curved that fabulous mouth of hers and Nick had to force himself to keep from reaching for her again.

"Hi, kiddo!" She opened her arms for a hug from one sweaty, dirty little football player. And after he'd greeted Tasha, the boy looked up at Nick.

"Are you comin' with us for pizza again?"

"Nick's busy—" Tasha said.

"You bet," Nick said at the same time.

She frowned at him and Nick grinned. She could try to get rid of him, but he wasn't going to give up and go away. It took a hell of a lot for a Candellano to run up the white flag of surrender. So he'd be around. Close enough that neither one of them would be able to relax. Oh, yeah. It was at least some comfort to know that he wasn't alone in this twisted little hell of desire. If he was burning . . . *she* was, too.

Together, they were gonna build a hell of a bonfire.

"Run fast, run far."

"What?" Nick held the phone to his ear with one hand and shoved his hair back from his eyes with the other. He blinked wildly, trying to focus on the alarm clock alongside his bed. The oversize red numbers stared back at him. Eight-oh-five. Good God. He cleared his throat and gripped the phone receiver in a stranglehold. "Who is this?"

"It's Carla, you idiot."

His sister's voice registered at last and he pulled the phone away long enough to sneer at it before slapping the receiver back to his ear. "For Chrissakes, Carla. It's eight in the morning. On a *Sunday*." He rubbed one hand across bleary eyes. "Somebody better be dying."

Especially after the long, lonely night he'd spent. Sleep hadn't come until four or five in the morning, and even then, dreams of Tasha had tormented him enough that he felt as though he hadn't slept at all.

His sister choked out a laugh that even across the phone lines sounded strained. "Oh, somebody's dead meat all right. And that somebody's *you*."

Nick rolled onto his back and stared up at the open beamed ceiling over his bed. Thank God the Marconis had managed to fix the roof; otherwise, he'd have awoken in a puddle after last night's storm. Okay, he told himself, you're not focusing. And it was always wiser to pay attention when his sister talked.

"Carla, are you having a breakdown or something?"

"Or something," she muttered, so low he nearly missed it. Then an instant later, her voice cracked like a whip. "You'd better wake up fast and pull it together."

"What are you babbling about?"

She took a long breath and sighed it out. "Mama."

Nick sat up straight, his sheet and blanket dropping from his chest to pool in his lap. "What's wrong with her? Is she all right? Is she sick?"

"Nope. Just pissed."

Relief swept through his bloodstream. Pissed he could deal with. Besides, she couldn't be mad at *him*. He hadn't done anything, for a change. Then smiling, he said, "Well, that can't be good. Who's she pissed at?"

"You, mostly."

"Me?" Oh, man, it was way too early for this. A man needed coffee to deal with the Candellano women. "What the hell did *I* do? I wasn't even awake until you called me."

"She knows."

Dread coiled in the pit of his stomach like a cobra poised to strike. Nick's mouth went dry and every nerve in his body stood straight up. "*Knows?* Knows what exactly?"

"About Jonas."

The cobra struck.

Shit.

"Damn it, Carla. . . ." He threw his legs over the edge of the bed and jumped to his feet. Stalking naked around the room, he waved one hand in the air as if he could reach through the phone, grab his sister, and shake her. "You said you wouldn't tell her."

"I didn't . . . exactly."

"What the hell happened?" Christ, this was all he needed. Mama coming after him with both barrels blazing. Didn't he have enough to worry about?

"I was at Stevie's shop early this morning—"

"It *is* early this morning—"

"Earli*er* then." She blew out an exasperated breath. "Jeez, Nick, keep up. I went over to help Stevie with the Sunday baking, since I was already up. Reese has a head cold and she kept me up half the night hacking up a lung and—"

"Carla . . ." God, his sister's conversations were like runaway trains, jumping tracks at every intersection.

"Right." She took a deep breath and plunged ahead. "Anyway, Stevie and I were talking about Jonas and—"

Nick grabbed up his jeans from the floor and tugged them on with one hand. "And Stevie knew about Jonas . . . *how*?"

"Well, dumbshit, Paul told her. After you told him yesterday."

Shit. He rolled his eyes and slapped his forehead with the heel of his hand. Should have sworn Paul to secrecy. Then Nick realized that the whole marriage thing probably had a "no secrets" clause. "Fine. And . . ."

"And . . ." Carla said, and he could hear her gritting her teeth. Great. *She* was mad? Then she started talking again and he listened up. "*And* . . . we didn't see Mama come in the back door of the kitchen and I guess she was just standing there getting an earful while we talked about Jonas and you and what you're doing and how Jackson said you should get a DNA test, which you really should do, but that you didn't want to yet

because of the media—and is *that* egotistical or what?"

"Thanks for the commentary," he said, sarcasm dripping from his tone. "What'd Mama do?"

"You mean *after* the top of her head exploded and hit the ceiling?"

His chin hit his chest. "Ah, shit."

"Pretty much."

Nick opened the bedroom door and headed downstairs. Caffeine. Now. Absently he noted how things had been changing in the house. Like the shoemaker's elves, the Marconis seemed to do magic overnight. He was hardly home anymore, so when he was, he noticed the changes. A new mantel over the fireplace. The piles of crap gone from the middle of the floor. Glass French doors leading to the outside deck. He made a left at the foot of the stairs and walked into the kitchen, the new blue-and-white linoleum cold against his bare feet. The countertop was finished, the blue-flecked granite spotless—but for the coffeepot in a place of honor—and gleaming. The new sink and goosenecked faucet shone in the overhead light.

Nice job, ladies.

But all he really cared about at the moment was coffee. And heat. Damn, it was cold in here. He backed up into the hallway and tweaked the furnace. From somewhere deep within the house, the heat kicked on in full force, and Nick sent a silent thank-you to Mike Marconi, master of plumbing and heating. Or was that mistress?

He shook his head while he walked back into the kitchen and hit the power button on the coffeemaker. Carla was still babbling, something about Italian curses and Mama planning an execution. He let her go and stared blindly out the back window at the lake while she rattled on in a stream of consciousness that would have been really impressive if he'd been more alert.

"You are *so* not Mama's favorite person today. All you are today is the son who's been hiding a grandchild. And don't you have anything to say?" she finally demanded, and then went quiet.

The silence got his attention more than anything else.

He shot a glare at the drip coffeemaker and mentally willed it to drip a little faster. Rubbing his eyes with the tips of his fingers, he muttered, "What am I supposed to say?"

"I don't know . . . a prayer, maybe?"

"Too late for prayers, if Mama's on the warpath."

"I could send a priest over to give you Last Rites," Carla offered cheerfully.

"I love you, too."

"Nick, Mama said I should tell you that she wants Jonas at her house. Today."

Crap. Reaching into a cupboard, he grabbed down a cup and quickly pulled out the glass coffee carafe and replaced it with the coffee cup. He couldn't afford to wait for a full pot. He'd take the jolt of caffeine in straight sludge.

Sunday dinner at Mama's.

With Jonas.

"I don't know if that's such a good idea."

"Well," Carla said, "it's that or hit the road and keep on runnin'."

She was right, he thought. Mama, now that she knew about Jonas, wouldn't quit until she'd met him and enveloped him with the kind of love only she was capable of. Would it make things tougher for Nick to settle this situation? Oh, yeah. Was there a way out—

short of selling his house and moving to Peru?

Not a chance.

"Mama said to tell you she's having a picnic at her house," Carla was saying. "She wants everyone there today by one o'clock."

"A picnic?" He stared out the window again at the drifting wisps of fog clinging to the surface of the lake. Steel gray clouds hovered low overhead and the naked limbs of the trees added to the whole "dead of winter" atmosphere. "It's gonna be sixty today and she's having a picnic?"

"She thought it would be easier on Jonas. Being outside, meeting his cousins—"

"Oh, man. . . ." Nick grabbed the cup, shoved the coffeepot back into place, and took a long, hot swallow of the poisonous brew. The caffeine hit him like a hammer and he almost wished it hadn't. This whole thing would be a lot easier to take if he could tell himself it was a dream.

"Oh and, Nick," Carla said, "if I were you . . . I wouldn't be late."

"You should have told me all of this before." Angela Candellano fixed her son with a steely look.

"I know." Nick finished talking and sat back with a sigh. He'd managed to get the whole story out and he was still alive. A plus.

"Just look at him," Angela murmured with a shake of her head. Jonas looked so much like her own boys had when they were small, she felt a twinge in her heart as memories flooded her eyes and filled her soul. Oh, his features were a little more refined than Nick's had been when he was a boy, but that Jonas was her grandson was never in doubt.

Jonas sat across the yard from her, eating a barbecued hamburger and sharing his potato chips with Debbie, Stevie's younger sister. Reese and Tina were sitting close by and Tina had given the boy her favorite dolly to hold. Already he was becoming one of them. As he no doubt should have been for years.

"Ah, Nicky," Angela said, and reached over to slap the back of her son's head on principle. "Is good that you brought him to his family. Finally."

"Thanks, Mama," Nick said, reaching up to rub the throbbing knot on the back of his skull.

"What's the matter with you?" she demanded suddenly, turning and fixing him with a glare that had been known to turn her children to stone. "Why do you keep him a secret? You're ashamed?"

"No," he said, and shifted farther down the picnic bench. Out of reach. "Mama, I didn't even know about Jonas myself until a couple of weeks ago."

Her lips flattened into one grim line that made him want to get up and run. God, what was it about parents, he wondered, that they could still hold such power over you even when you were grown?

She clucked her tongue at him and Nick cringed. He'd rather have her shouting and taking a swing at him than have her staring at him in disappointment. He'd seen that particular look too often in his life.

"It's . . . complicated, Mama," he said.

"Not so complicated you couldn't tell Jackson. And Paul. You should have told me."

"I would have."

"When?"

"When everything's settled, Mama," he said, and

glanced around the yard, desperately hoping that one of his brothers would stroll up and rescue him. No such luck. He was on his own.

"What's to settle? Look at him. So much like you."

Nick sighed. "Mama, it's not that easy."

"I know, I know." She threw her hands high, then let them land in her lap again. "You already told me. His foster mother is gone somewhere and . . . Tasha? Yes, Tasha doesn't want Jonas upset. She's a smart girl. No one wants him upset. We just want him to know his family."

Nick's gaze drifted across Mama's backyard. She'd had her picnic, winter or no winter. Even the weather couldn't stop her when Angela Candellano had her mind set on something. Smoke from the barbecue twisted like gray silk in the wind off the ocean. Paul, Tony, and Jackson slapped at it with spatulas and laughed over beers. *Chimineas,* outside fireplaces, bristled with red-hot embers at either side of the yard, sending streams of warm air sliding across the grass. Stevie, Carla, and Beth were huddled around one of them, laughing and talking together while the kids sat apart, eating. Reese, Tina, and even Debbie seemed enthralled with Jonas, and to give the boy his due, Jonas fit right in with everyone.

The kid had been excited at the idea of ending his shopping trip for Tasha's birthday with lunch at Mama Candellano's.

Tasha.

Nick wished she was there. With the family. Laughing with Carla, Stevie, and Beth. Playing with the kids. Teasing his brothers. Talking to Mama.

Smiling at him.

Nick scowled to himself. He'd never wanted to

bring a woman home to Mama's before. Hell, in his family, inviting a woman to dinner was tantamount to getting engaged. His mother would be buying a dress and calling the priest.

Everything in him went on red alert and he practically leaped off the bench. "We've gotta go, Mama."

"So soon?" she said, and stood up, already walking toward Jonas for the ritual hug and long Italian good-bye. Italians didn't just wave and leave. There were traditions to be upheld. If you wanted to leave at three o'clock, you had to start saying good-bye at two-thirty.

There were kisses and hugs and plates of food to prepare so you wouldn't starve on your drive home from a seven-course meal. There were stories to be told, promises for the next visit made, and memories of past visits to share.

Since he was used to it, Nick took his time, strolling toward Paul and Tony. Mama would be busy for a while, fussing over Jonas and the other kids.

"He lives!" Tony said as he approached and lifted a beer bottle in salute.

"It was close," Nick admitted, lifting a hand to touch the sore spot on his head.

"Hey, no obvious bruising, I call that a win," Paul told him with a laugh.

"Sympathy from the family. It's so touching."

"You want sympathy?" Tony said, chuckling. "You're in the wrong family."

Nick grabbed Tony's beer and took a long drink. "Duh. Christ. The KGB should know about Mama."

"She's too tough for those guys," Tony said, taking his beer back.

"Amen," Paul muttered, clearly delighted that Mama was mad at his twin this time, not him.

"So," Jackson asked, "have you decided what to do yet?"

"Yeah," Nick said, looking at his brother-in-law. "I think it's time to do what you wanted to do in the first place." It was past time, he thought, half-turning to look at Jonas, being enveloped in a Mama Candellano hug. The boy's arms wrapped around her thick waist as she bent her head to kiss the top of his head.

If Jonas was his son, he wanted the boy to know his family. If he *wasn't* his son . . .

"Good enough," Jackson said. "I'll call the kid's lawyer. Set up the test."

"The kid has a lawyer?" Paul asked.

Nick sighed and waved at Jackson. "You explain. I'm tired."

Tony laughed and slapped him on the back.

"Tasha!" Jonas shouted. "You came!"

Everything went eerily silent.

Nick did a slow, careful turn as the hairs at the back of his neck stood straight up. When he met her gaze, Nick gave silent thanks that looks really couldn't kill.

Chapter 16

Tasha couldn't breathe.

A cold, tight band wrapped around her heart and squeezed until she nearly winced from the pain. The icy wind slicing in off the ocean pushed at her with cold hands as if trying to keep her away from the tender family scene in front of her.

Jonas.

Her Jonas—surrounded by Nick's relatives.

Even as she stood there, watching, Jonas was being sucked deeper into the Candellano clan and being wedged further away from her. Pain, sharp and bright, tore at her and she blinked to keep sudden tears at bay. God, how could she hurt this much and still stand?

Still breathe?

When Jonas had called to tell her where he was, all she could think to do was drive to Chandler and claim him. To take him back home. To *their* home. And then she was planning on locking the doors. Maybe sealing the windows. Keeping the whole world—and especially Nick Candellano—*out.*

No more Ms. Nice Guy.

No more stolen kisses or dreams and visions of what might have been.

Just reality.

And the reality was that she had to keep Nick away at all costs.

Okay, a small, rational voice in her mind insisted, maybe she was overreacting just a shade. But not by much. Nick had moved in, shifted their nice little world into outer space, and then, without even telling her, dropped Jonas into the middle of an all-American family situation.

How could she possibly compete with that?

She stared at the frozen tableau in the backyard. It was as if they were all statues, frozen by Tasha's unexpected appearance. Then all at once, like a heart suddenly beginning to beat, everyone came to life at once. A golden retriever barked. Voices lifted. Jonas broke free of the older woman's hug and started toward Tasha.

Nick was headed her way, too.

Her stomach pitched.

If he'd had any sense, he'd have been moving in the opposite direction. Instead, he was coming right at her. Tasha pulled in a deep, cleansing breath and clung tightly to the hard ball of anger settled in her chest.

The big golden dog raced alongside Jonas as if there were a game in progress. She weaved back and forth in front of the boy as if she were trying to herd him, but Jonas kept coming, laughing out loud at the dog's antics.

Tasha's heart ached a little harder.

He was so at home here.

Nick's long legs allowed him to reach her first, but she didn't look at him. If she looked at him, she'd have to talk, and she was terrified that she'd start shouting instead.

"Tasha," Nick said, refusing to be ignored, "I can explain."

"I'm not interested." Good. No shouts. No curses. Short and simple. She looked past him at the boy and dog hurrying toward her. "Come on, Jonas, we have to go."

"Not yet," the boy said as he raced up and slid to a stop just in front of her. While he talked, he kept one hand stroking the dog's head, and the big animal's whole body quivered in delight at the attention.

He should have a dog of his own, Tasha thought.

"Nana's gonna give me some more of her cookies," Jonas said. "She makes great cookies."

Nana.

Oh God.

Tasha reached out and smoothed his hair back. She should have cut it, she told herself. All of these people. They'd think he didn't have anyone taking care of him. They'd think *she* didn't care. And oh Lord, she cared so much.

"Is it okay, Tasha?" Jonas practically bounced in place. "Can I go get the cookies?"

Everyone was watching her. She felt their gazes on her. If she grabbed him and ran, they'd all think she was nuts. A nut who didn't care enough to give Jonas a haircut. Well, she wouldn't give them any more ammunition to use against her.

"Fine." She forced a smile that felt as though it would crack her face. "Go ahead, honey. Get the cookies. I'll wait out front for you."

" 'Kay!" He was already turning and running back into the yard.

The big dog barked once as if saying hello. Everyone else started moving again. The older woman—

Nana—headed toward Tasha, a welcoming smile on her face.

But Tasha couldn't take much more. She was in no mood to make small talk and she didn't want to see any more of the big family gathering. Turning her back, she started for the front of the house, to where she'd left the van parked. She'd just sit in her VW van, roll up the windows, lock the doors, and wait for Jonas.

She didn't get two steps before Nick was beside her, taking her upper arm in a firm grip and holding on.

She yanked free and shot him a vicious glare. "Don't touch me."

"I know you're pissed off, but—"

She kept walking. Couldn't talk. Words gathered at the back of her throat, burning to be released. But she wouldn't say anything here. Wouldn't do the shouting that she so wanted to do. Because there were like a hundred Candellanos here and she was alone. Like always.

As she stalked toward the front of the house, she managed to nearly snarl, "And by the way, you don't know *anything* about me. Nothing."

"Whoa." He kept pace with her, his long strides easily matching her anger-fueled steps. "Take it easy, Tasha."

"Take it easy?" She whipped her hair back from her face and tore at it with impatient fingers when the wind kicked it back across her eyes. "You can say that to me?" She stopped, furious, and glared at him. "You take Jonas off for a day with your family and you don't even *tell* me?"

"Jesus. I didn't take him to South America."

She stomped off again. "That's not the point and you know it."

"You're right. I should have told you. But I figured you'd take it wrong. Clearly," he added wryly, "I was wrong."

Curling her fingers into a fist, she clenched it at her side and kept moving so she couldn't give in to the urge to punch that smiling face of his. One step, two, three. She turned on him again and he stopped short to avoid crashing into her. "Damn it, you had no right."

"It was a burger, Tasha, not a kidnapping."

"Oh, it's so much more than that," she muttered, and whirled around again, unable to look into those brown eyes any longer. Her steps pounded against the grass. "This wasn't lunch," she said, not caring if he could hear her or not. "This was bringing Jonas into your family. And you pulled out all the stops, didn't you? Introducing him to aunts and uncles and cousins and even a *Nana* for God's sake."

"Well, hell, somebody shoot me," he said under his breath.

"Oh, don't tempt me," she shot back. Fear chewed at her stomach. She held one hand to it in an attempt to ease the churning there. It didn't help. She kept walking, around the corner of the old house and into the teeth of the wind.

It slapped at her, stinging her cheeks, making her eyes water. The cold went bone deep. She shivered and felt as though she might never be warm again. Fear ran with her, pacing her steps, measuring her breaths. She was losing Jonas. Inch by inch, he was slipping away from her.

"Damn it, Tasha, stop." Nick grabbed her again and this time, when she tried to yank free, he didn't let her go.

"You stop, Nick." She congratulated herself silently

on keeping from screaming. "I don't want to talk about this."

"Too damn bad."

She gave him a look that should have warned him off. "Don't push me right now, football star."

"Okay," he muttered, tightening his grip on her arm, "that's it." He steered her away from the car and out onto the road in front of the house.

"Hey—" Tasha dug in her heels, but her old tennies slid on the damp grass. She had to walk. It was either that or fall on her ass and be dragged across the lawn.

"We're going for a walk." Nick kept moving, not even looking at her as he towed her along in his wake.

"Jonas will be waiting—"

"My mother's feeding him. Trust me, it'll be a while."

"Let *go.*" She pulled hard, and he released her, but stepped in front of her when she tried to go back to the car.

"Move."

"Not a chance." He met her gaze and stared her down. "We're talking. Now. We can do it in front of Jonas and my family, or we can take a walk."

Tasha inhaled sharply, deeply, and shot a quick look at the big old house sitting surrounded by trees and permanence . . . and history . . . and, hell. Everything she didn't have. Everything she could never give Jonas.

"Okay, fine," she said, keeping her distance from the man she wanted to kick. "We'll walk."

Nick rubbed one hand across the back of his neck and studied her as she walked stiffly in front of him. Her spine was rigid, her chin lifted. Her black sweater was long, hitting her jean-clad legs at the middle of her thighs. Her hair shone like dark fire and flew about her head like flames lifting off a torch.

Fury radiated off of her, but there was more. Something else feeding the hostility that made her green eyes look glassy with the emotions rattling through her.

Heading down the road, Nick kept pace with her furious steps, letting her walk off some of her mad before they talked.

She started first. "You shouldn't have brought him here."

"My mother found out about Jonas. She had to meet him."

Tasha shook her head as she stared up at him. "Your mom *found out*? You didn't tell her about him?"

He sighed. "No, I didn't tell her."

"Wow. Feel the warmth."

"Damn it, Tasha, why in the hell would I bring my family into this before I find out if—"

"If you're stuck?" she finished for him.

"I didn't say that."

"You didn't have to."

"You're just not gonna cut me any breaks at all, are you?"

"Don't you get it, Nick?" she countered, and planted both hands flat on his chest and shoved. He didn't budge. "You've already *got* all the breaks. You've got money. You've got a family, stability. You can give Jonas everything. I can't compete with that."

"It's *not* a competition, Tasha!"

"Of course it is." She shoved him again, and this time he staggered backward a step or two. "And *you're* winning. You don't even *want* to win and you're winning. How do I fight that?"

"Why do we have to fight at all?" he asked, stepping close to her again.

"You don't understand," she said, her voice dropping, the heat sliding from it. "But how could you?"

She turned and started walking again, as if needing to move. Nick measured his strides to hers. They walked past Carla's house and the Garvey cottage on the point. The ocean roared, calling them on, and Nick led her off the road and down the cliff path, toward the beach.

Here there'd be no one to hear. No one to watch. They could talk or yell or . . . He must be a sick man. As mad as she was . . . as much as she looked like she could cheerfully punch him dead in the face, he wanted her so badly he could hardly breathe.

Definitely.

A sick, sick man.

She stumbled on the path and Nick grabbed her arm. This time she didn't pull away but walked alongside him until they were on the sand. Then she stopped, and when he was sure she wouldn't bolt, he let her go, reluctantly.

She stared out at the ocean for several long, quiet minutes. The ocean thundered around them. Seagulls dipped and danced in the wind currents above. The birds screeched endlessly, the sound piercing, lonely.

But Nick could give a shit about the damn birds. Instead he simply stared at Tasha.

When she'd appeared at his mother's house, it was as if he'd conjured her with his thoughts. Although, Nick admitted silently, he'd been imagining her smiling and willing . . . not mad enough to melt steel with a glance.

She was breathtaking. Wild and fierce and so damn

beautiful it nearly hurt to look at her. Her flame-colored hair whipped around her head in the wind, and when she turned to look at him, he saw pain in her eyes that damn near doubled him over.

Until she started talking.

"You had no right."

"Tasha . . ."

"You don't deserve Jonas," she snapped, eyes flashing. "Where were you when his mom died and he went into the system, huh?"

"I didn't—"

"You weren't there when he used to cry himself to sleep at night. I was, though." She sucked in air like a dying woman. "Me and Mimi. *We* were with him. We were the ones telling him that everything would be okay. That he was safe. . . ." Her voice broke and she hiccuped in a breath.

Nick watched helplessly while tears filled her eyes, but before he could reach for her or say anything, she was on a roll again.

She angrily swiped away a single stray tear. "You weren't *there,* hero. And now it's too late."

"I didn't know about him before," Nick said, keeping a tight rein on his own anger. Fear and pain were driving her now, and to fight it with his rising temper wouldn't do any good for anyone. But God, it took everything in him to keep from shouting right back at her.

In his family, shouting was something you did.

Shouting just meant you cared enough to argue.

Shouting, to an Italian, meant love.

Love?

That thought brought him up short.

She snorted a choked-out laugh. "You didn't know

about him. Now *that's* something to be proud of."

"Okay, enough." He grabbed her, the fingers of both hands digging into her upper arms as he yanked her close. "I didn't know about him. I admit it. And I can't change that." Would he, if he could? he asked himself silently. And when the answer to that question didn't come, he pushed it aside to look at later. "But I'm here now. And if Jonas is my son, then I'm going to be a part of his life, whether you like it or not. And being a part of my life means being a part of my *family*."

"Your family," Tasha repeated. "Don't you see what this does to Jonas? It pulls him closer to you. Makes him want it all even more than he already does."

"What're you talking about?"

"This." She waved a hand, encompassing the beach, the ocean, the house on the cliffs, and the people in the yard. "The family. The big dog and the smiling kids and the barbecue in the middle of winter, for God's sake." She choked out a laugh that sounded as if it had hurt her. "He's never had that." She squirmed in his grasp but couldn't get free, so she settled again and pinned him with a cold gaze. "He was an only child. Then his mother died. And he was alone. You don't have any idea what *alone* is like, Nick. But I do. Alone is scary. Terrifying. And you look around and when all you can hear is the sound of your own heart beating . . . *that's* when you notice all the families. Kids and dogs and moms and dads and even the damn TV work on you, reminding you you're different."

"Tasha . . ." Her eyes were wild and bright, and it felt as though she was slipping away from him.

"And you want it all so much, you can taste it. You want the big house and brothers and sisters and people who give a damn." She dragged in a long deep breath.

"But all you've really got is yourself, so you make do. And then somebody comes along and dangles the dream in front of you and it looks so close that maybe it's okay to believe."

She talked fast, as if she couldn't stop the rush of words racing from her. And Christ, Nick wished she could. The images she created tore at him. He'd had the kind of life every kid should be able to claim while growing up. And Tasha—not to mention Jonas—had never known that kind of stability.

He wondered if she realized she was talking as much about herself as she was about Jonas. And Nick's heart ached for the little girl she'd once been. "Tasha," he said, his voice soft, soothing, "try to calm down."

"I can't." She swallowed hard and stared up at him, her green eyes haunted again and filled with memories of pain that he knew he would never totally understand. "You're dangling the dream in front of him, Nick, and he's too little to know how to protect himself from the disappointment."

"I'm not trying to hurt him," Nick argued. "I wouldn't do that. Not to him. Not to *you*."

"Accidental pain aches every bit as much as intentional pain."

She tried to pull free again, but it was no contest. Nick wasn't about to let go of her now. If anything, he wanted to pull her closer, hold her tighter, soothe away the shadows in her eyes, and make sure they didn't come back. Instead, he held her firmly, refusing to give ground, forcing her to look into his eyes.

"And if he's not your son?" she asked finally. "Then what?"

He blew out a frustrated breath. "It's time we found out one way or the other." Might as well get it all out there where she could chew on him for everything at once. "Tasha, we're going to do a DNA test."

Something flashed across her eyes and was gone again before he could identify it. Fear?

"DNA," she repeated hollowly.

"It's the only way." He stroked her arms, rubbing, soothing. But he sensed that she wasn't going to be soothed. Not now, anyway. "It's what we should have done two weeks ago."

"Maybe," she said softly, her voice disappearing again beneath the sounds around them. "At least then, we'll know."

"Exactly. Then we can decide from there."

"And if you're not his father?" she asked her question again, then answered it for him. "You disappear? Leaving me to sit with him while he cries again? Is that your plan, football star?"

He sighed. "Stop calling me that, damn it."

"It's who you are."

"Who I *was,*" he countered, and felt the solid truth of those words slam home. Damn, for the first time since having to retire, he'd actually put football in his past. Where it belonged.

It was as if a giant weight had just sloughed off his shoulders. Nick steadied himself and waited for the panic that was sure to follow. But it didn't come. He was an *ex*–football player. And that was, very suddenly, *okay.*

His grip on her loosened a bit, temper sliding from him like air from a balloon with a slow leak. "Tasha, can't we at least agree that we *both* want what's best for Jonas?"

She looked up at him and shook her windblown hair back from her face. Her skin looked like the sheerest porcelain. White, creamy, the few golden freckles standing out like gold dust scattered in milk. But her eyes were haunted again and he felt the pull of them right down to the bottom of his soul.

She inhaled slowly, deeply, air shuddering into her lungs. When she spoke, her voice was nearly swallowed by the roar of the ocean and the howling wind.

"We want what's best for him, Nick. We just don't agree on what that is."

"Maybe we won't be able to figure that out right now, Tasha. But we have time. Time to work this through together."

Together.

Tasha stared up at him and knew she'd lose in a battle with him. If it came down to a battle for custody, a rich man with an extended family would look like a straight flush—where an ex-runaway beautician with eight thousand bucks to her name wouldn't even equal a pair of sixes. She couldn't win. She couldn't take him on and keep Jonas. She couldn't fight the state and keep Jonas.

There was no win here for her.

And maybe, she thought, it was time to stop worrying about winning and time to consider that her losing Jonas might be the best thing for Jonas. Pain stabbed at her again, stealing her breath, tearing at her heart.

Her world had changed—and the old one was gone forever.

And there wasn't a damn thing she could do about it.

"That hurt," Jonas muttered the following afternoon as he and Nick left the small lab outside Chandler Community Hospital.

"No more than a hard tackle, though," Nick said, "right?"

"I guess." Jonas looked down at the small round Band-Aid on the inside of his left elbow. It was gross, watching the blood fill up that tube, and his stomach had gotten all swirly until the nurse told him to stop watching.

But it was okay. It was worth it. 'Cause now everybody was gonna know that Nick was his dad for real. And then he could go and see Nana all the time if he wanted to. And Reese and Tina weren't too bad, even if they were girls. But it would have been good to have a boy cousin.

"Do I have any more cousins?" he asked suddenly, glancing up at Nick.

"Not yet." Then Nick paused, thought about it, and said, "Well, you've got a few in Omaha. One of 'em's about your age."

"Cool. Where's Omaha?"

Nick just stared at him. "Don't they teach you anything at school?"

"You sound like Tasha." Jonas laughed, then kicked a rock in his path. It went skittering across the parking lot until it slapped against the tire of a blue truck. Thinking of Tasha made him think of something else, and since he and Nick were all alone, it was probably a good time to talk about it. "How come you kissed Tasha?"

"What?" Nick stopped beside the Corvette and looked down at him.

Jonas shifted his gaze to the toe of his tennis shoe and watched while he scraped his shoe against the asphalt in a slow circle. "The other night? I saw you guys kissing, so how come you did it?"

"Jonas . . ."

"Are you gonna tell me I'll understand when I'm bigger?"

"I was thinking about it," Nick admitted, smiling.

"I know all about that stuff, you know."

"What stuff?"

"You know, how babies come and everything."

"Jesus."

"And I kinda wanted to know if you and Tasha are gonna make a baby."

Nick cleared his throat and rubbed one hand over his face as if trying to make himself disappear. But that wasn't going to help. Hell, he'd never expected to be having this conversation. But then, he'd never planned on being a father, either, had he?

"Jonas, sometimes people kiss just because . . ." Help me out here, he pleaded silently for intervention from whoever happened to be listening. As he recalled, his own father had done a pretty good job in situations like this, so, *Papa, if you're listening* . . . "Well," he finally said lamely, "because it's nice."

"Kissing girls?" The kid's face screwed up like he'd just been given cough syrup.

"Yeah." Nick hid a smile and wondered how long it would take for Jonas to change his mind about the whole girl thing. Then he wondered if he'd be around to see it. And suddenly he really *wanted* to be.

Tasha's outburst from yesterday was still with him. He'd thought about it all night and into this morning. He hadn't been able to forget the look in her eyes when she'd spilled her guts. He hadn't been able to dodge the question she'd thrown at him. *And if you're not his father? You disappear?*

The truth was, he didn't want to disappear from their lives. And he couldn't imagine Jonas *or* Tasha disappearing from his.

Jonas spoke up again and shattered Nick's wayward thoughts. "Was kissing Tasha nice?"

Memories flooded him. Hunger reared its demanding head and took a bite of him. "Very nice."

"Did she like kissing you, too?"

He inhaled sharply, remembering the touch of her lips, the eager puff of her breath on his cheek, the press of her nipples against his chest. "Yeah, I think so." Although, after yesterday, he couldn't be sure she'd still enjoy kissing him.

Yet he was eager to find out.

"So, are you gonna make a baby?"

Man, kids were a real killer. Nick squirmed uncomfortably in his seat and tried not to allow the image of Tasha pregnant with his child into his mind. But it came anyway and, surprisingly enough, didn't terrify him. What's up with that? He pushed the image aside. "Wasn't planning on it, why?"

Jonas shrugged and leaned against the Vette. "Just 'cause I was thinking if you guys made a baby, then we could all be together and I'd have a brother or something, too, besides a mom *and* a dad."

Aw, God. The hole Nick was in just kept getting deeper and deeper. Pretty soon, he'd probably have dug straight through the earth and he figured he'd wake up and be speaking Chinese.

It couldn't be any more confusing than his life was right now.

"I mean," the boy continued, not looking at Nick at all now, "I just thought you should know that I think it's okay. I mean, you and Tasha kissing and stuff. At first it was kinda weird, but it's okay now."

"Thanks, I'll keep that in mind," Nick said, ruffling the kid's hair. It really *was* too long, he thought idly, and wondered how he could convince him to cut it. And then questioned if he had the right to interfere. According to Tasha, he sure as hell didn't. But according to his feelings, he did. Damn, this was a mess. Staring down at the boy who'd so invaded his life, he saw the promise of a future staring back at him.

Granted, it wasn't a future he'd planned on. But then, how many people actually planned and then *got* the future they outlined for themselves? Jonas's big brown eyes were trusting and Tasha's words flitted through his mind again. *He's too little to know how to protect himself from the disappointment.* And why should he *have* to know? Nick asked himself. Shouldn't it be the right of every kid to have a home and love and stability? Shouldn't this boy, with his gentle heart and loving nature, be able to count on a few simple things? Like family? And a home?

Nick sucked in a gulp of air and let it slide from his lungs on a sigh. "Get in the car, Jonas," he said softly. "I'll take you home."

" 'Kay." Jonas sprinted for the other side of the car. The kid did nothing slowly. He opened the door, climbed in, and slammed the door after him. Nick winced but didn't bother to say anything. Kids and slamming sort of went hand in hand, as he remembered.

God, Jonas was trying to set him up with Tasha. To keep them all together, Nick thought, and figured Mama would be proud. Nothing his mother liked better than a little matchmaking. She'd get a real charge out of knowing her possible grandson was taking up one of her favorite hobbies.

Once they were buckled in, Nick fired up the engine and backed slowly out of the parking space. Traffic moved in concert—lurching forward, then stopping—as they left the lot. While Jonas fiddled with the radio, ending up with some god-awful rock station, Nick's mind continued to work over everything he and Jonas had been talking about—until at last something occurred to him.

"Jonas?"

"Yeah?"

"You were saying how you'd like you and me and Tasha to be together?"

"Uh-huh."

"Well, I was just wondering—"

" 'Bout what?"

"About Mimi," Nick said, shooting a sidelong glance at the boy and noting the sudden closed, worried expression on his usually wide-open face. "She's your foster mother, right?"

Jonas's gaze dropped to the floor of the front seat. He studied the toes of his shoes with a concentration that could only mean one thing. He didn't want to answer that question.

"Jonas," Nick asked quietly as they came to a stop at a red light, "where's Mimi?"

Slowly, the boy lifted his head to look up at him. Tears shimmered in his dark brown eyes and his bottom lip quivered.

Shit.

Chapter 17

"Ms. Flynn," Evelyn Walker said sharply, "this has gone on long enough."

Well, that was plain enough.

Tasha had managed to avoid this little confrontation for months. But she'd known all along that Social Services wouldn't go away and they wouldn't forget. If there was one thing the bureaucrats were good at, it was biding their time before snapping their red tape traps shut on the unwary.

Well, Tasha was plenty wary. She'd had to be. But even she couldn't produce Mimi, which was the only thing that would call off this particular bureaucrat.

Tasha's brain raced, considering, then discarding one idea after another. Bribery wouldn't work. Even if she had enough money to try, Evelyn Walker would never go for it. The woman held "the Rules" close to her abundant breasts like her own personal Bible. Tasha could hire someone to pretend to be Mimi, but then, there had been only *one* Mimi Castle and no one else could come close to impersonating her. Besides which, Ms. Walker was a pain in the ass. She wasn't stupid. She'd know a fake Mimi right away.

So what was left?

Playing the game. Making nice with the woman who held all the power in this meeting. Tasha had to try to stall long enough to give her time to come up with a new plan. One that had, say, some small chance of success? "I don't know what you mean."

One gray eyebrow lifted in a dismissive arch. "Please don't insult my intelligence," Ms. Walker said tightly. She flicked at a nonexistent piece of dust, then frowned distastefully at the surface of the dining room table.

Tasha bit down on her tongue to keep from saying something she'd undoubtedly regret. She'd already done enough of that yesterday, with Nick. Oh God. Everything she'd said to him had come back to her time and again during a long sleepless night. She still couldn't believe she'd unloaded like that. To *him* of all people. For God's sake, didn't he have enough on his side? Had she had to point out all of the differences in their situations? Did she have to give him more to hold over her head?

Reaching up, she rubbed the bridge of her nose and tried to push that confrontation to the back of her mind. No point in reliving it any longer. It was done. Over. Too late for regrets. Now she had a brand-new situation to worry over. And there was still time to save this one.

"Honestly, Ms. Walker," she said, and mentally crossed her fingers—as children did, to take the sting out of an outright lie—"I'm not trying to—"

"You are *trying*," Ms. Walker interrupted impatiently, "to stall. It won't work."

Tasha poured the woman a cup of Mimi's best tea and tried to smile. It wasn't easy. These surprise visits always caught Tasha off-guard. As, no doubt, they were meant to.

Heck, just hearing the distinctive putter and cough of Ms. Walker's green Volkswagen in the driveway was enough to send cold chills racing along Tasha's spine.

Of course, today's jolt of adrenaline carried an extra punch since she was already on edge. With Nick and Jonas off getting blood tests and the future hanging by a slender thread.

"Mimi Castle has not responded to my inquiries in six months."

"Mimi's still in Paris." Tasha snatched at her only diversion. She set the flowered china pot down, picked up the latest postcard from Europe, and handed it over. "See?"

Ms. Walker took the postcard, stared down at the photo of Sacré-Coeur, then handed it back. "Lovely. The fact remains . . . Ms. Castle continues to show a lack of interest. She should be available for meetings with Social Services, as well she knows."

"Yes, but—"

Snapping her briefcase shut, Ms. Walker stood up, ignoring the steaming cup of tea. Meeting Tasha's gaze, she added, "Ms. Castle either shows herself for an interview at my office in one month's time—"

"Or . . ." Tasha held her breath, since she was pretty sure she wouldn't be able to draw another once that statement was finished.

"Or," Ms. Walker said, her gaze narrowing, "Jonas Baker's living arrangements will have to be reconsidered."

"You mean you'll take him away."

"Not I, Ms. Flynn," the woman said, picking up her

small black plastic handbag. "Social Services."

"It amounts to the same thing."

Lifting one hand to smooth steel gray hair that had been shellacked into complete submission, the woman admitted, "Why, yes. I suppose it does."

The earth shook beneath Tasha's feet. Not a real earthquake, of course, just an emotional one that rocked the foundations of her life. Her stomach pitched. Her mind reeled and her heart felt as though it was being torn from her chest. There it was. Out in the open. The one thing she'd been dreading for months. The inevitable showdown.

Tasha had one month before the world as she knew it ceased to exist.

"I think we've concluded our business, Ms. Flynn," Ms. Walker said, turning and heading for the front door.

Tasha watched her go. One small, stiff woman in an ill-fitting black suit. How was it, she wondered, that a woman who cared so little about a child's heart was the one person who had the power to break it?

Fear crouched in Tasha's belly like a rabid dog, sending out angry swipes of its paws. Pain stabbed at her. Panic gnawed on her. And she was forced to behave—for now—as if everything was all right. If she gave in to the urge to tell the truth, then plead and cry for mercy and understanding . . . all that would happen was that Ms. Walker would take Jonas *today.* She'd lose the last month she had.

And she couldn't do that.

There were still thirty days.

Anything could happen.

She could still take Jonas and run.

Before Ms. Walker reached the door, it flew open.

Late-afternoon sunlight speared into the room, slanting across the floor. Jonas raced into the house, then skidded to a stop when he saw the enemy.

"Jonas," the woman said, inclining her head like queen to peasant.

"Hello." One word, squeezed reluctantly from a boy who looked as though he'd rather be anywhere but there.

"I see Ms. Flynn has neglected to trim that hair of yours again."

He lifted his chin defiantly and swung his fall of hair back from eyes that glittered with revolution. "I like my hair like this." That said, he sprinted for the stairs and ran as if a vampire were hot on his heels.

"Of course." She'd already dismissed the boy and continued her march toward the door.

From outside, Tasha heard the throaty roar of the Corvette's engine as Nick drove away. Deep within her, disappointment battled with relief. Though a part of her ached to see him again, despite the embarrassment of facing him after yesterday's meltdown . . . a larger part of her was grateful that he hadn't come inside. If he'd met Ms. Walker . . . if Jonas had introduced the man as his father . . .

"One month, Ms. Flynn," the woman said from the open doorway. "I'll expect to see Mimi Castle at my office in one month."

The door closed after her and the quiet *snick* of the lock engaging had more of a sense of finality than a slam would have. Tasha sighed, folded her arms across her chest, then rubbed her upper arms briskly. It did nothing to dispel the chill within, but she hadn't expected it to. She turned and shifted her gaze to the stairs and the second floor where Jonas sat in his bedroom.

One month.

Molly's suggestion floated through her mind. *Marry Nick and both of you have Jonas.* For one brief moment, she actually considered the notion of seducing Nick. After all, she was *very* attracted to him, despite her best efforts to deny it. And he'd shown more than once that he was interested in her. She could probably do it. If she could get past the whole nervousness thing.

Wouldn't that be something? The world's oldest living virgin seducing a player like Nick. Her stomach pitched again and slid into a wild spin that seemed to settle a heck of a lot lower than her stomach. Oh God. Even if her brain was confused about what to do, it seemed that her body had a plan of its own. She blew out a breath and headed for the dining room. There she sat down, picked up the last card from Paris, and stared at it. Say she *did* seduce him, what then? A good idea in theory, she thought.

But sex didn't mean love.

Not to someone like Nick, anyway. And the reality was, Nick Candellano would never marry her. Not that she wanted him to, of course.

God.

All she wanted was for her family to be safe. Was that really so much to ask?

"Happy birthday, Tasha!" Jonas hit the light switch and Tasha sat straight up in bed, blinking wildly, trying to focus.

Heart racing, she scooped her hair back from her face and looked at the little boy standing in the open doorway. The smile on his face was bright enough to read by. He held a glass of orange juice in one hand and a badly wrapped present in the other.

"Happy birthday!" he shouted again, and Tasha thought she heard the window rattle in its frame.

"Good morning," she said, her voice creaky.

He sprinted across the room. OJ sloshed over the rim of the glass, ran down across his hand, and splattered in fat orange drops onto the floor. Tasha didn't care. Birthday traditions must be upheld. This one . . . possibly their *last* together, more than anything.

He set the glass down on the bedside table, then shook the OJ from his hand before thrusting the gift at her. "Open it."

"Don't I get a kiss first?"

"Oh. Sure." He leaned in, kissed her cheek, then climbed up onto the mattress beside her.

Tasha scooted over a bit on the old double bed, but stayed close enough that she could feel the boy's denim-covered knee pressed into her leg.

"Come on, Tasha. Open it." An impatient grin creased his face and she smiled back at him.

"Okay, don't rush me. This is big stuff, you know."

"Yeah, I know. And I wrapped it myself this year," he said proudly.

She would have known that anyway, she thought. There was probably a whole roll of Scotch tape on the neon green paper dotted with smiling baseballs and footballs. The big red Christmas bow, complete with fake snow and plastic candy canes, had no doubt been snitched from the attic. Tasha's smile softened as she looked at him. Reaching out, she cupped his face in her palm and leaned forward to kiss him on the forehead. "Thank you, honey."

"For what? You didn't even open it yet."

"Thanks in advance then, okay?"

" 'Kay. Come on. Open it."

"Right. Enough mushy stuff." She dug in, as she knew he would expect her to. No neatly unwrapped packages in Mimi Castle's house. Here it was a free-for-all. Paper torn, ribbon scattered. Mimi used to say it just wasn't a present if you weren't excited to get into it.

When the paper was pulled off, despite the yards of tape, Tasha smiled at him again. "I love it. *Sleepless in Seattle* is my favorite movie."

"I know." His proud grin widened. "And the DVD has lots of neat stuff on it, too." He promptly snatched the movie from her, flipped it over, and started reading aloud the list of extras. Tasha just watched him. Her gaze etched his face, this moment, into her mind. Dozens of years from today, she would be able to pull this memory from her mind and relive it all. The scents, the sound of his voice, and the solid warmth of him pressed against her. Tears filled her eyes and she blinked them back. She didn't want anything to dim this moment.

"And there's something else, too," he said when he'd finished reading. Reaching into his pocket, he took out another small package, wrapped just as artistically as the first.

"Jonas," she said, taking it from him, "you didn't have to get me two presents."

"Yeah, but it's fun that I did, huh?" He grinned and swung his hair back from his eyes.

His delight shone from those dark brown eyes and Tasha felt warmed through by his love. This child of her heart meant more to her than her own life, and the thought of losing him was almost more than she could bear.

"Open it."

"Okay," she said, sniffing. Once the paper was gone, she held a tiny bottle of cologne, and without even opening it, she knew what it would be. Jonas's favorite. Orange blossom. She twisted the cap free, tipped some cologne onto her fingertip, then patted the inside of her wrist. Holding it up for him, she asked, "Well?"

He smiled again. "Smells good."

"This is wonderful, Jonas. Thank you so much."

He shrugged and eased off the bed. " 'Sokay. You were surprised, huh?"

"You bet," she said, holding her gifts tightly to her. "You did good."

"Yeah, I know." Then he stopped grinning and pulled something else from his pocket. "Oh, and Nick wanted me to give you this."

"Nick?" Pleasure shifted into something else. Something she didn't want to pin a name on. "When did he give you this?"

"On Sunday when we went shopping."

A tiny envelope, it was the kind of thing people usually enclosed with gifts. When she opened it, she saw a plain yellow gift card. But inside, it read, *Happy birthday, Tasha, you and Jonas be ready at seven. Love, Nick.*

She warily looked at the boy in front of her. "Ready for what?"

"We're going out to dinner," he said, and started for the door. "Nick said to tell you not Taco Bell but not Four Seasons, either."

"Nick said? What else did Nick say?"

"Gotta go catch the bus, Tash!" Jonas yelled as he

left the room and hit the stairs running. "Happy birthday!"

Dinner? With Nick?

Tasha fell back against the pillows and stared blindly at the sun-washed ceiling. She told herself that the racing of her heart meant nothing. But even *she* wasn't buying it.

Nick was as eager as he'd been on his first date. Hell. *More* eager. That first date had been with Stevie. Someone he'd already known for years. There had been a comfort zone on that maiden voyage that was missing now. With Tasha, there was *no* comfort zone. Only the sizzle of electrical charges that zapped him whenever he was near her. And that sizzle kept bringing him back again and again. But it was more than sexual heat drawing him to her. There was something about Tasha that reached into all of the dark, lonely places inside him. Those corners of his heart and soul where old dreams died and new dreams began.

"And damn, I'm getting philosophical in my old age," he murmured. "Who would have believed it?"

He steered the SUV he'd borrowed from Paul for the night into Tasha's driveway and turned off the engine. Almost instantly his cell phone rang. "Yeah?"

"Nick, it's Tony."

"Hey, big brother. What's up?"

"Wanted to let you know . . . Coach McIntyre is in the hospital."

"What?" Nick's high school football coach had always seemed invincible to him. A big, burly man with a booming voice, Coach "Mac" had been at Chandler High for nearly thirty years.

"What's wrong?"

"Heart attack," Tony said. "Mild, but still . . ."

"Yeah." Was this the end of an era? Nick wondered.

"Anyway," Tony went on, "his wife called my office, said Coach wanted to talk to you."

"Me?"

"Yep."

"Why?"

"Dunno," Tony said. "Guess you'll have to go to the hospital and find out."

"Right." Nick hung up and promised himself he'd do just that—in the morning. But now there was Jonas and Tasha and . . . that sizzle.

By the end of the evening, Tasha felt as though every nerve in her body was standing at attention, screaming. Every square inch of her skin felt electrified, as if she'd stuck her finger in a light switch. Even the air around her hummed with excitement. Expectation.

They'd enjoyed a wonderful dinner at Masiello's, a lovely Italian restaurant on the Coast Highway, just outside Chandler. After leaving the restaurant, they'd walked along the harbor, watching the lights on the fishing boats sparkle like diamonds on the water's black surface.

Romantic?

Not with Jonas there, to dangle off the edge of the boat dock trying to catch the silvery fish darting just out of reach. But it was still . . . magical, Tasha thought, her heart filling with emotions rich and deep.

Just yesterday, she'd actually considered seducing Nick for Jonas's sake. She'd thought about surrendering her virginity, the one thing she'd been able to hold on to during her life on the streets, in the name of saving her family. But she knew she never would have been able to do it. Not even for Jonas could she have set aside her own hard-won self-respect.

But tonight, standing beside Nick in the soft fog-shrouded light, she realized it wasn't about seduction. It was about love.

She was in love with Nick Candellano.

Shock rippled through her.

Nick took her hand in his as they continued on the boardwalk lining the harbor. Tasha hugged her new discovery close and felt the warmth of his touch right down to her bones. When he smiled at her, the impact of it dropped on her like a stone.

"Did I tell you," he asked, "that you look gorgeous?"

"I think you might have mentioned it." At least five times since the moment she'd opened the front door to him. One look at his reaction to her had assured Tasha that it had been worth the two hours she'd spent getting ready.

"Good," Nick said, and reached to smooth his fingertips along her jaw. "Because . . ." His gaze dropped, admiring her again as he took in the short, flippy black skirt and the deep V neckline of her long-sleeved black lace blouse. "Really," he said. "Beautiful."

Her stomach took a slow slide toward heaven. "Thanks."

His hand tightened on hers. On the waterfront, wooden boats in their slips creaked and rocked gently in the water, as if soothing babies to sleep. Lights shone from some of the cabins, and shadows moved past the curtained windows. Running lights on the boats farther out in the bay winked on and off as the encroaching fog misted and cleared around them.

"You grew up here, didn't you?" Tasha asked while keeping a sharp eye on Jonas, now chucking rocks into the water.

"In Chandler, yeah," Nick said.

"Must've been nice." She tipped her face into the wind, tasting the salt in the crisp air, feeling the mist brush against her skin with a chill kiss.

"Where're you from?"

She stiffened, but Nick's thumb began to stroke the inside of her palm.

Tasha blew out a breath. "Chicago. But that was a long time ago."

"Not so long. Not if it can still haunt your eyes."

"It doesn't."

"Yeah, it does," Nick said softly.

She looked up at him. The three-inch heels she wore put them a lot closer in height. Close enough that his mouth looked far too tempting. "Not all of us grew up in la-la land, Nick," she said, and tried to pull free.

He wouldn't let her go. And instead of rising to her bait, he only smiled. "La-la land, huh? My dad used to work down here sometimes, on the harbor." Nick tucked her arm through his and kept walking, holding her close to his side. He could feel the rapid beat of her pulse like a jackhammer through her rib cage. "We did, too, in the summer, my brothers and me, I mean. And that's one nasty job, swabbing down the decks of fishing boats. 'Course, Carla had to work at home, for Mama. I think we got the better end of that deal."

She gave him a half-smile, setting off sparks inside him.

"No la-la, then?"

"Not so you'd notice." But it had been good, he told

himself. A great place to grow up. Something he doubted she'd ever known, and a part of him wished she would trust him enough to tell him more about the past that was still chasing her.

"Hey, Nick!"

He stopped dead and shifted a look toward the boat on his left. A tall man, long wild hair shining silver in the weird half-light, shoved up from the cabin hatch and waved a hand.

"Antonio!" Nick called, grinning. "How's the catch coming this season?"

"Pretty good. I could use another deckhand!"

Nick laughed and pulled Tasha even closer. "No thanks. But I'll tell Paul."

"Ha!" The big man laughed loud enough to startle a sleeping pelican off its perch. The bird lumbered into the air, then spread wide wings and skimmed the surface of the water, looking for a late-night snack.

Nick lifted a hand and kept walking. He hadn't been down here in too long. And seeing it now with Tasha and Jonas was . . . nice. Pitifully small word for what he was feeling.

"Do you know everybody around here?"

"Just about." He gave her a brief half-smile, then let his gaze settle on her mouth. "You know, I've been thinking about kissing you since the minute you opened your door tonight."

She inhaled slowly, deeply, and he watched the swell of her breasts with interest.

"I've been thinking about that, too," she admitted.

"How about we do less thinking and more doing?" Nick pulled her into the circle of his arms just as an icy breeze kicked up off the water.

"Uh . . . what about Jonas?"

"Right." Nick's gaze moved over her face like a touch. "Jonas. Couldn't we just send him fishing with Antonio?"

Tasha laughed and the sound of it rose up into the night air and settled back down on him like a promise. "I don't think so," she said.

"Yeah. . . ." Nick groaned as he said it and readied himself for another long night of aching.

They walked again, a few more steps. Jonas stayed far ahead of them, inspecting every inch of the dock and the harbor with the curiosity only an eleven-year-old boy possessed.

"But," Tasha said softly, "he goes to bed early."

Nick stopped dead and looked down at her. Everything in him went still. Moonlight peeked around the edges of a silver-rimmed cloud and dusted the harbor with a silvery light. Nearby, one of the fog lamp streetlights glowed a hazy yellow. The soft light seemed almost ghostly, as if it were trying to wrap them together in a golden haze.

"He does, huh?" Nick studied her eyes. The eyes that had been haunting his dreams for weeks. He didn't want any mistakes here. If she was saying what he was hoping she was saying . . .

Tasha took another deep breath and nodded. "After that big dinner and all this fresh air, he should be pretty tired by the time we get home. Probably fall asleep soon."

"Wow." Nick nodded, sliding one hand up to caress the line of her throat. "Then for his sake, we'd better get going, huh?"

Her eyes closed briefly with his touch. "Yes," she said, her voice a whisper of longing, "he must be exhausted. I know I can't wait to go to bed."

"Right." Nick smiled, bent down, and gave her a brief, hard kiss. "Right." Turning, he shouted, "Jonas! Time to go!"

CHAPTER 18

Two hours later, Tasha was a woman on the edge. Nick was due back at the house any minute and she was doing some serious rethinking.

Mistake, she thought, pacing through the dark, quiet house. Mistake that hadn't happened yet, she reminded herself. She could still chicken out. She could still lock the door and refuse to answer when Nick showed up.

But her heart ached at the thought of *not* being with him. She loved him. "Oh God, how can I love him? I *can't.* He's the enemy, for Pete's sake. Loving him only complicates *everything.*"

But that didn't seem to matter.

Mouth dry, she tried to swallow and couldn't. God, it was like having a mouthful of dust. Something to drink, she told herself, and headed for the kitchen. Barefoot, her steps were soundless against the cold wood floors. She needed that chill, though, to balance the heat bubbling in her veins.

She opened the fridge and grabbed a bottle of Chardonnay. Wine. Good idea. She closed the fridge by bumping it with her hip. Then she reached down two wineglasses from a nearby cabinet before heading out to the dining room again.

In the dark, moonlight danced through the room, creating patches of shadows and light. Tasha poured herself a half-glass of the crisp white wine and downed it in a few long swallows. The resulting heat in the pit of her stomach felt good, so she poured herself another, then carried it with her to the window.

She stared up at the black sky, dotted with fast-moving clouds that sailed past clusters of stars like sailboats on an endless sea. Trying to look beyond the stars, she whispered, "Mimi, am I doing the right thing? Is this only going to make things worse?" In the following silence, she could almost hear Mimi. *Relax, Tasha. Enjoy life. Live it so you die with no regrets.*

And maybe Mimi was right. Maybe the way to look at this was that even if Nick disappeared from her life once the DNA test results were in . . . at least she would have this one night. She would have given her virginity to the man she loved.

Oh God.

She took a sip of wine, concentrating on the smooth taste and letting it soften the rough edges inside. Nerves skittered into life in the pit of her stomach, and Tasha drew one deep breath after another in a vain attempt to ease them. Nothing was going to calm her down. Not while she knew that Nick was on his way here to . . . Okay, thinking about that was *not* going to help.

Upstairs, Jonas was sound asleep. Tasha smiled to herself. He'd been known to sleep through 6.0 earthquakes, so she knew he wouldn't wake up when Nick arrived. When Nick . . . *stayed.* Oh God. She took another drink, and warmth swirled in the pit of her stomach. Good. That was good.

Of course, her brain was beginning to feel a little fuzzy, but who needed a brain, right?

Headlights.

"Oh God." Twin white lights sliced through the blackness. As the car pulled into the driveway, the headlights slashed across the dining room window and she felt like the proverbial deer . . . "He's here." She shook her head. "Just who the hell are you warning?" she muttered.

Still clutching her wine, Tasha moved through the shadow-filled house toward the front door. She opened it and stepped onto the porch in time to meet Nick, coming up the front walk. He'd changed clothes. The sport coat was gone, replaced by a dark red sweater over a pair of faded Levi's that made his legs look impossibly long.

She took another sip of wine.

Nick stared up at her from the bottom of the steps, and his throat closed. Hunger roared inside him with the ferocity of storm surf crashing against the shore. In the indistinct moonlight she looked otherworldly. Her flame red hair looked dark in the shadows. She still wore that black skirt and the low-cut black lace blouse. But she'd removed her shoes and black nylons. Barefoot, her skin was creamy, pale in the moonlight, and her ankle bracelet and toe ring reflected the light with tiny winks.

He wanted her more than he'd ever wanted anything in his life.

Taking the steps slowly, he stopped on the porch, less than an arm's reach from her. "Is he asleep?" he asked, and she heard the tightness in his voice.

"Yeah."

His gaze dropped to the glass in her hand. "Wine, huh?"

She inhaled sharply. "I was a little . . ."

"Nervous?"

"Okay."

He took the glass from her and downed what was left of the wine in one long gulp. "Good." Then he set the empty glass down on the porch railing and stepped closer to her.

"Nick . . ."

"Dance with me," he said, sliding his right arm around her waist while catching her right hand in his left.

"What?" Her breath dusted the base of his neck and its warmth shattered inside him.

He held her close, pressing the length of her body along his. For two hours, he'd been thinking of nothing but throwing her onto a bed and burying himself deep within her. And now that he was here, he wanted to simply hold her. To feel her body along his. To relish the press of her nipples against his chest. To slide his hand up and down her spine. "Dance with me. Here. In the moonlight."

He moved and she followed, swaying against him even as she said, "There's no music."

"Oh, there's music," he assured her. "You just have to listen for it."

He rested his cheek on top of her head and inhaled the light flowery scent of her. Orange blossoms. She smelled of springtime and promises.

Her steps mirrored his as they moved quietly in the darkness. The old porch creaked beneath them as the soft breeze caught a wind chime somewhere in the yard.

His hand slid down her spine, to the curve of her bottom, and she took a sharp breath. Nick's heart raced and his blood pumped with a fury that nearly choked him with need. But he refused to give in to it. He wanted these moments. These quiet, romantic moments with her in his arms and the silent shadow-filled night all around them.

She'd been driving him crazy for weeks. His dreams were filled with her, his days measured by whether he would see her or not. She was in his brain, his heart, and his soul. Tasha Flynn had broken through his defenses and made herself such a part of him, he couldn't imagine a world without her in it.

Releasing her hand, he wrapped both arms around her, holding her as he moved, cradling her small, curvy body close to him. Her breaths matched to his, her heart beat in time with his. And he knew if he didn't touch her soon, he'd lose what was left of his mind.

She moved her hands up his arms to his shoulders, then encircled his neck. Her fingertips brushed against his neck and he felt the rush of heat from her touch as surely as if she'd branded him.

"I want you," he whispered, and felt her shiver in his arms. "I need to touch you, Tasha." As he scooped one hand beneath the hem of her lacy shirt, his fingers slid across her skin like silk across ice.

She sucked in a gulp of air and squirmed in his arms, but she didn't pull away. Instead, she shifted, moving with his touch, turning in to him. Nick smiled to himself as he shifted both hands beneath her blouse, and swayed to music only they could hear. Sliding his hands up between them, he found her breasts, bare beneath the lace, and air rushed from his lungs as he cupped her.

"Oh my." She sighed and tipped her head back, closing her eyes as she allowed him easier access to her body. His thumbs dusted across her hardened nipples, and her mouth dropped open on a soft moan.

That sigh sliced into him and left him weak. Wanting.

"Oh, Nick," she whispered brokenly.

"Let me have you," he said as his fingers and thumbs tweaked the tips of her breasts, teasing, stroking, driving them both to the edge of control.

She moved and his heart clutched. She sighed and his soul shattered. She moaned and a fierce, overpowering urge to claim her rose up in him, strangling him with need.

Tasha couldn't open her eyes. She was surprised she was still standing. Her whole body felt liquid. Her knees wobbled and she locked them as he continued to rock her gently in a slow, circular dance. His hands on her body were warm, strong, and tender. Music played in her head and her heart.

And he was the song. He was everything. His breath dusting her cheeks was a blessing, sweet with the promise of more to come.

His hands dropped from her breasts and she wanted to weep for the loss of them. But in an instant he'd lifted the hem of her blouse higher, baring her flesh to the cool night air. Her eyes flew open. She stared at him as her skin hummed and her insides warred between excitement and embarrassment.

"Nick, people will see and—"

"No one can see us," he said, a small smile curving his mouth. "It's too dark. We're too far back from the road."

"But—"

"I want to see you in moonlight," he said, and she was lost.

He tugged her blouse up and over her head, and before she could feel the cold, he leaned down and claimed her breasts with his mouth.

Heat suffused her. Saturated her. Glowed inside her until she felt radioactive and wouldn't have been shocked to see light streaking from her fingertips. Her stomach flip-flopped wildly, then tightened into a hard knot of expectation.

She looked down and watched as he took her nipples, one after the other, with his lips and tongue. He lavished attention on her, tugging, nipping, licking. She held tightly to him, digging her fingers into his muscled shoulders, wishing she could feel his skin beneath her hands. Embarrassment fled. Nothing mattered but what he was doing to her. What he was making her feel. Then he suckled her and Tasha felt the world tip.

She groaned tightly. "That feels so . . . good," she said, her voice harsh, strained with the new feelings sweeping through her. She arched into him, offering herself to him, silently demanding that he give her more, take more.

"So good," he agreed quietly, the words muffled against her body. Again and again, his mouth worked her nipples, until the fog in her head descended completely, leaving her awash in muted sensation.

When he broke the intimate kiss, Tasha groaned again, this time in dismay. But he only straightened up, dropped one arm around her, and said, "Inside. We have to go inside for the rest, Tasha."

"Right," she said, breath staggering in and out of her lungs rapidly, as if she'd been running a marathon. She felt keyed up, every nerve on alert. As if she might shatter if she moved too quickly. And oh, she didn't want to shatter, yet. She wanted to feel more. Experience "the rest."

He snatched up her shirt from the chair where he'd tossed it and followed her into the house. Tasha took her blouse from him and held it to her as she walked across the room toward the stairs. He was right behind her. His hurried footsteps matched hers. His breathing was harsh, strained, and she knew he'd been as affected as she. At the top of the stairs, she turned left and walked the length of the landing, to her own room, at the opposite side of the house from Jonas's.

Stepping inside, she let Nick move past her, then she closed the door. He took her blouse and tossed it aside, then pulled off his own sweater and the T-shirt beneath it. Moving closer, he drew her up against him, and the warmth of flesh to flesh speared through her, stealing her breath again. Her hands moved over his broad back, loving the feel of his skin beneath her palms. He shuddered at her touch and Tasha smiled to herself, enjoying the rush of sexual power inside her.

"I need to have you, Tasha. Now."

She pulled her head back and looked up at him. In the indistinct light, his dark eyes flashed and she trembled. "I need that, too, Nick. I need *you*. I didn't want to. But I do."

He nodded, his gaze moving over her, lingering on her breasts before lifting to meet her eyes again. "From that first day, I knew we were headed here."

"From that first day," she agreed. It had been inevitable. The sizzling attraction between them had been leading them here. To this moment. To this familiar room where moonlight shone like the path to heaven.

He cupped her face in his palms and bent his head

to kiss her. His mouth took hers, his tongue sweeping inside, stealing what was left of her breath and giving her his. She took it, claimed it, and then gave it back.

Her mind drifted, shut down, and her senses took over. His hands were everywhere at once. Her skin was on fire. And she didn't care. All she wanted was to feel. To have him show her everything she'd ever dreamed of. To have Nick inside her.

He walked her toward the bed and, leaning down, grabbed hold of the quilt and tossed it to the foot of the mattress. Then he bent her backward, laying her down on the clean, fresh sheets and joining her there. His right hand swept down the length of her body and beneath the hem of her skirt. Up, up, his fingertips slid along her thigh, then drifted to the inside, higher, higher, until he reached the thin silk barrier of her panties.

He actually growled and rolled her onto her back. Levering himself up on one elbow, he looked down into her eyes and said, "These have gotta go."

She inhaled sharply. "You bet."

He grinned at her, then kissed her hard, before shifting his mouth to her chin, her neck, and down the line of her throat. Slowly, he slid along her body, like a river of fire. His mouth trailed kisses across her flesh, and she burned, flames licking at her skin. He paused at her breasts, long enough to taste her nipples before moving again, down her rib cage, across her stomach, to the waistband of her skirt.

"More," she whispered, and heard the break in her voice.

"Now," he said, and reaching beneath her, he undid the zipper, then tugged the flimsy fabric down and off.

Then he cupped her, his palm tight against the scrap of black silk still covering her.

Tasha moved, lifting her hips into his hand. His thumb traced over a so-sensitive spot and she whimpered even as tiny electriclike shocks shot through her body. Writhing in the patch of moonlight spread across the bed, she hungered for more. She reached for him, but he avoided her hands as he slid lower, off the edge of the mattress, then pulled her to him.

"Nick . . ." She went up on her elbows as he hooked his fingers under the elastic band and slowly pulled her black silk panties down her legs.

He looked at her, eyes dark and fathomless. "Just lay back," he said, "and let me have you."

"But—" Tasha wanted his arms around her again. She wanted to feel his body pressed to hers. Flesh to flesh, that brush of hard to soft. Her body ached as she watched him kneel and position her legs on either side of him. "Nick, what're you—"

His fingertips dusted the insides of her thighs, and Tasha bit down hard on her bottom lip to keep from whimpering. Then slowly, tantalizingly slowly, his fingers moved closer to the heart of her. She lifted her hips in anticipation. She didn't know what to expect. What to feel. What to do. God, why didn't she know what to do?

He touched her.

Tasha splintered.

His fingers smoothed across her most intimate flesh and she gasped drunkenly for air. Drawing her legs up, bracing her heels on the edge of the bed, Tasha looked at him as she arched into his touch, wanting more but not sure how to tell him. But he didn't need to be told. His hands guided her legs to his shoulders, and before she could take a breath and hold it, his mouth covered her.

"Nick!" Her head dropped to the mattress and her hands fisted in the sheets. She hadn't expected this. Hadn't thought of anything but opening her body for his. But this was more, somehow. More intimate. More devastating. His mouth took her, his tongue sweeping wild, long strokes across her center until she lay twisting, helpless beneath his touch.

Heels digging into his back, she arched, lifting into him. Sensation poured through her in a rush. Breath staggered. Eyes wide, she stared up at the ceiling, then shifted her gaze down to where Nick was loving her. She reached for him, stretching out one hand to touch his hair, smooth his forehead. He glanced at her, and the heat in his eyes scorched her. She moved again, arching, lifting herself into him. He pushed her higher, higher, until she struggled toward the peak she felt rising in front of her.

His mouth took her places she'd never imagined. His tongue stroked her so intimately, her whole body seemed to shimmer with a pulsing light that played out in time with the beating of her heart. She hadn't known. Hadn't guessed that pleasure could be so deep. So all-encompassing. His breath dusted her body and she sighed his name. His hands smoothed her legs, her bottom. He lifted her off the bed, cradling her as he pushed her higher, faster, up a mountain of raging emotion until she raced breathlessly for the peak. And he was still cradling her when she shattered, whispering his name.

Before the last of the tremors had died away, Nick eased her down onto the bed, tore his clothes off, grabbed a condom, and slid up the length of her body.

She humbled him. She touched his heart in ways he wouldn't have thought possible. And he needed her more than ever.

She turned her head and smiled at him. "That was . . ."

"Just the beginning," he said, and kissed her, shifting to cover her body with his. She welcomed him, opening her legs, her heart, and taking him home.

He entered her slowly, prolonging the pleasure, staking his claim on her body, her heart, inch by inch. She reached for him, sliding her hands across his chest, dragging her short, neat nails along his flesh. He sucked in air through clenched teeth and looked down into meadow green eyes dazed with passion.

She lifted her hips, guiding him home, and he surrendered, pushing himself into her warmth. But in the next instant, he froze, buried within her. *A virgin?* Heart pounding, brain screaming, and need hammering at him, he swallowed hard, looked down at her, and said, "You should have told me."

"You know now."

"When it's too late."

"It was always too late to stop this," she said, reaching up to cup his face.

He turned his face into her palm and kissed it. "Your first time should have been special. Should have been . . ."

"I waited for this until tonight, Nick," she said. "This one small part of myself I managed to hold on to, until now." She smiled up at him and rocked her hips, testing his control, pushing him past the edge of endurance. "And it *is* perfect. Or will be. . . ."

Nick bent his head to kiss her, humbled again. She'd given him the one piece of herself she'd protected, despite whatever troubles had plagued her life. She'd been, at the heart of her, an innocent. She'd fought him and changed him and forced him to rethink a lot of his life. And now Nick felt the enormity of it all crashing down on him. She'd become a part of him. The *best* part. "Oh, it's gonna be," he whispered, bending low to brush a kiss across her mouth.

He moved within her and she gasped at the sweet friction of bodies joining. Setting the pace, he rocked in and out of her warmth with a rhythm as steady, as all-consuming, as a heartbeat. He watched her eyes glaze, watched her breath hitch in her chest. She dragged her nails across his shoulders and down his back, and the gentle scrape tore away what was left of the shell he'd built around his heart.

He looked into her eyes and found what he'd been missing all his life. He rocked his body deeper into hers, and as she took him inside, Nick realized he never wanted to leave.

Tasha moved with him, catching the rhythm of his movements and following him in this dance as she had earlier, on the porch. Moonlight drifted through the window and played on his features with a gentle touch. His eyes shone dark and deep as he looked at her. She felt the magic surround her as he claimed her body, heart, and soul.

This time, they reached the peak together, souls shattering, becoming one, and they held tight to each other as they fell.

Minutes, hours, maybe *centuries* later, Tasha moved and Nick shifted his weight off of her, rolling to his back and dragging her along with him.

"Wow," she said softly.

"Yeah, that about sums it up." Nick smiled into the

darkness and stroked one hand up and down her arm as she snuggled in close. "Still wish you had told me."

She tipped her head back on his chest to look up at him. "It's not something you can just drop into casual conversation, y'know. 'Oh, by the way, I'm the world's oldest living virgin outside a convent.' "

He rolled to his side, draped one arm across her middle, and stared down at her. "Tasha, we moved beyond casual a few steps back. And still you didn't tell me."

She didn't look at him, letting her gaze slide to one side.

"Just like," Nick added, wanting to get everything into the open at last, "you didn't tell me that Mimi's dead."

She froze in his arms. Her body went stiff with shock and her features were suddenly blank. Unreadable. She pushed at his arm, trying to slip away from his hold, but Nick only tightened his grip on her, locking her in close to his body with an arm wrapped around her waist.

"Let me go."

"Not until you talk to me."

Her gaze snapped to his, and the passion shining there only moments before was gone, replaced by suspicion and anger. "How did you find out?"

"Jonas told me." That ride home from the DNA test had been a long one. He'd listened to Jonas's fears and tried to ease them, all the while knowing that he couldn't talk to Tasha about any of it. He'd wanted her to come to him, as Jonas had. To include him, to let him help. But no matter the closeness between them, she hadn't budged.

Tonight she'd allowed him into her body. . . . Now he wanted into her heart.

"Then you already know everything."

Apparently, though, it wasn't going to be easy. "I don't know why you didn't tell me yourself."

She pushed at his arm again, and this time he let her move. She slipped off the bed, snatched an old afghan off a nearby chair, and wrapped it around her before facing him again. Tossing her hair back from her face, she said, "I couldn't tell you. You might have told Social Services. Then they would have taken Jonas."

"You think I'd rat you out?" That was insulting. He sat up, grabbed the sheet, and drew it up to cover his own nudity. Easier to fight if you weren't worried about your body betraying you.

"How was I supposed to know what you'd do?"

"And now?" he asked, hoping to hell she knew him well enough now to know that she could count on him.

She scooped her hair back, threading her fingers through the thick mass and yanking at it in frustration. "Now?" Shaking her head, she turned around and sat down on the edge of the bed, shoulders slumped, her back to him. "I don't know anything anymore."

Nick reached out and stroked one hand up and down her spine. "Talk to me, Tasha. Tell me what's going on. Let me in."

Tasha stared out the window, but she wasn't seeing the night. Instead she was seeing snatches of her past. Snapshots of her and Mimi. Her and Jonas. She was seeing this house, her home, and her family. And then she saw it all taken from her. Her heart ached, and when Nick took her hand in his, she held on tightly, glad suddenly to not be alone in the dark.

Slowly, she started talking, and then found she

couldn't stop. She told him about Mimi's sudden death. About how her Social Security money was sitting, untouched, in a savings account. She told him about the postcards sent by Mimi's loyal friends and the fears that had haunted Tasha for months. She told him about her half-baked plan to run away again, and she felt his fingers tighten on hers when she said it.

She'd been able, always, to talk to Molly. But this was different. *Nick* was different. It felt good to get it all out. To hear herself put her darkest fears into words. To feel his hand on hers tighten in support and to hear him whisper words of encouragement as she poured her heart out to him.

And when it was finished, done, she felt like a popped balloon.

"A month," Nick said thoughtfully.

"That's it."

"You're not going to run?"

She thought about it, then remembered everything Molly had said about sentencing Jonas to a life like the one she'd tried to forget. "No," she said, feeling that one slim chance slip from her grasp. "I won't run."

"And I won't let them take Jonas from you."

"Oh," she said, shaking her head, "you don't know the terrifying Ms. Walker."

"We'll find a way," he said, and she wanted to believe him. She wanted to think that he could help. That he wasn't actually her enemy but a blessing instead. But hope—trust—came hard to a heart that had been battered too often.

She turned her head to look at him and found his gaze, soft and reassuring, on her. "I've been fighting two fronts," she said softly. "Social Services—and *you.* One of you will take him from me."

Nick pulled her to him, wrapping his arms around her and holding her as she cuddled in close to his chest. Her heartbeat thumped against his own and he felt her fear like a living thing in the moonlight. Resting his chin on top of her head, he said, "If he's my son, I swear you won't lose him."

"And if he's not?" she asked, her voice as hushed and soft as the light pooling around them.

"If he's not . . ." Nick didn't want to acknowledge that possibility. The boy and Tasha had become all-important to him and the thought of losing either of them was something he didn't want to consider. So he didn't. "We'll figure out what to do. Together."

Chapter 19

Three days later, Tasha stood at her bedroom window and watched Nick walk to his car. When he reached the Vette, he paused, looked up at her, and grinned. Stupid, but she felt a flash of heat rush through her.

God, he'd just left her bed. She sighed and leaned her forehead against the cold windowpane. He'd only just finished showing her what a shower could really be like . . . and here she was, raring to go again. What the heck was going on? She'd gone from virgin to raging sex maniac in a couple of days.

"Damn, it feels good."

Nick climbed into his car and roared off, leaving gravel spitting in his wake. Dropping the curtains, Tasha faced the mirror, grabbed a brush, and ran it through her hair quickly, then headed downstairs. Time to go to work. Time to face the knowing glances from her customers and at lunchtime, no doubt, another inquisition from Molly.

For the last three mornings, it had been the same. Jonas left for school, Nick showed up, they had an hour or so together, and then he left, both of them going to work. The only difference was, *his* co-workers didn't *know* that he was sleeping with her.

Here at Castle's, the situation was a little different.

Did she mind? She'd asked herself that more than a couple of times the last few days. And the answer remained the same. No. She'd put up with the teasing and she'd try to ignore Molly's foolish, romantic dreams of planning a big wedding. Instead, she'd decided to simply accept what was. She'd have this time with Nick no matter what.

And for however long she had it, she was determined to enjoy it. Mimi's advice continued to echo in her mind, and damn it, Mimi had rarely been wrong. There was something to be said for simply enjoying life. And Tasha hadn't had nearly enough of it.

The specters of DNA tests and Ms. Walker still hovered at the edges of her mind, sending ribbons of worry through her body at unexpected moments. But she held on to Nick's promise to face them together with her.

Togetherness was an unusual idea for Tasha. She'd depended on so few people in her life. Had trusted even fewer. And yet somehow she was beginning to trust Nick. And more than that, to depend on him. To count on him being a part of her life. *Their* lives.

Her steps slowed on the stairs, her fingers tightened on the cool, polished wood of the banister. *So* not a good thing, her mind whispered. If she counted on him, when he finally *did* disappear from her life, he'd take her heart with him. But he would anyway, she reasoned. It was too late to change that now. Too late to keep from loving him. Maybe it had been too late from the start.

Tasha's stomach twisted. He hadn't even walked out on them yet. How could she miss him already? she wondered.

"Tash! You alive?"

Tasha came up from her thoughts like a deep-sea diver, finally breaching the surface. Blinking, she looked down to the foot of the stairs, where Molly waited impatiently.

"What's up?" Tasha took the rest of the stairs and stopped at the bottom, beside her friend.

"You've got a customer waiting."

"Yeah, I know." Tasha laughed. "If it's Friday, it must be Margaret."

"Oh, no." Molly shook her head slowly and gave her a wicked smile. "This customer's new. And insistent on seeing you."

She frowned. "Did you tell her I'm booked today?"

"Yep. She didn't care."

Okay, something was clearly going on. Molly's eyes flashed with amusement and her lips were twitching. Obviously, the new customer was a barrel of laughs. Either that, or the joke was on Tasha. "All right, let's hear it."

Molly's eyebrows lifted into delicate arches. "Apparently," she said, dragging out the suspense, "Tassel Loafer has a mother."

"What?" Tasha shot a look at the dining room and the kitchen and beauty shop beyond. Oh good God. Nick's *mother* was here? Jesus. Would she be able to tell Tasha had just had sex with her son? She swallowed hard. "What did she say, *exactly*?"

"She *said* she wanted to see you."

"Why?"

"Hell if I know."

Tasha hadn't expected an answer from Molly. But the questions remained. Why was she here? Why now?

To warn her off? Oh jeez. "His mother. Here."

Tasha's spine stiffened. Memories of the picture-perfect family gathering she'd witnessed last Sunday danced in front of her mind's eye. She saw Nick's brothers and sister and their families and the kids and the dog and *Nana*. The cookie-baking nana who'd won Jonas's heart in a single afternoon.

"That's right," Molly told her. "Angela Candellano. Right there in the shop, chatting with Edna like they were twins separated at birth and by twenty years."

"What does she want?" Tasha heard herself ask the question out loud, for all the good it would do.

"Look, Tash, she seems really nice. I mean, you could do worse for a mother-in-law."

"Oh, crap, Molly. That's probably what she's afraid of. Probably here to tell me to stay away from her little Nick. Probably thinks I'm after his money or something."

"Well, yeah," Molly said, rolling her eyes and shaking her head. " 'Cause you look like an evil, painted-up city woman, out to bewitch poor innocent little Nick."

Tasha hardly heard her. *Fine.* If Angela Candellano was worried, then Tasha would just put her mind at ease. She wasn't trying to trap the woman's son. Heck, *Tasha* knew better than anyone that she would never fit into the *Leave It to Beaver* world Nick had grown up in.

"Yo, Tasha!" Molly grabbed her arm and shook it. "You're zoning again, girl. Good sex is supposed to *clear* the mind, not dissolve it."

Tasha slapped one hand across Molly's mouth. "For God's sake, don't talk about sex with his mother in the house."

Molly pried her fingers off and laughed. "Right, 'cause a woman with four children wouldn't know anything about sex." Walking back toward the shop, Molly waved one hand at Tasha. "You stay here. I'll send her out to you so you can stay out of gossip range."

"Thanks."

"But I'll want an update later."

"Naturally."

Tasha walked into the living room and leaned casually against the back of the sofa. *Okay, a little too casual, Tash.* Straightening up, she moved, and stood with her back against the wall, as if expecting an execution. *Oh, that's much better.* For Pete's sake, she was just Nick's mom. She wasn't the pope, as Mimi used to say.

Mimi.

Tasha drew a long, deep breath, steadying her nerves by remembering the woman who'd taught her to believe in herself. Mimi wouldn't be worried right now. So by God, Tasha wouldn't, either. This was *her* place. *Here* she did belong.

"Such a nice house." The voice floated in front of her as hurried footsteps echoed through the kitchen and into the dining room. Framed in a slice of watery sunlight slanting through the dining room window, Angela Candellano stopped dead and smiled at Tasha.

Short and well-rounded, Nick's mother had a kind face and warm brown eyes. Her graying black hair was piled in a loose topknot on the crown of her head, and with both hands clutching it, she held her pocketbook at her waist. Her green flowered dress was starched and pressed and her black shoes were glossy.

"Ah, Tasha." She smiled broadly and suddenly erupted into a lightning fast walk that carried her to Tasha's side in a flash. Freeing one hand from the pocketbook, she wrapped an arm around Tasha and gave her a quick, hard hug. "Is so good to meet you. We didn't get to talk when you came to pick up Jonas."

"Yes," Tasha said, coloring slightly at the memory. She'd yelled at Nick in front of his family, then stormed off like a petulant five-year-old. "And I'm sorry I just showed up and then left again without any warning, but I—"

"Pshht." Angela waved a hand, dismissing that statement as her gaze swept the old house. "Very nice house," she said, nodding in approval. "Feels warm. Loved."

"Yeah, I've always thought so." Tasha wasn't sure what was happening, but this wasn't exactly going the way she'd expected. Somehow, she'd thought Nick's mother would be fire and brimstone—she was more like hot chocolate and marshmallows. "Mrs. Candellano . . ."

"Oh." She waved one hand again and started roaming the living room, looking at everything with interested eyes. "Call me Mama."

"Thank you, but—"

"Mama is easier," the older woman insisted, pausing to look at a framed photo of Mimi, Tasha, and Jonas, taken last Christmas. "This is Mimi?" She shot Tasha a quick look. "She has a good face. Jonas, he told me about her. And about you."

"Mrs.—"

Brown eyes narrowed.

"Mama . . ."

Brown eyes smiled.

"Mama, I don't know why you're here, but if it's about—"

"Thanksgiving," the woman interrupted. "Is about Thanksgiving dinner. I want you and Jonas to come."

"Oh." Surprise hit Tasha hard and left her speechless.

"Families should be together, yes?"

"Well, yes, but—"

"My grandson should be there. His Tasha should be there, too."

Okay, this was slipping into bizarro world. She really hadn't expected to be fielding an invitation to a family holiday dinner. And now that she was, she didn't know what to say. Having dinner with the Candellanos was *so* not a good idea. First off, Nick probably wouldn't want her there anyway. Sleeping with her was one thing. Including her in the circle of his family, his life, was something else.

Besides, did she really want to dig herself deeper into a world she would, all too soon enough, not be a part of anymore? "It's very nice of you to ask," she started to say, "but I don't think—"

"My Carla's bringing rolls—she don't cook so much—" Mama frowned in disappointment. "Stevie, ah, Stevie is bringing cakes and things. That Stevie, you'll like her. She's a cook. She should teach Carla. Carla doesn't listen to me so much about cooking. But she eats."

"That'd be great—"

"Do you cook?"

"A little."

"Is good to cook. Makes the house smell like home, yes?"

"Mama—"

"Beth—that's my Tony's wife, such a good girl—is bringing cannoli." Mama shook her head and clucked her tongue. "Might not be so good, it's her first try. Still, we'll eat it. My sons, they eat everything."

"Mama . . ." It was like trying to empty a pool with a strainer. No way could she get into this conversation. She was just a bystander here. This small woman was a force of nature. And suddenly Nick's hard head made perfect sense.

"If you want, you could bring some wine. That would be nice."

"I'm sure Jonas would love to come." When the woman paused for breath, Tasha jumped in. Even though it pained her to think about Jonas spending Thanksgiving away from her, Mama Candellano had a point about families being together. And if Nick *was* his father . . .

"You'll love it, too. My Nicky, he can drive you."

"Nicky—" *Jesus.* "Nick might not want—"

"Nick is good boy." Angela tipped her head to one side and studied the young woman who looked so flustered. She'd wanted a better look at the woman who'd caught Nick's attention. She'd seen it in her son's face last Sunday. The moment this girl had arrived at the house, Nick had come to life. Whether he knew it yet or not . . . he was in love. Real love. For the first time in his life. And Mama was pleased. "You like my Nicky, yes?"

"Well, sure, but—"

"Ah, that's nice." Angela reached up and patted Tasha's cheek. She had her answer. The flash in the girl's eyes. The color in her cheeks. Nice to know that girls could still blush these days. "You're a good girl, Tasha. We see you on Thanksgiving. Wine, now. Don't forget."

"I—"

Turning around, Angela headed for the front door. The best way to win an argument, she'd learned more than forty years ago, when first dealing with her husband . . . was to act as if you'd won and let your opponent be stunned into silence.

She opened the front door and looked back over her shoulder. Poor girl looked so perplexed. Well, she'd get over it. "Say hello to my grandson!"

When the door slammed, Molly came racing back into the room. "What's going on? What'd she want? What'd she say?"

Tasha tore her shell-shocked gaze from the front door and turned it on Molly. "She invited Jonas and me to Thanksgiving."

"Are you going?"

Tasha threw her hands up in surrender. She wasn't sure how it had happened, but, "I'm in charge of wine."

Jonas didn't feel good. His throat was kinda sore and his head hurt, too. He thought about calling Tasha and getting her to come pick him up from school. But it was Friday and if he was sick today, she wouldn't let him go to the football stadium with Nick tomorrow.

Heading down the crowded, noisy hall toward his next class, he grinned when Alex slid into him. "Hi."

"Hi. Did you ask? Can I go to the stadium with you?"

"Yeah, you can. Nick says he's gonna take us to the locker rooms and everything."

"Cool." Alex grinned, then frowned. "How come you're still callin' him *Nick*? Why not *Dad* or something?"

Jonas lifted one shoulder in a tired shrug. "I don't know. Feels a little weird, still."

"But good weird, right?"

He looked at his best friend and blinked when Alex's image went a little blurry. He cleared right up again, though. Good. "Yeah," Jonas said, turning in to biology class. "Real good weird."

From his desk at the small local television station, Nick was occupied with myriad jobs that kept him moving but bored him senseless. How in the hell was he supposed to be interested in covering high school sports and local news when his life was twisting in the wind?

He leaned back in his desk chair and stared out the window at the lowering clouds outside. Gray skies, high wind, and a temperature drop let him know a storm was blowing in off the ocean. He had a sudden urge to go stand on the cliffs behind his childhood home and watch the waves pounding against the rocks below. He'd always been able to think there. And Christ knew he needed to think.

But he was trapped in this cubicle of an office for at least another hour or so. Around him, voices lifted and fell; a quick burst of laughter was followed by a warning to keep it down. Keyboards clattered under typing fingers, and ringing phones shrieked above the din. Nick shook his head and looked around the room. Some of these people had been here thirty years. Others, like him, were new at it.

But the new ones were eager. Hungry to make a name, build a future. He'd been that way once. When he'd first started in football, Nick had been the go-getter. The guy who ran instead of walked and never sat down during practice. He'd known what he wanted and he'd gone after it with a single-minded determination.

This place was different. . . . He couldn't imagine living his life in a series of rooms like this one. Closed off, sealed inside a building, worrying about scripts and assignments and ratings and the camera angle. . . . But if this wasn't what he wanted, what was?

Mind churning, he suddenly stood up and grabbed his jacket. "Screw this," he muttered, and headed out.

"Coach is gonna retire."

"No shit?" Tony leaned back in his chair and lifted his feet to cross them at the ankles on the edge of his desk. "Whoa. Does that make *him* old? Or *us*?"

"Oh," Nick said, "him. Definitely." Coach had even *looked* old. Lying in his hospital bed, surrounded by flowers and Get Well cards from his players. Old but not forgotten. The man had had a steady stream of visitors since being waylaid by a minor heart attack. The nurses at Chandler Community were working overtime just trying to keep a crowd out of the old man's room.

In the lobby, Nick had even run into a couple of the guys he used to play high school ball with. Word had spread about the coach, and it seemed everyone he'd ever had an impact on was turning out to make sure Mac knew how important he'd been in their lives. And during his visit with the coach, it had struck Nick hard that this one old man, working for peanuts in an obscure high school, had reached more people than Nick ever had with all of his celebrity.

Coach had made a difference.

Nick had made money.

"Good." Tony grinned. "Just checking. Didn't want to be *old,*" he said. "Not with another baby coming."

"You're kidding." Nick turned around and stared at his older brother. Tony's daughter, Tina, was just over two years old and the apple of her daddy's eye.

"Nope." Tony's grin got even wider as he unfolded his legs and stood up. "You're the first one to know in the family. Beth just told me this morning."

Crossing to him in a few long strides, Nick grabbed his brother in a fierce hug and slapped him on the back. Another niece or nephew. The Candellanos were growing. "That's great. Congratulations."

"Thanks," Tony said, stepping back and moving for the coffee. "Beth's hoping for a boy. But me, I'd like another girl just like Tina."

While his brother talked about babies and the future, Nick's mind wandered again. A family. Tony was a real family man. And Paul was on that road now, too. Soon enough, he and Stevie would be making babies. And as for Carla . . . Nick smiled to himself. When she heard about Beth being pregnant, his baby sister's competitive streak would show up and she'd be in a race for the maternity ward. And why not? She was a great mother to Reese, Jackson's daughter.

Six months ago, Nick would have been pleased for his brother but confused as hell about why anyone would want to have a family of his own. Freedom had been all-important then. Or at least, he'd thought so.

Now, though, it was different. He looked at Tony and the rest of the family and, hell. *Jealousy* was an ugly word, but it was the only one that fit. He envied Tony's happiness. Envied Paul and Stevie and Carla and Jackson. He was the lame duck in the group now. No wife, no children . . . there was Jonas, though. And the kid had become more important to Nick than he'd ever thought possible.

As had Tasha.

Oh, just thinking of Tasha was enough to weaken his knees and tug at his heart.

Damn it.

Why wasn't anything simple?

Why didn't he know what to do anymore? He used to know. He used to have all the damn answers. Now he didn't even know the right questions. Could a man like him change? Could he make it work? What if he failed at being the kind of man Jonas and Tasha deserved? What if he couldn't be the kind of man he *wanted* to be?

Tony put on another pot of coffee and Nick wandered around the inside of the sheriff's office. Steps slow, mind racing, he studied framed photos hanging on the wall, trailed his fingers through the dust on top of the file cabinet, then stopped by the wide window overlooking Main Street. He stared out at Chandler, already gearing up for the winter carnival.

Once Thanksgiving was over, the Christmas decorations would go up on the streetlight poles and storefronts. Strings of tiny white lights would be draped up and down the length of the street, shining in the darkness like ropes of fallen stars. By the middle of December, the kiosks would be lining Main Street selling everything from real roasted chestnuts to handcrafted jewelry. Tourists would flock to the town every weekend, soaking up "old-fashioned small-town charm."

He thought about bringing Tasha and Jonas to the carnival and how much he'd get a kick out of seeing the kid enjoy the show as much as he used to. There'd be a Christmas tree to pick out and decorate. Presents to buy. Secrets to keep.

The smile on his face slowly faded away as he realized that there was no guarantee Jonas would be around in December. And if the DNA tests proved he wasn't Jonas's father . . . then what? Would Nick stand by and let the state take Jonas from his home?

From Tasha?

From *him*?

Nick's blood rushed hot through his veins. Since when did a blood test make family? Since when did a piece of paper decide who loved whom? That DNA test would tell him the truth.

But it couldn't tell him what he was feeling.

Only he could do that.

And it was long past time he made that call.

Chapter 20

"You're sure he's spending the whole night."

Tasha grinned. "All night. We've got hours."

Hours, Nick thought. If he had *years,* he'd still want more time. He levered himself up on one elbow and stared down at Tasha. She ran her fingertips across his naked chest and he sucked in air through gritted teeth.

God. He couldn't get enough of her. For days they'd been meeting. Snatching stolen hours every morning, like teenagers hiding from their parents.

Until tonight.

Nick had spent the day with Jonas and Alex, dragging them all over the Saints stadium. Or rather, *being* dragged. The boys had inspected every square inch of the place, from the locker rooms to the luxury suites to the concession stands. Nick had visited with a few friends, bought the kids lunch, then dropped both boys off at the Medina house.

"And," Tasha added, "Rose Medina always makes a huge breakfast on Sunday mornings, so Jonas won't be back home till almost noon."

"How will we kill that much time?" Nick bent his head to kiss her, hungry for the taste of her again, though his body had barely stopped buzzing. The brief brush of her mouth against his rekindled the embers within, startling him with their intensity. She was in his blood. In his soul. She'd touched him in ways he hadn't thought possible. Shone lights in all the dark, empty corners of his heart.

He couldn't lose her now. At least, not because he was too shit-scared to tell her how he felt. To take the leap. He'd thought of little else since leaving Tony's office the day before. Over and over again, he'd weighed the gains with the risks, and always the answer had come up the same.

Tasha.

Always, Tasha.

"What're you thinking?" she asked, reaching up to cup his cheek.

"About you," he admitted. "About *us*."

"Nick—"

"No, wait, Tasha." God, he didn't want to blow this. He wanted to get this right. To have the right words. The setting couldn't be better. Moonlight and bare skin. But how to tell her everything he was feeling? Everything he wanted for her? For them? Finally, though, he realized it was just important to get the words *out*. "I love you."

Her eyes clouded, her hand dropped from his cheek and she turned her head on the pillow. Staring toward the window and the night beyond, she said quietly, "Don't do this, Nick."

Not the reaction he'd been hoping for. Or even expecting. "What?" His fingertips on her cheek turned her face back toward him.

"Don't spoil it."

A curl of sheer panic spiraled through his guts. "Spoil it? Loving you is spoiling it?"

She inhaled sharply and pushing his hand aside, she slid off the edge of the bed, drawing the quilt along with her. The house was cold, as old houses were. Moonlight speared through the window and dazzled her in a silvery light that made her seem suddenly unapproachable. And Nick wanted to make a grab for her, just to reassure himself that she was still there. Still within reach. But she must have read his mind, because she took another step away from him.

Tasha shook her head and shoved one hand through her hair. Then swiveling her head, she looked at him. And her breath caught. Whatever she'd been about to say died unspoken. A man shouldn't be able to look *that* good. His dark brown hair tangled from her fingers, his eyes were hooded, still heavy with the passion shimmering in the air around them. His broad chest looked as if it had been sculpted from golden oak. The sheet pooled on his lap as he pushed himself up to stare at her in disbelief.

Oh God.

"What's wrong?" he asked, his voice a low rumble of sound that vibrated within her and set off small electrical charges in her bloodstream. "What's going on?"

Her stomach swirled with what felt like thousands of butterflies, all trying to take off at once. Nerves danced along her spine, and a chill that had nothing to do with the temperature of the house shook her to the bone. Mind racing, Tasha told herself to stay calm, but a part of her wanted to shout.

"You don't have to say that."

"Say what?" he demanded. "'I love you'?"

She winced and shook her head again. "Stop. You

don't mean it. Not really." A stray tear coursed down her cheek and she reached up to impatiently swipe it away. "You're just saying what you think I want to hear. Well, I don't. I don't want to be lied to."

"Now I'm lying to you?"

Tasha heard the anger in his voice, but she couldn't stop now. "Nick, I know you probably mean well, but—"

"Mean well. Thanks. That's great."

"Don't you see?" She kept staring at him and felt herself weaken. She'd known all along that this wouldn't last forever. Right? She hadn't expected him to treat her like the other women who'd sailed across his bed. Giving her meaningless words just to make sure she stuck around for another tumble. And oh God, it wouldn't hurt nearly this bad if she didn't love him so much.

"I just don't want to be another one of the crowd."

His eyes bugged out. "There's a crowd, now?"

She ignored that. "I want what we have. For as long as we have it."

"And that's all."

His voice was flat, but she wasn't fooled. Anger churned in his eyes, and even in the indistinct light, she had no trouble seeing it. "It's been enough, hasn't it?"

Actually, she thought, it had been more than she'd ever expected to find. And she wanted to cherish the memory—not ruin it by wishing it could have been something else. Something more.

"Nick," she said, trying to make him understand, "I don't want promises you can't keep—or regrets when you leave. I don't expect anything from you." *Just the pain when he was gone.*

His jaw worked, his eyes narrowed.

She breathed deep, blew it out in a rush, then said, "Just don't lie to me. I won't be lied to."

"I *haven't* lied to you."

She forced a smile that nearly cracked her face. Maybe he actually thought he'd meant the words. But sooner or later, day would dawn and he'd want to cut his own tongue out. "Let's just forget all of this, okay?"

"Forget it?" He grabbed the sheet and dragged it with him when he pushed off the bed. Wrapping it around his waist, he stood, feet planted wide apart, arms folded across that broad chest, and glared down at her. "I tell you I love you and you want to forget it?"

"It's best that way." Please stop. Please stop saying it.

Nick laughed harshly. "This is some kind of karmic joke."

"What?"

"On me." Shaking his head, he reached up and scraped both palms over his face, then looked at her. "My whole damn life, I've avoided saying those words to anyone but my family."

"Nick—"

"You had your say. *My* turn." He walked past her, searching the moonlit room for his damn pants. So much for hours to play. The game was over and he'd ended it by wanting it to be more than a game. Perfect. "I was worried, ya know." Muttering as he stalked around the room, he continued, "Worried about saying it all just right. Telling you how much you mean to me."

He spotted his jeans. Dropping the damn sheet, he stalked naked across the room and snatched them off the floor. Turning around, he faced her while he tugged them on. She was so damn beautiful it was all he could do to keep from going to her, yanking her to him, and *making* her hear him. "Those three words aren't a *chip* I play, Tasha. They mean something."

She sighed. "You don't love me."

"Really?" He snapped and zipped the jeans, then planted his hands on his hips. "What *do* I feel for you, Tasha?"

She shrugged and damn it, she looked too small wrapped up in that quilt. Fragile—as if she could be broken with a harsh word.

"I think you like me," she said. "And you love Jonas."

He stabbed his index finger at her. "No, you don't. Don't bring him into this. This is between you and me."

"There *is* no you and me."

"Why? Because you say so?"

"Because I'm not the kind of woman a man like you falls in love with."

Nick's head snapped back as if she'd hit him. And that's how it felt. "Is that right?" He walked toward her slowly, because everything in him was calling for foot-stomping fury. "What kind of woman is *my* kind?"

She tipped her chin up and met his gaze squarely. Even if she was an idiot, she wasn't a coward. So much for thinking her fragile.

"Someone educated," she said. "Someone with a career. Money. Style. Like those women in magazines." She flipped her hair back from her face. "Rich men don't find love with beauticians. Men with strong families don't fall in love with nobodies."

He looked down into the eyes that had haunted him for weeks. Nick fisted his hands at his sides to keep from grabbing her just to shake some sense into her thick head. "How can a smart, capable, fiercely independent woman be so *dumb*?"

"I'm not dumb." She stared up at him. "You just don't want to admit I'm right."

He fought for calm when every instinct was to shout. "Because I have money, I don't love you. Because I have a family I love, I don't want you. All we have is sex. That it?"

"Yes," she said tightly, pain radiating from her in thick waves. "That's it. Anything else is you trying to be nice."

His blood actually boiled. He cupped her chin in his palm and leaned in close. "Trust me, honey, I'm not feeling *nice* right now."

She jerked away and he let her go. He was too pissed to be rational at the moment anyway. Turning from her, he scanned the room for his shirt, and when he found it, he grabbed it and pulled it on. Stepping into his shoes, he picked up his jacket and shrugged into it.

She hadn't moved.

He didn't go to her again because if he did, Nick knew he wouldn't be able to let her go. And damn it, he wouldn't *beg*. Her words rattled around inside him until a response burst from him. "Tasha, you're a snob."

"What?"

"You heard me. Your family sucked and mine didn't. We both grew up anyway. Rich guy can't love you? Well, that's bullshit, babe." He stuffed his hands into his pockets and fisted them. "I've got money 'cause I worked *hard* for it. Spent years getting my ass kicked. Blew out my knee by doing my *job*. I worked.

Hard. Just like *you* do and my parents did and my brothers and sister. You think that bank account puts me higher than you? Well, that's your hang-up, Tasha, not mine."

"I didn't say—"

"You said plenty, believe me." Nick cut her off with a harsh laugh that tore at his throat. Jesus, this night had gone to hell in a hurry.

Tasha stared at him. His eyes gleamed darkly in the moonlight and the soft scent of his aftershave reached for her, even though he didn't. The night seemed darker, blacker, than it had such a short while ago. And Nick seemed further away from her than ever.

Tasha was cold. God, so cold. Pain rose up inside and threatened to swallow her. She couldn't breathe. Couldn't seem to draw air into lungs screaming for it, and a part of her didn't care. What did breathing matter when your heart was shattered?

She wanted to believe him. Wanted to think he *did* love her. But how could she? Besides Mimi and Jonas, no one had ever loved her. Tears pooled in her eyes and she hoped to God he couldn't see them from across the room. She wasn't a snob. She was rational. A realist. And the simple truth was, a man like him would never want a woman like her.

It was the situation with Jonas that had set him off. The three of them had spent so much time together, Nick had gotten *used* to the semblance of a family. He'd started thinking of them as a unit. Of him and Tasha as a couple.

But it wasn't real.

It would never be real.

And knowing that was killing her.

Nick blew out a frustrated breath. "I was going to tell you this later."

She looked at him.

"The station's sending me to Dallas. To interview some of the players before the Cowboys' game on Thanksgiving."

"Congratulations," she said softly. "It's what you've been hoping for, isn't it?"

His mouth thinned into a line sharp enough to draw blood. "Yeah. I'm a real lucky guy."

He was leaving. Just like that. Walking away. So much for love, huh? Tasha buried her pain, refusing to let it out until she was alone. She wouldn't cry in front of him. She wouldn't let him know how much she hurt. "How long will you be gone?"

"Be back before Thanksgiving."

"I'll tell Jonas."

"You do that, Tasha." He took a step toward her, then stopped. "And while you're at it, tell yourself that I love you. And keep telling yourself, till you believe it."

"Nick—"

"Damn it—" He stomped across the room, jerked his hands from his pockets, and took her face between his palms. She looked up at him through watery eyes, and when he bent his head to kiss her, she leaned into him. She felt the heat of him slip inside her, and when he broke the kiss, she wanted to beg him not to stop. But he didn't give her the chance.

"Think about that, Tasha," he murmured, stroking her cheeks with his thumbs. "We'll talk when I get back."

Then he was gone and the house was quiet. Tasha was alone and she told herself she'd better start getting used to it.

. . .

Monday morning, he stood outside and watched the last of the Marconi crew pack up.

"It's a great house, Nick." Jo Marconi slid her toolbox onto the bed of her truck, then slammed the gate shut with a metallic clang that echoed in the stillness. Turning around, she leaned against the dusty black truck, looked at him, and smiled. "An A-one Marconi family project if I do say so myself."

Nick stared up at the place by the lake and took in the new deck, new roof, and new paint job. "You guys and your dad do good work."

"Thanks." She straightened up and walked to the driver's door. Her dark brown ponytail swung in a wide arc with every step. Opening the door, she paused and said, "Like I said. Nice house here, Nick. Enjoy."

She drove off, gravel and dirt fishtailing behind her. When the truck's engine roar had died off, all that was left were the sounds of the wind blowing through the trees and a few stray ducks making a racket on the lake. "It is a nice house," he murmured, letting his gaze sweep over the structure. "But it's still not a home." And wouldn't be, if Tasha insisted on being an idiot.

With that pleasant notion clanging in his head, he walked to his own car to make the drive to the airport. Two days in Dallas suddenly sounded like a good idea. At least he'd be so busy, he wouldn't be tempted to call her.

"I don't feel so good," Jonas admitted when he walked in the door that afternoon.

"You don't *look* so good, either," Tasha said, and instantly swept her palm beneath his hair to test his forehead. "You're burning up, kiddo."

He looked up at her through glassy eyes. "My head hurts, too, Tash. Really bad."

Worry tingled in every cell in her body. Jonas *never* complained. *Ever.* Mimi used to say the kid's arteries could be spurting blood and he'd apologize for the mess he was making. So if he said his head hurt, Tasha was willing to bet there was something more wrong than a simple headache. Worry jelled into fear and took a quick slide toward panic.

There was no one to ask if she was overreacting. No Mimi. No Nick. So, if she was overreacting, she'd apologize to the doctor and be embarrassed. But either way, Jonas would be safe.

She took his backpack from him and tossed it onto the closest chair. "Wait here a sec," she told him before turning and sprinting toward the beauty shop. Sticking her head in the doorway, she ignored the customer with her head in the sink and called out, "Molly? Jonas is sick. I'm taking him to the doctor."

"Poor kid—" Molly nodded. "Sure, go ahead. I'll lock up here when I'm finished."

"Thanks." Then she was racing back to the living room, grabbing her purse and keys off the dining room table as she passed. Stopping beside Jonas, she ran one hand over his hair, then tipped his head back. New panic jumped inside her when he winced. "Your neck hurt, too?"

"A little," he said, and one small tear squeezed from the corner of his eye.

Tasha's mouth went dry. Could just be a pinched

nerve, she told herself, but even she didn't believe it. "It's okay, sweetie. The doctor'll fix you up. It'll be okay."

He nodded and walked beside her, squinting into the late-afternoon sunlight as they stepped onto the porch. Draping one arm around his shoulders, Tasha pulled him tightly to her side and kept him there as they walked to the car.

Dr. Weston had been around forever. At least, that's what he claimed. The man looked as old as time, but his smile was young and bright and always comforting.

Until today.

He stepped out of the examination room, drawing Tasha with him. Looking back at Jonas, he said, "Sit right there, champ. We'll be back in a minute."

When the door closed quietly, Tasha blurted, "What is it?"

The old man took off his glasses and cleaned them on a white hanky he was forever pulling out of his breast pocket for just that purpose. Tasha had long suspected he used the action as a stalling tactic while trying to figure out what to say to worried families. Today he proved her right.

Setting his wire-framed lenses back into place, he looked at her, reached out one hand to lay on her forearm, and said, "I think it's meningitis, Tasha."

"Meningitis?" She took a step back, as if distancing herself from the man would distance her from his diagnosis as well. She'd been hoping for flu. Would have accepted strep throat. Would even have settled for mono. But this? Oh God.

"Don't know what kind yet. Could be either viral or bacterial." He was talking to himself now, as well as her. "I'm admitting him to the hospital right away. Get some tests done. Find out what we're dealing with."

"Hospital?" Fear, wearing tiny metal spikes, ran up and down her spine, delivering pain and panic. "Tests?"

The doctor nodded grimly but continued to pat her hand absently. "It's probably viral," he said, his voice that practiced soothing monotone doctors seemed to develop in medical school. Did they teach classes in that stuff? "If it is," he continued, "we'll send him home with some antibiotics and he'll be fine in a few days."

"And if it's not . . . ?" She wanted to know it all. The bad and the good. How could you possibly panic properly without all the facts?

He sighed wearily. "Bacterial carries a new set of threats, up to and including possible brain damage."

Tasha staggered backward, slamming into the wall behind her. Breath rushed from her lungs. Her eyes filled and then spilled over with tears she was helpless to stop. Her gaze shot to the closed door behind which sat Jonas. Alone. Scared. Sick. Breathe, Tasha, she told herself. Breathe.

"I'm not saying that's what this is," Dr. Weston said sternly, "or that that's what will happen. But I wanted you to know going in what to expect."

"Does *he* know?" she asked, unable to shift her gaze from that closed door.

"Not yet." Dr. Weston's fingers squeezed on her arm until she looked at him. "I'll tell him. But, Tasha, I want you to get a grip. He's going to need you. He'll be scared and I want you to be able to help him through what's coming."

She nodded. "What *is* coming?"

"A spinal tap."

"Oh God. . . ." Nick, why aren't you here? Oh God, she wanted someone to hold on to right now. She wanted . . . *needed* Nick. He loved Jonas, too. He'd know what she was feeling. He'd help her keep the screams that wanted to rush from her locked inside.

"It's the only way to find out what we're dealing with," he said. "Now. I'll make the call to set things up. Which hospital do you want to take him to?"

Santa Cruz, she asked herself, where the only person she knew well was Ms. Walker? . . . Or Chandler Community? Nick wasn't there. But his family was. And suddenly she *so* didn't want to be alone anymore.

"Chandler," she said, then looked at the doctor. "After the spinal test . . . how long before we know?"

He shrugged. "If the lab's not too backed up, a few hours."

Hours of not knowing. Hours of prayer and hope and panic. Tasha dragged air into her lungs, then reached up and rubbed away her tears. She didn't want Jonas to see her crying. "Okay then," she said. "Let's do it."

He patted her arm again, gave her a wink, then turned back to the examining room to break the news to Jonas. Alone in the hall, Tasha looked up at the ceiling and murmured, "Mimi, do what you can to look out for our boy, okay?"

Then she headed outside to use her cell phone to call Nick.

Chapter 21

Fear perched on Nick's shoulders on the long flight home from Dallas. It whispered in his ear. Taunted him with visions of disaster. Fear dragged icy fingers along his spine and twisted his guts into a tight knot.

Would it be easier if he were there, in the hospital, with Tasha? Would it help to worry as a team? He didn't know. All he was sure of was his desire to *be* there. With her. Holding her.

Praying with her.

When Tasha called his cell phone, Nick hadn't thought twice. He'd looked the producer in the eye, said, "I quit," and hit the road running. Suddenly football and a shot at national TV coverage seemed small. Pitiful. All he could think of was an eleven-year-old boy, lying in a hospital bed. And Tasha, terrified and alone.

He couldn't help the terrified part, but on the cab ride to the Dallas airport, he took care of the alone part of her situation. One phone call to Paul had alerted the Candellanos, and Nick knew his family well enough to know that Tasha would be taken care of until he could reach her. But it should have been him. He should have been at home when he was needed.

Why was Texas so damn big? If it had been a regular-size state, he'd have been a hell of a lot closer to California. To home. To Tasha. He never should have gone for the stupid interview. He didn't even *care* about it anymore. Didn't wonder when his agent would call. Didn't see his career as the all-encompassing ego massage he once had. There were other plans flitting through his mind now. Better plans.

But they included Tasha and Jonas.

And without them, the plans alone would be meaningless.

The four-hour flight seemed to take forever. At the airport, he'd sprinted for the front door and grabbed the first cab he saw. Now all he had to do was survive the forty-minute ride to the hospital. Tasha's voice repeated over and over in his mind, breaking up until only certain words echoed through his brain. *Jonas. Hospital. Spinal tap. Meningitis.* Nick closed his eyes and mentally hurried the damn cab.

The Candellanos circled the wagons.

Just like in those old westerns you could catch on late-night TV, Tasha thought. They drew together, protecting each other with a strong line of defense.

And for the first time since losing Mimi, Tasha was on the *inside* of a tightly drawn circle of love. From her seat on the mint green Naugahyde couch in the waiting room, she shifted her gaze across the people waiting with her.

Tony, still in his sheriff's uniform, was standing in the far corner, talking to Nick's twin brother, Paul. Their sister, Carla, was making yet another coffee run with Stevie, Paul's wife. Tony's wife, Beth, since she was pregnant, and Tony didn't want her near the hospital with its sea of germs, had been left at home to watch the kids. But Mama hadn't left Tasha's side since the family arrived, responding to a long-distance call from Nick.

Nick.

Come home, she thought, wishing he were there already. Knowing all of this would be easier to bear if he were there beside her. Love? Yes, she loved him. And whether he really loved her or not, she wanted him there. With her. With Jonas. His family was kind and supportive and . . . wonderful. But they weren't Nick.

Tasha pushed up from her chair and paced. She already knew the dimensions of the waiting room where a handful of people—besides their group—sat, reading, watching the muted TV in the corner, and drinking god-awful coffee. Thirty paces long, ten paces wide. She walked it again. Then one more time. Nerves jumped inside her. She was supposed to be on a break. Since Jonas was sleeping, everyone said there was no need to sit beside his bed.

But she needed to be there.

She *needed* to watch each shallow breath rushing in and out of his chest. Besides, if he woke, she didn't want him to be alone.

"I'll be with Jonas," she muttered to no one in particular, and headed across the sparkling cream-colored linoleum, her tennis shoes squeaking like tiny screams. Tony and Paul came away from the wall as one unit, each of them turning toward her, concern etched into their features.

Tasha smiled tightly but kept walking, headed for the long brightly lit hallway. Outside, it was twilight, a cool November evening. Here, in the hospital, time meant nothing. Day and night blended together beneath the glare of fluorescent lights. The air smelled of disinfectant and fear. Tasha hugged herself and drew a tight rein on her imagination. Televisions in the rooms she passed flickered in weird flashes of light. Someone moaned and her eyes squeezed briefly shut in sympathy.

She stepped into Jonas's room and paused just inside. Shadows crouched in the corners, but from directly over the bed where the boy lay sleeping, a bright light poured down on him. His sweaty hair clung to his forehead. Needles attached to IV poles were stuck into his arms. Machines measuring his heart rate, blood pressure, and blood oxygen levels blinked in a series of numbers designed to confuse worried families. And beneath the blankets, his narrow chest lifted and fell in a regular rhythm. Tasha drew in a long, shuddering breath and didn't even turn when a voice spoke up from behind her.

"He will be all right."

"You sound so sure."

Mama sighed heavily, then walked up beside her, taking Tasha's hand in hers. "I *am* sure," she said. "Jonas is young. And strong. And the doctors are good."

Tasha stared at the child who meant so much. Outside, clouds were gathering for a storm and families gathered for dinner. Life moved on in the universe beyond the hospital corridors. But here, in this one corner of the world, everything felt as if it had been frozen. As if clocks had stopped. As if the world had taken a breath—and held it. "He's never been this sick before."

"Children get sick, families worry." Mama's hand

squeezed around hers. "Is the way when you love."

"It's hard." Tasha closed her eyes briefly and felt a stray tear snake down her cheek.

"It is."

Tasha appreciated that Mama hadn't tried to buoy her up by saying, "Don't worry." Her words were simple, quiet, and filled with a sympathetic unity that made Tasha feel a little better despite the fear curled in the pit of her stomach. She'd done the right thing by admitting Jonas to Chandler. Here she wasn't alone. Here there were people who cared—and though Nick wasn't here, it was a comfort to at least have his family standing beside her.

She took a breath and shifted a look at the older woman beside her. Stoic, she thought. Unflappable. *Mimi would have liked her.* "Nick thinks he loves me," she blurted in a harsh whisper, and couldn't imagine, after it was said, what had prompted the words.

Mama only smiled. "This I knew."

"You knew?"

"I can see it in him."

Tasha watched the woman's eyes for signs of disapproval, and when she couldn't find any, she felt compelled to make Mama understand. She pulled her hand free. "Well, he has to stop."

Mama's smile darn near glowed. "You love him, too."

"That's not the point."

The older woman chuckled. "Love is *always* the point."

"Not this time," Tasha murmured. "It can't work. Nick has to stop this."

"Why?"

"Because . . ." What was the use? Tasha threw her

hands up. "You guys are impossible to argue with."

"Is nothing to argue about. Tasha," Mama said, reaching for her hand again, "the heart knows what it wants. What it needs. Listen to yours, as Nicky listens to his." She gave her hand a squeeze, then said, "You're a good girl, Tasha. Strong. Smart. Don't turn your back on love. Is a gift that only gets bigger and better with time. When love comes, embrace it." Mama handed her a clump of neatly folded tissues. "Now dry your eyes and blow your nose. Your family will be here when you need us."

Tasha's vision blurred as Mama left the room. Turning her gaze heavenward, she whispered, "Hurry, Nick, I need you. *We* need you."

"Now that's what I call timing."

"Nick?" Tasha whirled around and saw him, standing in the doorway. His hair stood on end, no doubt from hours of him jamming his fingers through it. His eyes were tired, and a shadow of whisker stubble dotted his jaws. And no one had ever looked better to her.

Hope and joy and relief clashed together in her chest and Tasha surrendered to the wonder of it. Her breath left her in a rush and her heartbeat thundered in her ears. Just hearing his voice had made everything easier. Less terrifying somehow. Now all she needed was to hold him and be held.

He took one long step into the room and met her as she threw herself at him. Nick's arms came around her and he buried his face in the curve of her neck. "How is he?"

She burrowed in closer to him, as if trying to climb inside his skin. "Not good. His fever's still high. He doesn't seem to be responding to the antibiotics."

His hands stroked up and down her back, soothing,

comforting. "Do we at least know what we're dealing with?"

"No." Tasha pulled her head back and looked up at him. Worry glittered in his eyes, and seeing it made Tasha come out of her own fears to try to help ease his. "I mean, we know it's meningitis. We just don't know if it's viral or bacterial."

He sighed and shot a look at Jonas. "When will we know?"

She shook her head. "The lab's been backed up. Dr. Weston says we should know soon, though. They did a spinal tap, Nick." She swallowed hard. "They stuck a needle in his *spine*. Jonas cried."

"I know, baby."

"I couldn't help him."

"You did that just by being here, Tasha."

Nick shifted his grip on her, cupping her face in his palms, scraping the pads of his thumbs across her cheeks. His gaze moved over her and he took his first easy breath in hours. He knew no more than he had when he'd left Texas—but being here, with Tasha, made the uncertainty more bearable. He hadn't felt *whole* until he'd stepped into this room and found her waiting. Now that they were together, he knew they could beat anything. "He'll be okay."

One corner of her mouth quirked briefly. "That's what your mother said, too."

"Well then," Nick said, pulling her close for a hard hug as he swallowed back his own fear, "that settles it. Mama's never wrong. Just ask her."

Tasha held on to him, wrapping her arms around his middle and looking back over her shoulder at Jonas, so still and quiet. "I'm so scared, Nick."

"Me, too, baby," he said, keeping one arm around

her shoulder as he moved her closer to the bed. Jonas looked pale and small and so damn young. Nick's heart ached as an unseen fist gave it a squeeze. Spinal taps and hospital gowns. Some things no kid should have to know anything about. But he would be okay, Nick reassured himself. Jonas was tough.

He *had* to be all right, because Nick couldn't imagine his life without the small boy who'd turned it upside down.

Seconds ticked into minutes and minutes into hours. Time crawled past, with Nick and Tasha sitting side by side in the darkness. Nick held her hand tightly and watched Jonas's chest rise and fall with each shuddering breath. Nurses came and went with silent steps and glances filled with empathy.

Candellanos drifted in and out of the room in a show of solidarity—then leaving Tasha and Nick alone to stand guard.

The boy's cheeks and forehead were flushed and dry. Machinery positioned on the other side of Jonas's bed flickered with lights and readings that Nick couldn't understand. All he heard, all he concentrated on, was the steady *beep* marking each of the child's heartbeats.

He heard the music in those beeps and clung to the steady hope of them. Jonas would be fine. He *had* to be. It couldn't all have been for nothing. Jonas had found Nick. He'd brought them all together. He couldn't *die*. Not now. Not ever.

"How does this happen?" Nick said, and was almost surprised to hear his own voice. He swallowed hard. "I mean, a few days ago, the kid was great. Touring the stadium, planning Thanksgiving—the camp-out next month. And now . . ."

Tasha's grip on his hand tightened. "I don't know. I don't know why. Or how. I don't know why *any* kid has to get sick."

"It sucks. Big-time." Nick's back teeth ground together. "He looks so damn little. And helpless, damn it. I want to do . . . *something.*"

"You did," Tasha whispered, and leaned into him. "You came home."

Home. She was right in the most basic way. Wherever she and Jonas were, that was *home.* Nodding to himself, Nick held on to Tasha's hand as if she were a lifeline. "He's got to be okay, Tasha. He *has* to be."

And reaching through the metal railing, Nick caught Jonas's limp, dry hand in his and linked the three of them. As they were meant to be.

They all gathered in the waiting room.

"It's viral," Dr. Weston said, that comforting smile back in place.

Tasha's heart quickened, grasping at the relief she saw shining in the older man's eyes. Behind her, the Candellanos took a collective breath and Nick choked out a short relieved laugh. "And that means . . . ?"

"You can take him home in a couple of days." The doctor reached out and patted Tasha's shoulder. "I want to keep him another day or so, rehydrate him and get his fever down. Then he'll be good to go."

The air left her in a rush. Turning in to Nick, she was swept up in a hug that nearly broke a rib. But it was worth it. Relief bubbled through her veins like fine champagne. She heard another quick burst of laughter and a back being slapped, but she dismissed it all as the doctor started talking again. She turned in Nick's arms to face the older man again.

"We've got him on a strong antibiotic IV now, and I want to keep him a day or so. But he's going to be fine, Tasha."

She nearly melted against Nick and was grateful for the strong arms that wrapped around her middle. "Thank God."

"Amen."

For the first time in too many hours, Tasha relaxed. Everything was fine. Good. As it should be. Nick's hands stroked up and down her spine and she only half-listened as Nick spoke to the doctor. She didn't *have* to be in charge now. She could share the burden. And the joy.

Minutes ticked past, but she wasn't counting anymore. It was enough to know that Jonas would be all right again. Shifting slightly, she rested her head on Nick's chest and listened to the steady beat of his heart. It soothed her jangled nerves and steadied her racing pulse.

Moments later, when Tasha finally eased out of his embrace, she found they were alone in the waiting room. "Where'd everybody go?"

He grinned. "Where all good Italians go to celebrate. To get food." He stroked her hair back from her face, his fingertips lingering on her skin. "They'll be back."

"Good." She couldn't stop looking at him. "I'm so glad you were here today, Nick. I . . . *needed* you with me."

"Glad to hear it," he murmured, then blew out a breath. "The doctor said Jonas won't wake up for a while yet. So take a walk with me."

Nodding, Tasha walked to the couch, picked up her

purse, and as she did, her gaze dropped to the manila envelope tucked inside. She hadn't even thought about it in hours. But now that the crisis was over . . .

Outside, the night was clear and cold, and the stars hung overhead like lanterns at a party. A soft wind sighed past them. Tasha stopped and pulled the envelope from her purse. Handing it over, she said, "It's the DNA results. They came through earlier today."

He took the envelope. "Did you look?"

"No. It's got your name and Jonas's on it. Not mine."

Nick nodded slowly, thoughtfully, his fingers smoothing over the surface of the envelope. Here it was. The answer to the question that had started this whole thing three weeks ago. He started to open it, then stopped again. Shifting his gaze to Tasha, he said, "Before I open this, I want you to know something."

"Nick—"

He cruised right over her interruption. "Being in Dallas when you and Jonas needed me . . . well, it brought home a couple of things I've been thinking about lately."

"It doesn't matter. You came. You were here. For both of us. You're here *now*."

"Yeah. And I'm staying here."

"What?"

"My old high school coach has offered me his job at Chandler High." Her eyes widened and he smiled at her surprise. "I know what you're thinking. 'Football star' will never survive without the cameras and the fast life."

"That's not what I was thinking," she said. "Not even close."

Nick started pacing, moving around her in a tight

circle. "I've made lots of money, Tasha. I've had the star treatment. I've been all over the world. Now I want to be here. I want to make a difference." He laughed shortly. "I want to someday be an old man and have kids I coached thirty years before come back and tell me I made a difference." He stopped and looked at her. "Am I nuts?"

"No," she said softly.

He grinned. "That's a relief, since I already quit my job."

"You did?"

He shrugged, remembering. "I was about to go on air when I got your call. I unhooked the mike, pitched it at the producer, and said, 'I'm outta here.' They said, 'If you leave, you're fired.' I said, 'No problem, I quit.' "

"I don't know what to say," Tasha admitted, clearly stunned.

"I believe that's a first." He grinned again and Tasha's heart fluttered.

"Jonas is fine. You have a new job. All that's left is . . ." She pointed at the envelope.

"Right." Nick's future was stretched out in front of him. He could already see him and Tasha and Jonas in the house by the lake. Jonas would go to Chandler High, just like his old man. Hell, Nick would be coaching his son at his own old high school. And there would be other kids, too. They'd have a big family, he told himself as he pried up the metal tabs and slipped out the single sheet of paper inside.

Life was good and about to get better.

Then he read the paper. "I don't believe it." His gaze lifted to hers. "I'm not his father."

"What?" Tasha snatched the paper from him. She

looked it over, then turned dazed eyes up to him.

"I'm not Jonas's dad." Nick felt the shock ripple through him from his head right down to the soles of his feet. He'd been so sure. So absolutely positive. For the first time in his life, he understood the saying "you could have knocked me over with a feather."

Not so long ago, he would have felt a surging sense of relief at this news, Nick realized. He'd have hopped into his car and gone right back to the life that now felt foreign to him.

Only a few weeks ago, he would have killed to get that interview with the Cowboys. Today, all he'd done was curse the fact that Dallas was too far away from the people he loved. From Tasha. From his *son.*

When this whole thing had started, he'd been determined to prove that Jonas was no relation to him. And now that he held the proof in his hands, all he felt was . . . empty.

"We'd better go in," Tasha said, her voice barely more than a whisper. Handing him the piece of paper that defined their futures, she said, "Jonas will be waking up soon."

"Right." Nick followed after her. Carefully he tucked that paper back into the envelope and flattened the copper tabs back into place.

Jonas woke up slowly. "Tasha?"

"I'm here, sweetie."

Blinking at the light, Jonas turned his head on the pillow and smiled at Tasha. Then he noticed the man beside her. A weak grin lit his face. "Nick, you're here, too."

"You bet, sport."

"Can we go home now?"

"Maybe tomorrow," Tasha told him.

" 'Kay." He let out a jaw-cracking yawn.

"Jonas," Nick said, his voice soft and low, "the DNA test results came back."

Tasha sent him a look, but Nick was done waiting. Tests or no tests, this kid was his *son*. And he'd fight anybody who tried to say different.

"Yeah?" Jonas asked. His eyes were glassy. His fingers nervously plucked at the blanket covering him. "What'd it say?"

Nick leaned forward, bracing his elbows on the upper bar of the guardrail edging Jonas's bed. The overhead fluorescent light spotlighted the bed and the boy lying in it. Shadows crouched in the corners of the room.

Staring down into brown eyes so much like his own, Nick handed the envelope to Jonas and said, "This is yours and you can decide what to do with it after I tell you something."

Jonas held the envelope tightly but kept his gaze on Nick.

Tasha moved in closer to Nick, as if to protect the boy. Well, Nick thought, that's just what he was trying to do.

"Tests don't mean a damn thing, Jonas," Nick said, meeting the kid's gaze and holding it. "To me, it doesn't matter what those test results are. I *choose* you to be my son."

Jonas blinked.

Tasha inhaled sharply.

Nick continued, despite the knot in his throat. "I love you, Jonas. In every way that matters at all, I am your father. I love you." He said the words again, drilling them home and enjoying being able to say them to the boy who meant so much to him. "That's what counts—the love—so I have my answers. The tests don't mean a thing to me. I don't even care what's inside that envelope. Now it's up to you." He took a breath, then blew the air out and said, "You can look in the envelope and know what the tests say. *Or* you can *choose* to be my son and tear up the envelope. Up to you."

Jonas looked from Nick, to Tasha, and back again. Seconds ticked past until finally, "I choose you, too, *Dad.*" Then quietly, slowly, the boy tore the envelope in half.

Nick grinned at him, gathered up the pieces, and tossed them into the trash. Then he reached down to ruffle the kid's hair. "Now that that's settled . . . you're getting a haircut as soon as you're well."

"Aw, man. . . ."

"And as for you," Nick turned toward Tasha and held out one hand, "I'm going to say this again. Here. In front of Jonas. *Our* son."

Her breath caught.

"I *love* you, Tasha." He flashed a grin at her. "And I *know* you love me."

Jonas made a gagging noise—but he was smiling.

Tasha blinked and bit down on her bottom lip.

"This isn't the most romantic proposal ever made," Nick continued, his voice dropping to a low scrape of sound, "but it's real. The most real thing I've ever done. I love you and I need you to believe that. To trust that. I can't imagine my life without you."

"Wow," Jonas muttered.

"I want you to marry me." Nick stared into her eyes, willing her to see his love. Willing her to see that she held the key to his happiness. To their future. To the world they could make together. "It's your turn to choose, Tasha. Help me raise *our* son. We'll adopt him legally together. And together, we can give him a big family. Love me, Tasha," he added in a whisper, "and let me love you."

Tasha's heart lifted. Actually lifted. If her rib cage hadn't been holding it in, she thought it just might have floated to the ceiling. All her life, she'd been on the outside. If Mimi hadn't found her, Tasha would never have learned the joy in loving Jonas. And if Jonas hadn't sued Nick, Tasha would never have discovered the wonder of *being* in love.

Fate had twisted and turned to bring her to this spot. This point in her life, where she could choose to cling to a past that continued to haunt her—or she could take the risk of trusting the only man she'd ever loved.

And suddenly the choice was easy. She set her hand in his and felt the solid warm strength of his fingers close over hers. "I do love you."

"And . . ." he nudged, smiling.

"I choose you, Nick," she said, stepping into his embrace. "I choose love."

EPILOGUE

Two months later

For the first time in maybe *ever,* Castle's Salon was closed.

Temporarily, at least.

From downstairs came the crash of hammers, the whirring buzz of saws, and the shouts of every last member of the Candellano family. Tasha smiled, shook her head, and stepped into Mimi's old bedroom, closing the door behind her and muffling the noise from below.

Nick's brilliant idea of turning the Victorian into a posh day spa was becoming a reality. Soon they would be able to offer on-site masseuses, manicure/pedicure rooms, and luxury facials. There would be hot stone therapy, aromatherapy, and mud wraps. Castle's would be the best spa in Central California—if Tasha could get Nick to stop arguing with Jo Marconi about how to design the place.

"You'd love this, Mimi," she whispered, and picked up the framed photo of her, Jonas, and Mimi that stood on the lace-covered dresser top. Staring down into the woman's smiling eyes, Tasha smoothed her fingertip across the cold glass and said, "I just wish you were here to see it. To know that Jonas and I are all right. That everything turned out better than I ever hoped for."

Her gaze landed on the four-carat diamond that Nick had placed on her finger just two weeks ago. It glittered and sparkled in a stray ray of sunlight spearing through the partially opened blinds. She was married. It was still a little hard to believe, but the ring twinkled at her whenever she doubted it. Not to mention, Tasha thought with a smile, having Nick remind her a couple of times each night.

So much had changed so quickly.

Jonas and she had moved into Nick's house by the lake and Nick was already planning for spring training at the high school. Jonas was the proud owner of a completely rambunctious puppy—the last of Carla's dog Abbey's litter. Ms. Walker at Social Services had been *very* nice ever since Nick's lawyer—Carla's husband—had set Jonas's adoption in motion.

And Castle's was about to be changed forever.

The rest of the house had been picked up, packed up, and moved, either to Nick's house or into storage. But Tasha had left Mimi's former bedroom for last.

Cardboard boxes were stacked in short brown towers all around the room. The rug was rolled and propped against the far wall, and the bed had already been taken apart and carried down to the waiting truck. All that remained was the dresser and the few framed photos on top of it.

"No sense putting it off any longer." She pulled the top drawer open and was instantly surrounded by Mimi's scent, lifting from the potpourri she'd kept in her clothes drawer. Tears stung Tasha's eyes as she took Mimi's things out and set them aside for Goodwill. Just touching them made the older woman feel close again. And despite the happiness filling Tasha's life these days, she still carried the ache of missing Mimi.

Methodically she cleaned out the first three drawers, and when she reached the last one, she was relieved to have it almost over. Then she pulled the drawer open and found it empty—but for two sealed envelopes, one with her name scrawled across the front and the other with Jonas's. Both were in Mimi's flowery, generous handwriting.

"Oh my God," Tasha whispered, and reached for them with suddenly shaking hands. It was as if Mimi had suddenly reached out from beyond the grave to connect with Tasha one more time.

Cradling the twin envelopes in her open palms, Tasha stood up and carried them across the room to the window. Then she raised the blinds, letting in a flow of watery January sunlight. She set Jonas's sealed letter aside and carefully broke the seal on her own envelope before pulling free the single folded sheet of lilac-colored paper.

Nick watched his sister and Stevie planning the future spot for the Leaf and Bean's spa concession. Paul and Jackson were tearing out the kitchen cabinets, and Mama and Hank Marconi were laughing over old times while the Marconi girls got down to the business of overhauling the Victorian. Outside, Jonas, Reese, and Tina were playing with Abbey and her puppy, Goliath.

"In other words," Nick muttered, headed for the

staircase just off the living room, "I can find everyone but my wife." Chuckling, he took the stairs two at a time. "Wife. Hell, who'd have guessed it?"

He hit the top of the stairs and called, "Tasha?"

"In here—"

Her voice barely carried over the racket from downstairs, but it didn't matter. He let his instincts lead him to her. Opening the door at the end of the long hall, he stopped on the threshold. "What's wrong?" The tears in her eyes had surprised him, but not enough to keep him from her for long. He stalked across the cluttered room to grab her upper arms. "Are you okay?"

"I'm fine," she said, and gave him a smile despite the tears tracking down her cheeks in a silent flood of emotion.

He wiped her tears away with his fingertips. "Sure. I'm convinced."

"You don't understand. I found . . ." She glanced at a piece of notepaper in her hand, then held it out to him. "Just—" She swallowed hard, took a breath, and blurted, "Read this."

"This is why you're crying?"

Tasha blew out a breath, ruffling the hair that fell across her forehead. "Read it, Nick."

He looked from her tear-washed eyes to the paper in his hand, then started reading. . . .

> *My Sweet Tasha,*
>
> *I'm writing a letter to both you and Jonas, because I'm not getting any younger, you know. And one of these days, I might wake up dead.*

Nick chuckled, and glanced at Tasha. Her smile quivered, but there was a peace in her eyes he hadn't seen before. "Go on," she urged.

Not that I'm planning on dying anytime soon, but you just never know. But I didn't want to talk about me.

Tasha honey, you're a wonderful girl. You've been the daughter of my heart since that rainy night in LA ten years ago. I knew then we were destined to find each other. Of course, I figured that I was supposed to help you. To teach you. But you taught me, sweetie. You taught me that a true diamond can't be crushed no matter how many hits it takes.

And when the bruises around your heart finally heal, I hope you find someone who deserves you. And when you find him, grab him, Tasha, and hold on tight. If you have to choose between being safe and being loved . . . always choose love.

As I chose to love you.

Mimi

Nick blew out a breath. "She wrote one of these to Jonas, too?"

"Uh-huh. It says he's not to open it until he's eighteen, so God knows what she said to him," Tasha said with a choked-off laugh.

"She was really something, wasn't she?" Nick lifted his gaze to Tasha's.

"You would have liked her." Tasha took the letter

and tucked it carefully into its envelope. "She would have *loved* you."

"As long as *you* love me, baby," he said, pulling her up close, "that's all I'll ever need."

Tasha wrapped her arms around his neck and held on. Her heart felt lighter than it had in years. Her future was stretched out in front of her and she saw love in Nick's eyes. A few short months ago, she'd been terrified of losing her only family.

Now she had more family than she knew what to do with. And yet, there was always room for one more.

"So," she asked, keeping her gaze locked on his, "what are you hoping for—girl? Or boy?"

He laughed and kissed the tip of her nose. "Girl or boy what?"

Tasha just smiled at him and counted off the seconds until realization dawned on Nick's face.

"Are you—"

"Yep."

"You're sure?"

"Way sure."

His eyes were wide enough to pop out of his head. She hoped they didn't. Her stomach was a little queasy just thinking about it.

"When?"

"In about seven months."

"Shouldn't you be sitting down?" he asked, looking around the room but coming up empty.

"I'd rather be kissed."

"We can do both." Nick bent down, scooped her up into his arms, and cradled her against him. *Then* he kissed her.

And Tasha held on for the ride of her life.

#1 BESTSELLING AUTHOR
MAUREEN CHILD

FINDING YOU

Carla Candellano has faced a tragedy she'd like to put behind her, but no one has been able to penetrate the wall she has built around herself—until she meets six-year-old Reese Wyatt. Reese hasn't spoken since her mother died last year, and it's friendship at first sight for Carla and little Reese. But it's the girl's worried father, Jackson, who arouses Carla's curiosity, and passion, in ways she never imagined . . .

"An absolutely wonderful contemporary romance. A delightful blend of humor and emotion, this sexy love story will definitely keep readers turning the pages."
—Kristin Hannah, author of *Distant Shores*

"Heartwarming, sexy, and impossible to put down . . . Maureen Child always writes a guaranteed winner, and this is no exception."
—Susan Mallery, author of *Married for a Month*

AVAILABLE WHEREVER BOOKS ARE SOLD FROM
ST. MARTIN'S PAPERBACKS

#1 BESTSELLING AUTHOR
MAUREEN CHILD

KNOWING YOU

Ever since Stevie Ryan was a young girl, she was in love with her best friend Carla's older brother Nick Candellano. But Nick had to complicate things by growing up gorgeous—and breaking Stevie's heart. Now she's convinced that forgetting him is the way to go. And it's working out fine . . . until she and Nick's brother, Paul, spend one sultry night together. Has the right brother been under Stevie's nose all along?

"Maureen Child infuses her writing with the perfect blend of laughter, tears and romance. Her well-crafted characters, humor, and understanding of what it means to be part of a family makes each of her novels a treat to be savored."

—Jill Marie Landis, author of *Magnolia Creek*